THE RENEGADES
OF PERN

THE RENEGADES OF PERN

ANNE McCAFFREY

BALLANTINE BOOKS ▸ NEW YORK

THE DRAGONRIDERS OF PERN is a trademark of Anne McCaffrey.
Reg. U.S. Pat. & Tm. Off.

A Del Rey® Book
Published by Ballantine Books

http://www.randomhouse.com/delrey/

Library of Congress Catalog Card Number: 97-93885

ISBN: 0-345-41939-1

Design by Ann Gold
Map by Shelly Shapiro

Manufactured in the United States of America

First Hardcover Edition: November 1989
First Mass Market Edition: September 1990
First Trade Paperback Edition: September1997

10 9 8 7 6 5 4 3 2 1

JOHN GREENE

Maréchal de logis

1958–1988

"O, Johnny, why did they do ye?"

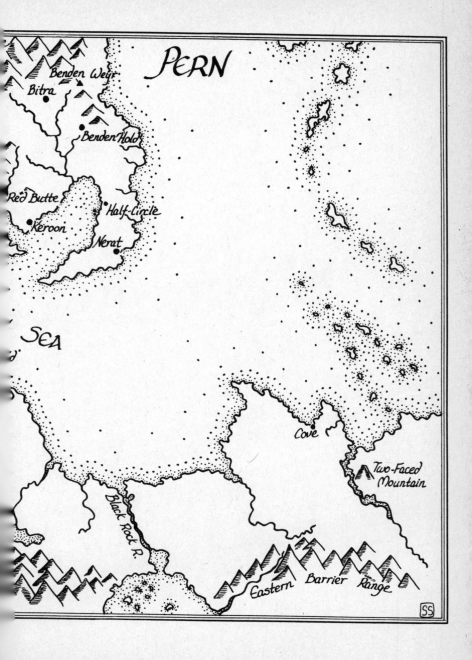

CONTENTS

▼▼▼▼▼▼▼▼▼

INTRODUCTION

▼▼▼▼▼▼▼▼▼

When Mankind first discovered Pern, third planet of the sun Rukbat in the Sagittarian Sector, they paid little attention to the eccentric orbit of the Red Star, another satellite in the system.

Settling the new planet, adjusting to its differences, the colonists spread out across the southern, more hospitable continent. Then disaster struck in the form of a rain of mycorrhizoid organisms, which voraciously devoured all but stone, metal, and water. The initial losses were staggering. But fortunately for the young colony, ''Thread,'' as the settlers called the devastating showers, was not entirely invincible: Both water and fire would destroy the menace on contact.

Using their old-world ingenuity and genetic engineering, the settlers altered an indigenous life form that resembled the dragons of legend. Bonded with a human at birth, these enormous creatures became Pern's most effective weapon against Thread. Able to chew and digest a phosphine-bearing rock, the dragons could literally breathe fire and sear the airborne Thread before it could reach the ground. Able not only to fly but to teleport, as well, the dragons could maneuver quickly to avoid injury during their battles with Thread. And their telepathic communication enabled them to work with their riders and with each other to form extremely efficient fighting units.

Being a dragonrider required special talents and complete dedication. Thus the dragonriders became a separate group— set apart from those who held the land against the depredations of Thread, or those whose craft skills produced other necessities of life in their crafthalls.

Over the centuries, the settlers forgot their origins in their struggle to survive against Thread, which fell across the land whenever the Red Star's eccentric orbit coincided with Pern's.

There were long intervals, too, when no Thread ravaged the land, when the dragonriders in their Weyrs kept faith with their mighty friends until they would be needed once more to protect the people they were pledged to serve.

One such long interval is coming to a close at the opening of our story; though with a decade to go before another Pass of the Red Star, few are yet aware of its ominous approach. Indeed, few believe Thread will ever fall again. And in the false comfort of that belief, people have grown complacent. With that complacency, discord has arisen in Hold and Hall, setting in motion a chain of events that results in renegades on Pern!

THE RENEGADES
OF PERN

PROLOGUE

_{▼▼▼▼▼▼▼▼▼}

In the northwestern province of High Reaches, an ambitious man has just begun a campaign of territorial acquisition that will make him the single most powerful Lord Holder on all of Pern. His name is Fax—and he will become legend.

Meanwhile, in the hills of Lemos Hold, in the eastern mountains of Pern . . .

"He's here again," the woman said, peering out the dust-grimed window slit when she heard the clatter of hooves on the cobbles in front of the cothold. "I tol' ya he'd come back. You're for it now." There was a certain note of sly anticipation in her voice.

The slovenly man at the table glanced contemptuously in her direction. His belly was full, though he had grumbled with every mouthful that porridge was no dish to serve a grown man, and he had just decided to do a little fishing.

The metal door of the hold was vigorously pushed in, and before the cotholder could get to his feet, the room was full of determined men, shortswords prominently at their belts. Uttering little shrieks of dismay, the woman flattened herself in the corner of the inner wall, oblivious to the clatter of pans and cups that spilled from the hanging cabinet.

"Felleck, you're out!" Lord Gedenase said in a cold, harsh voice. He stood, fists on his belt, his dark leather riding cloak fanned by his arms, making him appear much larger than life.

"Out? Out, Lord Gedenase?" Felleck stammered, staggering to his feet. "I was just going out, Lord, to fish for our evening meal—" His voice changed to a plaintive whine. "For we've naught to eat but boiled grains."

"Your hunger no longer concerns me," Lord Gedenase replied, swiveling to examine the filthy room with its rickety furnishings. His nostrils flared briefly in disgust at the musty smell of accumulated damp and dirt. "Four times you have failed to tithe, despite generous help from my steward to replace your moldy seed grain, your broken, misused tools, and even a draft animal when yours developed foot rot. Now, out! Gather your belongings and get out!"

Felleck was stunned. "Out?"

"Out?" the woman's voice quavered.

"Out!" Lord Gedenase stepped aside and gestured sternly toward the door. "You have exactly one half hour in which to gather your possessions"—the Lord Holder's eyebrows twitched with scorn as he glanced about the sordid dwelling—"and leave!"

"But—but—where will we go?" the woman cried despairingly, but she was already gathering up pots and pans.

"Wherever you wish," the Lord Holder said. Turning on one heel, he strode out of the place, kicking aside a pot lid. He motioned to the steward to oversee the eviction, mounted his runnerbeast, and rode off.

"But we have always been beholden to Lemos," Felleck said, sniveling and twisting his face into a piteous expression.

"Every hold supports itself and tithes to the Lord Holder," the steward said impassively, folding his arms. "Yours doesn't! Twenty-five minutes left!"

Sobbing loudly, the woman dropped her apron-load of pots and covered her ears to block out the implacable verdict. Felleck cuffed her, snarling in bitter rage. "Get the packsack, you stupid pig. Go roll up the bedding. Get moving!"

The eviction was accomplished on time, and Felleck and his woman were driven, staggering under their burdens, down the narrow track, away from their cothold. Felleck turned back once, before the bend hid his former home from sight. He saw the wagon then, drawn up near his empty beasthold; saw a woman holding a babe, an older child beside her on the seat; saw the neatly packed belongings, the sturdy burden beasts yoked to the trace, the milk animal tied to the wagon gate, and he cursed fluidly and fiercely as he pushed the stumbling woman before him.

Under his breath he vowed vengeance on Lord Gedenase—and on all at Lemos Hold—for his humiliation. They would be sorry, they would! He would make every man jack of them sorry!

Fax's lightning campaign has been successful: He has made himself Lord Holder of High Reaches, Crom, Nabol, Keogh, Balen, Riverbend, and Ruatha, having gained possession by dint of marriage or murder or the ferocity of his marauders. Tillek, Fort, and Boll have called in every ablebodied man, armed them, and drilled them in defensive skills. Beacon fires have been placed on hilltops, and fleet-mounted messengers recruited to bring word of any incursion into their borders. But news of those calamitous events has seeped slowly to the more isolated holdings . . .

Dowell always knew when visitors were on their way up the wagon track to his mountainhold: shod hooves echoed as noisy clatters from the next valley down.

"A messenger comes, Barla," he called to his wife as he laid down the plane with which he had been smoothing a fine piece of fellis wood, destined to be part of a ladder-back chair he was making for Lord Kale at Ruatha Hold. He frowned as his ears told him that more than one rider was on the way—and at speed. Then he shrugged, for guests were infrequent, and Barla loved visitors. Though she never complained, he often thought he had been unfair to take her so far up the mountains during spring and summer.

"I've fresh bread and a bowl of berries," she said, coming to the entrance of their hold. At least he had given her a right smart and commodious dwelling, he often assured himself, with three large rooms cut into the rockface on ground level, and five above. There was a good beasthold for their runners and the two burden animals he used to haul timber from the woods, and a drying loft for the timber he had seasoning.

The visitors, ten or more men, brought their animals roughly to a halt in the clearing. One look at the unfamiliar sweaty faces and Barla stepped instinctively behind Dowell, wishing that her face was smudged with flour or soot.

The leader's eyes narrowed, and his smile turned ugly. "You're Dowell?" The leader did not wait for a reply as he dismounted. "Search the place," he snapped over his shoulder.

Dowell's fingers curled, wishing he had the plane still in his right hand, but he straightened his shoulders and sought his wife's hand with his left. "I am Dowell. And you?"

"I'm from Ruatha Hold. Fax is now your Lord Holder."

Dowell heard Barla's swift intake of breath, and he squeezed her hand hard. "I had not heard that Lord Kale had died. Surely—"

"Nothing's sure in this world, carpenter." The man strolled casually up to the pair, his eyes all the time on Barla. She wanted to bury her face in Dowell's shoulder to escape the look in those lewd eyes.

Suddenly the troop leader hauled her away from Dowell's side, cackling as he forced her to turn and turn and turn until she was dizzy and had to grasp the nearest thing—him—to stay upright. To her horror, he pulled her against him. She could feel the gritty dust of his sleeve and shoulder, and saw the dried blood on his collar. Then his stubbled, coarse-skinned face was far too close and a blast of his foul breath hit her before she could seal her eyelids shut and avert her head.

"I wouldn't, were I you, Tragger," someone said in a low voice. "You know Fax's orders, and she's already plowed for this year."

"No one's hiding, Tragger," another man said, pulling a weary runner behind him. "They're here alone."

Barla was spun free, and with a stifled cry, she lost her balance and fell heavily to the ground.

"I wouldn't, were I you, woodman," said the same low voice that had cautioned Tragger.

Fearfully, Barla looked up to see Dowell straining to reach Tragger. "No, oh no!" she cried, staggering to her feet. Those men would think nothing of killing Dowell, and then what protection would she have, with her kinsman, Lord Kale, dead?

She clung to Dowell as Tragger ordered his men to mount. He wheeled his beast, glaring at her through narrowed eyes, an evil smile drawing his lips across his teeth. Then he gestured with his arm, and the troop sped down the track from the mountainhold, leaving Dowell and Barla shattered by the brief encounter.

"Are you all right, Barla?" Dowell asked, embracing her tenderly, a gentle hand on her waist.

"I've come to no harm, Dowell," Barla replied, patting his hand over her gravid womb. Echoing in the silence was the next word: "yet."

"Fax is Lord Holder of Ruatha?" Dowell muttered. "Lord Kale was in excellent health when . . ." He trailed off shaking his head.

"They murdered him. I know it. That Fax! I heard about that jumped-up High Reacher. He married Lady Gemma, and it was a unpopular hurried wedding. That much the harpers said . . .

quietly. They called him ambitious, ruthless.'' Barla shuddered at the thought. "Could he have murdered all in Ruatha Hold? His lady? Lessa and her brothers?" She turned scared eyes on him, her expression bleak.

"If he has massacred those at Ruatha . . ." Dowell hesitated, and his fingers flexed over his wife's stomach. "And you're second cousin but once removed in that line."

"Oh, Dowell, what shall we do?" Barla was truly terrified— for herself, for her babe, for Dowell, and for those who had died in blood.

"What we can, wife, what we can. I've skill enough to see us well settled anywhere. We'll go to Tillek. We're not that far from its borders even now. Come, Barla. We'll go have some fresh bread and berries, and make plans. I will not be beholden to a lord who kills to take another's rightful place."

F*ive Turns after Fax's astounding coup, Tillek still maintains a full compliment of men-at-arms, though the novelty has long since worn thin and boredom is a fierce problem in the barracks. Wrestling contests are frequent, keeping the participants fit and offering entertainment at Gathers, when the champions of the different barracks are pitted against one another . . .*

The moment the man's head cracked ominously on the cobbles, Dushik sobered. Then, with his next breath, he was on his knees beside the body, feeling the neck vein for a pulse.

"I didn't mean it. I swear I didn't mean to hurt him!" Dushik cried, glancing at the ring of men around him and noting the sudden hostility of their expressions. Hadn't they been encouraging him? Taking bets against his strength? Hadn't he been taunted enough at this Gather? There had been plenty to hand him wineskins and flagons!

A burly Gather steward elbowed his way into the clear space of the circle. "Is he dead?"

Dushik stood up, bile rising in his throat. All he could do was nod his head. This was the third time, his wine-dulled brain reminded him. The third time.

"This is the third time, Dushik," the steward said, tugging on his sleeve. "You've been warned often enough about your sort of brawling. . . ."

"I'd too much wine." Desperately Dushik tried to assemble a defense. "The third time" meant that he would be denied the Hold, his cot, and the work he was trained to do. Three deaths from brawls, no matter how they occurred, also meant he would have no luck applying to any other Holder. He would be banned—holdless. "They—they put me up to it!" He tried to lay blame to those in the circle, the ones who had bet on his prowess as a wrestler. "They—they made me!"

Suddenly Lord Oterel himself pushed into the circle. "Now, what's this?" He looked from Dushik to the motionless body on the cobbles. "You again, Dushik? The man's dead? Then, off with you, Dushik. The Hold is closed against you. All Holds are closed against you. Pay him off, steward, and escort him to the High Reaches border. Fax uses men of his sort!" Oterel snorted with contempt. "Clear this up. I don't want an unpleasantness to spoil the Gather!" He turned on his heel, and the circle respectfully parted to let him pass.

"He didn't listen to me," Dushik cried, turning vainly to the steward. "He didn't understand."

"Three men dead because you won't hold your punches, Dushik, is one too many. You heard Lord Oterel."

Suddenly three more strong stewards bracketed Dushik. He was marched to the barracks, allowed to collect his gear, then locked for the night in the small holding cell situated at the back of the beasthold. Even Lord Oterel would not force men to forego a Gather to escort an unwanted man to the border. But the next morning, those who escorted him were neither talkative nor forgiving for the journey.

"Don't come back to Tillek, Dushik," the leader said in farewell. But at the last moment he handed over Dushik's sword and long knife and a sack of journey rations.

After seven Turns, Fax's usurpation has become more or less accepted—except by the Harper Hall. The Masterharper, Robinton, has been hearing unsettling reports from his harpers that make him mistrust this uneasy peace. Fax is ambitious, and with all but Ruatha Hold prospering under his harsh management, it is entirely possible that he will look eastward, to the broad and fertile plains and the mines of Telgar. As if aware of Harper Hall scrutiny, Fax has begun to turn harpers out of his Holds and Halls for the most spurious reasons. Whatever teaching the harpers have provided, Fax says, the young will learn from his deputies. He has challenged authority—and succeeded. What will he challenge next?

As if there is an infection in the very winds that sweep the Northern Continent, others are challenging long-established ways. In Ista Hold, certainly one of the most conservative, a young man defies parental authority . . .

"I don't care if everyone else in the family have been happy on High Palisades Island for every generation since the First Record—I want to see what the mainland is like!" Toric separated the last five words with emphatic thumps on the long kitchen table. His father, a Masterfisher, regarded him in shocked amazement that gradually turned to frozen anger as his second son openly—and in front of the younger children and the four apprentices—defied him. "There's a lot more to Pern than this island and Ista!"

"Oh, Toric," his mother began, appalled. She had argued with him, trying to soothe him, and had even tried to placate her angry husband.

"And how, might I ask," his father began, holding up his hand to stem his wife's interference, "do you think you're going to support yourself away from this hall?"

"I don't know, Father, and I don't care, and never fear, it won't cause you any embarrassment because I'm not staying around this place for the rest of my life!" Toric stepped over the bench on which he had been seated for yet another unendurable meal. "There's a whole continent out there, and I'll see what else I'm able for. I've asked you fair for my journey-man's badge. You won't give it, so I'll leave on the trader."

"Leave on that filthy trader, Toric—" His father rose as his eighteen-year-old son strode to the hall door, scooping his weather-gear off its peg. "Leave," he bellowed, "and you will have neither hall nor hold, and all men's hands will be turned against you. I'll have the harpers read it!"

The door slammed shut so hard that the latch bounced up, and it swung open again on squeaky hinges. The others at the dining table simply sat, stunned at such an unexpected drama at the end of a tiring day. The Masterfisher waited, hearing the progress of steel-tipped bootheels departing across the exterior flagstones. When all sound had died away, he sat down again. Looking across to his oldest son, who was still gape-mouthed, he said in a tight, bitter voice, "That hinge wants oil, Brever. See to it after your meal."

His wife could not completely choke back a sob of dismay, but her husband paid her no attention. He never mentioned Toric's name again, not even when five of his remaining nine children followed their brother, irrevocably, off High Palisades Island.

K*eroon Hold—Winter—two Turns later . . .*

"Light-fingered she is, and I've told you that time and again, husband. She's not to work in this hold ever again."

"But it's winter, wife."

"Keita should have thought of that when she filched a whole loaf of bread. What does she think we are? Stupid? Rich enough to stuff her guts with more than she needs to do her work? Out she goes tonight. She's holdless as of this moment. Let her remember that, as well. She'll have no recommendation from Greystones if there is anyone fool enough to hire the slut."

At Keroon, on the first high spring tides in that eighth Turn after Fax's rise to prominence, a battered ship finally makes safe harbor, her rigging torn, mainmast snapped, bowsprit broken; and several of the crew vow to find a less hazardous occupation. The third mate cannot look forward to employment of any kind . . .

"Now, Brare, I've added a few credits to what's yours by rights, but a footless man's no good in the rigging, nor on the nets, and that's a fact. I've asked my brother who's Portmaster to see you healed and healthy. Talk it over with him, see what work's available in the port holds. You were always a good man with your hands. I've a good word for you, too, in this recommendation. Any Lord Holder will see you're an honest man who's had a trade taken from him by injury. You'll find a place. I'm sorry to have to beach you, Brare, real sorry."

"But you're doing it anyway, aren't you, Master?"

"Now, let's not be bitter, fisherman. I'm doing my best for you. It's a tough enough life for an ablebodied man, let alone . . ."

"Say it, Masterfisherman, say it. Let alone for a cripple!"

"I wish you wouldn't be so bitter!"

"Leave it to me then, Master, and get back to your ablebodied fisherfolk! You'll be missing the tide if you wait too long!"

All through the summer, rumors of impending Threadfall are spreading. Someone suggests that Benden's lone Weyr is circulating the rumors, but that idea is scoffed at: The precious dragonriders of Benden never show their faces outside the old mountain. And yet the possibility of Thread's return begins to dominate all conversations . . .

As the harvest in Southern Boll was particularly heavy that year, Lady Marella and her steward were constantly in the groves and fields, overseeing the pickers who were prone to slack off if given any opportunity.

"We must be thrifty with the earth's products," Lady Marella kept repeating, urging the pickers to increase their efforts despite the heat of the waning summer days. "Lord Sangel expects a fair day's labor for the marks he pays."

"Aye, he's wise to be storing the plenty while the skies are clear," one of the foremen remarked, picking hand over hand at a rate that astonished Lady Marella.

"Now I want no talk of that nature here . . ."

"Denol, Lady Marella," the man filled in courteously enough. "And it would settle our minds some, lady, if you could assure us that sort of talk is nothing but sundream."

"Of course it is!" she said in her most decisive tone. "Lord Sangel has looked into the matter thoroughly, and you can rest assured that Thread will not return."

"Lord Sangel's a good and provident man, Lady Marella. You ease my mind. Pardon me for mentioning it, lady, but iffen someone, say like some of the children, could bring us empty sacks, and iffen the cart could come between the rows to pick up the full ones, we could move much faster down these rows."

"Now, Denol," the steward began in an admonitory tone.

"No, no, that's not a bad idea," Lady Marella replied, noting the numbers of men and women plodding to the top row with full sacks. "Only children above ten Turns," she added, "for the younger ones must attend the harper and learn their traditional ballads."

"And we appreciate their opportunity, Lady Marella," Denol said, his hands darting with incredible speed from the fruit to the sack in front of him. "Moving about as we has to means they don't get their learning. Tradition means a lot to me, lady. It's the backbone of our world."

His sack was full, and he respectfully bowed as he trotted down the row to deposit it on the cart and pick up an empty sack. He was back and picking again within seconds, moving with diligent energy.

She went on down the rows, noting how often pickers had to leave their rows, the steward silent behind her. When they were out of earshot, she turned to him. "Implement the change tomorrow. It would speed things up. And give that man an extra mark for his suggestion."

The steward kept his eye on Denol throughout the harvesting, somewhat annoyed that he had not had the idea himself. But he could never catch Denol slacking the pace he set, either among the bushes, or in the groves, or when they started the backbreaking labor of digging the tubers. Denol still logged in more sacks than any other picker. The steward had to concede that the man was an excellent worker.

When the harvest was done, Denol approached the steward. "If my work has been satisfactory, steward, is it possible that me and my kin could stay on here over the winter? There's still a lot to be done with the pruning and wintering of the land."

The steward was startled. "But you're a picker. You'll be needed next at Ruatha."

"Oh, I won't go back there, not no way, steward," Denol said, looking apprehensive. "Ruatha's no place to go anymore since Lord Fax took it."

"But there's Keroon . . ."

"Aye, and the new lord's a fair Holder. But I've a mind to settle." He glanced up at the sky. "I know what the lady said, steward, that we wasn't to pay any mind to the gossip, but, steward, I can't get it out of my mind now. What with my nippers coming home and practicing their Harper Ballads and reminding me of what can happen does Thread fall."

The steward was frankly contemptuous. "Harper ballads are for teaching children their duty to hall and hold . . ."

"And Weyr. And they're smart ones, my nippers, steward, to be brought up in a trade, not wandering where Thread could fall out of the skies on them and eat them up like they was no better than ripe fruit."

The steward felt a shiver go down his spine. "Now, then, you heard Lady Marella tell you to stop such gossip."

"Would you speak to the lady for me, please, steward?" Denol slipped the bonus mark into the steward's hand, his look imploring, his manner suitably self-effacing. "You know I'm a hard worker. So's my woman and my oldest son. We'd work harder still for a chance to stay in such a fine hold as this. Finest one this side of the world."

"Well, I don't suppose there'd be any harm in your staying the winter . . . provided—" The steward swung a warning finger on the man. "—you do work hard and show no disrespect. And stop that nonsense about Thread."

By the autumn of the ninth Turn, the rumors are well spread: whispered in Gathers, on back roads, in wine cellars, in kitchens and lofts. Trouble is coming, and not just that this Turn's harvest is unaccountably poor after last Turn's bounty. But then, Keroon has experienced grave drought, and Nerat terrible torrents, and two mines in Telgar have collapsed—so the pessimists are certain that this is only the start of some tremendous calamity . . .

"There'll be a Pass?" Ketrin first stared at the carter, then frowned. "They said Thread would never come again. I don't believe you." He knew Borgald as a pragmatic, unimaginative sort, and a responsible carter, worried only about his precious burden beasts, the great horned bullocks that pulled his wagons. But the trader sounded convinced.

"I don't *like* to believe it," Borgald replied, looking dolefully at the line of carts as the drivers urged them into Telgar Hold. He nodded, absently counting, as each passed. "But with so many people sure it will come, I believe in taking precautions."

"Precautions?" Ketrin repeated, giving Borgald a startled look. "What precautions could you take against Thread? Do you *know* what Thread can do? Drop out of a clear bright sky on a man and eat him, boots, balls, and all. It'd devour your biggest herdbeast quick as you could snap your fingers. Start at one end of a prime field of wheat and roll across it, leaving not so much as a straw!" Ketrin shuddered. He was scaring himself with that old harper description of Thread devastations.

Borgald gave a snort. "Like I said, I'd take precautions. Just like my great-greats when they were hauling. The Amhold train has serviced holds since the very first Pass, and Thread didn't stop my ancestors. It won't stop me."

"But . . . Thread kills . . ." Ketrin was becoming worked up over the mere thought of its return to Pern's skies.

"Only if you get a direct hit; and no fool stays *out* in it."

"It eats through trees and flesh and anything not stone or metal . . ." Then Ketrin made a dismissive gesture. "Nah, can't be true. You've been too long on the track, Borgald, to listen to fool's talk. And I don't take it kindly that you're spilling such tripe at me."

" 'Tain't tripe!" Borgald replied, sticking his chin out defensively. "You'll see. But don't worry. I'll still haul your supplies up from Keroon and Igen. I'll be safe with my precautions. I'll put thin metal sheets over our carts and shelter the animals in caves. Thread won't score man nor beast in the Amhold train."

Ketrin shuddered as if he felt the hot score of Thread down his back.

"You holders," Borgald added with good-natured scorn, "you have it too easy. Thick walls and deep passages"—he gestured to the mighty prow of Telgar Hold—"make you soft and easily scared."

"Who's scared?" Ketrin drew himself up. "But you wouldn't have any place to shelter if Thread caught you out across the plains."

"There's mountain routes to take—longer, you understand, but never so far from caves. Look you, though." Borgald rubbed his chin. "It's going to raise the cost of hauling. Extra time, change of relay stations, the expense of converting the carts—all that adds up."

"Raise the carting costs?" Ketrin burst out laughing. "So that's what it's all about, my friend. Naturally you'd have to raise your charges, with all this *rumor* of Thread coming again." He slapped Borgald affectionately. "I'll lay you odds to evens, Borgald, that this is no interval, that Thread is gone. Ended."

Borgald stuck out his big fist. "Done. Always knew you had some Bitran blood in you."

They were interrupted by the hearty voice of Ketrin's Master. "Ho there, Borgald! Had you a good trip?" He did not wait for a reply. "Are you bringing me those supplies? Here, Ketrin, bring Carter Borgald up to the Hall. Where are your manners, man?"

"I'll trade you, Borgald," Ketrin muttered.

In the spring of the next Turn, Fax meets his death in a duel at the hands of F'lar, rider of bronze Mnementh, and Benden Weyr goes on Search for a woman to partner the last queen egg, hardening on the Hatching Grounds. While every Lord Holder heaves a sigh of relief for the death of the tyrant, they find themselves uneasy at this resurgence of the dragonriders. For though the rumors about the return of Thread died down during the winter, the Search has revived them, reminding folk of all they once owed to the dragonriders. In some folk, Fax's death and the impression of the new queen have awakened old longings and dreams . . .

"And you will not reconsider, Perschar?" Lord Vincet demanded, amazed, almost infuriated by the artisan's continued refusal. Vincet bore in mind that the man was an absolute genius with brush and color—Perschar had faithfully touched up all the fading murals and produced perfectly splendid portraits of all his family members—but there was only so much he could, in conscience, offer the fellow. "I thought the terms of the new contract were most generous." Vincet permitted his chagrin to border on the irritated.

"You have indeed been extremely generous," Perschar replied with the mournful smile that one of Vincet's daughters found affecting but which, at the moment, annoyed the Lord Holder. "I do not fault the terms of the contract or wish to haggle over incidentals, Lord Vincet. It is merely time for me to travel on."

"But you've been here three Turns . . ."

"Exactly, Lord Vincet." Perschar's usually long face crinkled in a happy smile. "Actually the longest I have stayed in any major Hold."

"Really?" Vincet was easily flattered.

"So it is time and a half for me to be off to a different clime, to explore more of this marvelous continent. I need stimulation, Lord Vincet, far more than I need security." The artist bowed in a self-deprecating apology.

"Well, if travel is all you wish, take this summer off. Good season for getting about. I'll have my Fishingmaster arrange passage for you. You wouldn't need to be back here until—"

"Good Lord Holder, I will return when it is time to return," Perschar said ambiguously. With a second graceful half-bow, he turned on his heel and left Vincet's office.

It took a full hour for Vincet to realize that Perschar's deft rejoinder had been a firm good-bye. No one had observed which of the many trails leading from Nerat's main Hold the painter had taken. Lord Vincet was quite upset for the rest of the day. He really could not understand the fellow. Here he had a full set of rooms; a workshop where he had, it was true, trained several talented holders to his craft over the past three Turns; a seat at the high table; plenty of marks in his pocket—*and* three new suits of clothing, shoes and boots as required, and the use of a sturdy runnerbeast.

Eventually, having heard the artisan's parting phrase repeated by her affronted spouse for the twentieth time in an evening, the Lady Holder of Nerat said, "He did say he'll return when it is time, Vincet. Cease fretting. He's gone for now. He'll be back."

In Telgar Hold, two Turns later, when the Lord Holders are becoming increasingly aware of and annoyed by the Weyr's ascendance, Lord Larad is trying to make a suitable disposition of his rebellious sister . . .

"Larad, I'm your sister—your *older* sister!" Thella shouted while Larad signalled vigorously for her to lower her voice. With his eyes, he appealed to his mother to support him, but Thella raged on. "You will *not* marry me off to some niggardly, foul-mouthed, snaggle-toothed senile old man, just because Father agreed to such a travesty in his dotage."

"Derabal is not senile or snaggle-toothed, and at thirty-four he is scarcely old," Larad replied behind clenched teeth. Being a brother, even half-brother, he did not appreciate the defiant stance of her magnificently proportioned body, athletic and fit in her riding gear. To him, the high color in her cheeks, the flash of the hazel eyes, and the contemptuous curve of her sensuous mouth meant merely another stormy session with her. It did not help that she was within a half span of his own height, so that in the high-heeled long riding boots she preferred she was eye-to-eye with him. At that moment he would have liked to throttle her challenge and reduce her to compliance with the good beating that was long overdue. But Lord Holders did not thrash dependent kinswomen.

Thella had always been the most contentious of his sisters, both half- and full-blooded: argumentative, arrogant, willful, and stubborn, making far too much use of the freedom their father had granted his adventurous and daring daughter. Larad had sometimes suspected that their father had almost preferred Thella, with her aggressive high-handed manner, to his son's more considerate, reflective ways. Lord Tarathel had even looked the other way when Thella had beaten a young drudge to death. He had, however, taken her to task for riding a promising young runner into the ground. Valuable animals could not be wasted.

Or perhaps as Larad's mother had suggested, Lord Tarathel had given the girl special consideration since her mother had died giving birth to her. No matter the reason, the old lord had encouraged his first-born child in her hunting, riding, and exploring pursuits; it had amused Tarathel to encourage her to defy convention. Thella was also eleven months Larad's senior, and she made as much of that seniority as she, a daughter, could. She had even challenged Larad at the Conclave of Lord Holders, demanding that she, Tarathel's first born, be considered first for the Holdership. She had been politely, in most cases, and dismissively, in others, told to take her "rightful" place with her stepmother, sisters, and aunts. Telgar Hold had rung for weeks with her complaints at such injustice. The drudges bore new lash marks daily as she vented her frustration, and some fled the main Hold on any pretext they could invent.

"Derabal is a minor holder, not even a lord . . ."

"Derabal holds an impressive spread from river to mountain, my girl, and you'll have more than enough to occupy you if you would *deign*"—Larad allowed some of his feeling to color that word—"to marry the man. His offer is in good faith, you know. . . ."

"So you keep telling me."

"The jewels he offered as a bridal present are magnificent," Lady Fira put in with some envy. She had nothing half as good in her own coffers, and Tarathel had not been a stingy man.

"Have them!" Thella swept that consideration aside with a contemptuous flick of one hand. "But I will not accompany his guard of honor—" She sneered openly. "—back to Hilltop Hold as a meekly submissive bride. And that, my dear Lord Holder,"—for emphasis she slapped her riding stick against her high leather boot—"is my final word on the subject."

"Yours, perhaps," Larad replied in such a harsh tone of voice that Thella looked at him in surprise. "But not mine." Before she could guess his purpose, he grabbed her by the arm and marched her to her sleeping room. Giving her a hard push inside, he closed the door and locked it.

"You are a right fool, Larad!" Thella called through the thick panel. Son and mother heard the thud of something heavy being thrown against the door, and then there was silence, not even broken by the curses with which Thella usually answered confinement.

The following morning, when Larad relented enough to allow

food and drink to be brought to Thella, there was no sign of the recalcitrant girl. Thella's gowns remained neatly folded in their chest, but all of her rough-wear gear was gone, along with the bed fur. On investigation, four runnerbeasts—three good mares already in foal and Thella's strong and willful gelding—were missing from the beasthold, as well as a variety of gear and sacks of journey food. Two days later Larad found that several bags of marks were missing from the safe-hold in his office.

Discreet inquiries by Larad revealed that Thella had been seen leading a string of horses, heading southeast to the dividing range between Telgar and Bitra. There was no further report of her after that.

To Derabal, Larad sent a younger half-sister, a rather sweet and certainly biddable girl who was quite happy to have a decent hold of her own, and a husband who would give her such beautiful gems. Certainly Derabal would later thank him for a remission from the tempers and terrors of Thella.

When Thread did, indeed, begin to fall on Pern, and the Lord Holders threw all support behind the Benden Weyrleaders, Lady Fira worried about Thella.

When she first heard reports of rather peculiar thefts occurring along the eastern mountain trails and the Igen River track that carters had been forced by Threadfall to use, she nursed very private suspicions about Thella. For a long while, Larad never once connected the thefts with his half-sister. He persisted in blaming the holdless, the dissenters, those turned out of hold and hall for violent acts or robberies: the renegades of Pern.

1

EASTERN TELGAR HOLD,
PRESENT (NINTH) PASS, FIRST TURN,
THIRD MONTH, FOURTH DAY

Jayge had hoped his father would stay longer at Kimmage Hold. He did not want to leave as long as he and his shaggy mare were doing so well in races against the holder boys' runners. Fairex looked so clumsy with her winter hair that it had been easy to fool the other lads into wagering against her. And to give the Kimmage boys their due, they had not warned off any of the outholders who came in with their fathers to visit the main Hold. So Jayge now had a most satisfactory collection of credit bits, almost enough to trade for a saddle when next their wagons encountered those of the Plater clan. He needed only another race or two—just a seven day more.

The Lilcamps had been at Kimmage all through the wet spring. Why did his father want to move out now? No one argued with Crenden. He was fair but tough, and although he was not a very big man, anyone who had experienced his fist—and Jayge still did at times—knew that he was far stronger than he looked. Just as a holder, major or minor, was the final authority on his property, so Crenden was obeyed by his kin. A shrewd trader, a hard worker, and honest in all his dealings, he was welcome in those smaller, less accessible holds that were unable to get to the main Gathers on a regular basis. To be sure, some Crafts sent travelers on regular routes to take orders for their Halls, but they rarely ventured up the narrow tracks into the mountains or across broad plains too far from water. Not all of Crenden's goods bore a Crafthall stamp but they were well-made, and cheaper than Crafthall products. Crenden also had a fine memory for what his clients might need and carried a varied stock, limited only by the space of the wagons.

So, early that morning, bright and clear, Crenden gave the order to break camp, and by the time a hot breakfast had been eaten and everything was once again neatly stored in the wagons, the teams were harnessed and all the Lilcamps stood ready to move out.

Jayge took his position by the lead wagon; now that he was ten, he rode courier for his father on the nimble Fairex.

"I admit it's a fine day, Crenden," the holder was saying, "and the weather looks to hold fair awhile, but the roads are hub deep in mud yet. Stay until they've dried out enough to make travel easier."

"And let other traders make it to the Plains Hold before me?" Crenden laughed as he swung up onto his rangy mount. "Thanks to your good fodder and hospitality, my beasts—and my folk—are well fed and rested. That lumber's going to fetch a fine price at Plains, and we'd best be on our way with it. The track is downhill most of the way from here, so the mud won't be a problem. A little gentle exercise will work the winter fat off all of us, get us in shape for the hills again! You've been a good host, Childon. I'll have those new clamps for you when we're back this way in a Turn or two, as usual. Be in good health and heart in our absence." He stood in the stirrups, looking back over the train, and Jayge, seeing the look of pride on his father's face as he surveyed his clan, drew himself straighter in the saddle.

"Move 'em out!" Crenden cried, his deep voice reaching

to the last of the seven wagons. As the beasts leaned into their yokes and harnesses and the wheels began to turn, there was waving and cheering from the holders lining the flagged apron in front of the entrance. Some of the holder boys raced up and down the line, yelling and snapping their drive-whips, showing off the proper *pop!* they had learned managing the Kimmage herdbeasts. Jayge, who had long since proved his prowess with the lash, kept his long whip neatly tied to his saddle horn.

Above Kimmage Hold, the hills were covered with fine stands of the timber that, lovingly nurtured and wisely logged, brought Kimmage holders their income. Once every five years they made the long journey to Keroon Hold to sell the timber that had seasoned in their work cavern. The Lilcamp clan had traded labor with Kimmage Hold for many generations, chopping and hauling timber, or, in the worst of the winter season, helping to enlarge Kimmage Hold into its rock fastness. Now the trees that the Lilcamps had felled five Turns before were loaded on the wagons. A good profit would be made of that lumber.

As Jayge leaned back to check his bedroll, a lash whistled past his ear. Startled, he swiveled to catch sight of the rider going past him and recognized the holder boy he had bested in wrestling the night before.

"You missed," Jayge called cheerfully. Gardrow would have bruises today, for Jayge had given him some hard falls, but maybe the boy would not be so eager in the future to bully the little kids into doing his chores for him. Jayge hated a bully, almost as much as he hated someone who abused animals. And it had been a fair fight: the lad was two Turns older than Jayge and two kilos heavier.

"I'll match ye again when we come back, Gardrow," Jayge cried, and managed to duck out of the saddle as the other boy wheeled his pony, lash swinging above his head for another attempt.

"Unfair, unfair!" two holder boys yelled.

That caught Crenden's attention. He hauled his spirited mount back to his son. "You been fighting again, Jayge?" Crenden did not approve of any of the Lilcamp folk brawling.

"Me, Father? Do I look like I've been fighting?" Jayge concentrated on looking surprised at the question. He had never mastered the air of genuine innocence that his sister could turn on.

His father gave him one long, undeceived look and held up a scarred, thickened forefinger. "No racing now, Jayge. We're on the move, and that's no time for foolery. Steady in the saddle. We've a long day ahead of us." Then Crenden let the runner have his head and moved forward to lead.

Jayge had to fight down temptation when the holder boys begged him for one last race. "Just down to the ford? No? Then up over the spur trail? You'd be back before your father could miss you." Even the stakes mentioned were good, but Jayge knew when to obey. He smiled and, with a sigh, turned a deaf ear, even though winning would have ensured him the coveted saddle. Then one of the wagons caught a wheel in the side ditch, and he and Fairex were called to help get it back on the track. When he looked over his shoulder to ask the boys to help, they had already scattered.

Good-naturedly Jayge looped his towrope through the haul bar on the side of the wagon and urged his sturdy runner-beast forward. The wheel came free all of a sudden, and clever Fairex danced out of the wagon's way. Recoiling his rope and knotting it on the worn nub of his saddle horn, Jayge glanced back at Kimmage Hold, impressive in its bluff that overlooked the energetic Keroon River. On the other side the home herds grazed eagerly on the new grass. Sun warmed Jayge's back, and the familiar creak and rumble of the wagons reminded him that they were moving on to Plains Hold where, he consoled himself, there surely would be someone who would underestimate Fairex. He would have that new saddle the very next time they passed the Platers.

Ahead of him strode his father's big mount, leading the

way along the track by the riverbank. Jayge settled himself deeper into the saddle, stretching his legs in the stirrups and only then realizing that he would need to lengthen the leathers. He must have grown a half-hand since they pulled into Kimmage Hold. Shards, if he had grown too tall, his father might switch him off Fairex, and Jayge was not sure what his father would have him up on next. Not that any of the Lilcamp runners were slugs, but they would not fool other kids the way Fairex had.

They had been several hours on the trail and were nearly ready for a nooning stop when the cry went up: "Rider coming fast!" Crenden raised his arm to signal a halt, then swung his big mount around and looked back the way they had come. The messenger, racing after them, was plainly visible.

"Crenden," the oldest Kimmage son cried, yanking his runner to a stop. His message came out in gasps. "My father says—come back—all speed. Harper message." Hauling a scroll out of his belt and thrusting it at Crenden, the boy gulped, his face blanching, eyes wide with fright. "It's Thread, Crenden. Thread's falling again!"

"Harper message? Harper tale!" Crenden began dismissively until he noticed the blue harper seal on the roll.

"No, really, it's not a tale, Crenden, it's truth. Read it yourself! Father said you'd need to believe it. I can't. I mean, we've always been told that there'd never be more Thread. That's why we didn't even need Benden Weyr anymore, though Father's always tithed because he's beholden to Lemos and we've more than enough to do it out of charity since the dragonriders *did* protect us when we needed it—"

Crenden cut the boy's babbling off with another gesture. "Quiet, while I read."

All Jayge could see was the black-inked words bold on the white surface, and the distinctive yellow, white, and green shield of Keroon Hold.

"You can see it's real, Crenden," the boy rattled on. "It's got Lord Corman's seal and all. Message has been on the way for days because the runner popped a tendon and the messenger got lost trying for a shortcut. He said Thread's fallen over Nerat, and Benden Weyr saved the forests, and there were thousands of dragonriders over Telgar for the next Fall. And we're next." The boy gulped again. "We're going to have Thread right down on us and you've got to be inside stone walls 'cause only stone, metal, and water protect from Thread."

Again Crenden laughed, not at all dismayed, although Jayge felt a spasm of cold uncertainty shiver down his spine. Crenden rolled the message up again and thrust it back at the boy. "Thank your father, lad. The warning is well meant, but I'm not falling for it." He winked at the boy good-naturedly. "I know your father'd like us to help finish that new level in the hold. Thread, indeed! There hasn't been Thread in these skies for generations. Hundreds of Turns. Like the legends told us, it's gone now. And we'd best be going now, too." With a cheerful salute to the astonished boy, Crenden stood in his stirrups and roared out, "Roll 'em!"

There was such a look of total dismay and fear on the lad's face that Jayge wondered if his father could possibly have misread the message. Thread! The very word caused Jayge to squirm in his saddle, and Fairex danced under him in response. He soothed her and argued with himself. His father would never let anything happen to the Lilcamp train. He was a good leader, and they had wintered profitably. Jayge's pouch was not the only one that was reassuringly plump. Still, it was hard not to be scared. His father's response had surprised him. Holder Childon was not the sort to play jokes; a straight man, he said what he meant and meant what he said. Crenden had often described him so. Childon was a good deal straighter than some holders who looked down on trains as feckless folk little better than thieves, too lazy to carve out a hold for themselves and too arrogant to be beholden to a lord.

Once, when Jayge had been in a fearful brawl and his father

had given him a thorough hiding, he had justified the fight by saying that he had been defending his Blood honor.

"That's still not a reason to fight," his father had said. "Your Blood is as good as the next man's."

"But we're holdless!"

"And what's that to mean?" Crenden had demanded. "There's no law on Pern that has ever said a man and his family *had* to have a hold and live in one place. We can't invade another man's property, but there's land no one's even set foot on all around us. Let those who are weak or scared shiver in four walls . . . not that we've to worry about Thread anymore. But, lad, we've been holders in our time, in Southern Boll, and there're Bloodkin living in it still who're glad to claim us as relatives. If that's all you need to keep from brawling, take no taunt on that score."

"But—but Irtine said we were only one step above thieves and pandlers."

His father had given him a little shake. "We're honest traders, bringing good wares and news to isolated holds that can't always get to a Gather. We travel from inclination and choice. This is a broad and beautiful world we live in, Jayge, and we'll see as much of it as we can. We spend long enough in one place to make friends and understand different ways of doing things. That's far better, to my mind, than never moving out of one valley all your born days, and never hearing a new way of speaking or a new way of doing. Keeps the brain blood circulating; shifts ideas and opens eyes and hearts.

"You're old enough to know how welcome we are at every hold the train stops at. You worked along with us at Vesta River Hold, extending their upper story, so you know we're not lazy folk. Now, hold your head up proud. You've a good Bloodright. And don't let me catch you scrapping again because someone teases you into it. Fight for a good reason, not such a damfool prideful reason. Now, you've taken your punishment. Get to your bedroll."

He had been only a kid then, but now he was nearly a man

and had learned to ignore silly taunts. That had not stopped him from using his fists and his naturally agile body, but he had learned which fights to get into, and how to protect himself well enough to avoid the too visible marks of a brawl. And pride in his Bloodline gave him an air of confidence that only a real fool would challenge. Jayge liked the kind of life his family led: never staying long enough in one place to grow weary of it. There was always something new to see, new friends to make, old ones to reencounter, and, for the time being, races to be won on Fairex.

The trail turned abruptly south, skirting a granite outcropping and affording a wide view of the other shore and the low foothills that would culminate in the immense Red Butte. Suddenly Jayge was conscious of the odd sky to the east, a lowering, threatening gray. He had seen plenty of bad weather in his ten Turns, but never something like that. Glancing toward his father, he saw that Crenden had also noted the strange sky, slowing his mount's walk to study the grayness.

Suddenly Readis, Jayge's youngest uncle, came tearing up from the rear, shouting at Crenden and pointing to the cloud. "That came up sudden, Cren. It's like no weather I've ever seen before," Readis cried. His mount circled Crenden's as both men scanned the horizon.

"Looks like a local storm," Crenden said, marking the discernible edges of the cloud.

Jayge had joined his father by then, and the first wagon was slowing, but Crenden waved them on down the track.

"Lookit!" Jayge's arm shot up, but Crenden and Readis had also seen the flashes of fire that proceeded in bursts along the edge of the cloud. "Lightning?" He was unsure himself, for he had never seen sparks that flared and remained airborne like that. Lightning always connected with the surface!

"That's not lightning," Crenden said. Jayge saw the color drain out of his father's face, and his runner began jigging under him, snorting with fear. "And it's been awful still. Not a single wherry or snake around."

"What is it, Cren?" His brother's uncertainty was making Readis nervous.

"They warned us. They did warn us!" Crenden hauled his runner up on its hindquarters, yelling at the top of his lungs and gesturing with his head for Readis to get to the rear. *"Get moving! Get 'em rolling! Challer, whip 'em up. Get that rig moving!"* He kept turning his mount, his eyes scanning the wooded hillside. "Jayge, get down the track. See if there're any ledges we can shelter under. We've got to find some shelter. If even half of what they say about Thread is really true . . . we sure the flaming hell can't stay out here in the open!"

"Couldn't the lighter wagons make it back to the Hold?" Readis asked. "Borel's team's fast. Dump everything. Put the children in it and go like hell!"

Crenden groaned, shaking his head. "We're hours down the track. If I'd believed the message . . ." He pounded his saddle horn with his clenched fist. "Shelter. We've got to find shelter. Go, Jayge. See if there's any shelter at all."

"Then timber, Cren, slanted against the wagon . . ." Readis suggested, his mount sliding about the track and narrowly missing the edge overhanging the river.

"Thread eats wood, too; that'd be no use. Stone, metal . . . *water*!" Crenden stood in his stirrups, pointing down to the river that frothed along its rocky bed.

"That?" Readis responded. "Not deep enough, and far too fast!"

"But there's a pool, a big one, near the first cascade. If we could make that . . . Jayge, scoot along. See how far away that pool is. Challer, whip up that team and follow Jayge as fast as you can. Readis, unhitch the beasts from that timber wagon. We can't save it, but we'll need the beasts. *Move out! Whip 'em up!"*

Jayge dug his heels into Fairex's side. Why did they have

to be caught on this part of the track? On the one day's trek through forest and hill that could provide no real shelter? He knew the pool his father meant—it was a good fishing spot, and it would be deep with all the winter rains shedding from the hills. But a pool? That was no real shelter from Threadfall. Jayge knew the Teaching songs as well as any kid of Pern, and it was stone walls and stout metal shutters that one needed during Threadfall. As the track rose to the crest of a hill, the deep basin came into view, its waters sparkling invitingly. Thread could devour flesh. How deep did one have to be under water to be safe?

Jayge lifted Fairex into a hard gallop, counting in rhythm with the little beast's strides so that he could judge the time it would take to reach the pool. He kept watching the banks and the track, hoping that he might notice a rock ledge or even a burrow. They could put the babies in the burrows. How long did a Fall last? Jayge was so agitated that he could not bring the Traditional Duty ballads to mind.

It would have to be the pool then, he thought as he and Fairex plunged down the incline. Fifteen minutes even for the biggest, heaviest wagon. And there was a line of big boulders that formed a natural dam—he could see the current flowing smoothly over the lip. He kicked Fairex on into the water to test its depth. The gallant little mare was swimming in moments, and Jayge plunged off her back, shuddering at the chill in the water and bobbing under as his feet found no purchase. Deep enough! Everyone but the wee babies could swim. But swim where? Jayge yanked on Fairex's rein, and obediently she circled to face the river's edge. When he saw her hit the bottom, he swung himself up into the saddle and started her back the way they had just come.

He could hear the sounds of the train echoing loudly down the valley: the thunder of hooves and wagon wheels, the urgency of strident calls. Jayge thanked the Dawn Sisters that all the wagons had been scrupulously checked before they had left Kimmage Hold. Now was not the time for a wheel to

ANNE MCCAFFREY

spin off or an axle to break. He only hoped the burden beasts
could be forced out of their usual plodding pace.

Jayge kept his eyes on the cloud as he raced back. What
were those gouts of flame? It looked like thousands of flame-
flies, the nocturnal creatures he and his friends had tried to
capture in Nerat's lush jungles. And then he realized what he
was seeing. Dragons! Benden Weyr's dragonriders were flying Thread! As dragonriders should! As dragonriders always
had and now were again, protecting Pern from Threadfall.
Jayge felt a surge of relief that was instantly overwhelmed by
confusion. If the dragonriders were already flaming Thread
from the skies, why would the traders need the river pool?

"Worlds are lost or worlds are saved, by those dangers
dragon-braved?" The verse sprang to Jayge's mind, but it was
not the one he wanted. "Lord of the hold, your charge is
sure, in thick walls, metal doors, and no verdure." But Lilcamp folk were holdless.

Then his father came galloping around the bend, Challer's
rig nearly at his heels.

"The pool's just down this hill . . ." Jayge began.

"I can see it myself. Tell the others!" Crenden waved his
son back down the line.

The other wagons were strung out, their canvas tops swaying dangerously from side to side. Already bundles had top-
pled—or been tossed out—on the roadside, and Jayge started
to pull Fairex up in order to retrieve something.

"Don't stop!" his father ordered.

Habit warred with that order: Lilcamp folk never littered
their path with discards. Jayge made his way back to the next
wagon, halting Fairex only long enough to shout to Auntie
Temma, always a clever driver, who actually had her two
yokes clumping along at an awkward canter. He had to jump
Fairex up into the woods to avoid being caught up in the
stampede of the loose runners and stock. He saw the deserted
timber wagon, rocks propped under its wheels, and, lumber-
ing along behind the loose animals, the eight yoke of burden

beasts that had pulled the Lilcamp payload. Borel, his oldest uncle, had all his kids prodding the bawling creatures, who bucked and kicked against the sticks instead of moving forward until the two drovers began to flick weighted lashes at the knobby rumps.

Jayge cantered on down the line, passing Auntie Nik and her husband, who were riding burden beasts and hauling others by their nose rings. The last wagon had been switched to runner teams and was picking up speed. Jayge swung in behind it, making Fairex sidle as he punched at crates perilously close to falling out. He did pick up some lost baggage, scooping it up and lobbing it into the back of the nearest wagon. He also tried to keep in mind just where the strewn belongings had landed, so that after all the fuss was over he would know where to retrieve them. Traders learned to be very good at marking places. Once Jayge had been somewhere new, he could always return, the way was so clearly printed in his head.

By the time the Lilcamps were all in the pool, the gray mass of Thread was nearly upon them. The pool was full of floating debris from the wagons that had been driven into the deepest part. Crenden and the uncles were trying to make certain that the animals would not drown themselves, for the burden beasts were bawling and the runners were neighing in panic. Some of the yoked beasts were trying to climb up onto the far bank.

Jayge had swum Fairex to the dam side of the pool, where some boulders loomed above the water. The mare's eyes were wide with fright, her nostrils distended. Only his stubborn hold on her reins kept her from swimming off. He was treading water, one hand locked desperately around a rocky knob.

The scene before him would be forever etched in his mind: people thrashing in the water, their yells and shrieks no less terrified than those of the animals; bundles floating free and going over the dam; mothers holding young children onto the tops of submerged wagons; Crenden, in the shallows, rushing from one side of the ford to the other, enforcing orders with his lash, yelling that they were only safe *under* the water, that when Thread fell they all must hold their breath under the water! Forever Jayge always would remember the scene framed by the sight of the inexorable approach of Thread— and the dragonriders flaming it.

Then, not wanting to believe his eyes, Jayge had his first glimpse of Thread. Three long spears of the stuff slapped into the tall standing trees on the bank. Their trunks flared briefly and then began to vanish. So did the brush and trees on either side. Jayge blinked, and there was a bald patch and something disgustingly pulsing, rolling—and with every turn more of the thick mulch disappeared and more trees fell. Suddenly a fountain of flame washed across the spot. He saw the long twisting *thing* in the center of the flame turn black and burn quickly, adding an oily yellow smoke to the clean fire. Jayge almost missed seeing the dragon at all, he was so caught by the terror of the Thread burrow. But the dragon hovered briefly, to be sure of the destruction, so Jayge caught the sight of the huge golden body as the dragon—gold was for queens, wasn't it?—beat strongly upward and flamed again, farther up the hill. There was another dragon farther down the river valley, another gold. But someone had told him that gold dragons did not fly. And there was only the one queen in Benden Weyr.

Before he could puzzle that, he heard hissing, the sound of something hot entering the pool. Fairex thrashed, shrilling in terror, and Jayge saw the thick rope of Thread coming down almost on top of them. Diving for Fairex's head, he ducked them both under the water, working his arms violently to ward the stuff away from him.

Something hit Jayge on the back of his head, and his warding hand came into contact with a pot, floating free from some wagon. Flailing to the surface, he found himself in the midst of cooking wares. Fairex had her head above water again, snorting to clear her nostrils. The current pulled at Jayge, and he grabbed at a floating saddle tie and yanked himself to the mare. He guided her away from the break, water pressure pushing them against the boulders. The pot, and a big lid, clanked against the stones beside him.

The screaming about him took on a new note, shrill with fear and pain, both human and animal. He looked over his shoulder and saw Thread falling across the pool, falling on everything. Where were the dragonriders? He craned his head up and saw the wriggling, falling *things*. Then there was a dreadful hiss and a terrified bawl from Fairex beside him told him that a thick tendril of Thread was attacking. Jayge grabbed the pot and scooped up the hideous thing, then plunged pot and its contents under water. The lid bounced against him, and Jayge grabbed it and held it as a shield over his head and that of his frantic mare. When he felt something hit it, he yelled and gave a frantic push to dislodge the Thread, pro-pelling himself backward and kicking water over Fairex's head in case that would do some good.

He had no sooner done so than he caught sight of flame and was aware of a tremendous whooshing noise, followed by a shout that his ears heard as "You bleeding fools!" Then there were more licks of fire while Jayge huddled under his pot lid, one arm around his mare's neck. Blood ran from her rump and turned the water pink. He also saw, disbelieving, the blackened head of a runner, turning idly and then disap-pearing as the current caught it and took it over the dam. Then he was far too occupied with fending Thread off himself and his mare, trying to keep any of the drowning stuff from touching him. His leather pants were reduced to shreds, and his boots, he found when he was able to examine them, were Threadscored.

Much later, Jayge learned that it took about ten to fifteen minutes for the full Threadfall to overpass a stationary point, and that the dragonriders did not always overpass rivers and lakes because Thread drowned in water—and that the Oldtim-ers, who came from an earlier time when Thread had been a constant menace, were resentful of having to protect so much forestry.

That terrible noon, when Jayge finally led an exhausted Fairex out of the water, the pool was filled with lifeless bobbing bodies, animal and human, and the pitiful remnants of the prosperous trader train.

"Jayge, we'll need a fire," his father said in a dull voice as he followed his son out of the water, dragging the sodden gear he had removed from the body of his rangy runner.

Jayge looked up the bank to the forested slope, amazed to see that fine stand of trees reduced to smoldering trunks and charred circles, black and oily smoke rising ominously. The rich, dense woods had been changed to barren smoking poles, branchless and charred.

The hillside hid from view the continuation of Fall and dragonfire, and once again the sun blazed down. Jayge shivered. He paused long enough to take the saddle off Fairex who stood, all four legs Threadscored, head down and uncertain, too tired to shake water or blood from her body.

"Move it, lad," his father muttered, starting back to the pool to help Temma, who was carrying a still form out of the cold water.

Muted sobbing and louder cries of grief followed Jayge up the slope. It took him a long time to find enough unconsumed wood to start any sort of a fire. He walked very cautiously, terrified that a tendril of Thread might have survived the dragonfire. When he got back to the river, he kept his eyes on the fire he was starting, unwilling to look at the still forms lying on the stony verge. He was immensely relieved to see that his mother was there, bandaging someone's head. He saw Aunt Temma, too, but he had to turn away from the sight of the hideous raw marks, like something cut by the claws of the biggest wherry ever, on Readis's back, Aunt Bedda was rocking back and forth, and Jayge could not bear to find out if his baby cousin was injured or dead. Not just yet.

As soon as he got the fire going, he took the rope from his

saddle and brought Fairex with him to bring more wood down to the shore. On his way back, he made himself see the extent of the tragedy. Beyond the new piles of soaking bundles and wet crates, there were seven small bundles, three very small and three larger ones. No, the babies would not have made it. They would not have known to hold their breath under water. Nor would his younger sister, or his youngest cousins.

Tears streamed down Jayge's face as he piled the wood by the stones that surrounded the fire. Two dented kettles were heating water, and, astonishingly, a soup pot had been recovered. Saddles had been placed in a ring around the fire to dry. Someone was splashing in the pool, and he saw there, for the first time, the metal bands that had once spread the canvas wagontops, like the ribs of some great water snake. Aunt Temma burst to the surface and began to tug on a rope. He saw his father struggling with something still under the rope. Borel and Readis, despite their wounds, were desperately pulling at yet another submerged article.

Jayge had just turned to untie the wood piled on Fairex' back when abruptly she wheeled and dashed back up the slope, racing away from the camp as if a wherry had attacked her. Then dirt and sand flew around him, over the fire and into the soup pot. Startled, Jayge looked up, unable to imagine what new hazard faced them.

A huge brown dragon was settling to the top of the track above the pool.

"You there, boy! Who's in charge of this ground crew? How many burrows have you found? These woods are disastrous!"

At first Jayge could not understand the words rattled at him. There was an odd inflection in the man's voice that startled him. The harpers kept the language from altering too much, his mother had once told him when he had first encountered the slower speech of the southerners. But the voice of the dragonrider, so small up there perched between the neck ridges of the big beast, sounded strange to Jayge's ears. And the man did not really look like any man Jayge had ever seen. He seemed to have huge eyes, and no hair, and leather all over. Were dragonmen different from the rest of Pern's people? Realizing that his mouth had dropped open, Jayge clamped his jaws shut.

"You can't be ground crew. You're much too small to be any use! Who's in charge here?" The rider sounded offended, annoyed. "This isn't what I'm used to, I assure you. You'll have to do better than this!"

"Will we just?" Crenden strode forward, Borel right behind him along with Temma and Gledia.

"Lads *and* women! Only two men! You can't have efficient ground crews if this is all you can provide us," the rider continued. Suddenly he took off a close-fitting cap, revealing a face that was quite human, if creased with a deep scowl and accentuated by the soot marks on his cheeks.

Jayge stared, aware of many details that he would recall later and with cynical accuracy: except that the rider wore his hair cropped close to his scalp, he was really like any other man. Under other circumstances and with later knowledge, Jayge might have forgiven him his irascibility, and even some of his scathing disapproval. But not that day.

However, it was the dragon that fascinated Jayge. He noted the dark streaks of soot on the dragon's brown hide; the two damaged ridges; the rough scars on its forequarters—long thin scars, darker brown, many of them along its barrel and back—and the thickening of tissue along several wing vanes. But it was the ineffable weariness in the dragon's eyes, whirling slightly and coloring from a purple to a blue-green, that Jayge noted particularly. Those eyes whirled in Jayge's dreams for many nights thereafter—but his strongest impression was of the weariness, a fatigue that he himself certainly felt down to his very bones.

Although it was the dragon who dominated that first moment, the rider soon took center stage with his strong words and the contemptuous tone in which he delivered them. He spoke to Crenden as if the trader were a drudge, an unperson of no importance but to serve the dragonrider's orders. For his father, and for himself, and for the shattered remainder of their kin, Jayge resented that tone, that dragonrider, and all he stood for. And he hated the dragonrider for all he had not done to protect them.

"We aren't ground crew, dragonrider. We're what's left of the Lilcamp train," Crenden said in a hoarse voice. Those behind stared wearily up with unspoken resentment.

"A train?" The dragonrider was contemptuous. "A train—out during Threadfall? Man, you're insane."

"We knew of no Threadfall when we left Kimmage Hold."

Jayge drew in his breath. He had never heard his father utter a falsehood—yet that was not a true lie. They had not heard of Threadfall at the time they had set out from Kimmage Hold. And it was right for his father to shame the dragonrider.

"You should have known!" The dragonrider would not accept responsibility. "Word was sent out to all holds."

"It didn't reach Kimmage Hold before we left." Crenden was equally determined to set the blame.

"Well, we can't protect every stupid trader and isolated spot, you know. And I'm beginning to wonder why we bothered to come here at all, if this is all the gratitude we receive! Which lord are you beholden to? Take it up with him. It was up to him to be sure you were warned. And if there're no ground crews from Kimmage, this entire area could be at risk. C'mon, Rimbeth. Now we've got to check the whole bloody area!" He glared at Crenden. "It'll be your fault if there're burrows here. You hear me?"

With that, the dragonrider replaced his helmet and took a firm grip on the straps that fastened him into position. In the brief moment, Jayge was certain that the dragon was looking directly at him as he stood there by the fire. Then the big beast turned his head, spread his wings, and launched himself into the sky.

"Rimbeth's rider, I'll know you again! I'll seek you out if

it's the last thing I do!'' Crenden's words were a fierce shout
as he raised his fist skyward.

Jayge watched, incredulous, as first the dragon was there,
and then it was not. Dragonriders were not what he had expected them to be, what he had been taught they should be.
He never wanted to see another dragonrider in his life.

The next morning, they managed to get four wagons out of
the pool, along with as much of their baggage as remained
usable after the immersion. Their foodstores had been destroyed, or swept away by the current. Many of the lighter
bundles and crates had either been burned up, or had floated
loose and been lost. Three of the twelve surviving beasts had
lost eyes to Threadfall; all were savagely scored across their
backs and the muzzles they had lifted out of the water to
breathe. But they could be harnessed, and without them the
retrieval of the wagons would have been impossible. Only
four of the loose runners made their way back, badly scored
but alive.

Jayge counted himself and Fairex very lucky indeed when
he had time to think about anything but the appalling tragedy. His mother seemed scarcely to realize the loss of her two
youngest children. She kept looking about her, a puzzled
frown on her face. Even before Crenden had made the decision to seek help from Kimmage Hold, she had begun to
cough, a soft, apologetic cough.

The second morning, with patched harness and wagons still
damp, the Lilcamps turned back to Kimmage Hold. It was an
uphill journey, hard on animals with open sores on their
backs, and on people weighed down by grief and despair.
Jayge led his little mare as she trudged patiently with Borel's
three small weeping children on her back. Their mother had
shielded them from a tangle of Thread that had eaten her to
the bone before her lifeless form had slid into the pool,

drowning the voracious organism. Challer had died trying to protect his prize team.

"I don't understand it, Brother," Jayge heard his Uncle Readis murmur to his father as they trudged up the road. "Why did Childon not send someone to help us?"

"We survived without them," Crenden said emotionlessly.

"I can't call the loss of seven people and most of our wagons 'survival,' Cren!" His voice was rough with anger. "Simple decency requires Childon—"

"Simple decency flew out of the hold when Thread fell. You heard that dragonrider, clear as I did!"

"But . . . I heard Childon beg you to stay. Surely they'll need us more now."

Crenden gave his younger brother a long cynical stare and then shrugged, plodding along in boots that had split open with the wear of the last few days. Jayge squirmed inside himself, and his hand went to his little hoard of credits. There would be no new saddle now. Other things would be needed more. Young as he was, Jayge knew that everything had abruptly altered. And young as he was, he also recognized the essential injustice that Childon, and all Kimmage Holders, imposed on the Lilcamps when they returned. Where before they had been honored guests, valuable partners in a logging venture, the Lilcamps had lost most of their assets—wagons, livestock, and tools.

"I've my own folk, beholden to me, to provide for now, for the fifty long Turns this Pass will last. I can't take in any holdless and improvident family to apply to me," Childon said, never once looking Crenden straight in the eye. "You've wounded and sick, and kids too young to be useful. Your stock's all injured. Take time and medicine to heal 'em. I've got to provide ground crews for every Fall, to support not only Igen Weyr but Benden when they call on us. I'm going to be hard-pressed to look after my own. You must understand my position."

For one long hopeful moment, Jayge thought his father was

going to storm indignantly out of the hold. Then Gledia coughed, trying to smother it in her hand. That was the moment, Jayge later decided, when his father capitulated. His wide shoulders sagged and he bowed his head. "I do understand your position, Holder Childon."

"Well, just so's you understand, we'll see how things go on. You can bed down in the beasthold. I lost a lot of stock that're going to be very hard to replace. I'll talk about compensation for yours later, for I can't waste fodder on the useless, not with Thread falling I can't."

No Lilcamp was really surprised when Readis, unwilling to accept such humiliation, left during the night. For many nights afterward, Jayge had nightmares involving dragon eyes shooting fire lances through his uncle's twisting, bloody body. Later that spring, Jayge's hoarded credits helped pay the healer for Gledia's treatment. But Gledia died before full summer, while all the ablebodied men, including Jayge, were out as ground crew.

2

NORTH TELGAR HOLD TO IGEN HOLD, PRESENT PASS, 02.04.12

Thella heard about the spring Gather at Igen Hold on one of her dark-night forays to Far Cry Hold, where she had gone to acquire seedlings from their starting beds to renew the small garden she had just begun. Hiding behind bales of dry fodder, she overheard a conversation between the beast-master and the barnman; both were plainly envious of those chosen to make the trip to Igen, despite the dangers of such a journey during a Pass.

Knowledge of a Gather was very reassuring to the renegade Telgar Blooddaughter. Before she could hope to attract folk to work in her high mountain hold, she would have to supply basic needs, and legitimately. In one trip to a large Gather, she could quite possibly acquire all she needed. She was already making plans as she waited for the men to leave so she could sneak to the greenhouses and help herself to the seedlings.

It had taken her all that first Turn to recover from the shocking frustration of Threadfall. Thella did not cope well with failure. Not only had she lost two of her fine runners to the

disgusting stuff—well, the animals had panicked with dragons flying over them and run off a precipice—but all her careful and ambitious plans had had to be abandoned. The
disappointment had plunged her into a deep roiling depression. She had planned so carefully: if Thread had only held
off until the following Turn, she would have established herself in her own hold.

She had found the place during one of her ramblings in the
high country. Someone had once lived—and died—there, for
she had removed twelve skulls, the only part of the dead that
mountain snakes had been unable to masticate. What had
killed the holders would always be a mystery, although Thella
had heard of instances where entire hold populations had
been wiped out by virulent disease. But they must once have
lived well. The hold still held wooden furnishings; the stout
slab table and the bedframes, dry and dusty, were usable. The
metal fittings and utensils had a thin coat of rust, but that
could be sanded off. There were cisterns for water and basins
for bathing. Most of the south-facing apertures, protected by
deep embrasures, had retained their glass. Four good hearths
for warmth and cooking needed only to be cleaned to be used.
In her initial investigations as a young and optimistic girl as
yet unthwarted by the Threadfall that had destroyed her
plans, Thella had even found cloth, brittle with age, in the
stone storage chests of the sleeping quarters and grain in the
beasthold. There were stone walls around enough highland
pastures to support adequate meat animals, and pens were
set into one side of the cavern. Thella knew the Masterherdsman had hardy strains that would thrive on mountain fields.
She did not like the notion of sharing her living space with
beasts, but she had heard that it was one way of generating
additional warmth. One would need all the heat one could
get in these hills.

But the hold could have been completely reestablished and
hers! Hers! If she had just had the Turn or two. The ancient
Contract Law of Pern gave her that right. She could have in-

sisted that the Conclave of Lord Holders permit it, once she could prove her competence. Her father had told her, in answer to discreet questions, that anyone could form a hold, so long as it could be proved to be self-sufficient and remained well managed. And a discreet check of the record hides told her that a Benamin Bloodline had once established that mountain hold, but that it had been untenanted since before the last Pass.

Only Thella's determination to prove her competence—and her pride as eldest daughter of one of the proudest Holds on Pern, direct descendant of its founder, in whom the best qualities of her Bloodline were manifest in her beauty, intelligence, and skill—had kept her alive that first Turn. But she had been reduced to a hand-to-mouth existence which even traveling folk would have scorned. Cursing every step of the way, she had been forced to leave her mountainhold that first winter, before the snows blocked the one trail down, or leave her own skeleton for snake fodder.

Insult was added to injury as once again all of Pern, Hold and Hall, had to rely on those wretched dragonriders who should have been thoroughly redundant. Her father had held that opinion. No dragonrider had minced through Telgar's Hold since that last Pass had ended. It was all part of a giant concatenation of circumstances ranked against her, Thella of Telgar. But she would prove her durability and resilience. Not even Thread would thwart her in the end.

So by the coming of the second spring of that improbable—but actual—Pass, Thella had finally wintered comfortably, having located three secure, well-concealed caves that were small but adequate for shelter. She had left each of them provisioned for reuse should she require them again. By that time she had become deft at extracting supplies from minor holds in Telgar and Lemos. Except for boots. She had hard-to-fit feet—rather long, wide across the ball, and narrow in the heel—and no matter where she had looked, she had been unable to find suitable footwear. Before she had always had the hold cobbler to supply her boots and shoes; she had left behind a locker full of them, and as hard wear had lacerated worn leather, she regretted her lack of foresight. But then, she had not anticipated living in the rough for nearly two full Turns.

She had acquired all other items of clothing as needed. There were quite a few tall men in Far Cry and one of the other nearby holds, so clothes were plentiful. She took only new trousers and shirts, of course—not even in extremity would Thella of Telgar wear used clothing. She had no trouble getting her hands on an appropriate jacket, a shaggy winter hide, and she had lifted furred sleeping bags, one for each of her three boltholes. Those supplies, along with the food she took, were after all no more than a modest portion of the tithe due a Lord Holder's family, so she had no compunction about her acquisitions; she merely did not wish to be seen— yet. But boots . . . boots were another matter, and she might have foregone principle to get decent boots.

A journey to Igen Hold for a Gather would be the best way to end the footwear problem and satisfy one or two other minor needs that would fulfill the rudimentary requirements of her prospective holders. Perhaps she would be able to hire a likely herdsman, preferably one with a family to supply her with drudges. They could camp in the beasthold section and not interfere with her privacy. She had not wanted to take on anyone local, and Gathers were an excellent place to find suitable, and reliable, persons.

Igen's Gather was slated to begin in ten days. The maps she had taken from Telgar—and had committed to memory— gave the position of camping caverns all the way down the Lemos Valley to Igen, so she did not expect the outward bound journey to pose her any problems. According to what she had overheard, there would be one Threadfall—falling to the north over High Telgar—and she would have to wait out another one hitting Keroon and Igen. She wished, and not for the first time over the past eighteen months, that she knew exactly when Threadfall was due. She had had some very narrow escapes—both from Fall itself and from being seen by ground crews and sweepriders. It did not suit her—yet—for any suspicion of her whereabouts or plans to be known.

She made the trip with both runners, switching from one to the other so that she could set a good pace. She would quickly outdistance the Far Cry travelers whom she did not wish to meet on the trace, although they had a head start. She had been forced to alter her overnight plans when one of her intended campsites proved fully occupied. But her fury over that was diverted when she discovered a hitherto unmarked cave with a small stream making a pool by its inner wall—she had been able to hobble the runners inside and treat herself to the luxury of a bath. She marked the spot unobtrusively so that she could find it again, secure in her infallible memory for places.

From then on, she made a point of finding secondary caverns and thus avoided any unnecessary encounters. An astonishing number of folk were on the move—understandable, since this was evidently the first spring Gather held in the new Pass.

By the night before, she was no more than an hour's quickstep from Igen. In the dawn darkness, she had watered her runners at the wide river and left them hobbled in a blind ravine, its slopes greening in the swift verdant growth of the desert springtime; her gear she stored behind a boulder. From a careless cotwife she had acquired the voluminous draperies worn by desert holders, contrived a suitable band to secure the headdress and conceal her sun-streaked blond hair, begrimed her face, and used charcoal to thicken her eyebrows, giving her a grimmer cast. Then, with the traditional waterskin of the desert holder slung across her back, she was jogging along the high ground above the river even before she could make out the Gather flag flying from the drum tower of Igen Hold.

She quickly overtook groups of excited chattering folk

headed in the same direction and merely grunted acknowledgment of their greetings; desert folk tended to taciturnity,
so conversation would not be expected of her. And as she had
elected to run, she passed all those who were proceeding at
a less demanding pace to their destination.

She arrived in full dawn to find the Igen Gathergrounds
well populated and gave an ungrudged quartermark for several pockets of hot bread, fresh cooked on a metal sheet over
a crackling hot oilbrush fire. Slices of a soft cheese inside the
bread made a filling breakfast. She was a bit irritated when
she was grossly overcharged for a misshapen clay mug for
klah. But it was pay or go without, and the smell of the bev-
erage after long abstinence was more than she could endure.
She had never had to bring utensils to a Gather, having always been accommodated in the Lord Holder's hall, and she
had not thought to bring any from her travel pack. Fortunately, though the mug was imperfect, the klah was freshly
made, not something that had aged on the hearth all night.
Nearby, cooks were busy trussing a dozen herdbeast car-
casses onto spits over glowing firepits, the aromas soon to
remind Gatherers of the excellent spices that always seasoned
Igen roasts.

Replete, she strolled toward the great, colorful Gather tents,
her critical gaze noting storage creases and recent repairs to
tunnel-snake holes. Igen Gathers had unusual accommodations. With the sun at near equatorial intensity by midday,
traders could not have endured its fierce glare, so stalls were
erected under a square of tented corridors, where flaps could
be rolled up to provide both ventilation and quick exit. Thella
had already noted scrawny brats sneaking in and out. At the
first corner entrance the Gathermaster was overseeing the setting of the poles for an awning against the vicious noonday
sun. The air inside was still cool from the chilly desert night.
Already many stalls were ready, journeymen enticing the
trickle of Gatherers walking the tented square.

Thella gave the tannercraft stalls a cursory glance, noting

that a workbench had been set up and a variety of trial lasts and tools laid out, ready to ensure perfect fittings. Apprentices were still unpacking travel panniers under the eyes of the Master, who was arranging attractive displays of his wares, and an older journeyman was fussily adjusting the price boards attached to the tentpole. Thella walked on, suddenly taking in the meaning of the sign announcing that the Master's leathers were Threadscore-proofed. She snorted. Threadscore-proofed indeed!

She ignored weaver and smith craft stalls for the moment and stopped to fill the wretched mug with fruit juice. It was so refreshing that she stayed for another, wondering how soon the porous, badly fired clay would begin to leak. The tent, despite ventilation, was beginning to warm up as more people pressed in to do their buying before the noonday heat forced everyone to rest. She walked the entire square and then, to assuage her wrath against the extortionate potter, picked up a rock that someone had used to pound in tentpegs and lobbed it deftly over her shoulder at his stand. As she slipped back into the tent, she heard a satisfactory shattering and pained outcry, and smiled.

Feeling equable again, she was ready to see about boots. When the Mastertanner politely turned her over to a journeyman so that he could serve some better dressed clients, she seethed once more and wondered how she could repay his discourtesy; but her mood altered as the journeyman, a soft-spoken man with big hands, fingers scarred from leatherknife and needle, was soothingly deferential and efficient. He fitted her immediately to a good stout pair of midcalf hide boots and a pair of ankle-high wherhide semiboots, then took careful measurements for full leg boots, assuring her that they would be sewn and ready before high noon. She paid him for the hide boots, which she immediately put on, and the semiboots, which she tied onto her waterbag, and gave him half of the price of the third pair. That way, if her plans altered and she could not pick up the boots, she would not be out too much credit. She waited as he summoned an apprentice to begin cutting the sole to the pattern he had just made. Then, appeased, she left the stall.

It was during her second stop at the bake fire that Thella noticed the big man. Even at a Gather he was exceptional—exceptionally ragged, too, with a brooding angry look that made people give him a span or two of distance from themselves. There was something almost pathetic about his air of aloofness, as if he knew, and even expected, to be shunned and avoided. He grudgingly gave up a quarter credit to pay for bread, carefully choosing the biggest of the pieces on the metal sheet, then waiting for them to finish baking. But he was very strong, and that commended him to her. She would need strong men, preferably ones who would be very grateful to her for taking them on.

Suddenly it came to her that there seemed to be an unusually large number of holdless at the Gather, if their status could be judged by their scruffy appearances. Few actually ventured into the Gather tent, which was as it should be if they had no marks to pass, but they circulated freely among the crowds outside. Her belt pouch, full of good Telgar currency, was hidden from view under her loose robes, but nevertheless she unobtrusively shoved it under her shirt as she looked about for the guards Lord Laudey ought to have posted to forestall disturbances and deal with petty theft. And this Gather was particularly crowded, it being the first spring Gather in the Pass.

Ah, that was it, she realized. There were always more holdless during a Pass. Holders, with absolute authority over those within their walls, made sure that everyone they supported in such parlous times was efficiently worthy of his or her keep. A holder, major or minor, could withhold shelter from travelers even if the leading edge of Fall was close. In such times, people worked harder and obeyed right sharp, or they lost their sanctuary. As it should be, Thella thought with complete approval.

If she had only had a little more time before the Pass had started, she would have been able to exercise such time-honored options. She still would, or die in the doing. In one way, the Pass might work to her advantage. For the promise of shelter within stone walls, there would be those eager to work even in a high isolated hold. She began to scrutinize the holdless with an eye to the shoulder knots of their crafts, assessing their strength and desperation. Her holding might not be much yet, but it had possibilities. She wandered around the stall square again, keeping an eye on the progress of her third pair of boots and listening for any news or helpful information.

What she heard was better than a harper's tale. A lot had happened since Thread had started falling on Pern again. Benden Weyr had tried desperately to cope with the Falls. Then, in an act of heroism unparalleled even for Pern's legendary heroes, Lessa, rider of Ramoth, Benden's only queen, had risked her own life and the life of her dragon in order to bring the five lost Weyrs of Pern forward, going back 400 Turns to a past time when there had been six full Weyrs and persuading them to assist the seemingly doomed present.

Thella found the mechanics of the feat hard to believe, but the fact was clearly demonstrated by the appearance of swaggering dragonriders wearing the colors of Telgar, Ista, and Igen Weyrs, as well as Benden. And all too clearly, Hold and Hall deferred to them in everything.

On a later circuit, when she saw the apprentice in an ingratiating pose with an Ista dragonrider, she gave him a stern glare. The young man blanched, apologized, and returned to stitching her half-finished boot. The very idea of his deferring work for a Telgar. . . . Reluctantly Thella realized that she no longer had that Blood advantage and stalked away in a savage mood.

Those dragonriders! Acting as if the Gather had been put on just for their benefit. She saw girls surrounding most of these dragonriders, and juveniles hanging on the words of

the others! Insidious group! And yet, despite her disenchant-
ment, Thella noticed a definite difference between riders from
Benden and those of the other three Weyrs. The—what was
the term she had heard? Oldtimers?—the Oldtimers walked
with the unmistakable swagger of those totally assured of their
eminence, while equally obvious was a certain eager, almost
apologetic deference in the Benden riders. Thella approved of
neither stance. Without the Lord Holders' support, the Weyr—
Weyrs, she corrected herself, though she still found it difficult
to believe in the restoration—could not have continued to
exist.

It was becoming stuffy in the tented square, but by the time
she had eaten her nooning under the canopies that had been
raised near the firepits, her boots were receiving a final polish.
The Mastertanner stamped his approval on the finished product, and she paid over the second half. Her boots were handed
to her, neatly encased in a rough cloth bag that she hung with
the other packages.

During her circuit of the Gatherstalls, Thella had purchased
seed for late-maturing root vegetables, guaranteed by the
Masterfarmer in attendance to give a good yield. She also purchased spices; a few small sacks would not weigh down her
runners and would be very welcome to season wild wherry
meat. The noon sun was pouring down on the tents, making
the air within uncomfortably hot. People were beginning to
look for places in the lounge areas to wait out the worst of
the heat. Though she had not yet hired any workers for her
hold, Thella had half a mind to leave, but it was an impossible
time to travel. So she found a space in the western course of
the Gathertent and, despite some long moments brooding
about possibilities, made herself as comfortable as possible,
her new boots forming a pillow. Then reassured by the sight
of guards patrolling to protect the nappers, she fell asleep.

A sense of movement near her outstretched hand awoke
her. She had become sensitive to the slightest sound, even
the near-silent approach of tunnel snakes, in the past Turn or

so. Opening her eyes, she saw a small figure bending over a sleeping man just beyond her, a dirty hand reaching with a knife to cut the bulging pouch. Stupid of him not to conceal such a temptation, she reflected. Her knife was instantly in her hand, jabbing at the bent back. She shoved the blade deftly into the fleshy part of a thigh, heard a stifled intake of breath, and the figure bolted, slipping under the tent flap. She looked back at the owner of the pouch, whose round wide open eyes were on her bloodied blade.

"You're quick indeed," he said, shoving his pouch into his shirt and rearranging his clothing to hide the bulge. His Craftknot, Thella saw, identified him as an Igen herder.

"You should have done that before you slept," Thella muttered, disgruntled. She hated being aroused, and she had been sleeping deeply. She wiped her knife on the tail of someone else's cloak, aware of the almost suffocating blanket of heat even though a little breeze stirred the tent flap. She would never get back to sleep again, and it was still too hot to think of returning to her runners.

"I had it under me. I've turned in my sleep," the herder replied, equally disgruntled. He waved one hand over his face, courting the breeze. "I'm not that green, I'll have you know. I chose my spot among honest men and women," he added in a querulous aggrieved tone. "Look at the guard, fast asleep on both feet." But even as he spoke, the guard could be seen eyeing them. "It's getting so honest folk"—he gestured to their sleeping mates, who were indeed a prosperous-looking lot, wearing the brand-new knots of minor Igen and Keroon holds on their best Gather clothes—"can't be protected at Gathers with so many holdless about. It's time to complain about this shocking disregard for privacy. Make some examples. Should be stopped. The more of us who speak out, the sooner there'll be a remedy to such behavior. You'll speak, of course?" His voice had grown louder with each sentence, and some of the sleepers stirred. The guard warned them with a hand gesture to be quieter.

"Speak?" Thella was briefly astonished at the man's audacity. "No." Then, seeing that she had offended him, she added, "I must be on the road at dark. Shocking problem, I agree." It cost her nothing to be conciliatory.

He seemed suddenly indecisive. "A long way to go?"

She nodded, ostentatiously settling herself to resume her rest.

"North, perhaps, along the western bank?"

Thella gave him a long look of surprise, quite forgetting for the moment that she wore rough guise and was tall enough to be mistaken for a man.

"For a ways." She thought of that pouch, bulging with credits. He was much older than she was, and did not look particularly fit. Get a ways out of earshot, knock him on the head, and she could have that pouch and whatever he carried in his travel sack with little trouble to herself.

"I'd make it worth your while to see me to my holding," he added, winking meaningfully. "You'd be there before the moons set. And a harper halfmark in your hand for your company."

"Aye, for that I'll match my steps to yours then," Thella agreed after a thoughtful pause. How easily deceived an honest man was, seeing his own honesty in others, she thought. She gave him a nod and closed her eyes. She would need the rest of her nap.

The murmur of renewed activity roused her the second time. She and the Igen herder emerged into the cooling twilight and made for the latrine pits. She eluded him in the general shuffle for privacy and sought him out at the washing basins.

Harpers were already playing in the Dancing Square, though no one would be treading any measures yet. The evening air was heavy with the tantalizing smell of roasted spiced meats, and by common consent, Thella and the herder joined the lines, waiting for a skewered slab of the seasoned meat. The herder paid for two cups of wine.

"A thanks for your timely intervention. Have you seen anyone limping?" the herder asked. Thella shook her head, but she had not been looking for the culprit; instead she had been watching the big man she had noticed earlier grab a fallen piece of meat and run off with it. Hungry enough to eat it, sand and all, she thought, irritated by the sight. Gatherers ought to be able to enjoy their food without such intrusions. Still, if the man were that far down on his luck, and that quick and strong . . . she wished she had not promised to accompany the herder.

Then, because she knew such courtesies were expected at a Gather even between new acquaintances, she bought a second round of wine. Drink made a man unwary. She also made certain as she dropped a halfmark in the vintner's wine-stained hand that the herder saw that she was well marked herself.

She bought several more slabs. "For my nooning," she told the herder, who then assured her that he would provide her with that meal.

"I thought you said we'd be at your croft by the moonset," she said, giving him a quick stare.

"To be sure, to be sure," the herder hastily agreed. He said no more as she folded the meat into the pocket of the water-skin.

But she had caught a note in his voice, an air about him, that she distrusted, though she was quick enough not to give him any clue of her suspicion. He bought them both more wine, and she let most of hers leak out of her cup while she pretended to match him sip for sip. Winking at Thella, he paid the vintner to fill his travel bottle. She was beginning to find him tedious indeed.

Well, no one was likely to miss him when she took him out, so she set off with him, leaving the Gather site, passing the encampment which by then was nearly as merry as the square, and joining the wide track by the river, which sparkled in the light of Timor Moon. Belior, the speedier moon, was just beginning to rise. Soon the way would be as bright as daylight and considerably kinder to the eye.

They had gone along the track for some minutes before senses sharpened by the adversity of the last months told Thella that they were being followed. They were well beyond even Igen's own beastholds and the cots that ranged on either side of the main Hold. There were no travel lanterns in either direction anymore. She judged the follower to be on their left, taking advantage of the slope and the sparse groundcover.

"What a magnificent night!" she exclaimed, throwing her arms out and swiveling on one heel so that she got a good circling turn. Yes, there was someone to their left about four lengths behind them.

"Yes, yes," the herder agreed. "And Belior just rising. We must hurry."

"Why?" Thella demanded, deliberately acting contentious, as if she were slightly inebriated from all the wine he thought she had drunk. "We've made a good Gather, I've new boots"—she slurred her speech—"and if I hadn't so far to go, I'd've stayed longer with such good company. Whoops!" She feigned a stumble on the stony track. As she rose, she came up with her belt knife shoved up one sleeve and a smooth stone in the other hand.

"Easy now," the herder said, ranging himself on her right side, hands outstretched as if to support her. He spoke more loudly than he needed, and she knew it was not the wine that caused it.

Ahead of them a rocky spur jutted out, causing the track to veer back toward the river. So, someone thought they could drop her. Well, she would see about that.

They were in the shadow of the shelf when she heard the faint scrape of shoe in sand. Every sense alert, she waited a fraction of a moment longer, then grabbed the herder and yanked him over just as a body hurtled through the air, dagger flashing in the moonlight. She grinned as the herder cried out once, the assailant's knife slicing his throat. Then she acted, her own knife on the nape of the attacker's neck, pricking his skin as she shoved a knee in his back and pushed his head down, half smothering him in his victim's cloak and travel bag.

"Don't!" a muted voice cried. Slowly he held out his knife hand, letting the dripping blade fall to the ground.

"Easy now. Don't make me nervous," she said, roughening her voice. She grabbed his wrist and, when he made no resistance, flipped his arm back and up, twisting it tight against his shoulderblades. She could feel the thick muscles and wondered that she had mastered such a big man. But he was breathing shallowly, obviously unfit for such exertions. She gave his arm a painful twist, hearing him grunt where a lesser man might have cried out—she knew how to use such a hold to her advantage. "Was I marked out?"

"Aye, you were."

"Any others? It's early on a Gather evening." When he had been silent long enough, she twisted again, and he grunted. "Any others?"

"Aye, he'd marked others. Finish you off and go back for another."

"A fair Gather for you. What'd he promise?" Thella thought the big man simple to trust the herder and go back to the Gather. The herder could as easily turn his helper in to the guard.

"Half what we took. He said it'd be enough to buy into a hold."

"*Buy* into a hold?" In her surprise, Thella forgot to deepen her voice.

"Yes, there're holds where you can buy a place for a season. If you satisfy, you get taken on regular. I'm good with a flamer. I just don't like it with Thread falling and me with no place to shelter." The phrases came out in grunts, but he made no attempt to struggle against her hold. She was be-

ginning to wonder how long she could continue to exert the
pressure necessary to cow the man. He was big. He could
easily be the one she had noticed in the morning, but she
had not seen the herder in anyone's company during the
afternoon so the scheme must have been arranged earlier.
Well, at least he was not whining about wrongful treatment
and holder abuse.

"And how much loyalty could a holder expect of you—and
your knife?" She felt his body twitch beneath her knee.

"Lady, give me a hold during this Pass, or shove your blade
in." His muscles seemed to relax, as if he was tired of striving
against the odds of life. He was at her mercy, and she was
tempted to see if she had the strength to kill him, as she had
had the wit to subdue him.

"But it's so easy to kill to live," she said, her voice coax-
ingly smooth.

"Aye, easy enough to kill, but not easy to live holdless.
Not easy at all." He sounded very weary indeed.

"Your name?" she asked. "And previous Hold?" It was
customary to circulate the names of brutal murderers,
shunned from Holds, to all Lord Holders to protect them from
taking on such offenders.

She could feel his muscles tense and wondered if he would
lie to her. If she felt he was not telling the truth, she just
might push home that knife. But she needed a strong holder
more than she needed the gratification of a kill.

"I can, of course, tie you up and go back and get Laudey's
guards," she said when he did not answer immediately. She
wanted to make him sweat a little longer. Such power gave
her a sense of ineffable superiority.

"Dushik, I was called. I was beholden to Tillek."

She recognized the name from a list sent around several
Turns back and smiled, somewhat disappointed. Well, she
must keep even the bargains she made herself. And he would
be more useful to her alive.

"Ah, so you're the one," she said as if she remembered

more than the name. "Mind that I can still turn you in, Dushik," she said, releasing him. "And during a Pass, you can be chained out in Fall as execution, for it is my word against yours."

"Aye, lady, I understand. But I acknowledge you with heart and mind as Lady Holder and will give loyal service."

He actually sounded as if he meant it, so she released her hold on his arm and jumped backward, replacing her belt knife with her dagger in a fluid motion but ready to throw both at him if he made a suspicious move.

He waited a long moment, slowly working his arm down and around. He got first to his knees and then to his feet, his movements indicating deep weariness.

"Throw me his pouch, Dushik," she said, holding out her left hand. He gave her a long measuring look before he complied and then stood waiting for her next order.

As she thrust the bulging sack into her shirt she realized that the scuffle had loosened her headcovering and her braided hair had fallen forward.

"Now, see what else he had that's useful," she ordered, gesturing curtly with her dagger.

By the time Belior had risen, Dushik had exchanged the corpse's clothing for his own and, on Thella's orders, had heaved the body into the river. She made him discard the bloodstained cloak.

"There seemed to be plenty of other holdless wights at the Gather," she said disdainfully. "Would you say that any of them could be trusted to do a good day's work for their keep?"

"For you, lady," he said deferentially, going down on his knee to her, "I would see that they will."

Thella was well pleased.

3

SOUTHERN CONTINENT,
PP 11.04.06

There has to have been someone going through the sack,"
Mardra, Weyrwoman of Southern Weyr, insisted. She
stared accusingly at Toric, Southern's holder.

"Couldn't the fastening have loosened during the journey,
Weyrwoman?" Saneter asked, though the elderly harper's
desire to placate the Weyrwoman was stretched as thin as the
holder's temper.

"Then why, I ask you, *why*—" She set her goblet down so
hard on the table beside her that the stem broke and the remaining wine dripped onto the floor. "Now, look what you've
made me do!" She beckoned to a fat drudge pretending to
tidy the surface of the sideboard. "Quickly! Mop it up before
it attracts a horde of fly-bys."

If Saneter hoped that the mishap would distract Mardra, he
was quickly disappointed. She never lost an opportunity to
aggravate Toric.

When Saneter had been posted to the Southern Hold, Master Robinton had briefed him fully on the situation.

"You've been chosen for more reasons than merely trying to ease your joint-ail, Master Saneter," the Masterharper had said. "I can rely on your discretion and soothing manner, as well as your common sense, to keep me informed of any untoward occurrences." The Masterharper had paused significantly, his clear eyes meeting Saneter's. "The Southern Weyr was actually initiated some ten Turns before Threadfall, though that is not general knowledge, and volunteer holders went to assist them. When this Pass started, the Southern Weyr and Hold were temporarily abandoned. Then, as you know, with T'bor as Weyrleader and the ill-fated Kylara as his Weyrwoman, it became an excellent situation where injured dragons and riders could recuperate. You know the more recent history, I'm sure, with the discontent of some of the Oldtimers, and the exile of the incorrigible dissidents to Southern where they could do little harm.

"Toric, who was holding rather an extensive area, elected to stay on. He's rather well situated, mind you, though there were restrictions put on both the Oldtimer dragonriders who were exiled and any commerce between north and south." The Masterharper cleared his throat and gave Saneter yet another enigmatic look.

Saneter had been so relieved that he could continue to function as a harper, even in the south, that he would have been willing to do much more than exercise his diplomatic talents.

"Toric puts up with Mardra, T'ton, T'kul—who is, in my opinion, the worst of the lot," Robinton went on. "He'd have no such autonomy in the north, but I will want to hear what sort of friction develops . . . if you understand me, Saneter?"

"I do, Master Robinton. I believe I do."

Saneter often chided himself for his innocence. But a man learned as he lived. Once, when Saneter was just settling in to Southern Hold, Toric's lovely young sister, Sharra, had mentioned that Mardra fancied her brother, but that Toric wanted nothing to do with the Weyrwoman. Mardra's attitude toward Toric reflected a deep and vicious antipathy, a desire to humiliate and demean.

"I ask you *why*, Toric, my queen fire-lizard, who is far more reliable than a watchwher, distinctly informs me that someone was there and crept away." Having made her point she glared at the Holder, who said nothing, though Saneter could see his fingers alternately clenching into fists and releasing into grasping motions. "Look at me when I'm speaking to you, Toric," she added, leaning forward on her couch, her bleary eyes and features missing nothing of his attitude. When Toric moved his head fractionally, Saneter could see her deciding on a further insult.

With a harper's appreciation for valor, Saneter thought sadly of that glorious day when the Oldtimers' Five Weyrs had arrived. Every man, woman, and child on Pern, saved from certain death by the reinforcements, had been grateful to their wings. He had been a harper at Telgar and had seen Mardra and T'ton, the Fort Weyrleaders, a handsome pair, so pleased with their reception. T'kul, High Reaches Weyrleader, had appeared to be an energetic and knowledgeable leader, if slightly condescending to F'lar and Lessa. After four Turns of dealing with the disaffected Oldtimers, Saneter found their decline increasingly painful to deal with. Mardra had become a raddled, blowsy old woman, constantly wine-sotted; and T'kul, stringy with age and potbellied, spent his time endlessly recounting spectacular Falls which he had seemingly charred with only his dragon Salth's aid.

"Look *at* me," Mardra repeated, command still ringing in her voice, her eyes piercingly intent on the holder. Again his head moved fractionally, and Saneter, judging by the furious set of the Weyrwoman's lips, suspected that Toric had adopted his very disconcerting habit of seeming to look right through her. "She saw someone. Someone who shouldn't have been there. Someone who tampered with that sack. Find me that someone! I want to know what he or she took from that sack. Those were Crafthall tithes to this Weyr, and I hold you, all of you—" For the first time she glanced at the other Masters who had been summoned with Toric. "—responsible for any losses. Now hop it out of here!"

There was a murmur of righteous protest from the other Masters—farmer, fisher, herdsman, and tanner. Saneter, too, would have backed any retaliation. Craftsmen had the right to withdraw their services from a holder—and, by law, from a Weyr, though such an extreme action had never been recorded. The harper caught his breath, slightly frightened of the consequences of such an act—they were, after all, in the early years of the Pass—but just when he could no longer stand the suspense, Toric whirled and strode out of the Weyrhall, his heels thudding loudly against the wide floorboards. There was a hint of frightened relief on Mardra's face. If she realized that there were limits past which she could not go, then the morning had had a positive outcome. Saneter cleared his throat, gave Mardra a brief nod, and followed Toric. If the others could just contain their fury long enough to get out of the Weyr Hall, they would have brushed out of the incident without irrevocable damage. All for some trivial bauble!

Saneter did not let his breath out until he reached the hall entry, just as Toric strode down the broad steps without seeming to touch them. Quickly the other Masters overtook the harper, as much to get out of the Weyrwoman's presence as to support Toric's example. Saneter did not consider himself a choleric man, but he was as livid as Toric. The farther the holder got from the Weyrhall clearing the louder his curses grew. By the time he reached the well-trod path skirting the cliffs around the beach, he was bellowing out inventive damnations, his voice rising above the complaints of the others.

"We're here by choice, not tradition," Gabred, the Masterfarmer, cried. "Even Kylara was better behaved than that twat!"

"I'd use her guts for bait if I thought fish would take it!" Osemore the Fisher said, his weatherworn hands closed into thick and dangerous fists. "Chain her to the beach and let the leeches eat her."

"Old baggage," was Maindy the Herdsman's contribution. "Useless slug. Salt 'er, I would."

"If only they didn't ride dragons," Torsten the Tanner said. He shuddered. He was as incensed by the incident as the others, but by temperament he was a cautious man. His words stemmed the flood of invective. When the wounded northern dragons had been quartered at Southern, the holders had become all too acquainted with the agony of a dragon whose rider had died, and the forlorn, gut-twisting keen of those that heralded the dragon's suicide.

Though Saneter winced at the idea, he was grateful once again to Osemore. Dragonrider inviolability was deeply ingrained in them all—even a renegade holder like Toric. Which was why Toric had had to leave the Weyrhall before a total rupture of discipline occurred. But by Faranth's First Egg, it had been close. If they had not been in a Pass—not that Southern's dragonriders did more than mount a token flight. . . . Saneter shook his head, deploring the situation.

"*Their* shipments of who knows what arrive," Toric began again in a savage tone, "dumped down by *their* dragons, and suddenly it's *my* fault that one sack arrived open. She doesn't even blinding know what was in it, much less if anything *is* missing. We're summoned—summoned like apprentices—"

"More like drudges, at anyone's beck and call," Gabred put in sourly.

"To account for a possible, not provable, theft on the word of a fire-lizard? If she and that slovenly lot can't keep track of what comes in and out of their Hall, why should I? And how? When I'm never informed of shipments or Weyr requirements unless they run out of something in the middle of one of their carousals." Toric threw up both arms in his exasperation, hitting the fronds that draped gracefully to shade the path. He tore down branches and began shredding the leaves, needing some way to release his fury.

The last four Turns since the Oldtimers had been effectively exiled to Southern had been all too frequently punctuated with such scenes: the dragonriders demanding explanations for matters of which Toric had no knowledge whatsoever. There would come a day, the harper knew, when Toric would not respond to a summons. Saneter did not like to think about that day. The Oldtimers could not leave the south—and Toric would not.

The situation deeply distressed Saneter and his ingrained respect for the traditional values and duties. He did not understand why the Weyrleaders would want to replace Toric. The man was an excellent holder.

Unless the aim of those constant nuisance summonses and Mardra's needling were being deliberately designed to force Toric out of the hold and replace him with someone more accommodating or obsequious. The Weyrleaders had misjudged Toric and his ambition in that case. Toric had long-ranging plans for his holding, more extensive than those of the Weyrleaders, who did not appreciate the potential of Southern's bounty. Until just recently, the holder had seemed impervious to the demands and the pettiness, telling Saneter that it was easier to do whatever he was bid and get on with the next job. Toric had then shocked Saneter's harper-trained sensibilities by remarking that the dragonriders would all be dying off soon enough, preferably before his patience with them was exhausted. But any residual loyalty Saneter had once felt had been totally compromised by the most recent episode. From then on the harper would support Toric completely, with no further comments about a holder's duty to his Weyrleaders.

While Toric and his folk thrived in Southern, the Weyrleaders were visibly decaying. While Toric sent teams out to discover the extent of the southern lands, the dragonriders kept to their quarters, venturing no farther than the lake or the nearest beach to bathe their dragons.

Just then Toric stopped abruptly in the path, and the Masterfisherman tripped over his feet to halt, spreading out his arms to stop the others. Toric turned, eyes glinting narrowly with his fury, and made a scissoring motion with his hands.

"Anyone . . . anyone at all . . ." he said, jaw working as he let his angry green eyes fall on the hastily assembled work party. "Anyone"—he brought open hands together in a resounding smack—"who gives over fire-lizard eggs to Oldtimers gets thrown out of Southern. No excuse, no appeal. On the next boat north! Have I made myself plain?"

"I shall post a notice to that effect—" Saneter began, and then broke off. Why would Toric forbid an occupation that had earned the hold occasional marks? Fire-lizard eggs were in constant demand from northern traders and any seafolk pausing in Southern's deep harbor. Surely not because Mardra's little creature had played a part in this affair? But the moment was not right to question Toric; the holder had resumed his furious pace, the Craftmasters doing their best to keep up with him.

Saneter dropped back, as much because he wanted to absorb the meaning of that order as because there was no way he could keep that pace. He no longer had the energy he had once enjoyed, and despite the improvement the mild southern climate had made in the joint-ail in hip and shoulder, the exhilaration of anger was giving way to exhaustion. He mopped his face, sweating even in the shade of the leaf-canopied trace, and let his pounding heart and the thudding pulse in his temples subside to a calmer rhythm.

He wondered if he would send a message to the Masterharper about the latest uproar. Robinton already knew that Toric despised the Oldtimers; probably knew more about T'kul, Mardra, and the rest of the Oldtimers than Saneter ever would. Perhaps he ought to be informed about Toric's new order. The amount of marks offered for the contents of a gold fire-lizard queen's nest was more than most holders earned over three or four good Turns. Granted, not that many gold nests were generally located, but the demand for the creatures always seemed to increase. Well, they were more than pets, Saneter thought fondly, hoping his little bronze would perceive that he was no longer in Toric's angry company and it was safe to return to his usual perch on the harper's shoulder. He had also told Master Robinton that the Oldtimers were exacting far more than a normal tithe, and that the deliveries did not occur at the customary times or by the usual carriers: it had been moon-dark last night. And he had not seen a single dragon active that morning. But why would Toric forbid his holders to sell fire-lizard eggs to the Weyr?

On the other hand, Saneter decided, a long account of that day's incident, when viewed in a calmer frame of mind, was nothing to bother the already burdened Masterharper with.

Mardra had sent them all to see that one sack in their delivery hung open. Saneter had looked closely enough to identify it as a northern weave, probably Nabolese. Certainly the hemp that closed the sack mouth was of Nabolese manufacture. There had been wine—one could smell the spill—souring in the hot sun. The Mastervintners of both Tillek and Benden sent more than a fair tithe of their pressings to the Southern Weyr, but then, Saneter thought uncharitably, Southern Weyr consumed far too much.

Another bellow—only Toric could roar like that—startled him into a limping jogtrot. Who under the sun had been stupid enough to add fuel to Toric's rage? Saneter hurried along. And to think that the Masterharper had implied that Southern Hold would be a pleasant sinecure, with just enough activity to keep him from boredom. Well, boredom was the least of Saneter's worries.

When he emerged into the clearing on the bluffs above the beach, he groaned. Two ships were anchoring, their decks plainly crowded with people and parcels. The last thing in the world Toric needed at that point was to deal with yet another shipment of useless northern discards. There might indeed be—there usually were—some useful workers with craft skills or general handiness, but far too many of those making the trip were as aimless as the Oldtimers were.

Yet, when Toric roared again, Saneter heard a glad note in the bellow, and the way the holder was making for the harbor steps, waving his arms over his head and yodeling, gave every appearance of welcome and pleasure. Quickly the harper walked across the intervening space just in time to see Toric, arching majestically in the air, dive from the high point of the cliff into the deep clear blue-green waters of the anchorage and swim with powerful strokes to the larger of the two ships. It flew Rampesi's pennant.

"That'll help cool him down," a cheerful voice said at Saneter's side. He looked over and saw Sharra, her fire-lizards chirping excitedly before they made a straight-line dash to the boat. "Hamian must be aboard." She flashed her lovely smile at Saneter, and suddenly the morning was bearable again. "Remember? Osemore brought us a message that he was on his way from Telgar Smithcrafthall. My brother, an accredited Mastersmith!" She hugged herself, smiling with pride and anticipation. "Oh, Hamian has to be onboard. What was the old woman's gripe this time? I ducked away when I saw him shredding mandamos."

One of the others present would undoubtedly spread the story, but the harper had some respect for his position. As he watched Toric's arms flashing in a vigorous crawl toward Rampesi's ship and its passengers, he shook his head. "I hope he's doing the right thing, luring people to the south. We aren't getting the folk who're settled and craft-trained. Mostly the holdless. And why are they holdless?" Saneter wondered if he dared slip away for the rest of the morning. As harper he really should not countenance the human importations, yet he knew how desperately Toric needed bodies to cut through the jungle growths, clear more land, and secure his ambitions.

"Toric won't care, as long as they're still breathing. Not if

Hamian's also aboard. I was wondering how on earth we were going to get him out of his black humor this time." Sharra's ability to cool her brother's tempers was appreciated to the point where Southern holders dreaded her absence on forays into the wildness. She was, in her own way, as much of an original as her older brother, though her skill ran to healing rather than holding. She harvested the bounty of medicinal plants that grew to luxuriant size and in amazing quantity in the Southern Continent. She had no compunction about pursuing her particular interests, whether or not Toric forbade her to go out alone on the long searches she enjoyed. Suddenly she began to jump up and down, waving vigorously. "Look, Saneter! That has to be Hamian on the rail. And he's not going to let Toric outdo him!"

Saneter shaded his eyes, squinting across the brilliant sea. He had just one glimpse of the figure posed on the weather-rail before the man seemed to hover in his graceful dive, cleaving the brilliant blue water and bobbing up safely a moment later to swim energetically toward his brother.

"Hamian's return couldn't be better timed," Sharra remarked. "But I hope Rampesi got a good price for our last cargoes."

Saneter shook his head. Toric was not supposed to trade with the North. If someone ever checked to see how many ships had "been forced to seek shelter from storms in Southern coves"—always the one cove—there could be real trouble with the Northern Lord Holders and the Benden Weyrleaders. He was positive that if Toric approached the Masterharper, presenting the problems and the possibilities inherent in the magnificent continent, some proper arrangement could be made.

Sharra began to shout impartial encouragement to her brothers, and even those who knew of the latest encounter of holder and Weyrwoman left their tasks to swell the hurrahs. Osemore was ordering crews to the sturdy fishing boats to ferry cargo and passengers ashore. When Saneter saw several more dive clumsily in to swim ashore, he felt somewhat encouraged by their enthusiasm.

Meanwhile Toric and Hamian had met midway, with much splashing, ducking, and shouts of challenging laughter. Saneter decided not to worry until he had good cause. As he turned back to Sharra, his bronze fire-lizard settled to his shoulder.

"Well, at least a few of those passengers have a measure of courage. Or maybe they're just tired of smelling themselves. Either way, Sanny, I take it as a good sign they'd try to swim in," she said, smiling. "I'd best warn Ramala that we'll need more than fruit and rice on the table tonight."

"I can do that," Saneter said. "Surely you want to be here to welcome your brother after three Turns' absence?"

"Oh, I'm not hanging about while they pretend to be shipfish," Sharra said with a negligent wave. "They won't come in until they've half drowned each other. And I can see that Master Rampesi's launched his dinghy. There'll be messages for you to sign for, Saneter. They'll be here long before my brothers." She turned on her heel toward the hold's cool caverns, and Saneter made his way to the harbor stairs.

Sharra knew her brothers well, for Saneter and Master Rampesi were exchanging greetings before Toric and Hamian hauled themselves, laughing and breathless, out of the water. Toric had lost his bad humor in the exercise and was grinning broadly as he watched his younger brother strip sodden shirt and pants from a big frame made more powerful by three Turns of smithcrafting.

"You were enough of a threat to the girls before you went north, Hamian," Sharra yelled, throwing down dry short pants. "Have the goodness to cover it decently before you get up here."

"Sharra, my lovely. I've brought you some samples of northern men. Maybe one you'll like," Hamian shouted at her and ducked as she lobbed a ripe redfruit at him.

"Any likely ones among the passengers?" Toric asked as

he wrung the water out of his own brief garment. If Hamian worked as competently as he looked, he would be well worth the marks his absence had cost the hold.

"Half dozen maybe," Hamian replied, losing the width from his grin. "I did my best to leave the scum. I'll be fair—Master Rampesi and Master Garm wouldn't have some of them aboard. We picked the likeliest. There was supposed to be a dragonless man. . . ."

"Dragonless?" Toric stared at his brother in dismay. "Benden Weyr?" Though he still respected them, Toric was at odds with the Benden Weyrleaders over many of their decisions. He relaxed visibly when Hamian shook his head.

"No, from Telgar Weyr. A blue rider. The harper said that a heavy tangle caught the dragon on the left side. Somehow he managed to land with G'ron, his rider, but the man's riding straps had been scored clear through, and he hit the ground so hard they thought he was dead. There was nothing they could do for the blue. He went—" Hamian broke off. He had seen good dragonriders in plenty at Telgar Weyr over the last three Turns, counteracting his experiences with the Oldtimers, so a dragon's death was a felt loss.

Toric said nothing until Hamian, in a swift change of mood, turned apologetic. "Look, I know we didn't get the quality of settlers we need, but they're all able bodies. Some of 'em had journeymen's knots and a couple were apprenticed to trades. I'll take 'em all with me to the mines and work their butts off. If they don't like it, they'll be far enough away from here not to bother you. In fact," Hamian said, his smile a fair match for Toric's at his slyest, "I'll take anything that can breathe and walk to get those mines started. We—" He clapped his brother on the shoulder with such a resounding smack that the noise startled those struggling to step to the pier from the rocking cockleboat. Five fell into the water. "We will also teach you how to swim!" he finished unexpectedly, grabbing the nearest floundering man by the shirt and lifting him easily out of the water. Then, when Toric shoved him toward the steps,

Hamian bounded up to wrap powerful arms about his sister and swing her about in an exuberant embrace.

"How's Brekke? Did you see her? Mirrim? F'nor?" Sharra was asking with what breath the crushing hug had left her.

"I've letters for you, and I just gave you one message from Brekke. She said she needed numbweed the most and were you going to harvest soon."

"Good, I shall supervise that myself!"

"And make a side trip down to your lake again," Hamian teased her. "Catch any new sports? No? Well, then—" He hooked an arm about her shoulders and started for the caverns. "F'nor and Canth were at Big Bay to see me off, so all news is fresh. Mirrim's a pain in the neck, but she'll change if she lives and has her health. And," he added, lowering his voice for her ears alone, "I also saw Mother. She still won't come though Father's dead more than three Turns. Brever would no more leave the Crafthall to hold here under his younger brother than I could swim the Currents. Our other three sisters won't leave her, though I tried very hard to get them and their husbands to come. But they won't if she won't, and she won't if they don't. It's all very well for Toric to want all his Bloodkin here—but if he thinks he can trust them all on that score, he's wrong. Frankly, I don't think any of them would do well here anyhow."

Saddened by the thought that her mother would never live in Toric's beautiful hold, Sharra leaned her head against her brother's broad powerful chest, sea cool from his swim, and walked with him in silence for a few moments.

Toric had been the first to leave the family's High Palisades seahold. He had left the lonely island off the western side of Ista and gone to the mainland, out and about and away from the hard labor of the Fishercraft. He had been in Benden Hold when F'lar had become Weyrleader and turned back the Lord Holders' attack. For perhaps the only time in his life, Toric had acted on impulse and had presented himself as a candidate for Ramoth's first clutch. Disappointed in that wish, he had volunteered to follow F'nor in founding the timed Weyr in Southern, and had remained on when that project had been abandoned. Once he had established, with much hard work, his hold he had come back to Keroon and talked first Kevelon and Murda, then Hamian and Sharra into joining him. Their mother had been proud of Toric's achievement, but not of her children's desertion.

"Would she change her mind if Toric becomes official Lord Holder? D'you think then she'd forgive him, and us, for leaving Father?" she asked softly.

Hamian cocked his head down at her. Sharra was tall for a girl, but she was dwarfed by her huge brother. "There's not much activity on that score, Sharrie. Lord Meron of Nabol's dying, and though he's got Bloodkin enough, there's going to be a real ruckus over that succession. No time to be upsetting the incumbents. What's the matter?" he asked when Sharra began to shake her head.

"One day they'll be sorry. One day they'll see their mistake in not confirming him, in leaving him out of the Conclave."

"Sharra, he *is* Lord Holder in all but title," Hamian argued. "And that's not today's good news. There're a couple of good honest Masters come to join us."

Sharra's hazel eyes glanced at him with irritation, and she ducked out of Hamian's embrace. "Not you, too. I tell you, Hamian, if you've said one word to anyone, especially Toric . . ."

"Me?" Hamian reared back, hands warding off a blow, his expression one of amiable surprise at her reaction. "I assure you I learned my lesson before I went for my mastery. Southern Hold women marry when and where they choose."

"And Toric had better remember that!"

"With you reminding him whenever marriages occur, how could he forget? Now," he said, blocking her not-so-playful blow, "can I please have something to take the tang of sea from my throat? We'd rough enough weather crossing the

Currents that I shouldn't have to take the rough of your tongue the moment I climb the steps home!''

''Ramala's been squeezing fruit since I went for your shorts. And look, here's Mechalla to greet you. Bring her with you.'' Grinning slyly, Sharra slipped away from her brother's side to allow the first of the girls who had grieved at his departure to flirt with him on his return.

No one clouded that evening with any mention of the morning's meeting with the Weyrwoman; the entire hold immediately got to work to settle the newcomers so that all could enjoy Hamian's return. Even the scruffiest of the new arrivals, having survived Toric's scrutiny, were determined to make the most of so much food and honest hospitality. Even Saneter put aside the thick rolls of messages, most of them dealing with the exiles, to enjoy roasted meat on the strand.

''Any murderers in this lot, Saneter?'' Toric asked, guiding the harper down the beach away from the feasting. People were still gorging themselves, and Toric wanted to know how well his private assessments of the new settlers jibed with the official reports.

''Only one,'' Saneter replied, ''and he claimed self-defense.'' The harper was not convinced, having spotted the rather surly-looking fellow off to one side, shunned by other passengers. ''Fifteen were apprentice-level, and two more got as far as journeymen in their crafts, and were turned out of their places for constant pilfering and theft; one was caught selling Crafthall goods at a third of their worth.''

Toric nodded. He was desperate enough to take any help to clear Southern lands, even to the extent of circumventing the Benden Weyrleaders' restriction on any intercourse between the interdicted Southern Weyr and Hold. So Toric was smuggling people in from the North. Some desperate holdless folk heard whispers that he would not turn them away from the Southern shores, but he was getting too many useless folk for his trusted settlers to absorb quietly. He needed more skilled men, trained in hold and hall management—and he had to keep his illicit settlers from the Oldtimers' notice.

"Two were caught stealing unmarked herdbeasts. There are, however, some honest settlers," Saneter continued, hurrying on to the good news. "Four couples with good crafts, and nine singles of varied backgrounds, some of them with very good recommendations. Hamian vouches for four of the men and two of the women. Toric, I'll say it now and get it off my chest: you should apply to the Masterharper."

Toric snorted. "He'd tell Benden—"

"And the Benden Weyrleaders, if you approached them with Master Robinton, would be the first to assist you. They wanted to explore this whole land," Saneter said, sweeping his arm wide, "and they would have, if the Oldtimers hadn't—well, you know all that." He broke off. "But some young, eager, *trained* holder sons who know they're not going to get any place north during a Pass would certainly see the advantages to coming south. Even if we have to sneak them in when the Oldtimers aren't looking." Saneter gave Toric a quick glance to see his reaction. Toric's head was down, and Saneter could tell nothing from his profile.

"You certainly don't have to mention what you've already discovered. I haven't, I assure you, Lord Holder," Saneter went on. "But if ore is to be useful to you as a trading medium, it's got to be known. As I'm sure Hamian told you, the Mastersmith is desperate for all the iron, nickel, lead, and zinc he can get. Mine production in the north is at full pelt."

"You're remarkably well informed for a harper sent south for his health," Toric said, giving the old man a long hard look.

"I am indeed harper," Saneter agreed, drawing himself up and returning Toric's stare. "And that has always been more than simply singing teaching songs to *children*!"

"We've got to mine; we've got to transport the ore. And that's going to take muscle. At least Hamian's brought back three good journeyminers and another Master.'' Toric rocked on his heels, jamming his thumbs in his shirt belt. There was a cool northerly breeze blowing across the strand. ''They'll have tonight's celebration, then we'll muster them all tomorrow morning, first light''—Toric's grin was calculating as he thought of the stronger southern brews that were guaranteed to give the unwary vicious hangovers—''and give them the usual warnings. The useful will remember, and the foolish will forget, and then cause neither us nor the Lord Holders who sent them further grief.''

Toric's callous attitude had once bothered Saneter, but he had been at Southern too long not to see its merit. Southern was a bizarre, often cruel, land, and those who deserved its bounty learned to survive its dangers.

''Those dragonmen were supposed to explore,'' Toric declared. ''They haven't. I am. Flood, fire, fog, or Fall, I'm going to find out just how big Southern really is.''

Saneter forebore to mention either Sharra's competence in exploring down the Big Lagoon River or her eagerness to go as far as she could. For all the innovations Toric had made in his hold, he retained some traditional views, especially about his sisters. Murda had been acquiescent; Sharra was not. The harper cleared his throat to voice a suggestion, but Toric went on.

''Even a dragon has to fly straight the first time he goes to a new location. Why did F'lar recall all the good riders?'' His tone was so disconsolate, suddenly so weary and hopeless, that Saneter almost felt sorry for the man.

Giron was so drunk that for most of the first day he slept. The carter did not bother to check his load of barreled salt fish when he pulled into the cave site, so Giron had slept on undiscovered. Later, when all sheltering there were sound asleep, Giron rolled off the uncomfortable barrels and went in search of water. Slaking his thirst at the stream, he settled himself as comfortably as the rocky ground permitted and slept again. He stole food from campers the next evening, still disoriented, not remembering that he had marks enough, tucked inside his waistband, to buy whatever he needed. He kept trying to remember what it was he had forgotten: something he should have but was missing. Something he would never find again. There was an ache deep inside that would never stop hurting.

The next day, another carter recognized the empty-faced stranger as the dragonless man. He brushed his clothes, fed him, and when Giron demanded wine, he let him have the wineskin, surprised that the former dragonrider did not complain about its raw acid taste. The carter took him up on the seat of the wagon, because he conceived that he had a duty to protect one who had been a dragonrider. There were too many holdless rogues about who would rob even their mothers of marks. The carter endured the pathetic, silent man all the way across the mountains and to the door of the Master-tanner's Hall. There Master Belesdan had his drum tower communicate with Igen Hold and Igen Weyr. Finally Lord Laudey sent an escort with a spare runnerbeast.

"We're to take him back to the Hold," the escort said. "He was supposed to go to Southern Hold. Cracked his skull, you know, and doesn't think straight yet. We'll get him there safely."

Halfway there, Giron saw sweepriders, and, as the escort reported to Lord Laudey, "He seemed to take a fit. He was screaming and yelling, and he whipped up the poor runner-beast so hard, we couldn't catch up. Last we saw of him he was swimming across the river. I don't know if he was trying to catch up with the dragonriders, or what."

"Go across to the caves. Tell them to watch out for Giron. Let them know who he is and that if anyone does him any harm, they'll answer to me—and to all the Weyrs of Pern."

The urgent requests brought by Master Rampesi from Brekke and the Healer Hall were all the excuse that Sharra needed to force Toric to allow her to go harvest the numbweed bush. She made it very clear that a quick trip just to harvest the bush would mean cooking it in the hold. Allowed a longer trip, the complete job could be done entirely on the site. Toric hesitated, and Sharra's heart sank. She knew that he wanted her to spend time with some of Hamian's new arrivals, but she was not ready to settle down, and she was afraid that she might actually find she liked one of them.

"I feel I ought to accompany her this time," Ramala said suddenly.

Catching her hard stare, Toric yielded, knowing that if he refused them both, he would have little peace. "You be careful, Sharra," he said, wagging a finger in her face. "Smart and careful."

With a teasing smile she caught the finger. "Brother, why won't you, too, admit that I'm the Mastercrafter out back?" She left it at that, and he stalked out of the family hall, muttering about ingratitude and dangers she could not imagine.

Ramala grinned and, her husband out of the way, added travel-packed foods to Sharra's pile of gear. "We can make the morning tide. I've three boats."

"Three?" Sharra was both surprised and delighted. "How'd you manage that, Ramala?"

Ramala shrugged. "No one can ever have too much numbweed. Garm took the coast route to check on the growth, and it's very good this year. I saw the total of Brekke's needs. You go after the unusual herbs. I'll manage the cookout. I need a respite."

Sharra laughed with genuine amusement. Ramala was a quiet woman, competent, perceptive, and gifted with all the attributes Sharra knew herself to be deficient in, especially patience. Ramala was not a pretty woman but she exuded an indefinable air that caused people to turn to her for advice and help. Sharra did not know much about Ramala's past—

except that she had been in a Healer Hall in Nerat before she came to Southern; the other woman had bought her own place in Southern, and Toric had seen such worth in her that he had invited her to join him permanently in his hall. Ramala never complained, but Sharra could quite easily see how she might like a short break. Toric's hard ambition and driving energy were wearing. He would be occupied with Hamian in setting up the miners' train, Saneter could fend off the Weyr, and Ramala's four children were old enough to be useful on the trip.

Sharra completed her packing, throwing in a second pair of the double wherhide high boots with reinforced toes that she preferred when tramping through Southern's undergrowth and streams and adding her tough cotton shirts and knee breeches. She filled the many pockets of her vest with the minor tools she had found most handy to carry on her person at all times, then packed a doublecoil of new hemp rope; dagger, implement knife, and a short blade that fit in one boot; the roll of waterproof cotton that had acted as tent, raingear, or bedding; and the broad-brimmed hat that shielded her eyes from sun glare.

The three boats sailed with the tide, heeled over and flying as the stiff easterly wind caught the red sails. Most people were singing, and some of the younger boys, who regarded the voyage as the best part of the outing, had lines cast over the side, each hoping to catch the biggest prize. Shipfish picked up their customary bow positions, flipping and careering and generally making a show of themselves to the delight of the passengers. Their appearance augured a good, quick voyage, and Sharra felt the shadows that had fallen over the hold lift. Damn the Oldtimers! Damn them right *between*. Those stupid restrictions were all their fault.

She glanced quickly around as if someone could have heard her thoughts. Meer and Talla, her fire-lizards, crooned softly from their perch on the cabin. Still, one ought not to ill-wish dragonriders. Not all of them were like the Oldtimers, but those were enough to sour life in Southern.

They came around the headland, and Sharra jumped to the sheets when the skipper had to take in sail to avoid being driven too close to the rocky coast. They would be at the Big Lagoon by the next morning, at which time they could negotiate its hazards in broad daylight and on the tide.

Once they had landed and all the gear had been brought to a good site, Ramala told Sharra to get herself lost but to be back in ten days.

"That won't take me much farther than I've been before," Sharra complained, but at Ramala's fond, stern look, she hefted her pack to her back, called Meer and Talla from the fair doing wingdances across the plain, and trotted off to make the most of her freedom, muttering cheerfully about restrictions.

She had nearly reached the first stands of trees surrounding the plain when Meer, describing lazy loops above her head, gave a hopeful chirp, a sound that indicated to Sharra that he had seen a gold. He was one of the randiest bronzes in the hold. Then his chirp altered briefly in surprise, and he returned to her shoulder. Talla took the other side, both of them alert. So when Sharra heard the sounds of someone stumbling about in the forest and the scolding of a queen fire-lizard, she was more annoyed at a possible curtailment of her ten-day holiday than she was surprised to find a stranger so far from the hold.

Her annoyance fled at the sight of a scruffy lad, hunkered down in the brush and peering at the activity of the camp, one arm about the neck of a runt runnerbeast while a young gold fire-lizard had her tail firmly wrapped about his sunburned neck. He seemed disgusted that his queen had not warned him of Sharra's approach, but he was willing enough to talk. His name was Piemur, he said, and all on his own he had already survived three Threadfalls in Southern.

Sharra was impressed with his resourcefulness, and it occurred to her that here might be someone Toric could use. He
was young and alone and clever—and she liked him. Resisting
an impulse to ruffle his sun-streaked tangle of hair, Sharra felt
a pang of sorrow for whatever mother had lost this young
rascal. A heart-grabber, he was. Now, if she could find someone with his charm, say ten Turns older . . .

His cocky resilence decided her. She did not have to take
him back to the shore yet. She could have her browse around
and get the stuff Brekke had asked for—and she would have
a chance to see just how capable a Southern holder he could
be. Toric would listen to her evaluation. Maybe if she had a
capable apprentice to take along, Toric would let her do some
real explorations.

As if he could read her mind, Piemur offered to help her
with her herb-gathering. Pleased, she motioned for him to
follow her deeper into the forest.

By the time they returned to the coast, Sharra had formed
a high but qualified opinion of Piemur. He was the born rogue
and scoundrel she had suspected, and she was certain that a
discreet inquiry to the North would prove that he was a Craft
apprentice, absent—for a dare, she rather thought, that had
gone badly wrong—without permission from his Hall. He had
probably been in a major Hall or near a major Hold, because
he was knowledgeable about attitudes and issues that the av-
erage boy was unlikely to know about. His mind was as quick
as his tongue, and he had a wry sense of humor and fun. His
voice had almost settled to an adult baritone, so he was older
than he looked.

Piemur was also possessed of a finely tuned memory and
never forgot her traveling lessons on herbs or travel safety.
He had an instinct for self-preservation that rivaled that of
his fire-lizard. And, like Sharra, he had an exploring turn of

mind. They would have been halfway to the snowy mountains if they had not had to be back to make the voyage home. He was exactly the stuff of which good Southerners were made.

His main worry then was that his runnerbeast—whom he called Stupid and who was anything but—could not be accommodated on one of the ships. He had sworn he would walk back to the hold if he had to, but he would not just let Stupid loose. Sharra had eased his apprehensions on that score, promising that a couple of strong sailors could easily lift the little runnerbeast into one of the sloops, but on the hike back to the coast, Piemur had become more and more laconic. Something was worrying him, and to Sharra, it confirmed her notion that he had not been entirely truthful with her.

"We don't care what people left behind them, so long as they work hard here. It's a great place to start all over, Piemur," she said when they were within hailing distance of the camp. She waved to Ramala, who had just noticed them. "I think we can even manage to get a message North—discreetly—if there's someone who should know you're alive and kicking here."

Instead of appearing relieved, Piemur looked away. "Yeah, I'll have to do something about a message, Sharra. Thanks." But he did not look at her, pretending to adjust a chin piece of the halter he had made for Stupid out of the varicolored grasses they had found in the swampland.

Sharra introduced him as the survivor of a shipwreck whom she had encountered in the wilderness. "Toric will love him as a prime example to the faint of heart in that latest group. If a kid can live rough, they can manage, too," she told Ramala.

"He'll need boots," Ramala commented. "Too bad his feet aren't as tough as the rest of his hide."

Sharra laughed. Piemur's skin had taken a deep tan to the ragged waistband of his tattered pants. He had mended the worst rents with patches Sharra had in one of her pockets, but he desperately wanted a waistcoat like hers, with "sockets and pockets and gussets and gores where a fellow could store anything he needed on the trail."

Though he sported a few scrapes and scratches, he was less marked than some of those who had gathered numbweed bush. The stench of the cooked weed hovered like a miasma on the plain, but the tubs and buckets of the salve were already stored in the sloops. Fresh fish had been caught from the outer barrier reef, and roots and fruits had been gathered. There would be a good evening meal.

On the sail back, Sharra heard Piemur asking casual questions of the other youngsters. Somehow the questions always got around to the matter of the Oldtimers. Whatever he really wanted to know, Sharra thought, he did not seem to have found out by the time he could see the Weyr cliff itself.

Sharra instantly recognized a small skiff riding at anchor, with its Harper Hall colors on the stern. It was not the first time that Menolly herself had come from the Fort Hold Healer Hall to collect Master Oldive's share of Sharra's medicinal gatherings. Menolly might be seahold bred, but she had never before made the journey alone. Could Sebell have come with her? Toric was standing, elbows cocked, on the stone wharf; they would have to unload the ships before she got a chance to see Menolly and her unidentified shipmate.

Getting Stupid unloaded and up the steps proved easier than Sharra had thought. Ramala helped distract Toric—Piemur could be introduced later when Toric had had time to count the large number of full tubs and see how much had been gathered. But when Sharra had gotten the boy safely to the entrance to the cavern, he had nearly dropped the load he was carrying.

"A drum!" He caressed the edge of it.

"That's an addition," Sharra said. She was surprised not only by the drum, a section of one of the huge mandamo trees that were large enough to shelter a fair of fire-lizards, but by the mixed emotions that rippled across Piemur's expressive face: familiarity, yearning, and calculation.

He looked up and out, northwest across the sea. Then, before she could tell him not to, he pounded the drum in a complicated sequence. After that, he picked up the feather ferns he had dropped and looked politely at her for directions.

The two of them had just reached her workroom when they heard the shout, echoing down the cavern aisle. *"Piemur report!"*

"Sebell?" The look of utter astonishment on the boy's face lasted no more than a fraction of a moment. He dashed from the chamber, Sharra hard on his heels. Her castaway boy knew Master Robinton's messenger? When she got to the main hall of the hold, she found Piemur being embraced by Menolly and Sebell. Only after Toric had shouted them all quiet, demanding explanations, did Sharra hear an accurate account of Piemur's adventure.

Piemur had gone with Sebell to Nabol Hold, trying to locate the source of so many fire-lizard eggs. It was believed that the deceased Lord Meron had had illicit dealings with the Oldtimers. Piemur had managed—and Sebell gave his apprentice a scowl for the worry he had caused the Harper Hall—to get into the Hold and audaciously steal one of the eggs hardening on Lord Meron's hearth. Forced to hide in a sack to escape discovery, he had awakened in Southern, panicked at the sound of voices, and again escaped discovery.

"There is no way under the sun that you will get me to admit to Mardra, Loranth's rider," Toric said, his expression forbidding as he faced Sebell, "that someone really had been in her bloody sack!" He scowled fiercely at Piemur, who looked alarmed.

"Well, she's forgotten the matter long since, I assure you," Ramala remarked calmly. "I think we should concentrate on this enterprising young fellow."

"He's got the makings of a good Southerner, Toric," Sharra said.

4

<hr>

LEMOS AND TELGAR HOLDS,
SOUTHERN CONTINENT, PP 12

It took Thella and her seventeen raiders seven days to make their way to her objective, Kadross Hold in the forested hills of Lemos. For four days they rode; then they left their runnerbeasts in a well-hidden cave with a guard and made the final leg of the journey to a cramped hole in the mountainside an hour's climb from Kadross Hold.

As they ate cold travel rations—they would not risk smoke being sighted by Asgenar's sharp-eyed foresters—she reviewed her plan once more. Some of the new men still resented her. That would end after they learned that a good plan meant good results. With her dagger, she sawed off a sliver of the smoked meat, but she did not sheathe the blade. Instead she began flipping it in her right hand as she walked. It never hurt to remind them all that she had acquired a convincing accuracy with any sort of knife, and she was not shy about displaying that skill to maintain discipline.

"Resist the urge to take anything else that might come to your hand," she said, "or you'll take a short walk with Dushik." She paused again, letting the significance of that threat sink in. "The raids I plan," she went on, thumping her chest with the hilt end of her dagger, "secure us everything we need to make us quite comfortable and—" she paused, letting her attention fall on Felleck until he looked at her, startled "—Allow us to show our faces at most halls, holds, and Gathers," she finished.

One of her recruits, Readis, had contacts with traders, which Thella had made good use of. She generally knew what trains were moving where between Falls. She always knew what each was likely to carry—and had mapped the best places on every route to lay an ambush, snatch what she needed, and disappear. She had no hesitation about lifting Craft messages from couriers while they slept in the way-caves that were thought to be safe from robbery. Like most Bloodline Holderkin, she had been taught drum rolls and understood most of the messages she heard, pounding back and forth in the valleys. She had profited in very unexpected ways from her Turns in a major Hold.

"Remember that?" And she made a dramatic turn as she reached the back of the cave. "We can't always rely on paid mouths to tell us what we need to know. Some of the holdless would sell their mothers and profit more by informing on us.

"I don't foresee any need for violence, either. Thread will fall early in the morning across Lord Asgenar's prime forestry. As soon as leading Edge passes this cave, we move out." Some of the men muttered. She shot a look at Giron, the dragonless man, who had unexpectedly volunteered to come on the raid. It had been an encouraging change from his months of apathy; she had expected to get some use out of him a lot sooner. "We move into position and wait until the Kadross people leave on ground crew duty. Their track leads downhill. They always feed their stock before Threadfall, so we're not likely to run into anyone coming out to check. There're only elderlies and a few kids left. Asgenar doesn't realize how helpful he'll be tomorrow!"

The men laughed or smiled, as they were supposed to. She

encouraged their disrespect of tradition and smiled to herself as she turned again. Her boot caught briefly against Readis's flamethrower tank. He immediately shifted it. Readis was the link to too many sources of information for her to object to his obsession. She had seen the Thread scars on his back, so she permitted him to bring the flamer when they would be out in Fall. It was perhaps a wise enough precaution, and he never slowed them up, even lugging that deadweight.

"Now, settle down. We all need sleep. Dushik, sleep over here. Then if you snore I can kick you off your back." She drew sour laughs from those who knew the big man's habit. As usual he grinned at her as he arranged his blanket. She turned away, satisfied. "Readis, you'll wake us all at dawn?" The man nodded and took his place.

She lay down by the low opening to the cave, where she would not have to endure the smell of many bodies in a confined space. The others soon settled, Dushik breathing heavily. But tired as she was, Thella could not slow her mind sufficiently to fall asleep. She was always exhilarated just before a strike; anticipation was usually the best part as she waited to see her plans work, proving once more to her men just how good she was!

And to think that once she would have settled for having a Hold of her own, to be acknowledged by the Conclave as a Lady Holder in her own right. So much had changed since she met Dushik. She had found far more to excite her: the thrill of planning and executing a raid, and taking exactly what she had set out to acquire, but no more. Success inspired her to set more hazardous goals, more difficult puzzles. Dushik was beginning to snore, and she prodded him with her heel. He grunted and turned over.

Since that Gather day she had found a far more satisfying challenge: choosing victims instead of being one. When she and Dushik had returned to the Gather tents to hire some carefully selected holdless men and women, she had already begun to plan. There would be many laden runners and carts leaving the Gather, and if all went well—and why would it not?—not all of them would reach their original destinations. She and Dushik would choose what they needed to supply her mountainhold—and the desperate holdless who hovered on the edges of Igen's Gather would bear all the blame.

The success Thella had since achieved with successful, well-spaced raids across the eastern Holds gave her immense satisfaction. If brother Larad held any suspicions that it was his own sister who was plundering his prosperous minor holds, he certainly had not mentioned it to the other four Lord Holders. Not that those thickwits would have believed him or taken any punitive action. Yes, it was inordinately satisfying to plunder in Telgar. But not too often there, or anywhere else.

By bribery and threat, Thella had obtained copies of detailed maps of the Holds in which she wished to operate, just as she had taken Telgar's master charts from her brother's office. While those were useful to her, she became increasingly adept in drawing out information from unlikely sources, and in attracting valuable men like Readis—and Giron, now that he seemed to be recovering.

Four Turns earlier one of her men had brought her a copy of the Harper Records on Lord Fax's activities in the Western Ranges. Now there had been a man whose vision and grasp she could admire! A real pity that the man had died so early in what had promised to be a spectacular Holding. With cunning, he had outrageously taken over seven holds. Several times she had used his surprise tactics, scaling the heights of well-positioned holds and coming stealthily in through upper windows just at dawn, when the watchwher's night vision was useless. He had probably been tricked into the duel that had killed him. Or good judgment had deserted him—no one challenged a dragonrider. Dragons had unusual powers, and they did not let their riders get injured. She still hoped to learn exactly what dragons did for their riders, apart from going *between* and fighting Threadfall. Giron would not talk about Weyrlife—yet. She would have to encourage him.

The most depressing part of that harper account was that no one had attempted to take charge of what Fax had so ingeniously secured. Ruatha Hold had been given to a baby, Meron had taken hold only of Nabol, and the other five had been reclaimed by Bloodkin of those Fax had supplanted. Then Meron, who ought to have learned more from Fax, had become enamoured of Thella's half-sister, Kylara. Well, Kylara had not been very smart in Thella's estimation: she had lost her dragon queen. And Meron was dead, too.

Dushik's crescendo of snores distracted her, and she kicked him twice.

In her ceaseless quest to reduce risks and improve the profit of her strikes, she had thought long and hard about acquiring some fire-lizards, as they were said to hear dragons. One constant threat to her plans was the possibility of sweepriders noticing unusual numbers of mounted men and loaded animals on unfrequented tracks. If she had some way of knowing when dragons were approaching, she would have time to reach proper cover. But at her first encounter with fire-lizards at a Bitran Gather, she had realized that they were much too noisy for her purposes. The success of her raids very often depended on stealth.

She prided herself that she probably knew more about their Holds than the Lord Holders did themselves. Except perhaps Asgenar, Lord of Lemos. Word had come to her that he was beginning to see the seemingly unrelated thefts as a serious problem. Any attempt to infiltrate his Holding would be too risky, but Sifer, Lord Holder of Bitra, was a much poorer manager. Seeing her chance, she had sent Keita to live with one of his stewards. It was proving necessary to get the flirt away from camp because she would not leave off teasing the woman-hungry men. In Bitra she could satisfy her itch and listen to Thella's advantage.

Dushik began to snore again, but before she could kick him, the man on the other side did. Finally she fell asleep.

The next morning Readis roused them at false dawn. They

ate, washing down the dry rations with water fetched from a nearby stream. When the men slipped out to attend to private needs, she reminded Dushik to keep an eye on Felleck. Neither trusted the man who had complained throughout the entire trip, but he had proved to be an expert at snaring wherries and knew the most edible of tunnel and rock snakes, and had been chosen because of his strength.

Perschar would be at Giron's elbow. Thella still had not figured out why the dragonless man had volunteered for the foray. Over the last months his awareness had increased, his disturbingly blank expression becoming more alert. Readis had found him in the Igen caverns where so many holdless sheltered, thinking that a former Weyrman might prove useful to Thella. Perscher, who was capable of patching wounds and setting bones, suggested that Giron's vagueness was probably the result of the long head gash. And, of course, once he had entered her hold, even Thella would not be so cruel or stupid as to turn him out. Meanwhile his improvement had been steady, if slow. With more animation in his face, he was also rather attractive and quite intelligent, though he rarely offered information. As a dragonless man, he was held in a certain respect by the other men. She had resented that at first, but she was beginning to think that she could make use of it.

The first indication of Threadfall's leading Edge was a darkening of the bright day. There was a noticeable shift to the rear of the cramped cave. Readis armed his flamethrower and stood across the opening. Incurious and unafraid, the dragonless man hunkered down behind him.

Although every man could see that trailing Edge was flowing across the valley, Thella had to threaten Felleck and three others with her whip before they moved out of the cave. Readis had already signalled that their descent held no Thread horrors, and he and Giron were on their way down. Thella was furious that the others had not moved at her word. So much depended on being in position before the ground crew left Kadross Hold.

But at last they had all made the descent and were safely hidden behind the ridge. She crouched where she had a clear view of Hold, beasthold, and the track that dropped down into the valley, the track the holders would soon follow.

What was taking those wretched holders so long to organize themselves? Thread was well past. She could see no more dragonfire bursts in the sky. Then she heard the grate of metal and saw the hold door swing out, and she could not suppress her inadvertent gasp. Excitement raced through her veins, her senses heightened with a singing in her blood, and her hands reset themselves on dagger hilt and lash handle. She could feel the pounding of her pulses. She contained that energy as she counted the men and women who emerged from the safety of their hold. Good, they were trudging innocently out to do their duty, leaving behind one old uncle and two aunties to take care of the smallest children.

When the ground crew were out of sight down the hill-track, Thella gave the signal to move toward the beasthold. From her spies' reports she knew that the holders fed and watered their animals before Fall. No one was likely to check until the ground crew returned late that evening. She watched her raiders advance, all of them keeping low and pausing behind cover just in case someone did open one of the shuttered windows.

Dushik and Felleck reached the thick metal-clad door and carefully opened it just wide enough to admit them. Instantly the next group, five men led by Giron, slithered across the open ground and were safely inside. Thella joined the third group, and the fourth slid in behind with no trouble.

"Just look at this," Felleck said, lifting handsful of the golden grain that they had come for. It was of good quality, Thella thought, noticing that no dust drifted away. Giron gave Felleck a prod in the ribs for unnecessary chatter. Felleck scowled, but he took the pail Giron gave him and began scooping grain into the sack that the dragonless man held open. The others worked in silence.

The grain that was disappearing into sacks and out of Kadross beasthold would enable her to load her runnerbeasts up with enough feed for raids at a safe distance from her main bases. She already had a large band of holdless folk to be fed and quartered that winter, but she needed more she could count on, strategically placed in the five Holds. Any dimwitted renegade could steal, but few could acquire exactly what they needed exactly when they needed it. Thella, Lady Holdless, could.

When Dushik caught her arm, she realized that she had been distracted from the progress of the raid. The last of the sacks was filled. Most of her men had filed out, heading for shelter where they would wait out any alarm. She took one of the remaining sacks and heaved it with a practiced motion to her shoulder. Dushik grabbed two, then turned to help her secure the bars across the door. They moved as fast as they could to the rocks. The return climb to the cave took longer, but they were well below the far ridge when Thella heard the rumble of drums.

"Calling Lemos Hold," Giron surprised her by saying. So far she had been the only one knowledgeable about drum messages.

"Shards!" Thella stopped, listening hard to the sequences. But the ridges distorted the sounds, so she could not make out the content of the message. She could guess, though. She wiped the sweat from her face, furious at having the theft discovered so soon. She would have to alter her plans, move more cautiously to deposit the grain where it was needed.

Giron grunted. "No dragons'll come looking today. Too tired," he said. Adjusting the sacks on his shoulder, he continued his descent.

The next day, she had her raiders split up into groups of three and four, each group headed for a different destination. They had orders to try to hide the grain if they saw any signs of pursuit and then return to the main Hold by a circuitous route.

My minor holds are constantly being raided," Asgenar told T'gellan, bronze Monarth's rider, who had conveyed the Lord Holder back to Lemos after the Fall. "Kadross is not the first to have suffered but probably the quickest to let me know." He grimaced, crumbling the drummed message in one fist as he strode to the map on the wall of his office. "Grain today, harness there, blankets stolen where they dried at a streamside, tools from a miner's hold, seasoned timbers carefully stored in a cavern that the holder was certain no one knew about. Little things, but it's no longer minor pilfering by the holdless. It's well planned and executed, and it's beggaring my small holders."

T'gellan scratched his head—though he kept his hair cropped short, his scalp still itched with sweat after a long Fall. He had been hoping to get himself and Monarth back to their weyr, and a bath, but Lord Asgenar was scrupulous in his duty to the Weyr, so T'gellan could not skimp the courtesies. He took another sip of the excellent mulled wine that had been served as soon as they walked into the Hold. The Fall—a fourth in the new pattern—had been right over Asgenar's cherished forestry, and F'lar had borrowed extra riders from Igen and Telgar to be certain that the invaluable trees were adequately protected. There had been additional ground crews, conveyed in from "safe" areas, to be sure that whatever Thread might possibly escape the dragonriders in the air would never burrow in the forest. It had been a very properly managed Fall, on the ground and in the air.

"Kadross Hold?" the dragonrider said. "And while they were all out on ground crew? Just grain?" He joined Asgenar at the wall chart, noting the meticulous detail of the terrain, the contour and height of every ridge and hill, and the type and size of every forest plantation. He wished once again that Lords Sifer and Raid were half as well informed as Lemos's young Holder.

Asgenar laid his finger on the spot, then moved it so that T'gellan could see the tiny numbers jotted in the square of the hold complex. "No, not *just* grain. Half their winter's supply. Ferfar received the grain only yesterday morning. I'd sent two escort riders—at the carter's request. He's had trouble with holdless raiders recently and was fearful of a long, unprotected trek."

"Someone spoke out of turn, d'you think? Or was the thief just lucky?"

"Thieves. They emptied four barrels, so there had to be a good few in on this," Asgenar replied, gesturing for T'gellan to hold out his winecup to be refilled. "There have been too many—ah, how shall I put it?—timely thefts—to be good luck. These thieves know what they want and where to get it."

"And no doubt in your mind that Ferfar is honest?"

"Not the day after receipt, with extra marks spent to insure safe delivery." Asgenar gave a snort of disbelief. "The escort saw no one on the track, coming or going. And with Threadfall, who'd be on a trail?" He grimaced, having answered himself. "Clever thieves! With all the able-bodied members of the hold out on ground crew. We wouldn't have known of it today, but Ferfar's uncle needed something in the store and saw a spillage. He was on the drums immediately."

T'gellan frowned, and at first Asgenar thought that the bronze rider would prefer to ignore the report. Then T'gellan looked him straight in the eye. "I've asked Monarth to tell everyone still airborne to do a low-level return. If they see any movement or anyone traveling, they'll get a closer look and report it to me. Tell me, have you any idea where the thieves'd be headed? Men heavily laden with sacks of grain won't be able to move quickly or far."

"That's another problem. All this part of Lemos, and well into Telgar—" Asgenar pointed at the various-sized brown stars that dotted the map "—is pocked with large and small caves. We mark any new ones we discover. There're probably plenty we haven't found. But my foresters report recent fires and occasionally buried trail supplies in off-trail caves. Far too frequently to be coincidence." Asgenar rubbed at his face and then massaged the back of his neck. "I'm not of a suspicious nature, but there is a pattern, not in the raids themselves, but in what is stolen. Certainly more food and practical items than valuables. There are renegades somewhere in those mountains who are living very well without doing a stroke of work. I resent that. And so do my holders."

"Indeed, they should," T'gellan agreed warmly. Lemos Hold had generously tithed to the Weyrs even before Fall.

"I don't have enough guards or holders and foresters to keep any sort of a watch on so many caves. And I'm beginning to think that some of the holdless accused of theft were indeed, as they claimed, innocent."

T'gellan looked thoughtful. "How many such innocents do you have in safekeeping at the moment?"

Asgenar grunted in disgust. "Far too many. You can't turn whole families with toddlers away. And I need all the able bodies I can get to fill out ground crews."

"Any you could trust for light duty? Like doing regular rounds of the more likely caves for a while to see who turns up?"

A smile replaced the anxiety on Asgenar's face. "By the First Egg, T'gellan, I'm disgusted I didn't think of that myself. What the holdless want most, after all, is a place to live and enough to eat. A minor holding in exchange for work well done. I can provide that," he added with a pleased smile.

I am perhaps far more aware of the problem," Masterharper Robinton said, peering around at the sober expression of the five assembled Lord Holders, "than any of you. My harpers keep me informed of major thefts so valuables can be restored. This list—" Robinton flicked the sheets that Asgenar had compiled for him beforehand. "—is most unsettling." He paused briefly, to let his sympathy and concern be noticed. "I'm glad that you approached me on this rather than tax your Weyrleaders. It is essentially, I think you will agree, a holder problem and must not interfere with the primary responsibility of the Weyrs." He made a mental note of Sifer's frown.

"But the dragonriders would be invaluable in tracking down these renegades," Corman said, banging the table with his big fist, his rugged features stern.

"In those copious free moments they have between Falls," Master Robinton replied drolly.

"At T'gellan's suggestion," Asgenar said to indicate that Benden Weyr was helpful, "I've put trustworthy holdless families in the caves nearest regular trader routes."

"And what good will that do?" Sifer demanded. "They'd be in league with thieves. I don't trust holdless men. Won't have them hanging around in Bitra, you may be sure. Why, I ask you, are they holdless in the first place?"

"I'll tell you," Laudey said, pointing a bony finger at the Bitran Lord Holder. "Because the elderlies and the crippled were turned out of their rightful places as soon as the Pass started, to make room for ablebodied men and women. Those caves on my eastern banks are full of that kind of holdless folk."

Sifer plainly did not approve of Laudey's altruism.

"You and your lady have been exceedingly generous," the harper said to Laudey.

"My men have their orders," Laudey said with a tinge of defensiveness in his voice. "We don't let just anybody shelter there."

"I'll bet some renegades get in no matter how good your guards are," Sifer muttered. "But I want the men responsible for these raids found and punished. It'd be an example to others with any idea of making Threadfall an excuse for indiscriminate pilfering."

"It's my opinion that we should be looking for a well-organized and well-informed band," Asgenar said. "They know what they want and they take it. We didn't find so much as a speck of grain leading from the Kadross Hold the next morning. They had to have gone up the mountain and reached shelter somewhere, or they'd've been seen by T'gellan's wing on their way home. Fifteen, twenty men would have been needed to carry that much grain. That raid was accomplished with clever planning, good information, and discipline."

"Then how do we track 'em if not by dragonriders?" Sifer asked. "Besides, the holdless are too spineless to do any of that." He pointed at the long list of thefts the Harper had set in the middle of the round table. "In fact, I'd lay odds against it being holdless." He leaned forward conspiritorially, across the table. "I'll bet it's those Oldtimers, striking back at us across the sea, whipping away what they can't tithe out of Hold and Hall." He peered around the table to gauge reactions.

"I don't think I'd take bets on that, Lord Sifer," Robinton said, his tone courteous. "When you consider that Benden dragonriders would know if any Oldtimers appeared in the north for any reason."

"Harper's right, you know," Corman agreed, giving Sifer a cold and quelling look. "We've some advantage in Keroon, being wide open. You can generally see travelers a good distance off. My sons have been riding, at random, from hold to hold, and since they started that, we've had fewer incidents." He looked at Asgenar. "Wouldn't work as well in your Hold, though, being up and down."

"Chased 'em out of Keroon up into Bitra is what you've done," Sifer said in outrage, his face flushed.

"Stop griping, Sifer," Laudey said with impatience. "Igen's only across the river from Keroon, and the living's easier—so I don't think you're as put upon as you think."

"There's a very old saying," Robinton began, raising his voice to stop the exchange. "Set a thief to catch a thief." His devious smile was not lost on the others. Asgenar and Larad leaned forward attentively.

"Catch what?" Sifer looked scornful. "Not if the first one's on to a good thing like this."

"Not a real thief, Lord Sifer," Robinton went on, "but a clever journeyman of mine with a knack of mixing in with all sorts of people. As Lord Asgenar said, the targets are all well chosen, and the raids show considerable familiarity with trade routes, unoccupied caves, and the routines and management of Holds and Halls." Because he was looking in Larad's direction, the Harper noticed his fleeting look of apprehension and dismay.

"He'd do well to start in those caves of mine," Laudey said, drumming his fingers irritably on the surface of the table. "All sorts of folk come and go, though, as I said before," he added defensively, "my guards keep order. The cave system is vast—lots of corridors and tunnels no one's been bothered with. I did block up as many of the smaller entrances as I could, but I've had other priorities, you know."

"With as many as you're sheltering, Laudey, there'd be someone to want a few marks in his hand for noticing irregularities or sudden prosperity," Asgenar said.

"Nonsense, most of the holdless wouldn't think twice about concealing a thief for a spill of his takings," Sifer said. "I've seen the way they operate myself."

Robinton raised his eyebrows in affected surprise, and Corman snorted since it was rather a joke that Bitrans drove bargains hard enough to be called cheats.

"Then you'll permit me to see what my journeyman can find out?" Robinton scanned their faces. They wanted something done without extending their already strained resources. It was as well, he thought, that he had anticipated their agreement. In actual fact his spy was already in place, harper sources having informed him of the situation well in advance of the Lord Holders' appeal. "I suggest that we keep this matter to ourselves, with no exceptions outside this room."

"You've got clever men in your Hall," Corman said, adding hastily, "and women." He was exceedingly fond of Menolly. "But what if he should find something going on in one of our Holds and needs our help?"

"If he needs help, Lord Corman," the Harper said with a sly smile, "then he's not been as clever as he should be. Leave the matter with me for this cold season. There's too much snow around for anyone needing to hide his tracks."

"I wouldn't bet on that," Sifer muttered.

Keita's orders from Thella included reporting any break in the usual Hold routine. Keita did not know much more than that Lord Sifer had been away overnight, conveyed by a dragonrider to his destination, but she did hear that upon his return he ordered his warders to let him know of any traces of occupation in way-caves or sites, and in particular of any tracks on back trails. The Bitra drum tower had been busy, but she did not know what the messages were about, as they had not used an open code.

Thella read and reread that message, almost pleased that she would have the challenge that the search would offer. Sifer did not worry her; his guards were more fond of gambling and prodding the holdless beyond Bitra's borders. But he was more likely than Corman, Laudey, or Asgenar to drop useful information if he was irritated.

Come to think of it, lately there did seem to be more sweepriders doing low-level flights above the forested hills and ridges. She had not quite counted on that. She gave orders to keep travel to a minimum—her storerooms were well stocked, so that meant no hardship—and gave strict instructions that those who did move across open areas must cover their tracks as they went. Dushik, Readis, and Perschar carried those orders to her other bases. For a while she would lie low.

It was Readis who returned six days later to tell her that

the Masterharper had been seen at Lemos Hold, along with Corman, Laudey, Larad, and Sifer.

"So, they've called the Harper in for advice. So what?"

"He's no simpleton, Thella," Readis said, frowning at her casual dismissal of what he considered disturbing news. "He's the most powerful person on Pern, next to F'lar."

Thella widened her eyes in mock surprise and alarm. "Spare me!"

"The Harper Hall knows things. You pride yourself that you've got ears all over the Eastern Range, Thella." Readis wanted to shake the complacence out of her. "Well, he's got ears, and drums, all over this continent and, some say, in the southern one, too."

"Harper Hall doesn't even have guard units!" she scoffed.

But even Dushik looked worried. "Harper doesn't need them," he said. "What the Harper knows gets around, if that's what he wants." He scowled. "I had to come east to get away from Harper words."

"I know, Dushik, I know." Thella said. Her voice was testy, but she smiled placatingly at her devoted crony. "You check over anyone who suddenly gets the urge to join our stalwart crew. Harpers always have callused fingertips from plucking strings all the time."

Dushik nodded, reassured, but Readis frowned.

"I wouldn't leave it at just that, Thella," he began.

"Who's holder here, Readis? Aren't we living well and far more comfortably than most lousy mountain holders? Certainly far better than any other holdless?" Her voice rang out, echoing down the tunnels to other chambers. She liked the effect, liked the vibrant sound of her own voice, and it never hurt to remind her folk just how much they had acquired under her guidance. "It's taken the Lord Holders nearly twelve Turns to realize what's been happening."

Readis stared back at her. "Lady Holdless Thella, you did take great interest in Fax's doings in the west. Don't underestimate harpers as he did. That's all I'll say on the matter."

"Readis is right about harpers, Lady Thella," Giron said, surprising everyone by speaking up. "And that Robinton is the cleverest man on Pern."

"You have both made good points," Thella said, and beside her Dushik relaxed. He was very sensitive to any criticism of her. "We've been so very successful, and that can make one careless. Giron, how many of the harpers do you know?"

Giron shrugged. "A few. The Weyrwoman Bedella liked music. Harper Hall sent them to Telgar Weyr whenever she asked."

"I'd be far more concerned with those bloody sweepriders that we can't see until they're above us," Dushik said, pointedly looking at Giron. "They're the real problem."

Abruptly Giron left the chamber, and Thella turned angrily on Dushik. "You let *me* handle him, Dushik!"

Hamian!" Piemur called to the Masterminer, pointing toward the bluff on the right-hand side of the Island River. "Those mounds! They're not natural!"

"No, they're not," Hamian answered without even looking up from the line he was neatly coiling. Minercrafter he might be, but he had been a sailor from his earliest Turns both in Southern and at High Palisades. He would no more leave untidy decks than he would an untidy forge or shaft. "There're some more, farther down the river on the left bank. Don't know what they used to be, but the piles haven't been washed away."

"But don't you want to look?" Piemur was astonished by Hamian's disinterest. Sometimes he thought the man took for granted all the beauty and wealth around him.

Hamian grinned at the young harper. "I've enough on my

plate without haring off to look at ruins I can't waste time searching.'' His grin broadened, and he ruffled Piemur's sun-bleached hair. "I make good use of the ones in the open pit. They even marked the direction of the veins. I don't know how they did that!''

Piemur ducked away. "But who are 'they'? You said there wasn't any mention of Southern workings in the Smithcraft-hall records.''

Hamian shrugged. "That doesn't mean much. As far back as they're legible, they're all about mine yields and tons smelted, and who bought what and where it was shipped. Except for Master Fandarel, the Craftmasters didn't look much beyond the main hall. *Put your backs in it!*'' he roared at the oarsmen. Once past the delta region, he hoped for a good westerly breeze to fill the sails and make some headway over the broad portion of the Island River. He licked a finger and held it up. "The wind's picking up!'' He cupped his hands and yelled encouragement to the rowers. "Not long now!'' But to Piemur, he muttered, "Those shiftless mongrels,'' before he raised his voice again. "I can see who's leaning on his oars! Number four oar, you there, Tawkin—you and your part-ner, number six, put your backs into it, damn your hides, or there'll be no beer tonight unless you—that's more like it!

"I tell you what, Piemur,'' Hamian added, relenting as he saw the disappointment on the young man's face. "You and Stupid can investigate on our way back. An independent study to show Toric you're good at charting and measuring. Keep an eye on those starboard banks—'' He outlined the area he meant. "See how long that bank is. This shallow draft sloop is fine for river traffic but, as we both know, not all that great in coastal waters. If we'd a collecting point here . . .'' Hamian thought for a moment, then slowly began to grin. "We could set up a permanent hold up there, in those ruins, and transship ore direct to Nerat or Keroon Sea Hold. Save a lot of time and effort, and give some responsible man a proper hold. Hmm, yes, you do that.''

Hamian had already calculated that they had made better time coming east along the coast than they did beating around the Southern cape and having to wait for the tide to ride over the reef into the lagoon. They had enjoyed a couple of days of easy sailing down the Island River before they came to the fork where a smaller tributary came down out of the central hills to join the flow. Just beyond that conjoining was where Hamian hoped to set up a hold, if the river proved navigable that far.

Wanting to avoid the miserable haul down Lagoon River and through the swamps that his sister Sharra found so fascinating, he had taken several days off to sail east. Somewhere in that direction the Island River must start. It had been an easy trek down the foothills to a point where he could see the river shimmering in the distance. The terrain was perfect for a burden-beast route. It had taken some pretty sharp dealing with Toric, but with some subtle help from Sharra and their brother, Kevelon, he had convinced the holder to see the benefit of cutting down travel time. There had been another load of northerners to absorb, so Hamian had volunteered to take all of them off Toric's hands and put them to work building pier and hold above the spring flood level. There was enough grassland for herdbeasts, and the mountains were close enough to quarry stone.

Hamian was backing his own judgment about the alternate route. He needed to prove to Toric that someone else could know something about Southern besides the self-styled Lord Holder. Sometimes Toric's attitudes bothered Hamian; and Toric was always accusing him of being tainted by northern notions during his Turns at the Smithcrafthall.

Hamian had organized his arguments well. Lagoon River might appear to be the shorter route, but trying to pole ore-laden barges through the swampland halfway down the river made it quite another story. Hamian was not afraid of hard work, and he was remarkably effective in getting a similar effort out of his teams, but between trips, the channel markings got broken or swallowed by the shifting bottom mud. Hunting for deep waters, while being eaten by insects, bitten by swamp snakes, and harried by wherries who regarded anything that moved as fair game, was not an efficient use of available labor. Hamian had become infected by Master Fandarel's overriding compulsion for efficiency.

"Pull that oar, Tawkin, don't stroke it!" he yelled as the longboat began to veer slightly to port. Hamian intended to watch that fellow. He was getting to have as good an eye as Toric and Sharra for who would work out in Southern. "Now, there could have been some shipwrecked fisherfolk who built there," he suggested to Piemur as the mounds slowly slipped out of sight.

Piemur was shaking his head. "Fisherfolk don't build in stone, and that's all that would have lasted four hundred or more Turns. Besides, there was nothing about this place in the Harper Hall Records, which *are* legible a long way back. I know," he added, wrinkling his nose as if he could still smell the reek of decaying hides. "I had to copy 'em for old Master Arnor." Piemur drew in a deep breath of the forest-scented air as if cleansing his lungs of the remembered smell. He exhaled gustily.

Hamian laughed. "Well, you can see what your harper-trained eye makes of the mine fittings." The single big square sail of the wide-bellied narrow draft ship began to fill. "Belay that, lads!" he shouted to the rowers. "Make ready to take the longboat aboard," he ordered the nearest crewmen. "That's more like it. We'll make some headway today. Both moons are out tonight, so if the wind lasts, we'll be there in two days. That's a damn sight better than six trying to wade through swamp. Too bad we can't get as far as the Falls. They're spectacular."

"Falls?"

"Yes, Toric sent an exploratory party down this river, oh, just before I left for Telgar Smith Crafthall. They got as far as the Falls before they turned back. Sheer rock cliffs that no one could scale." He saw the determined look on Piemur's face. "Not even you, but maybe Farli. Look, you'd better go stand with Stupid. He's getting restless."

"He'd rather walk than sail," Piemur said, though the motion on the river was not as unpleasant as on open water. He never could understand why Menolly and Sebell were so enthusiastic about sea voyages. At the moment, Stupid was stomping on the deck, and Piemur hurried over to calm him. It would not do to put gouges in the smooth deck planks. Farli was still doing her lazy circles far above, and Piemur wished he had the view she had from up there.

He sat down, leaning back against Stupid's front legs—the best way to keep the beast still—and peered over the portside rail at the passage of the plain, wondering what lay in the dense forest beyond. Piemur hoped to prove his worth on this trip. Sharra had talked Hamian into taking him on in a scouting capacity and to record the alternate route. He had gotten a taste of exploring two Turns back and was becoming increasingly bored at setting up drum towers. He had done all he could, and Saneter was talking of sending him back to Harper Hall to get his journeyman's knot. But Piemur wanted to explore uncharted lands.

From the edges of the Swamp, down to Numbweed Plain and Big Lagoon, across that headland to Southern, and east along the coast to the Mountain Rift and Dry Holds, Toric had installed small settlements with men and women beholden to him for the opportunities. It had been fun for Piemur to teach drum codes to pupils so much older than himself. He had been diligent, too, because Toric was a totally different personality than Master Robinton, Master Shonagar, or Master Domick and his drum tower masters. Piemur had felt Toric's hard hand once and took great care not to feel it again. He knew that the Southerner was very ambitious, far more than anyone—except possibly Master Robinton—knew.

But the provident, beautiful, amazing, fantastic land that was Southern was more than the people who grabbed a hold on it. Looking to a seemingly limitless eastern stretch of forest and hill, Piemur wondered just how far Southern did extend—and just how much Toric thought he could take into one Hold under his orders! Soon Piemur's first loyalty to the Harper Hall was going to come into abrupt conflict with his sneaking admiration for Toric's ambitions. Or the ambitions of someone like Lord Groghe, who had that mess of sons to settle, or Corman, who had nine. If they found out how much good land was available, they might even defy Benden's orders. Saneter kept telling Piemur that Master Robinton was well informed of all Toric's doing, but Piemur was beginning to wonder if Saneter really *knew*!

Just then, Piemur gasped. Through the gaps in the weather rail, he had a perfect view of the port banks. There, lounging in the sun, unperturbed by the ship floating past, were two huge spotted felines. They were probably some of the sports that Sharra had mentioned. Piemur realized that he should call attention to them, but Hamian was on the starboard rail, watching the boat being lifted aboard. And somehow, Piemur did not want to share the moment with anyone, or scare the magnificent creatures away.

I came as soon as I could, Lady Thella,'' the bedraggled wight said through lips blue with cold. The first line of sentinels had passed him through to her hold guards. "I wasn't seen. I hide a lot. No tracks. See?'' He thrust a long-needled tree branch at her. "I tied this to my belt, and it swept up my tracks as I made 'em.''

Thella made herself relax, but she worried that the thickwit before her could have led searchers to her lair in his hasty rush to tell her some insignificant rumor.

"But this could be important, Lady,'' the ragged man went on, trying to stop his teeth from chattering.

Thella signalled to one of the cook drudges to get the man

a cup of klah. She could barely understand him as it was. If he had something important to say, she wanted to hear it quickly or dismiss him.

He nearly prostrated himself, all but spilling the klah when it was handed to him, but a few sips appeared to control his spasms.

"I mean, you always wanted to know just when Thread starts and stops," he said. "And which lord is going where, and more about the Weyrs then us'ns is supposed to know. Well, I got the way for you to hear dragons—all the time! This girl, well she can hear dragons! That's good, isn't it? She can hear 'em at a distance, too, and what they say to each other."

"I find that hard to believe," Thella said expressionlessly, glancing quickly at Giron. The dragonless man slowly swung his head around to look at the newcomer.

"Oh, no, Lady Thella. She can. She really can. I watched her. She'd call the children back into the caverns, telling 'em dragonriders was on their way over. The first time, she said they'd be coming to Igen Hold. I saw the dragons headed that way myself. I heard her tell her brother when they were on their way back to Benden Weyr. At least she said they were from Benden Weyr and there wasn't no way—no reason, either—to think she was lying. She did it all quietlike. She didn't know I heard 'er."

"If you were close enough to hear her do it all quietlike," Thella began sourly, "then why wouldn't she know you heard her?"

The man winked and grinned, an appalling sight since he had so few front teeth left. "Because in the caverns, I'm deef! I don't hear nuffing. I'm good at that, I am. I get fed 'cause I'm helpless." He demonstrated, saliva spattering from his loose lower lip.

"I see," Thella drawled. Awful man, cleverer than he looked. Readis often said that the holdless survived more by deception than by strength. The "deaf" man would not have passed her outer sentinels if he had not been an accepted spy.

She glanced at Dushik, who gave her a reassuring nod. "She has one of those little fire-lizards?"

"Her?" The man guffawed, and more spittle drooled from his mouth. He seemed to sense her disgust and swallowed, mopping at his mouth with the blanket someone had thrown across his shoulders. "Nah! Fire-lizzuds cost ya. The way I heard it, her dad and ma were chased out of Ruatha by Fax. The ma's still a looker, got big—" Hastily he caught himself, realizing he spoke to a well-endowed woman. "Fax did like a good piece to warm his furs. If the ma was Ruathan Bloodline like she claims, it could be in the Blood for the girl to hear dragons. The Benden Weyrwoman's Ruathan, you know."

In the face of her cold silence, he lost all brashness. He gulped down the rest of the klah as if afraid the cup would be dashed from his hand and looked warily about him.

Let him stew, Thella thought, setting her elbow on the armrest and cushioning her chin in the palm of her hand, looking anywhere but at the disgusting messenger. He was right: Ruathans had produced too many dragonriders—far more than any of the other Bloodlines. Lessa was the current insult.

"Tell me again," she ordered, gesturing for Dushik and Readis to listen carefully. Giron kept on watching, his face blank.

But the man seemed to be telling the truth. He had heard the girl's younger brother boasting of his sister's ability, that she always knew when Thread would fall "because the dragons talked to each other about it."

Giron nodded at Thella as he regarded the "deaf" man with incurious but seeing eyes, very much aware of what had been said.

"I think," Thella said after mulling over the risks involved, "I think I must speak with this fascinating child. Do you know her name, deaf man?"

"Aramina, Lady Thella. Her name's Aramina. Her da's Dowell, and he's a woodjoiner; her ma's named Barla; the boy's Pell, and there's another—"

She cut him off. "And they're all at Igen cave site?" At his hasty nod she asked, "Would they be likely to move?"

"They been there a good few Turns. He does work he sells at the Gathers, and makes furniture—"

"I don't need to know that, my good man," she said coldly. He had a gargling voice, as if phlegm constantly lodged in his throat; it was not only a disgusting sound but an irritating monotone. "They're not liable to take off?"

"Where to, lady?" he replied ingenuously, raising both hands in appeal.

She motioned to Dushik and Readis. "I'll go. Dushik, you must stay here." She looked at the dragonless man. "Giron, you'll come with me." She was annoyed that her words sounded more like a question than an order, but Giron nodded, an odd twitch pulling at his mouth. "You'd know if she can actually hear dragons, wouldn't you?" she asked him.

Ignoring his silence, which usually meant Giron's consent, Thella rose and left the room with Dushik. The smell from the informant warming up by the fire was offensive.

"Dushik, take care of him!" she ordered.

If deaf men could tell tales, dead men would not. Dushik obliged her, as always.

5

IGEN AND LEMOS HOLDS, PP 12

Thella was not pleased when she and Giron arrived at the labyrinthine Igen caverns to find that their usual discreet entrance had been blocked up again. She was angry enough to help Giron destroy the barrier.

"Someone didn't do a good job," Giron said as the hardset that sealed the stones crumbled at the touch of his steel.

"I'd skin a stoneman who did such shoddy work," Thella said through gritted teeth. She was tired, and she had counted on getting safely inside without being caught by the Igen patrol they had seen in the distance.

The site had been excellent for her purposes. A tangle of young sky-broom saplings partially concealed an opening just high enough to permit runners to enter. Inside, the ceiling was sufficient for tall men to stand erect. A small chamber to the right of the entrance made an excellent beast shelter, with water oozing into a pool. There were four other tunnels leading from the entrance, two of them falling into dangerous shafts; the widest led deep into the bowels of the cave system; the fourth and narrowest seemed to end within a dragon-length but, in fact, turned abruptly right and came out at one of the intersecting main passages of the inhabited portions of the cave system.

It was easy enough to get into the vaulted chambers where people congregated during the day without encountering any of Lord Laudey's guards. Although Thella contacted one of her regular informers, it took all morning before she caught a glimpse of her quarry. She was not impressed.

Aramina was a slender brown girl, her pants rolled to her knees, and traces of mud on her legs and arms. Her clothing was muddy, as well, and as she passed by Thella's vantage point, the odor of the mudflats lingered about her, along with the stench of the net full of shellfish she carried. A small, muddier boy tagged along, calling, "Aramina, wait for me!"— and Thella had the positive identification she needed.

She saw Giron's cold eyes following the pair, and the ominous expression on his face made her uncomfortable.

"I'll want some proof of her abilities," she said. "She's of an age to be difficult. Too old to be malleable, and too young to be reasoned with. Find out what you can about her. I'll see where she squats." She caught his arm as he turned away. "And be sure you eat before you come back. It looks like some scavenger smelled out the supplies we left here."

"Snake, more likely," Giron said unexpectedly, his gaze following the girl as she made her way among those sitting about the wide, low-ceilinged cavern.

Thella went in search of her most reliable source of information. As she made her way to a largish side chamber, not far from the main entrance, she realized that there were more folk living in the caverns than ever before. The place stank of its throng. Thella estimated that there must have been hundreds sitting or standing about. From snatches of conversation she overheard, she understood them to be waiting for the arrival of Lady Holder Doris, who came every morning with three healers to examine the injured or ailing and distribute the day's ration of flour and root vegetables. The ablebodied apparently added to those supplies, to judge by Aramina's net. Shellfish from Igen's tidal flats were very tasty. Those holdless drifters were living better than she, of Telgar's Bloodline, had in her first Turn of the Pass. Well, if the Igen Lord Holder and his Lady had food to give to beggars, then she would not mind lifting more of their goods in the future, Thella decided, skirting the crowd deftly. No one seemed to take note of her as she ducked down the passageway to Brare's squat.

"It's tough times," the footless seaman told her, and expected her to believe it as he dipped out a bowl of thick fish chowder for her, rich with roots, a variety of fish meats, and even some shellfish. "Laudey's men search now at odd times—you couldn't be sure when it's safe."

Thella gave a quick glance to position the exits from Brare's cave. "How recent a custom is this search? What can they expect to find in here?" Brare had been one of her first and most useful contacts. He despised Craftsmen and had few good words for Holders, despite the fact that he was living fairly well off the softhearted Igenish.

"Aye, last few weeks." He cocked his head and regarded her through slitted eyes, a sly smile on his face. "Aye, since all of Kadross Hold's grain was lifted one morning during Threadfall. Up Lemos way."

Thella did not change expression as she thanked him for the chowder and blew on the surface to cool it. "You make a great chowder, Brare," she said.

"I'd lay low were I the ones who cleaned out Kadross. I'd find a new shore to cast my nets. Lotta questions being asked, casual like."

"About me?"

"About likely souls who'd turn renegade. They seem to want to catch a good-sized, well-disciplined band. They'd pay high for a proper lead."

She smiled to herself, pleased that her skill had been noticed but irritated that the search had fanned out as far as Igen's caverns. Maybe she should not raid Igen, after all.

"You been real clever, Lady Thella."

He timed his casual use of her name well—she had just taken a mouthful of chowder, still too hot to swallow quickly. He grinned at her discomfort, but they were alone, and Brare was not fool enough to let her name drop where others could hear it. He had known who she was for the past few Turns and she wondered how much she would have to hand over before he would "forget" that he knew it.

"No fear, lady." Brare chuckled. "It's my secret!" He chuckled again. "I like a good secret. I know to keep it close, too. Here!" He patted his belt pouch.

Fair enough, and curiously she did trust Brare. She had paid him well over the last Turns. She took his hint and slipped him thirty quartermarks, coins he could most easily change without question. Readis had confirmed that the old fisherman had never been known to betray anyone. The old man, who moved only between his sunny place outside the main entrance and his cave, probably knew anything of interest that occurred throughout the eastern rank of Holds. She had used his information to advantage in the past.

His sharp gray eyes sparkled as his hand confirmed the new size of his pouch. "That's a tidy price for a cup of chowder, lady." He gave her a wide smug grin without opening his lips, screwing up the sun-scored wrinkles about his eyes.

"Not just chowder, Brare," she said, putting an edge on her voice. "What do you know about this girl who can hear dragons?"

Brare regarded her with widened eyes and an appreciative stare, pulling the corners of his mouth down knowingly. "Thought you'd hear about her. Who tol'ja?"

"A deaf man."

Brare nodded. "He was bound and determined he'd get to

you. I told him to wait. Too many looking to find you. He could lead 'em to your door.''

"He didn't. I've rewarded him well. Gave him a hold all his own for the winter." Brare accepted her lie with an amiable nod, and Thella pursued the information she needed. "About the girl?"

"Is that why you brought the dragonless man with you?"

It was Thella's turn to grin. He *did* have ears in the walls and eyes on every ceiling!

"He's improved in health since you told Readis he was here. The girl?" She did not intend to spend the whole morning chatting with a coy old man in a smelly inner cave, even if he did make a fine chowder.

"Aye, that's true enough. Our Aramina, daughter to Dowell and Barla. She hears dragons, right enough. Or so the hunters say, for they take her with them if there's any fear of Fall.''

"Where is she? I'm not prowling about in this warren without direction.''

"That's wise of you. Two passages to the right here, turn left. Follow the main branch—it's now lighted—to the fourth intersection. Family dosses down in an alcove on the right. Pink downers," he added, referring to the cave's stalactites. "Dowell carved me my stick, you know." He reached beside him and offered the crutch for her inspection. When she caught sight of the intricate carving, she grabbed the end for a closer look. Father, as well as daughter, would be useful to her. "Broom wood," Brare said with understandable pride. "Hardest wood anywhere. Not even Thread scores it. This came from a piece blown down by that big gale we had several Turns back. Took Dowell all winter to decorate it. Paid him what it was worth, too." His fingers caressed the dark wood, rubbed shiny by use.

"Fine work."

"Stout crutch. Best I've ever had!" Then bitterness seemed

to overcome him and he snatched it from her, throwing it down beside him and out of sight. "You've had your chowder. Get away from me. I'd be thrown out of the best berth a footless man could have if you're found in here."

She went immediately, and not to please him—once he started brooding on his injury, he turned maudlin. As she followed his directions, she mused on the idea that a man who could carve with such skill would be living among the Igen holdless. She would have thought he could find a place in any Hold.

Not for the first time, she wondered why no one had taken Igen's cave complex to Hold. There were plenty of large chambers, even if they were not so high and vaulted as those of Igen Hold itself across the river. Floodwaters washing into the main chamber would be a disadvantage, she admitted. Igen Proper stood well back from the river, on a high bank, well above any overflow.

The labyrinth was not so well ventilated, but some of the stalactites and stalagmites that formed natural divisions between alcoves had an eerie luminous beauty in their shaded layers. The deeper in she went, the more she was aware of the settled odors of damp and concentrated human living. She was glad of the glow baskets, for she would have been quickly lost without light.

The alcove with pink stalactites was empty but neat. Belongings were locked away in carved chests, straw pallets rolled up on top of them. Propped in one corner and chained to a stalactite was a heavy dray beast yoke, though with its distinctive carving anyone would be a fool to steal it. She stood in the center of the chamber, trying to get a feeling for its inhabitants. She would have to find out what pressures could be put on Dowell and Barla so that Aramina would come of her own accord.

When she heard the echo of cheering and many conversations, she turned inward, moving swiftly to less used corridors and back to her lair. She had taken another few hours' rest and was mulling over possibilities when Giron returned, calling softly to warn her of his coming. Wise man, she thought. She had already heard the scraping and had her knife out, poised to throw. He grunted when he saw her arm still raised and waited to enter until she had sheathed it. He had a covered earthenware bowl in one hand and a loaf of bread in the other.

"I waited for my share," Giron said, offering half the loaf to her. The tempting odor of steamed shellfish filled the little room when he opened the pot and peered in. "There's enough."

She wanted to say that she did not eat dole food, that Thella, Lady Holdless, did not accept Igenish charity, but the bread looked crusty and was still warm, and the shellfish would be succulent.

"You can bury the shells later," she muttered, reaching into the pot. "What did you hear? Was the place searched? Did you see her again? A reliable source tells me she's genuine."

Giron grunted, and his face had a closed expression, not quite concealing intense and conflicting emotions. She waited until they had both eaten before she prompted him again. She could not let his black mood take precedence over her requirements.

"She hears them, right enough," he murmured, eyes unfocused and features set. "The girl hears dragons."

His tone made her examine him more closely, and she got a sense of a bitter poignant envy, an unsettling rancorous anger seething in the dragonless man. They had done him no favors restoring his health. So why had he come with her, knowing her quest?

"She could be useful to me, then," she said finally to break the dense brooding silence. She spoke in a brisk tone. "Look to the beasts after you bury the shells. Save the pot. Were Igen guards in evidence? I'm told they search frequently and without warning."

He shoveled the shells back into the pot, then shrugged. "No one bothered me."

That did not surprise Thella. One look at his expression would have been sufficient to warn off questions, even from guards. She was sorry she had not brought someone else to leaven such dour company. She rolled up in her sleeping fur before he returned from his tasks. She knew he knew she was not asleep, but he settled himself for the night with a minimum of sound.

The next morning she changed to appropriate holder clothing, with Keronian colors and a beasthold journeyman's shoulder knot. With a knitted hat over her plaits, she strolled confidently to Dowell's alcove, giving a greeting at the entrance as she swiftly surveyed the occupants.

"Dowell, I've heard of your carving expertise and have a commission for you."

Dowell rose and gestured for her to enter, nudging the boy off one of the chests and telling him to get a clean mug for the holder. Aramina, in skirt and loose blouse, reached for the klah jug and poured a generous cup, which the woman, Barla, passed courteously to Thella.

"Be seated, holder," Barla said with the air of someone embarrassed to offer only a chest and struggling to hide it.

Thella took what was offered, thinking that the woman might well have been coveted by Fax: Barla was still a handsome woman, despite deep worry lines about mouth and eyes. The boy was goggle-eyed about an early visit; the youngest child was still asleep along the far wall.

"I don't come by much good wood, holder," Dowell said.

"Ah," Thella said, airily dismissing that consideration. "That can be remedied. I'm in need of two armchairs, in a fellis leaf pattern, as a bride present. They must be finished before snow blocks the pass to High Ground Hold. Can you oblige me?"

She could see Dowell hesitate and could not understand

why. Surely he took commissions. He wore no color or journeyman knot. He shot an anxious glance at his wife.

"It'd be worth a quartermark to me to see design sketches
by evening." Thella took a handful of marks from her pouch,
selected a quarter, and held it up. "A quarter for sketches.
We can discuss price when I've chosen what I like, but you'll
find me generous." She saw the anxious glint in the wife's
eye, saw her unobtrusively nudge her husband's arm.

"Yes, I can have design sketches for you, Lady Holder. By
this evening?"

"Very good. By evening."

Thella stood, dropping the quarter in his hand. Then she
turned as if struck by a sudden thought and smiled at Aramina. "Didn't I see you yesterday? With a net full of shellfish?" Why did the girl stiffen and eye her so warily?

"Yes, Lady Holder," Aramina managed to reply.

"Do you dig every day to fill the family pot?" What did
one talk about to timid girls who heard dragons?

"We share what we dig," Aramina said, lifting her chin
proudly.

"Laudable, most laudable," Thella said, though she
thought it rather odd that a girl who had lived holdless would
be so touchy. "I'll see you this evening, Master Dowell."

"Journeyman, Lady Holder. Journeyman."

"Humph. With the carvings I've seen?" She left the compliment like that. Dowell's family would need careful handling. She could hear the woman whispering excitedly to her
husband. A quartermark was a lot to a holdless family.

Now where, Thella wondered, was she going to come by
seasoned wood, the sort a prosperous holder woman would
gift a bride?

She was back that evening and expressed lavish praise for
the five designs he showed her. He was a good draftsman

and showed a fine range of chair types. She was tempted to do more than just string him along with promise of work in an attempt to gain the daughter's confidence. Such armchairs would be far more comfortable than the canvas affairs and the stiff benches which were all she currently had. The harp-back design could be easily transported in sections to her hold and then glued together. One design, with a high, straight back, wide, gracefully curved arms, and carved legs and cross-pieces, was particularly splendid.

All of a sudden, Giron came striding down in the passage-way, flashing her an urgent hand signal.

"Let me have a day or two to choose, Dowell," she said, rising to her feet and folding the sketches carefully. "I'll bring these back and we'll discuss this further."

She heard the wife murmur anxiously to the joiner. But Giron jerked his head for her to be quick, so she followed him down the next narrow alley.

"Searchers!" he whispered. Then she led him through dim corridors until they were safely out of reach.

Two days later, after she had Giron check to make sure there had already been a search that morning, she returned to Dowell's place. To her disgust the girl was not there. She discussed wood with Dowell and haggled over price. She finally gave him more than she thought she ought, but as she would probably never have to give over but half, and might even get that back, she could afford to seem generous.

Aramina, she discovered from Brare, had been sent out with the hunters. No one actually said that she had been taken along because she could hear dragons, but it did not take much wit to figure that out.

"How many people know about her?" Thella asked Brare, worrying that if the Weyrs found out about Aramina's talent, they would snap the girl up, thus ending all of Thella's grand plans. Her ambitions were great, and she was becoming increasingly convinced that they could not be realized without a guaranteed way of evading the dragonriders.

"Them?" Brare jerked his thumb in a western direction and snorted disbelief. "No one'll tell 'them.' It'd be worth their life here if they did. She's too useful to the hunters. Have to go much farther out in the hills to find wherry these days. Don't want to be caught out. I do like a bit o' wherry meat once in a while." He sucked in air past gaps in his teeth. Thella rose at once and left.

Over the next few days, Thella tried both to gain the girl's confidence and to lure Dowell into bringing his whole family to her hold. She and Giron had "found" the required lengths of wood handily enough, cautiously replacing what they stole with inferior planks.

"We're quiet in the mountains, I grant you," she told Dowell as she watched him meticulously carving the design on the chair back, the controlled motions of his short-bladed knife almost imperceptible. "But you can't want your children to remain in this warren. You could finish these chairs in my hold, comfortably. I've got a good harper-teacher as well." She managed not to smile at the thought of her so-called harper's morals.

"We're going back to our rightful hold in Ruatha, lady," Barla replied with dignity.

Thella was surprised. "Across Telgar Plains during Threadfall?"

"The route has been well planned, lady," Dowell said, intent on his work. "We shall have shelter when it's needed."

Thella caught Barla's slight, almost smug smile and read it as an indication that they were counting on their daughter's talent.

"Surely not at this time of the year, with winter approaching?"

"Your commission will not take me long, lady, now that I have the wood," Dowell said. "I shall have it ready for you and still make the journey. Winter comes later to Telgar coasts."

"Dowell is a journeyman; he practices his craft," Barla added, defensively. "The stewards sent by Mastersmith Fandarel and Telgar Lord Holder cannot draft him to the mines."

"Of course not," Thella agreed fervently, though she felt a jolt of apprehension at the thought of her brother Larad anywhere near. "I'm amazed that Lord Laudey is permitting any interference by outsiders in these caverns."

"Lord Laudey suggested it," Dowell said with a mirthless smile.

"I do not blame him," Barla said gently. "There are many here who could work who don't. Lady Doris is too kind."

"A fine generous woman," Thella agreed, beginning to think that perhaps Barla was the one she should concentrate on.

Giron had informed her that the searching was two-pronged: to sift any information that might lead to the capture of marauding bands and to collect ablebodied people to work at Smithcrafthall and Telgar's mines. The population of the cavern had noticeably decreased the first night. Sufficient folk, those with families particularly, had volunteered for the Smithcrafthall's various projects: not just the making of more agenothree flamethrowers and the maintenance of existing apparatus, but some scheme—and Giron was skeptical—of the Mastersmith's to provide better communications between all Holds, Halls, and Weyrs. Thella did not like the idea of mountain mines being reopened. The unused shafts made ideal refuges. Still, she could always give her scouts miner's knots to wear on their shoulders. They would then have an explanation for their presence in the shafts.

Just in case one of Larad's stewards might recognize her, even after fourteen Turns, she elected to keep out of sight. Being confined all day did not improve her temper at all. She had Giron keep one eye on Dowell's progress, and the other on the girl—and she made plans.

What Thella was waiting for was one of the foggy nights typical of late autumn. With Telgar's men around, she no longer had the time to talk the family into moving to her hold—not when slipping a little fellis powder into their dinner kettle would sidestep resistance. And the girl was the one she wanted. The others were useless baggage. When they were truly asleep, she and Giron would remove the girl. A few threats of vengeance would ensure the girl's compliance. She had Giron purchase a third runnerbeast and prepare to leave the area.

She was livid, two mornings later, when Giron came hurrying back to tell her that he had found the woodcarver's alcove occupied by six elderlies, none of whom understood his questions about the previous inhabitants.

Brare was astonished when he heard—and angry. "Aramina's gone? She'd no right. There's to be a hunt today, before the next big Fall. They were expecting her. They need her to help them hunt. And I had my mouth all set for roast wherry." He shoved his crutch under his arm and was halfway down the passage before Thella realized where he was going.

Giron grabbed her by the shoulder. "No! Guards around. Come."

"He'll find out where they've gone."

"He should have *known* they were going," Giron replied in a savage tone. "It'll be a warm day *between* before I believe that footless man again." He started to leave. "They can't have gone far, not with three children and a cart pulled by burden beasts."

"Burden beasts?" Thella followed him, not at first realizing that she was. She stopped. "Why didn't you tell me they had burden beasts?"

Giron halted and swung around to her, disgusted. "You're not usually slow-witted. You couldn't have missed seeing the yoke they had chained to an upper.'' He grabbed her by the hand. ''They'd beasts for the yoke—kept 'em at grass, south of the cavern.''

''Which way would they go then? They couldn't be mad enough to head toward Ruatha now?''

''I'll check with the clamdiggers. You get the runners ready. They can't have gone far, whichever way they went.''

Halfway back to her lair, Thella realized that she had followed Giron's orders without protest. She was furious with him, and with herself for losing control, and outraged that the meek-mouthed Dowell and his affected wife could have outguessed her. She only hoped he had taken the carved wood with him. She would have those chairs off him or his hide!

''They didn't strike off east,'' Giron said. ''The ferryman would have seen them.'' He had been running hard and had to lean against the wall to catch his breath. ''A train went out of here, three days ago, headed toward Great Lake and Far Cry Hold with winter supplies.''

''Dowell expected to join them?'' Thella tightened the cinch on her runner and gestured for Giron to ready his while she tied their supplies to the saddle of the third beast.

''They wouldn't want to be on their own. You don't lead the only renegade band in this area,'' Giron said, pulling the strap so tight that the runnerbeast squealed in protest.

''Watch that, Giron!'' She meant both noise and rough-handling. She did not hold with needless mistreatment of animals. She would have expected better management from a dragonless man—or maybe he was revenging his loss on other animals.

Outside the den, she signalled to him to stop and dismount. As much as she wanted to be on the trail of her quarry, she first had Giron help her replace enough of the debris to ensure that a casual look would see a blocked entrance. She might need that refuge again.

Then they mounted and were off as fast as they could safely move on uphill, stony ground and leading an animal.

The fourth day out of Igen, Jayge had lost all his bad temper. All he had really needed was to get back on the road again, away from holders, away from the shifting and shiftless masses in the low caverns and the constant appeals from the Smithcrafthallers and the Telgarans to "take a hold of himself," "be useful," "learn a good craft," and "make enough credits to bank with a Bitran."

He *liked* being a trader; he had always liked the open road, setting his own pace, commanding his own time, and being accountable to himself alone for what he ate and wore and where he sheltered. Jayge certainly would not have traded the hazards of life on track and trail, despite the horrors of Threadfall, for a secure life straining his guts and his back to carve rooms in someone else's hold. The three wretched miserable Turns at Kimmage Hold had been sample enough of holding. He could not imagine how his Uncle Borel and the others could possibly have chosen to remain at Kimmage as little more than drudges. The children for whom they were sacrificing themselves would not appreciate it when they got older. Not Lilcamps with the restlessness bred into the Blood.

Jayge strode out ahead of the train. He was walking point, checking the trail for any obstacles that might hinder the progress of the broad, heavily laden wagons. Their metal roofs made them cumbersome but safe enough—thanks to Ketrin and Borgald's ingenuity—if the train got caught out in a freak Fall, though that would be very bad trail management indeed. Since that first time, nearly thirteen Turns earlier, neither Jayge nor any other Lilcamp had suffered score. There were, he had discovered since that day, worse things than a mindless burning rain.

Jayge cursed under his breath. The day was too fine to sully by thinking of past problems. The Lilcamps were out and about again. Ketrin was with them on this journey, and they had ten wagons packed with trade goods to deliver to Lemos Great Lake and Far Cry Holds. The train had skirted the danger of the shifting soil, sand, and mud of the Igen River basin, but the track through the sky-broom trees could be even more treacherous.

The great trees, unique to this one long stretch of the valley, had root systems that radiated in a great circle around the trunk to support the soaring limbs and tufted heights. In the misty early morning light the sky-brooms had the appearance of skeletal giants with bushy heads of hair, and abnormally long arms that either reached for the sky or hung to knobby legs.

Only as Jayge passed them could he see the twined trunks; the more there were, the older the sky-broom. The short tufts of spiny leaves flattened out, often hiding wild wherry nests situated too high above the ground for snakes to reach and easily guarded from nest-robbing wherries. Often the crowns of coarse, short leaves would be eaten away by Threadfall. Some of the giants had fallen, leaving jagged stumps jutting high above the extensive plain. Sky-broom was a much-treasured wood, though very difficult to work, or so Jayge had heard from a Lemosan woodsman. Whole branches could be used as support beams in free-standing holds, strong enough to support the weight of a slate roof.

Jayge glanced up to see dragons flying above. The first time his little half-sister had seen the sky-broom trees she had asked if dragons landed on the flat tops. But Jayge found little humor in the innocent question. Even after so many Turns he could not help feeling a certain nervous tightening of his belly muscles whenever he saw dragons in the sky. He shaded his eyes to appraise the creatures.

"That's not a full wing," Crenden bellowed reassuringly.

Jayge waggled his hand above his head to indicate that he

had not taken alarm; he recognized from their leisurely pace and informal pattern that the riders were probably returning to Igen Weyr from a hunt, their dragons too full in the belly to fly *between*. Then he heard someone shrieking and turned to look behind.

On the lookout platform of the lead wagon stood his half-sister, screaming at the top of her lungs and waving her hands, trying to attract the high-fliers. The Kimmage Hold harper had made certain that Alda had grown up with her head packed full of tradition. His brother Tino, who was old enough to remember that horrific day, watched as impassively as Jayge.

Even dragons looked small silhouetted against the sky-brooms. But splendid! Jayge was honest enough not to deny them that. He could never erase the shock and disillusion of his first meeting with a dragonrider, even after he had met many dedicated, courteous and considerate Weyrmen, but watching the dragons flow across the sky, their wings moving in unison, he experienced his usual dissatisfaction with the walking pace of both humans and runnerbeasts.

He looked down, scanning the track ahead of him. That was his responsibility today, pointing a smooth track. One had to have room to stop burden beasts: they were slow thinkers and once they got their heavy loads moving, they were not easily halted, not with all that weight behind them. The Masterherdsman in Keroon could not seem to breed *all* the necessary abilities into one animal. One had to choose between speed and endurance, mass and grace; intelligence seemed paired with nervousness, placidity with slow reactions. Still, their present beasts would plod on and on through the night if necessary, without once altering the rhythm of their stride.

Jayge saw a large depression—a dragon-length wide and at least five hands in depth, enough to break an axle—and signalled for his father to swing the lead wagon to the left. Crenden was marching by the yoke, his wife Jenfa and Jayge's youngest half-brother astride the left-hand beast. Jayge trotted on ahead and stood on the far side of the dip so the other wagoners could begin to shift their line of march.

He saw the flank riders spreading the news down the long sprawl of the train. The rear wagon was just passing the first of the day's obstacles, a huge tree stump, and he noticed that someone had climbed it and was wagging his arms in the sequence that told Jayge and his father that riders were coming up on the train fast: two riders, three runners.

"I'll watch this, Jayge," Crenden shouted, prodding his yoke into the new direction. "Go see. We're a big group for any marauders to take on, but I'd rather know."

Jayge wasted no time, untying his runnerbeast from the rear of the wagon. Kesso woke from his somnambulance the moment Jayge's hand tugged on his reins and shook himself alert. From the moment Jayge swung up to the saddle pad, Kesso became a different animal, snorting, eager, and responsive. The rangy runner might not be as well bred as a holder's mount, but Kesso was still winning marks in any race Jayge could enter him in.

As he cantered back along the train, he called out reassurances. "Just two riders, three beasts. Probably traders. May want to join us." Every adult was descending to the ground, the children all packed safely inside wagons, weapons out of sight but ready to be seized.

Three wagons back Borgald raised a hand, and Jayge slowed Kesso, pulling him in to walk alongside his father's trading partner. "I don't even trust two riders," the older man said. "They could be sizing us up, you know. Those recruiters stirred up a lot of filth, made 'em nervous in the low caverns—desperate, too. Don't want 'em anywhere near us."

Jayge smiled and nodded. Why else had Crenden sent him back to check? Borgald and Crenden had a great partnership: Borgald talked, Crenden listened. But somehow everything got resolved to the satisfaction of both. Jayge nudged Kesso forward, seeing Borgald's oldest sons, Armald and Nazer, and his Auntie Temma already mounted and waiting for him down the line. He loosened his saddle knife. It was at such times that he wondered where his Uncle Readis had gone. Readis had been a wicked mounted fighter.

Jayge halted with Temma, Armald, and Nazer well back of their last wagon. He knew that they had a strong, well-manned train, and the sooner that was apparent to the strangers, the less trouble they would be likely to have.

The riders continued on at a steady, long-distance lope, coming at him in a straight line, jumping in and out of the root-sinks left by rotted sky-brooms—good riders on good horses.

Two men, Jayge thought, then changed his mind as they drew closer. A man and a woman, a tall one but, despite the dust cloth across the face, a woman. She pulled up just in front of the man, so Jayge looked to her for greeting.

"Bestra of Keroon Beastmasterhold," she said with the sort of condescending air that many holders displayed to traders.

"Lilcamps' and Trader Borgald's train," Jayge replied with terse courtesy. She did not even look at him, which would have been polite, but kept her eyes on to the line of wagons ahead. The man did the same, and there was something about his expression that made Jayge slide his gaze away.

"We're after a thief," the woman went on quickly. "A holdless man who took marks and six fine lengths of well-seasoned redfruitwood from me. Have you passed them out on the track? They'd be in a small single-yoke wagon." She could certainly see that there was no small wagon in the crooked line detouring past sky-brooms and root holes and heading toward the foothills of the Barrier Range.

"We've passed no one," Jayge answered curtly. He was aware, out of the corner of his eye, that Temma was circling her unusually restless mount. Hoping to get rid of the odd pair, he added, "We left Igen low caverns four days ago, and we've seen no one."

The woman pursed her lips, her eyes flicking past him, assessing the train in a calculating manner that Jayge did not like. Her companion looked straight ahead of him, with a rigidness that was a striking contrast to her quick scrutinies.

"Trader," she said, smiling ingratiatingly, "you'd know if there were other trails, back that way?" She pointed back over her right shoulder.

"Yes."

She snapped him a quick hard glance, holding his eyes. "That a single yoke could travel?"

"I wouldn't try it with any of ours," he answered, pretending to misunderstand.

Her frustration blazed out at him, startling Jayge in its force; the emotion was a complete contrast to her oblivious companion. "I'm asking about a single cart, a thief running away with my goods," she burst out. Startled, Kesso danced away, head high, tugging at Jayge's strong hand.

"That sort of rig could make most of the slopes all right enough," Armald answered, cheerfully helpful. "We're traders, lady, but we wouldn't harbor holdless folk. Everything in our wagons got dockets."

"There are at least ten switchback trails up to the foothills," Jayge said, signalling impatiently to Armald to let him do the talking. Armald, with a big frame and a threatening arrangement of thick features, was a good man to have at one's back, but he was not clever enough to spot menace unless it came at him, swinging sword or club. Jayge pointed. "We didn't see any new tracks, but then we weren't looking for any."

"Rained two nights ago. That'd help you find their tracks," Armald added, nodding amiably.

The harm was done, and Jayge shrugged. "Good day to you," he said and eased himself up out of the saddle, hoping that the pair would leave.

Lilcamps never got involved with local disputes and had learned to be very careful who traveled the road with them, but Jayge's sympathies were clearly on the side of those fleeing this woman. She hauled her mount around. Jayge saw the lather marks of hard travel and the exhausted look of all three animals—and kicked it toward the foothills. The silent man turned, jerking the pack animal into motion, and followed her.

"Armald," Jayge and Temma said at the same time over the noise of their departure. "When I do the talking, I do the talking!" Jayge continued, shaking his whip handle at the big man. "That was a Lady Holder. She was after thieves. Lilcamps and Borgalds don't harbor thieves."

"They weren't holders, Jayge," Temma said, her expression anxious. Her mount had calmed down, so Temma had been maneuvering to get a good look at the pair. "The man lost his dragon at Telgar Weyr some Turns back. He went missing from Igen a long time ago. And that woman . . ." Temma moved uneasily in the saddle.

"That's Lady Thella. I told you," Armald said. "That's why I told her what she wanted to know."

Temma stared at him. "You know, Jayge, he's right. I thought she looked familiar."

"Who's Lady Thella? I've never heard of her."

"You wouldn't," Temma said with a derisive snort.

"I knew her," Armald insisted.

Temma ignored him. "She's Lord Larad's older sister. The one who wanted to become Lord Holder when Tarathel died. She's no good. No good at all."

"I used to see her in Telgar Hold; always riding about, she was." Armald said defensively, in a sulk from the scolding. "She's a fine-looking lady."

Temma rolled her eyes. She was not a plain woman herself, but she was a good judge of her own sex.

"Angry sort," Nazer said, fastening his dagger back into its sheath. "Wouldn't bargain with that one and make a profit."

"I think we should see them out of our range," Temma said. "Jayge, wait until their dust dies, then follow. Make sure which track they do take. I'll tell Crenden."

"I'm point," Jayge reminded her. He would not relinquish his assigned duty.

"Armald'll finish the day for you." She gave Jayge a wink and a nod. "He is good at noticing holes in the ground."

"Point?" Armald's face brightened. "I'm a good point."

Nazer snorted. "Then get to it." Smiling, Armald started off and Nazer turned to Temma. "What say we ride flank?"

Temma shrugged. "I don't see the need. The mist's lifting. We'll get a clear view. We'll just hang back in the rear awhile." Then she grinned at Nazer, and Jayge, pretending not to see, ducked his head to hide his own smile. Well, Temma had been alone a long time. If she liked Nazer, Jayge would take himself off and leave them alone. Now that they were out and about, instead of in a hold, they could all spread out a bit. "Your saddlebags full enough?"

Jayge nodded, slapping the travel rations always kept on saddled mounts and, turning Kesso, began to walk him back toward the foothills.

When Giron's sharp eyes finally found the tracks of Dowell's cart, they had lost several more days. Thella was going to make that snotty young trader pay for his impudence. She was sure he had known exactly which of those many switchback trails the fugitives had taken. Giron said nothing that first day, still upset by the sight of those dragons, no doubt. When the creatures had appeared in the skies, winging directly toward them, he became all but paralyzed. Only because his mount was used to following hers did it keep on.

When they had stopped for the first night, she had had to make camp, force him to dismount, and peel back his fingers from the lead rope. She debated leaving him to recover on his own, but she might need assistance separating the girl from her family.

She was glad she had not left him because he did, in the

end, revive sufficiently to catch what she nearly missed: the mark of wagon wheels on the soft mud of the track.

"Smarter than I figured, for he must have tried to hide his tracks," she muttered, incensed by Dowell's shrewdness. She could not figure out why he had left so precipitously. She was certain that she had been tactful and careful—he had started work on the carvings just as if he had planned to finish them. Ten marks would have been a goodly addition for one planning a long journey.

Suddenly Brare came to mind. Had that crippled fool warned Dowell? Not likely, if the girl was as valuable to the cavern's hunters as Brare had said. They would not have done anything to scare her away. Could it have been Giron's surveillance? Maybe the dragonless man had unnerved the family. Giron could unsettle her from time to time, as he had yesterday going into that trance fit. Or perhaps someone had let slip her identity, and Dowell had panicked. Well, she would make sure of Brare's loyalty the next time she came to the Igen low caverns!

"Thread?" That was the first word Giron had said in three days, but for once he did not sound certain. He tried to see past the branches obscuring the sky. The forest was thick there, though a lot of it was new growth. Throwing the lead rope at her, he forced his runner up the bank and then, using the beast as a prop, agilely climbed a well-branched tree.

"Watch yourself!" she called when the trunk swayed with his weight. "Well, what do you see?" He gave her no answer, and she was ready to follow him when he started down. His face was bleak. "Dragons? Is there Thread?" He shook his head.

"Well, one dragon, two, how many? Hunting?"

"One, hunting. Hide."

The trace was not completely sheltered by the branches, and most of the shedding trees had lost their leaves. She and Giron would be visible from the air. Thella, urging her mount up the bank, was nearly pulled from the saddle by the recal-

citrant lead runner, but she got in among a copse of evergreens, while Giron, his body flattened against the trunk, kept
his eyes skyward. His mouth opened, almost as if he wanted
to cry out to the rider, to make himself known. Thella caught
her breath, but he seemed to thin against the trunk, as if all
the substance drained from him. He stood there so long that
Thella was afraid he was paralyzed again.

"Giron? What's happening?"

"Two more dragons. Looking."

"For us? Or Dowell?"

"How would I know? But they carry firestone sacks."

"You mean, there's Thread coming?" Thella cast about in
her mind, trying to remember the nearest shelter. "Get down
out of there. We've got to move!"

Giron gave her a faintly contemptuous look, but she said
nothing to challenge it, she was so relieved that he had not
frozen in the tree.

"These are Lord Asgenar's precious woods," he said.
"There'll be plenty of dragonmen to see no Thread penetrates
here."

"That's all well and good, and I'm no more afraid of
Threadfall than you are, but I can't say the same for these
runners. We've got to get them out of sight."

When they found it, the shelter was barely adequate,
but at least it was deep enough so they could fit the three
runners inside. What the stupid beasts did not see would
not upset them. By the time the Thread had passed, Thella
had fretted herself into a frenzy. As soon as Giron was certain that the final Edge had passed them, she insisted on
moving out.

"If that girl is Threadscored . . ." She left the threat hanging as she swung up onto her runner. She had an awful vision
of the girl's body twisting as Thread engulfed it. Seeing the
scorn in Giron's eyes, she clamped down on her anxiety, but
the thought that she might have lost her quarry to Thread
made her frantic to know, one way or the other.

"Thella," Giron said with unexpected authority. "Keep an eye skyward. They'll be extra-thorough over forest."

He was right, she knew, and she spurred the beast forward. "There's not much light left, and I need to *know*!"

It was she who saw the next telltale. Someone had rubbed out wheel marks, for the signs of sweeping were obvious once she had seen the cake of dirt, too obviously prized out of a wheel hub. Dismounting, each searched one side of the track; Giron found the wagon on the left, reasonably well hidden behind screening evergreens. He was peering within when Thella reached him and pushed him out of the way in her impatience.

"Rummaged around looking for what to take with them," Giron said.

"Then they're nearby."

Giron shrugged. "Too dark to look now." He held up his hand warningly as she jerked the reins on the runner to bring him close enough to be mounted. "Look, if they're dead, they're dead, and your stumbling around in the dark isn't going to revive them. If they're safe, they're not going anywhere now." The fact that he was right did little to soothe Thella. "I'll sleep in the wagon tonight."

"No, *I'll* sleep in the wagon tonight. You take the runners back to the cave. Join me at first light tomorrow." She took the blanket and journey rations out of her pack and sent him away. "First light! Remember!"

This might be even better, Thella thought. Stay by the wagon and see who comes by in the morning to check on it. Aramina was the oldest. That would be too much luck, she realized, chewing the dry food. But she would prefer not to be encumbered with the whole family. If she could just spirit Aramina away . . .

More dragonriders?" Thella was incredulous. "What are they doing around here?"

"How should I know?" Giron replied, showing the first sign of anger she had ever seen from him. He sank down, knees cocked, forearms lax across them, staring straight in front of him.

"But Threadfall was yesterday. They should be gone!" She shook his arm. How dare he look away like that! "A bad Thread infestation?" Accustomed as she was to Thread, her breath caught at the idea of a burrow taking hold in the forest anywhere near her. "Is that why?"

Giron shook his head. "If Thread had burrowed overnight, there wouldn't be any forest left. And we'd be dead."

"Well, then, why? Could that dragon yesterday have seen you?"

Giron made a mirthless sound and got to his feet. "If you want that girl, you'd better find out where she is. They can't have gone far. They wouldn't have left the wagon."

Thella was trying to marshal her thoughts. "Could the Weyrs have found out about her?"

"Weyrs have plenty of people who hear dragons," he said scornfully.

"She could have been Searched, couldn't she? I heard there were eggs on Benden's Hatching Ground. That's why. C'mon. They're not going to take that girl. She's mine!"

It was well they were on foot, the runners still hidden, for they were able to hide when the troop of mounted men rode by.

"Asgenar's foresters," Thella said, brushing leaf mold from her face. "Shells and shards."

"No girl with them."

"They were looking for us! I know it," she said, cursing as she veered around a thicket. "C'mon, Giron. We'll find that girl. We'll find her. Then we'll pay back that Lilcamp trader boy. Cripple his beasts, burn the wagons. They won't get as far as the lake, you can be sure of that. I'll get him for informing on me. I'll get him!"

"Lady Holdless," Giron said in such a derisive tone that

she paused in her furious progress. "*You'll* be got if you're not quieter moving through this forest. And look, someone's been this way recently. The bushes are broken. Let's follow the signs."

The broken bushes led them to the scuffed marks and prints on the track of horses, men, and dragons. Through the trees they could see movement and caught a glimpse of a man. He was not Dowell, for Dowell did not wear leather or a weapon's harness. They crossed the track carefully, working slowly uphill toward the edge of a nut forest. Then Giron pulled her down.

"Dragon. Bronze," he whispered in her ear.

She felt a flush of irritation with Giron. He had been right to be so cautious. That annoyed her almost as much as finding her quarry guarded by a dragon. Why had the dragonriders not just taken the girl away? Or was this a trap for Thella? How could they possibly know that she wanted Aramina? Had Brare spoken out of turn? Or that impudent fellow at the trader wagons? Did he talk to dragons, too?

Then she caught sight of someone moving through the grove. Picking nuts? Thella stared in astonishment. Yes, the girl was picking nuts. And there was a guard helping her. Thella closed her eyes to blot out the sight of her quarry so near and so unattainable. She and Giron would be lucky to get out of there with their skins. She pulled her arm away resentfully when she felt Giron tug at her sleeve. Then she saw him pointing.

The girl was moving farther and farther from the guard. Just a little farther, Thella thought. Just a little farther, you dear sweet child. And she began to grin as she indicated to Giron to help her outflank the girl. The guard was not looking downhill. If they were careful . . . they would be. Thella held her breath as she moved forward.

Giron got to Aramina first and grabbed her, one hand on her mouth, the other pinning her arms to her side.

"It falls out well, after all, Giron," Thella said, snatching a handful of hair and pulling the girl's head back, giving her a little pain back for all the trouble she had caused. Thella thoroughly enjoyed the fright and terror in Aramina's eyes. "We have snared the wild wherry after all."

They began to pull her back down the hill, out of sight of the guard. "Don't struggle, girl, or I'll knock you senseless. Maybe I ought to, Thella," he added, cocking his fist in preparation. "If she can hear dragons, they can hear her."

"She's never been to a Weyr," Thella replied, but she was struck with the possibility. She gave Aramina's hair a savage jerk. "Don't even think of calling for a dragon."

"Too late!" Giron cried in a strangled voice. He heaved the girl from him, toward the point where the ground fell away at the edge of the grove.

Thella let out a hoarse cry as the bronze dragon blocked the girl's fall. The dragon bellowed, his breath hot enough to startle Thella into running as fast as she could, Giron a stride behind her. As they slithered and fell, they could hear others calling. Thella spared one look over her shoulder and saw the dragon crashing among the trees, unable to dodge through them as agilely as the humans could. The dragon roared his frustration. Thella and Giron kept running.

6

SOUTHERN CONTINENT, TELGAR HOLD, PP 12

Master Rampesi arrived at Toric's hold, swearing and ranting about stupid northerners who thought the Southern Sea was some kind of mountain lake or placid bay.

"I'm bloody fed up with such idjits, Toric. I rescued another six—and there're twenty who drowned when the tub capsized—a day's sail from Ista. Any decent seaman would have warned them about the storms at this time of year, but no! They must set out in holey buckets and not a seaman among 'em!"

"What are you on about, Rampesi?" Toric interrupted the tirade with bad temper of his own. "Didn't you get the men we'd contracted for with the Mastersmith?"

"Oh, I've them, as well, never fear. But word got about that I was sailing south, and I had to move out of Big Bay Harbor and anchor in a cove to keep the clods from swarming aboard me. The situation's getting out of hand, Toric." Rampesi scowled, but he took the fortified wine that Toric poured him, knocked it back, and exhaled appreciatively. Then, some of his irritation soothed by the smooth spirit, he sat down, turning his keen eyes on Southern's holder. "So, what do we do to keep Benden and the Lord Holders off our backs? A little honest trading is one thing; a wholesale immigration of holdless another. And there's Telgar's lord trying to recruit more men for his mines, Asgenar wanting his forests patrolled against devilish clever marauders, and all kinds of queer goings-on down to Ista's Finger."

Toric pursed his lips, rubbing his palm on his chin. "You say it's become known that common northerners are let in here?"

"That's the rumor. Of course"—Master Rampesi shrugged, throwing one hand up, fingers splayed—"I deny it. I trade with Ista, Nerat, Fort, and the Great Dunto River." He gave Toric a slow, conniving wink. "I admit to being blown off course from time to time, and even to being blown as far as Southern once or twice. So far not even Master Idarolan has questioned that. But it's going to be harder to escape, shall we say, official attention."

"Clearly something must be done to stem the rumors . . ." Toric was annoyed; his arrangement with Masters Rampesi and Garm had been very profitable.

"Or sanction *proper* passage south."

Rampesi charged Toric hefty fees to transport Craftsmen to Southern, so he could well imagine the profit the mariner would realize on a regular service.

"You did tell me," Toric began, "last time you were here, that there is a shortage of lead and zinc?"

"And you know the prices you've been getting for what I've smuggled in. Those northern mines have been worked a long, long time." Master Rampesi caught Toric's drift. "I'm only a Mastermariner, Holder Toric, so I'm not in a position to speak out for you where it matters."

"Yes, where it matters. And I'd be taking Lord Larad's trade from him."

"Not Mastersmith Fandarel's though," Rampesi replied

quickly. "He's the one's crying for metals and whatnot for all those projects of his." Master Rampesi did not have a high opinion of them, but he was quite willing to supply the raw materials.

"But he's at Telgar . . ."

"Ah, but he's also Mastersmithcraft, and Halls don't need to 'please and yes' Lord Holders. They're as much captains in their Halls as I am on my *Bay Lady*. Were I you, I'd seek Master Robinton's help on this. He'd know best whom you should approach. I'm due to dock at Fort with this cargo so I can carry a message for you, and happy to do it. Wisest course is to sail straight into this one, Toric."

"I know, I know," Toric replied irritably. Then he remembered how dependent he was on Master Rampesi's services and smiled. "I may just have a passenger for you, Rampesi, when you sail."

"That will be a novelty," the *Bay Lady*'s Master remarked sardonically, holding out his glass for another charge of wine.

Toric found Piemur, as usual, in Sharra's workshop, laughing and chattering in far too intimate a manner to his liking. They were busy—so he could not fault them there—packing the medicinal supplies that Rampesi would take to the Masterharper. Toric would miss Piemur. The apprentice had been very useful indeed, setting up the drum towers; and his maps of the Island River stretch had proved as accurate as Sharra's, with shrewd notations of possible hold sites, natural plantations of edible fruits, and the concentration of wild runners and herdbeasts. But he was far too often in Sharra's company, and the young harper did not figure in Toric's plans for his pretty sister. Still, if Toric handled him astutely, the boy could serve him well. Piemur had been Master Robinton's special apprentice and was on excellent terms with Menolly and Sebell. He had all too often demonstrated his eagerness to remain in Southern. Let him prove it now.

"Piemur, a word with you?"

"What have I done wrong?"

Without answering, Toric gestured back down the hall to his office. He decided, as he followed the boy, that it was more to his purpose to speak plainly. Piemur did not miss much; he knew about the restrictions on commerce between north and south, knew how much leeway had already been tacitly accepted in the matter of Southern medicines transported North, and knew, from his own experience, of the illicit commerce carried on between the Oldtimers and Lord Meron in Nabol before the man's death had ended it. Yes, the boy did not miss much—but he had never, to Toric's knowledge, been indiscreet.

"Rampesi just brought in another bunch of shipwrecked fools trying to cross the Southern Sea," Toric said as he slid the door shut.

Piemur rolled his eyes at such folly. "Fools indeed. How many did he find alive this time?"

"Twenty, Rampesi says. With as many more trying to board the *Bay Lady* before he sailed."

"That's not good," Piemur said, sighing.

"No, it's not good. Rampesi's getting nervous, and we can't have that." When Piemur shook his head, Toric went on. "You and Saneter have often said that I should speak with your Masterharper about officially easing those restrictions. I've wanted nothing to do with the Northerners, but it seems they want plenty to do with me. And I must control the influx. There are thousands of holdless, useless commoners expecting an easy life here, and I won't have it. You know what I've created, what I'd like to do. You're no fool, Piemur, and I'm no altruist. I'm working for myself, for my Blood, but I want folk who're willing to work as hard as I do to hold for themselves. I can't permit all I've done to be wasted on the indigent."

Piemur was nodding agreement with most of his arguments. "You couldn't risk being absent from Southern for the length of a journey North. So I guess you're asking me to make the trip.''

"I think it might serve several purposes for you to go."

"Only if it's not a one-way trip, Toric." The boy looked him squarely in the eye, and Toric was slightly surprised. "I mean it, Holder Toric." A shrewd gleam in the young man's eye reminded Toric that Piemur was older in some ways than he looked. He also knew the stakes.

"I appreciate your point, young Piemur," Toric assured him candidly. "Yes, I would like you to explain how heavy those restrictions weigh on Southern's hold population—how an easement would profit the North in more ways than better medicines. You can admit to the mineral and metal deposits—" Toric held up his hand warningly. "Discreetly, of course."

"Always." Piemur grinned knowingly.

"There would be another reason why you ought to make the trip, besides, of course, your association with the Masterharper. If I can be blunt, you're overold now as an apprentice." Seeing that the boy was startled, Toric went on smoothly. "Saneter's getting older, and I prefer to have a harper who is sympathetic to my aims, especially one already familiar to the Oldtimers so that the substitution will go unnoticed. Get your journeyman's knot while you're back at the Harper Hall, and you're welcome back here when you've walked the tables. I promise you."

"And exactly what do you wish me to say to Master Robinton?"

"I believe I can trust you, journeyman-elect, to tell your Craftmaster what he needs to know?" Toric saw how quick the boy was to catch his slight emphasis on "needs."

Piemur winked. "Oh, definitely. Just what he *needs* to know."

When Piemur was gone, Toric began to wonder just what that impudent wink had meant. It never occurred to him that the Masterharper would sail south to find out for himself what he felt he needed to know before presenting the matter to the Benden Weyrleaders. And that voyage would have many repercussions.

Jayge fretted over the encounter all the way to Lemos Great Lake—especially after comparing his impression of the Lady Thella with descriptions he had heard of the worst of the Lemosan marauders. No one mentioned her by name, and fortunately Armald was not bright enough to make the connection. Lady Holders remained Lady Holders, just as traders remained traders. Armald was less certain about dragonless men, but that person would have unsettled anyone.

What worried Jayge was the knowledge that the renegade had command of a disciplined band that was well able to cause trouble for the Lilcamp-Borgald train. He had irritated her, and though Temma had called him foolish to stew over it, he could not help himself. He was also certain that Thella's appraisal had been too purposeful—and the trader train had a long way to go to get to Far Cry.

They had taken shelter from Threadfall not far from Plains Hold, and, as customary, Crenden and Borgald offered to send men for ground crew the next day. Nazer and Jayge rode into Plains Hold to find out where Holder Anchoram wanted them to crew.

To Jayge's surprise, Lord Asgenar himself came in on a blue dragon, dismounting with the ease of long practice, smiling, and greeting the many extra folk assembled at the Hold. He seemed popular, and Jayge halted his runner near the anxious trio of mountain holders Asgenar stopped to speak to. The Lemos Lord Holder was tall and slightly stooped in the shoulder, with a full head of blondish hair, slightly dampened from his riding helmet. He had an open face, a clear eye, and an easy manner—a different sort of lord to Corman, Laudey, or

Sifer, the other Lord Holders Jayge had seen. But Asgenar, like Larad of Telgar, was a relatively young man and not so hidebound as the others who had enjoyed the independence of Interval.

Listening, and Jayge prided himself on his keen hearing, he heard that the major complaint of the anxious holders was lack of adequate protection from raids.

"If they just came at us, fair and square, and it was a matter of strength or skill, Lord Asgenar, it would be one thing," a Beastmaster was saying. "But they sneak in when we're out in the far meadows or doing our Hold duty, and they whip in and are gone before anyone knows they've been. Like that Kadross Hold theft."

"All the eastern Lord Holders are being hit, not just Lemos . . ."

"And the Bitrans are turning honest folk away," someone muttered angrily.

"Some of you already know that I've started mounted patrols on random swings. I need your help. You've got to inform the Hold when you see anything unusual, have unexpected visitors of any kind, or are expecting carters or journeymen to deliver. Be sure to lock up your holds—"

"Shells, Lord Asgenar, they broke open all my locks and took what they were after," a mountain holder complained bitterly. "I live up yonder." He pointed to the north. "How'm I going to send you word in time?"

"I don't suppose you have a fire-lizard?" Asgenar asked.

"Me? I don't even have a drum!"

Asgenar regarded him with what Jayge thought was genuine sympathy and concern. "I'll think of something, Medaman. I'll think of something for folk like you." And Jayge could hear the sincerity in his voice. Then Asgenar raised his arms to quiet the sudden spate of questions. "Telgar, Keroon, Igen, Bitra, and I are convinced that all the major thefts are the work of one group, despite the range of their strikes. We don't know where they are based, but if any of you living up in the Barrier Range see any traces of large group movements, anything unusual, bring word to the nearest drum tower. You'll be compensated for your loss of time.''

"Will if we can, lord,'' Medaman said. "We'll be snowed in for the winter anytime now.''

"That's easier,'' Asgenar said, grinning broadly. "Just tack out a bright cloth—or your wife's Gather shawl—on the snow. F'lar and R'mart keep sweepriders out all the time now. They'll be told to check it out.''

That suggestion went down favorably, and Asgenar was able to continue on to the Hold. Jayge wanted to hang around a little longer, but Nazer, once he had packed the new ageno-three cylinders on the burden beasts, wanted to start back.

"I need my sleep if I'm to work ground crew tomorrow,'' the other man told Jayge with a huge yawn.

Jayge grinned and shooed one of the pack beasts back into line.

The ground crew did not have much to do, as extra wings of dragonriders had been assigned to protect Asgenar's forests. Only one tangle of Thread got through and was quickly flamed into char. Nevertheless, Borgald was punctilious about duties to the Weyr and never let members of his trains skimp ground crew service. Crenden complained of the loss of two days' travel but only to Temma and Jayge. A brown rider stopped to thank the crew, but though he was courteous enough, he kept the exchange to a minimum and flew off southeast instead of back toward Benden Weyr.

To make up for the time lost in discharging their Weyr duties, they started the train rolling again as soon as the massive beasts could be prodded out of the cavern shelter and yoked up. They kept on the road night and day until they reached their usual campsite on the far edge of Great Lake. A patrol from Lemos Hold stopped by for a cup of klah and general gossip but declined an invitation to stop the night.

"They offered us escort," Crenden told his son disdainfully. "All the way to Far Cry."

Jayge snorted. "We can handle ourselves."

"That's what Borgald said."

Jayge thought he caught a hint of uncertainty in his father's eyes. "They have a patrol. We can mount a patrol."

"We could also—" Crenden's eyes narrowed as he looked deep into the campfire's flames. "—Take a different route."

"If Thella hadn't been scared off by Asgenar's guards," Temma said, emerging from the darkness to join them, "I'd worry more."

"What say, Temma?"

She grinned as she hunkered down and swung the klah kettle over to pour herself a cup. "Chatted up one of the hold ground crew before we pulled out. Thella's quarry—those thieves of hers—are a harmless joiner and his family, and they're now in Benden's charge, you'll be glad to know." She winked at Jayge. "Let your conscience be easy, lad. Though it's a shame Asgenar didn't catch that pair." Temma pulled her mouth down in regret, then smiled. "But they didn't take the girl either. That's who Thella was after, the girl who hears dragons!" Temma looked skyward for a moment, her expression briefly envious. "That could make very useful listening in times like these. And more reliable than one of those fire-lizard creatures they're bringing up in droves from the Southern Continent."

"Southern?" Crenden regarded her in surprise.

"Brother, I think we're going to have to talk to Borgald. He's far too traditional in his attitude. I think we ought to look for trade possibilities with the south ourselves." Temma chuckled at Crenden's surprised reaction. "We'll get through this journey first and see what we hear at Far Cry. They're always up on the latest rumor." She rose. "Nazer and I will be first patrol. Wake you at second moonrise, Jayge. Get some sleep."

"Don't *you* fall asleep," Jayge countered with a snicker. "Private joke," he added as he felt his father's disapproval.

After resting the beasts three days, the Lilcamp-Borgald train yoked up to begin the final leg of the long journey up the Igen River Valley. The track ran partly through forest and partly along the riverbank. They did not have to worry about Thread, for they would not be far enough north to be involved in the Telgar Fall.

Halfway to Far Cry, just where the track narrowed, with a steep drop to the river on one side and rocky forested slopes on the other, the raiders struck. Afterward, Jayge realized that they had chosen the best possible point for an ambush. There was no room for his people to maneuver to avoid the rock-slides that were loosed, battering the lighter wagons and sending three down the drop into the river. Even one of the big ones, hit with an enormous mass of rocks, was tilted off-balance and fell, the legs of the helpless burden beasts pawing for footing.

It was just pure luck that everyone was out of the wagons at the time, lightening the load for the beasts straining up the slope. It was lucky, too, that no one had discarded their arms, even though they had felt a false safety so close to Far Cry.

Choking on the dust, listening to the bawl of frightened, injured animals, the screams of wounded people, and unintelligible shouted orders from both Crenden and Borgald, Jayge kicked Kesso past the milling runner and burden beasts he was herding. He reached the last wagon, one of the biggest, just as the raiders piled down the slopes, hollering and slashing at whatever was in their way.

Jayge saw an attacker leap to Armald's back from the height of the bank. Roaring, the big man tried to dislodge the raider who was stabbing at his chest. Jayge, trying to come to his aid, was beset by a half dozen, trying to pull him from his runner. Kesso was a fighter, hooves and teeth, whirling on his hindquarters so that no one could get within sword's length of his rider. But before Jayge could help, Armald had been overcome, a bloody lifeless lump on the ground.

Slicing at his attackers, Jayge broke loose just as he heard Temma and Nazer shouting for help. Individual fights were in progress up and down the wagonline. Jayge caught a glimpse of Crenden, Borgald, and two of the drivers trying to protect the animals. Some of the women and several of the older children had armed themselves with prod poles and were doing what damage they could.

There was no room to maneuver Kesso on the track, so Jayge spurred the excited beast up the steep hill, managing incredible leaps over the uncertain surface and then reversing, to skid down the slope to attack from behind the men opposing Temma and Nazer. Nine, Jayge counted. Wicked odds, and Nazer and Temma fighting brilliantly. Rising in his stirrups, he launched his belt daggers, each blade finding its mark in a back. Then, using his boot dagger, Jayge leaned over Kesso's left side and sliced the nearest man from buttock to shoulder just as he saw a spear catch Temma in the shoulder, pinning her to the side of the wagon. Nazer shielded Temma with his body, his swordwork dazzling as he tried to defend them both, but he was too close set and wounded in arm and leg. Jayge hauled Kesso to his hindlegs, walking him forward to drop him and bringing two more down. Then he flung his knife at the man with sword raised to slice off Nazer's head. As he dropped from the saddle, something came whizzing past his head, and he heard his sister Alda's triumphant shriek as a heavy iron pan caught a toothless woman in the chest. More heavy pots rained down on the attackers as Tino yelled encouragement. Kesso continued to kick back, effectively clearing Temma's right side.

"Knock them over! Knock them over!" The shout reverberated above the shouts and cries, the noise of fighting and bawling beasts. "Get as many over as possible!"

"No, leave off. Dragons in the sky! Leave off!" someone else bellowed. "Dragons!"

Abruptly the attackers fell back, scrambling up the bank. Jayge was of no mind to let a single one of them leave alive. He took Nazer's sword from the wounded man and retrieved his own daggers before he leaped over the debris. He had as much trouble finding good footing on the sliding bank as the retreating raiders, but he slashed and prodded, hoping to strike flesh and bone.

"Dragons? Where? Sear your hide!" Despite the distortion of fury and volume, Jayge recognized the voice. Thella! The raiders were Thella's! Temma would wish she had listened to him and been more wary. But they were so close to Far Cry Hold!

"In and out! A bronze!" was the answering shout, and Jayge, also recognizing the second voice, missed his next stroke. "Let's get out of here!"

Jayge could not spare time to find either speaker as he clawed up the slope, his quarry just managing to keep out of reach. He had to catch the man before he could disappear into the forest. There was enough sense left to Jayge to realize that it would be foolhardy to attempt pursuit there, unless the dragonrider returned to sweep the forest. With a desperate surge, Jayge felt the sword slice deeply across the raider's foot and heard the man's scream. But the man was suddenly hauled up and out of Jayge's reach. Jayge, overbalanced by his effort, rolled heavily down the bank, landing on a pile of rocks.

Dazed and winded, it took him a few moments to struggle to his feet. There were cries for assistance all along the train. Jayge saw her then, poised on a boulder that jutted out over the track, surveying the damage her ambush had caused. Then he saw her bring her arm back to throw. The dagger snicked across the tendon of one of Borgald's beasts, casting it to its knees. Filled with rage at such viciousness, Jayge launched one of his own blades. But Thella did not wait to be someone else's target. She whirled, leaping up the bank and disappearing quickly from view. And the last of her raiders had gained the heights and were quickly lost up the slope.

"No, don't follow," Crenden bellowed from the front of the train. "We've got people and beasts to help."

Cursing at his bad luck, Jayge clambered over dead raiders on his way to the last wagon. Tino was already trying to help Nazer, while Alda was making her way down from the wagon top.

"I got two," Alda was shrieking at the top of her lungs. "I got two with pans."

"You better find those pots," Tino told her firmly. "And fill them from the river. And bring out the brazier. We need hot water."

"Get the fellis first, Alda, and the numbweed pot," Jayge said, wondering how Temma could possibly be alive with that hole in her shoulder. Nazer was weak with blood loss from several deep wounds, but he insisted that they attend Temma first. Together Tino and Jayge stanched the flow as best they could until Alda brought them the medicines and proper bandages. Traders were accustomed to dealing with trail injuries, but more serious wounds would require a trained healer's skill.

"I'll get the hot water," Alda said when they had done all they could for Temma and Nazer. Sniffling back her tears, she went off to retrieve the pots she had thrown.

Sorrowful bawling reminded Jayge and Tino that there were other considerations almost as important as Temma and Nazer. Of the two yokes hauling the big wagon, both off-siders were dead, their backbones hacked in several places. Their bodies had, fortunately, afforded some protection to their yoke mates; both were bleeding, but the cuts were superficial. Jayge and Tino could not shift the dead beasts, but they slapped numbweed salve liberally over the wounds of the survivors, poked some fellis into the beasts' mouths, and hoped that would ease their torment.

It was only then that Jayge and Tino heard Borgald's loud complaint.

"If the dragonrider saw this, he *must* help us," Borgald was shouting, repeating the words like a chant as he bent over his prized burden beasts, patting them here and there, oblivious to the blood pouring from severed arteries onto the gravelly roadway. "Do you see them coming, Jayge?" Borgald raised a bloody hand to shield his eyes from the sun, peering forlornly at the sky.

Jayge and Tino exchanged pitying looks and walked on, carefully avoiding the hand and foot of a man buried under a rock slide. The little milch beasts had been caught by it, too. Jayge wondered if maybe he and Tino should try to round up the animals he had been herding along the track. They would be scattered all over, maybe even slaughtered, along with half the train's folk and burden beasts.

"Jayge!" Crenden came striding toward him, bloody but relatively sound. "Did that runner of yours come through this? Can you ride on to Far Cry and get help?"

"Maybe this time a dragonrider will help," Jayge cried.

"Dragonrider? What dragonrider?" Crenden mopped at the cut over his eye. Irritated by the blood dripping down his face, he tore a strip off his shirt and wound it around his forehead. "If you and the runner are sound, don't waste time." He paused, bending to examine a dead raider. "Dead. The ones they left are all dead. I saw that woman kill one herself, a man wounded in the leg." He kicked at the dead man. "No one's going to tell us anything useful. Ride, boy. What are you waiting for?"

Jayge swung up on Kesso, only then aware that his left leg was bleeding and it felt as if he had taken a wound across his right hip. He grunted as he settled in the saddle, and Kesso willingly darted forward.

No sooner were they around the bend than a figure jumped into the track. Jayge reached for his dagger when the man waved both arms urgently, limping toward him. A wounded raider, escaping from Thella's kindly knife?

"Jayge, you've grown—but I knew you," the man said, and Jayge remembered the voice that had given the dragonrider alarm.

"Readis, what in all the—" His uncle? One of Thella's marauders?

"Never mind that, Jayge," Readis said, hanging on to the stirrup leather, keeping one hand on Kesso's shoulder to prevent the restive beast from ramming him. "I'd no idea it was Crenden's train we were ambushing. She told me another name. I didn't even know you were back on the road again. Believe me, Jayge! I'd never hurt my own Bloodkin."

"Well, your *friends*," Jayge replied, letting scorn edge his voice and seeing his uncle wince, "have damned near done in your sister, Temma. Remember her? I don't know who else is dead for sure, but we've lost almost every burden beast we owned. I counted four smashed wagons at least."

Readis gave a grim smile. "The only thing Thella fears is dragonriders." He scrambled up the bank, grabbing a bush to help himself to the top. "I did what I could. I've got to catch up. But tell them I tried to stop it once I knew who you were."

"Don't try so hard the next time, Readis," Jayge yelled after him. The underbrush closed in after the hobbling man, and Jayge stared after him. So there had been no dragonrider in the sky! But he had to be grateful for the lie. "Come on, Kesso, we've got to get help."

The only reason Maindy was so quick to respond to Jayge's message was that the Far Cry holder needed the supplies the train was bringing. Why hadn't the train set out patrols? Jayge did not mention the offer from Asgenar's forester. Did Jayge know if the Weaver Hall's shipment was safe? If not, there would be no cloth to make warm winter clothes. But even as Maindy rattled on with Why didn't you? and What did they? he was organizing a rescue troop. He had ordered out the hold's healer, three helpers including his own lady, and every ablebodied man in the hold. He had seen that supplies and enough rope and tackle to lift even the heaviest wagon from the riverbank were packed onto runners, and a half hour after Jayge came in, he was ready to ride out.

"The dray beasts will take their own speed, but we'll be all ready to hitch them up when they do arrive at the gap," Maindy said confidently.

To Jayge's utter astonishment, they returned to find dragons and riders helping Crenden and the saddened Borgald, still mourning his losses. A brown dragon was in the process of lifting a terrified burden beast from the river gorge back onto the track. It was battered, but apart from being scared into dropping and watering all the way up, it would probably recover. But its yoke mate was already being butchered.

Jayge took care of his exhausted mount before he went to see Temma, who was lying, far too pale, in the wagon she had been protecting. Nazer was there, holding her hand, his own wounds bound and his dark skin as bleached as Temma's.

"You're back?" Nazer asked, face and eyes dull. Jayge nodded. Nazer carefully placed Temma's hand down on the blanket and patted it tenderly. "I'll clean you up. Raiders' blades often got snake glob on 'em."

When he emerged from Nazer's rough but thorough measures, Jayge was feeling no more pain, and his head was only a little dizzy from the fellis draught Nazer had made him swallow. He insisted on going with Maindy's troops and the green and blue dragonriders who intended to follow the tracks of the retreating raiders. Sufficient bloodstains had been found leading up the hill to warrant a search. Wounded men would not be able to travel fast or far.

But that hope ended when they found the bodies of six men

and the toothless woman with their throats cut. Their wounds had all been dressed, and they had probably been killed after they had been dosed with fellis. Jayge did not know whether he was glad, or sorry, that Readis was not one of the dead.

It was when the patrol began shifting the bodies to a shallow cave for interment that Jayge spotted the tight roll of sheets. He scooped it up before someone trampled it into the bloody ground.

It was strange enough to find sheets of Bendarek's precious wood-pulp leaves under a raider corpse, but examining the roll, Jayge had more shocks to absorb. Clearly written in a good clear hand was the message, "Deliver to Asgenar." The roll was neither sealed nor tied, and Jayge had no compunctions about taking a closer look.

What he found was artwork—sketches of people. He nearly dropped the package when he uncovered a likeness of his uncle. And there were more, including ones of Thella in arrogant poses; Giron, his face more startlingly empty than it had looked in person; and others, two of whom Jayge realized were among the dead. Dropping to one knee, Jayge surreptitiously sliced away his uncle's likeness from the page. Then he rolled the whole thing up as tight as he could and called out in surprise.

"Maindy, I think you should have charge of this," he said, holding it out.

After one glance, Maindy shoved it into his jacket, frowning. Jayge got very busy as far away from the holder as possible. But the incident added to the other puzzles he had to try to piece together once he got back to the ambushed camp.

Who could he talk to? Temma was holding her own, according to Nazer, but the man looked so distressed that Jayge held his tongue. He could not tell his father; so it would have to wait until he could talk to Temma. But on the long tramp back, Jayge decided that he owed Readis his silence. He was certain that if Readis had not raised a false alarm, the raiders would have killed them all.

Why? Because Jayge had not been helpful that day at the sky-brooms? Or because Armald had? That poor old clod was dead. Temma and Nazer had certainly been savagely attacked. Had Thella been after them in particular? Jayge would bet a Bitran any odds that the raid had been punitive. Most of the train's goods had been bulky items, hard to pack up that slope and into the hills. And it was not as if the area was cave-pocked, where goods could have been stashed temporarily. Thella had been out to destroy, not loot. Why? She would have been caught long since if she went after every wagoneer who answered her indiscreetly.

And what about those sketches, addressed to Lord Asgenar and cleverly left behind to be discovered? Clearly someone in Thella's camp was not her ally, and that was some consolation to Jayge as he listened that night to Temma's fevered breathing.

It was several days before the train could move out again. Maindy had to send back for wagons to take the loads from the ruined vehicles of the traders, and more wheels were called for to replace those damaged by the slides. All but one wagon left the site of the ambush, and twelve trader graves remained.

7

LEMOS HOLD, SOUTHERN CONTINENT, TELGAR HOLD, PP 12

As much to escape wintering at Far Cry Hold as to pursue his own search, Jayge hired himself and Kesso out to one of Lord Asgenar's roving troops. Temma and Nazer were envious, vowing to join him as soon as their wounds healed. Jayge tried to sound encouraging about that, but he had overheard the hold healer talking to Lady Disana outside the temporary infirmary and knew that it would be a long while before either recovered.

Crenden proved more resilient than Borgald over their losses—and Maindy, unlike Childon of Kimmage, was willing to strike a fair deal with the two trader captains. Replacing the dead animals would have to wait until spring and would take almost all their available marks. But in return for reasonable work in the hold, Crenden and Borgald would be allowed time and resources—including the assistance of the hold's carpenter and Smithcraft journeyman—to repair their damaged wagons. Borgald, Crenden, and their wives sat at the high table for the evening meal, and Maindy consulted them often. So when snow blanketed the valley, the traders willingly helped Maindy's workmen finish the interiors of extensions built that summer. Finally Borgald began to take an interest in the children orphaned by the raiders, and although his smile faltered when he inadvertently looked about for his son, Armald, he began to recover. Crenden, on the other hand, continued to brood over an attack which seemed to him to be totally unprovoked. Jayge decided that telling his father of his own suspicions would do nothing to improve the older man's depression.

Jayge went off with the troop without having had the opportunity to tell Temma about Readis and still pondering the significance of the sketches he had found so fortuitously. He assumed that one of Thella's wounded had dropped the roll, and it amused him to think that dead men *could* tell tales. Though he had not had much time to study the sketches, the faces were vividly burned into his memory. Some looked to have been more hurriedly executed than others, but all had been drawn with a clever economy of line capturing pose and character, and Jayge was certain that he would recognize every one of them, although he could name only Thella, Giron, and Readis. Thella was the one most frequently drawn, in different poses and angles and, in a few cases, in what Jayge realized were disguises. At night Jayge rehearsed those faces, all but the six dead, in his mind. If he saw any one of them, he would know them. He wondered what Asgenar had made of the sketches.

That first evening on the track from Far Cry Hold, once the stewpot was heating over the fire and the men were unrolling their sleepbags, the troop leader, a forester whom everyone, with varying degrees of respect and admiration, called Swacky, came over to Jayge. Swacky was a bull-necked man with massive arm and chest muscles from twenty Turns of logging; he had a bit of a belly on him from drinking ale whenever he could get it and eating huge amounts of food, but he was nimble-footed and long-eyed, with a sparse fringe of brown hair and a rough-featured, long-jawed face. When the men had been gathering wood for their cave fire, Jayge had seen Swacky throw an axe at a piece of wood, splitting it neatly down the center. He was told, and he had no trouble believing it, that Swacky could axe wherries out of the sky. The burly man wore a variety of blades, ranging from light throwing hatchets to the two-handed axe strapped to his saddle.

To Jayge's complete surprise, Swacky thrust a wad of well-thumbed sheets at him. "Memorize these faces. Them's who we're lookin' for. Any or all. Recognize any from your brush at the ravine?"

"Only the dead ones," Jayge said, but he studied each face carefully, matching it up with his memory. What he held were copies, executed so hastily that they had none of the vitality of the original sketches.

"How'd you know which was dead?"

"I was with the trackers when they found the six with their throats slit. That Telgar woman . . ."

Swacky caught Jayge's shoulder in a painful grip. "How'd you know that?" He had lowered his voice, and his expression warned Jayge to keep his answers soft.

"Armald, Borgald's son, one of those that got chopped down, recognized her when she met us."

"Tell me," Swacky said and sat, folding his legs up to his chest, his back to the others.

So Jayge told him, leaving nothing out but the fact of Readis's astonishing appearance. "I still don't know who saw a dragonrider," he added. "I heard later that a sweeprider saw the train stopped and thought it had been caught in a landslide."

"It had, hadn't it?" Swacky's eyes crinkled up in a mirthless grin. "I took a good look, trying to figger that ambush out so we'd avoid such like."

"And? I was pretty busy helping my folk."

"Well . . ." Swacky shifted his bulk, took a knife from his boot, and began to draw a diagram in the dirt. "That ambush was well planned. They was waitin' for you. How come you never put out no point?''

"We did. We found her dead, pushed over the bank. Couldn't ride flank. We were close enough to Far Cry by then.''

Swacky waggled the dagger point in admonishment. ''Until you're in the hold, you're not close enough. Any rate, there were ten deadfalls ready, spaced out to crunch each of your wagons.''

"If they'd been spaced out in the usual intervals,'' Jayge broke in, holding up his hand, ''as they had been on the flats at the sky-broom plain the day we met . . . she planned it then, I know it!'' And Jayge tasted hatred in his mouth, sour and acrid. ''If I catch her, I'll cut her throat.'' His hand went to his dagger.

"Then it's over too quick, lad,'' Swacky said, tilting his long head, his eyes glittering with a malice as savage as Jayge's. Then he tapped Jayge's knuckles lightly with his dagger. ''If you catch her while in my patrol, you turn her over to me. She hasn't killed often or lately in those raids of hers, but you're not the only one wants to see her dead. You was lucky your wagons was strung out up that steep slope. Another thing shows she's slipping. Your wagons didn't tip as easy as she thought they would. But—'' He held up the blade again. ''She's getting careless. Or desperate.'' Swacky did not sound so sure of that. ''Lord Asgenar's been over the waybills on the trade goods you carried, and he can't find anything she'd have such bad need of she'd take such risks to get.''

"How would Asgenar know what she'd steal?''

"*Lord* Asgenar,'' Swacky corrected, tapping him smartly on the knuckles, his expression severe. ''Even in your own head, boy. And Lord Asgenar knows 'cause he's been making it his business to find out what she's been lifting, what she's got in that base camp of hers, what she might need. Besides a little girl who hears dragons.''

Jayge was indignant. ''Thella only mentioned a thief she was after. And I doubted her then, but she was angry.''

''Is that what she told you?'' Swacky asked, surprised.

''A girl hearing dragons was the reason for attacking us?''

Swacky nodded his head wisely. ''That's what I was told by that young bronze rider. Such a girl would be very useful to someone like Thella, you can bet your last bootnail on that.''

''That'd be useful,'' Jayge admitted. He wondered why the Weyrs had not already Searched her out for one of their queen eggs. ''You know, Armald recognized her. But he only called her 'lady.' He didn't say her name to her face, though he told us later.''

''Well, Armald is now dead, you took your share, and you said yourself that your aunt and the fourth man who met her that day damned near got killed, too.'' He held his hand out to take back the sketches. ''You've seen her, boy—you'll be helpful. That runner of yours good on hills?''

''The best, and he'll murder roosting wherries, give him the chance.''

Swacky got up to return to his own bedroll. ''Well, that'd cause undue noise, boy, and we want to move as fast and as quiet as we can, never knowing what we'll find.''

''One thing, Swacky. The man who drew those sketches. How do we know who he is? We might kill him by mistake.''

''We're not to kill anybody is m'orders. Capture 'em. And keep looking.''

''What are we looking for?''

''Best possible find'd be their main base, but any caves, hiding places, are a help.''

''She won't be moving anywhere in the snow.''

''Aye, true, but cave holds stand out in snow, don't they? Then we map 'em, check 'em out, and if there're supplies hidden or buried, we fix 'em so they can't be used come spring.''

And with that Swacky moved off.

Toric in a rage at any time was a problem for his household. Toric fuming in the midday summer heat, without the calming influence of either Sharra, who had gone to the Healer Hall at Fort Hold, or Ramala, who had gone to midwife a difficult birth down the west coast, was a burning firestone looking for something to char.

Piemur and Saneter locked eyes and, with a few deft harper signals passing between them, elected to take a positive—and humorous—tack.

"Well, for sure, they're all inlanders. Never been in so much as a rowing boat before," Piemur exclaimed, casting a jaundiced eye over at the limp figures on Master Garm's deck. "Wilted, that's what they are. Wilted northern lilies. Ah, we'll take them in hand." He beckoned to a youngster hovering nearby. "Sara, go get some numbweed to slather on their sunburns and some of those pills Sharra uses for stomach disorders. Your mother'll know which ones."

"Master Garm," Toric said, seething with wrath and indignation. "You will pause only long enough to deliver the cargo from your hold and then you will take those—those excrescences back where they came."

"Now, Holder Toric," Garm began placatingly. The sea crossing had been rough, and his passengers had deafened him with their complaints, threats, and unwelcome eruptions. He was certain he would never get the smell out of his big aft cabin. He did not care how much he got paid to take the puny bastards south—he would *not* go through it again. Those he had smuggled in for Toric had kept their distress to themselves. The pampered lot he had just legitimately brought over had bitched the entire crossing! "Toric, they're still alive! When they gets over being so sick, you can get a lot of work out of them! Well growed! Fed well, too, to judge by what came up the first day out!"

Toric was scowling as blackly as ever. "The last thing I need here is a gaggle of spoiled useless turds who've never done an honest day's work and think they're going to walk into ready-made holds! I never should have agreed. That Harper talks so smooth . . .''

"Sure he does, or he'd be no good at being Harper." Piemur would not stand for anyone to denigrate Master Robinton. "But there's no reason you have to treat that stomach- and sunburn-sick bunch any differently than you've treated anyone else that fetched up in this harbor." He could not help grinning at the dawning comprehension on Toric's face. "You didn't promise F'lar or Robinton—nor would either of them expect it—to give these younger holdless sons preferential consideration. They can sweat right alongside everyone else here. If they thought they'd wander aimlessly, picking ripe fruit from the trees and basking in the breezes and southern sun, you'll soon put 'em right."

"But—" Toric stopped, flicking his angry eyes from the wretched young men on Garm's deck to the sandy coastline spreading east.

"No buts, Toric," Piemur went on while Saneter's fingers flew in a cautionary sign. "They get a day or two to recover, and then they get assigned tasks—" Piemur grinned slyly. "—suitable to their abilities. You're still Toric, Southern holder, and you've the right to hold any way you choose. At least they're used to jumping when a Holder says 'jump'— they're better disciplined than some of those holdless louts Garm's brought you. In fact, I'd say once those lads recover from sunburn and seasickness, they might surprise you." Piemur sounded very positive and sure of himself. Toric just kept looking at the figures sprawled on the deck and over the rails of Garm's ship.

"You whipped more into line than I thought you would, Toric," Garm said, beginning to warm to Piemur's line. "You can do it again. Just leave 'em loose. The good ones'll survive."

Toric was wavering. Then he scowled. "You'll take no messages back with you, Garm, that I haven't seen first. How many of 'em have fire-lizards?"

"Oh, five or six," Garm said after a moment's thought.

"They're all *younger* sons," Piemur added reassuringly.

"No queens or bronzes, then?"

"No, two blues, a green, and one brown," Garm answered. "The critters didn't hang around that long after the lads started getting seasick. And they're not back yet."

Toric snorted, his manner relaxing a trifle.

"Send 'em out to Hamian, or over to Big Lagoon. Most of 'em should know drum code." With Toric calmed down, Piemur was full of useful suggestions. He did not want to get stuck with another drum tower assignment, not when Toric had not yet kept his part of their bargain and let Piemur loose to explore. "Let 'em go. The smart ones'll want to learn. The dumb ones'll kill themselves off."

"Listening to them natter before we set sail, they all sort of thought they were going to be given holds," Garm put in hesitantly.

"First they've got to prove their ability. To me!" Toric jerked his thumb at his chest. "Oh, bring them in. Piemur, Ramala's not here. You know how to dose 'em. Saneter, see if Murda can find beds for them tonight. I'll see where to send 'em. Shards! Why did they have to get here so soon?"

"We had good winds," Garm replied, misunderstanding Toric's complaint as he wiped sweat from his weathered brow. "Made a nice fast trip." He caught his dinghy's painter and hauled the boat in for the row back to his ship.

"Too fast," Piemur said softly, catching Saneter's eye. They could have used a few more days to prepare Toric for the "invasion." "I devoutly hope that there are a few sensible ones."

"D'you recognize any of them?" Saneter asked as the two climbed the harbor steps. At the top small groups of children, having seen Toric's departure, began to line the railing, pointing to the ship. Piemur could hear their giggles and unkind comments.

"Not from here, or in their condition." Piemur shrugged. "I expect Groghe sent a couple. The one really smart son stayed at Smithcrafthall. A couple weren't bad. He kept 'em all, fosterlings and the Bloods, in line. Lord Sangel's would be accustomed to heat—might even know something about crops. Corman's lot are probably still charging around the eastern holds, looking for Thella, the clever Lady Holdless."

"Piemur! One day that quick tongue of yours is going to get you in trouble."

"It has," Piemur said, grinning wryly. Then his smile changed to one of unforced approval as young Sara came up with a basket full of lotions and vials. "Good girl. Pills for their ills. Go help Murda, sweetness."

Asgenar alighted from the dragon, landing heavily—which was exactly how he felt: heavy, disturbed, and knowing no other alternative to the problem. Certainly it was kinder for him, Larad's fosterbrother, to break the news.

K'van, looking no less enthusiastic but more determined, dropped lightly to the ground beside the Lemos Lord Holder. Heth turned his head toward the two, eyes glinting green-blue in reassurance. K'van gave him a solid slap on the shoulder and crunched over the newly fallen snow to the impressive steps leading up to Telgar Hold's main entrance. It was cold enough not to linger, and Asgenar followed the young bronze rider.

They reached the top step just as the door was opened and just as Heth took wing up to keep the watchdragonrider company on the sun-struck fire heights.

"A'ton sent word down that you were coming," Larad said, looking pleased to see them. "You'll be surprised at what a fine lad he is."

Asgenar was thrown off balance. "A'ton?"

"Your nephew. Or had you forgotten I've a third fine son?" Larad gestured diffidence. "You've other concerns. Good day to you, K'van. Are you part of this?"

K'van nodded, shedding his helmet and loosening his flying jacket, then making work of matching his gauntlets and tucking them into his belt.

"My office then, but surely you'll both have some klah or a mulled wine?"

"Later perhaps."

"Dulsay's close by, and I think I'd like to finish my cup while you explain this visit. Dulsay?" Larad called. His wife appeared with a tray and three steaming cups.

"I took the liberty, Asgenar, K'van. It'll help loosen the chill from your tongues," Larad said while Dulsay served them. Then she discreetly withdrew to the Great Hall, and Larad led the way to his private room.

"There's no way to buffer this one, Lar," Asgenar said, taking one of the chairs. He put down his cup, opened his double-fronted fleece jacket, and hauled out the sketches, which he dropped on the table. "Have a look at them."

Asgenar had put the sheet with the drawings of Thella on the bottom. Larad, his frown growing deeper as he examined each face, exhaled when Thella's likeness appeared and sank slowly to his chair. "I thought her dead since the Pass began."

"I'm sorry, Lar, but she's very much alive, and far too active."

Larad flicked the sheets back and forth, always returning to the ones of Thella. The fingers of his left hand drummed an irregular rhythm on the polished wood of his worktable. Then he tapped Giron's face. "This is R'mart's missing brown rider?"

"A dragonless man. Temma of the Lilcamp train—the one that was ambushed six days ago—identified him and Thella as those who were looking for Dowell and his family."

Larad looked baffled.

"Dowell's daughter, Aramina, hears dragons," Asgenar said.

K'van shifted restlessly in his chair.

"I fail to see a connection," Larad said hesitantly.

"A girl who heard dragons would be of inestimable help to a raider," Larad said after Asgenar had explained. "And you were her rescuer, K'van?"

"Not me, sir." K'van smiled, relieved that Lord Larad seemed disposed to be helpful. "My dragon, Heth!" Heth's bugle was audible even through the thick walls of the Hold.

Lord Larad merely nodded. "But I don't see why . . . why Thella"—he looked even more distressed, as if the use of her name amounted to an actual accusation—"would savagely attack a harmless wagon train."

Asgenar shrugged. "When goods were missing it was bad enough, but to kill innocent people . . ."

"I agree. A heinous crime. Inexcusable. Contemptible."

"You know we've thought that only one group was responsible for the systematic looting all along our eastern range."

"All Thella's work?" Larad was incredulous and obviously hoped to hear a negative reply.

"Certainly the largest part of it. She's the obvious leader of her own band."

"And—" Larad paused, then leaned forward and shuffled the damning sheets into a neat pile. "Who drew these? Someone buying leniency?"

"We're assuming it was a harper infiltrator. Robinton did say that he'd help all he could."

"Oh, yes, I recall that. So, how can I assist you?"

"She's found somewhere to use as a base camp," Asgenar said, gesturing to detailed Hold maps on Larad's wall. "She also uses others as waycamps, burying travel supplies and grain for her runners."

"The grain that was stolen from Kadross Hold?"

Asgenar nodded. He felt considerable sympathy for Larad,

who was still fighting against the evidence that his own Blood was responsible for the scavenging. "I'm hoping that you might know of a cave, somewhere in the mountains of Telgar, which Thella might be using."

Larad passed a hand across his face, but when he dropped the shield, his expression was obdurate, and Asgenar knew that he had made his difficult decision.

"When Thella left here, spring of the Turn before the Present Pass, she took with her copies of the Hold maps."

"Well, that explains a lot," Asgenar said admiringly. "She'd know every nook and cranny in your Hold to hide in. And don't be too upset. I'm certain she managed to get copies from me, Bitra, Keroon, and Igen. Nothing if not thorough, your sister."

"As of this moment, Asgenar—and K'van, you bear witness—she is no longer of my Bloodkin. I shall have the harper disown her."

Asgenar nodded acknowledgment of that rejection; K'van raised his right hand, accepting the witness.

Larad strode purposefully to the map and studied it fingerlength by fingerlength. Suddenly he stabbed his forefinger on one spot. "Here is where she is likely to be. Our father, Tarathel, gave her her own way in most things, mounted her well, and took her with him on his trips around the holds. She mentioned once in my hearing that she had a place she could hold against all comers. She often disappeared on her own for days at a time. She was seen several times by the herdsmen in that vicinity. I hadn't remembered it till now. She'd be entirely too familiar with the resources. She was bloody clever, you know!" There was a hint of respect in the level voice. "She didn't rob Telgar holds often enough to make me suspicious. Or, to be quite candid," he amended with a grim smile, "to be suspicious enough to take it further. I did think she was dead. We found a set of runnerbeast shoes in a ravine. Our farrier said he'd hot-shod those to one of

Thella's mares. I assumed she'd been caught by Threadfall at the same time.''

''Lord Larad, might it be a good idea to send one of your fire-lizards to see if anyone's in that hold?'' K'van asked. ''I'm always taught not to assume anything.'' He chuckled. ''Ass—you—me!''

Asgenar suddenly found that his ear was extremely itchy and ducked his head, while Larad gave K'van a long thoughtful look.

''Now, that is an extremely constructive suggestion, K'van,'' the Telgar Holder said. ''You'll make wingleader when you're grown. My thanks.''

''Our thanks,'' Asgenar said. ''She'd have a watch out for sweepriders but not for our clever little friends. If you can tell them just where to look?''

Larad called for his fire-lizard queen and Dulsay's bronze, cracking the door to let them in. ''I think I know a landmark to give them to find the place. I've not been in that vicinity often, but the map indicates a wide plateau. They'd have to be using the hearths, and in this chill weather, smoke, wood, or blackstone would be obvious.''

K'van approved of the fire-lizards' prompt appearance and the intelligence obvious in their attention to Larad's instructions. They chirruped happily, and Larad let them out his office window, a narrow slit, which the two fire-lizards navigated by flying up it sideways.

''This is marked as a holding. Are the inhabitants in her band, too?'' Asgenar asked.

''No one's held there for a hundred or more Turns. It was one of the places which a plague of those times wiped out. No one else was willing to take it over.''

''Is the entire complex marked? Would there be Hold Records showing the extent of it? I'd prefer to know exactly how to catch the whole gang.''

''I would, too.'' Larad walked his finger along the dates on the tomes of Records on his shelves before he took one down and placed it on the table. "These diagrams are exceedingly old, but we have them for almost every mine and cave system," he told them with a touch of pride in his voice.

Asgenar, examining the pages spread open for him, thought that Larad had every right to be proud. "By the First Egg, that's remarkable!" At first he had eyes only for the remarkable clarity of the drawing. "What sort of ink did they use? How old is this?"

"That I can't guess. Nor the substance used."

Asgenar ran respectful fingers along the edge of the opaque sheet.

Larad grinned wryly. "Thicker than your sheets, Asgenar, but no give to it. You can't erase or reuse it, either." He sounded as if he found that a disadvantage.

K'van had turned from the drawing to its legend. "Look, even the height of each section of tunnel is recorded." He gave a soft whistle. "Now that's mapping!"

"They knew how in those days," Larad said, beginning to shake off the shock of his sister's intransigence. "Telgar was the third Hold established."

"Yes, yes, some of those subsidiary shafts, even the narrow, low ones, would make ideal bolt holes," Asgenar said, eagerly addressing the real issue. He strode back to the map, examining the area around the suspect cave. "Yes, and access to it along a number of tracks. Larad, you don't need to feel obliged . . ."

Larad drew himself up straight. "I do and I am. We'll need copies of that quadrant of the area and of that old cave map. Who else have you asked to join us in this sortie?"

Asgenar grimaced, scratching his right ear. "I would rather we kept it between us, Larad. K'van volunteered, since he's already involved. The fewer who know, the better I'd feel. And I mean, just in this room for the time being. Now that I have your understanding and cooperation—" Asgenar conveyed his sympathy and respect by giving his brother-in-law's shoulder a brief, firm squeeze. "—it's a matter of organization and strategy, making sure none of them escape us. We both have trained men; I've roving troops of foresters in that general area right now. F'lar and Lessa—because of the girl—have offered Benden's assistance. So a quick in-and-out would see us in position at all these exits," he explained, tapping the relevant points, "and for a frontal assault. If we keep the whole affair between us, it could be managed quickly and with the least fuss."

"Lord Larad, that mountainhold you sent the fire-lizards to is definitely occupied," K'van surprised them by saying.

Larad looked at the window, then turned to K'van for an explanation.

"Heth listened," the dragonrider said.

Asgenar grinned uninhibitedly. "Lad, you're a marvel!"

"Dragons make useful go-betweens," K'van said in a droll voice. Asgenar stared at him for one second before he broke out in a peal of laughter. Even Larad, who was not quite as quick to see a pun, chuckled at last.

Wild happy chirps announced the return of the fire-lizards. They swooped to Larad's shoulders and made much of rubbing their cold bodies against his face. He stroked their delicate heads before finding tidbits for them in his pocket.

"Now sir," K'van said. "While you and Lord Asgenar discuss strategy, I'll make copies of these to take back to Benden for duplication."

Asgenar and Larad exchanged glances and then began to formulate their plans.

The dragonriders burst into the cold mountain air just at dawn, while the frozen sentry was nodding off to sleep. Alerted to his presence by a bronze fire-lizard, they were able to sneak up on him, and one deft blow turned sleep to unconsciousness. Men slid off dragon backs, slipping and sliding into position, while F'lar, T'gellan, F'nor, Asgenar, and Larad checked to be sure all were ready. The three wings of dragons then lifted with amazing quiet to nearby ridges, holding themselves ready to spot any escapees.

"And I thought *between* was cold," Asgenar muttered under his breath, flexing his gloved icy fingers and working his toes in his fleece-lined boots. He turned his face slightly so that the puffs of warm air from his fire-lizard kept his nose from freezing. A little trickle was running from one nostril, and he sniffed, then glanced to either side of him, wondering if the troopers had heard him. The lad on his right did not look old enough to be a veteran, but the burly man on his left was exactly the kind to guard one's vulnerable side. His name was Swacky, Asgenar remembered.

Larad had insisted on being in on the frontal assault, though any of the others would have been glad to spare him. The Telgar Lord had been like that as a fosterling, too, Asgenar remembered. He had hated to be gulled, and he had been dead keen to set matters right once he had learned that he had been made a fool of.

Day had never taken so long to come, Asgenar thought, feeling the cold eat through his heavy coverings. He was beginning to shiver and tried to control it.

"Sir," someone whispered from his left, and he saw a hide-covered bottle extended. "A sip'll stop that."

Asgenar gratefully accepted and gasped at the raw spirits. He had expected nothing more potent than hot klah.

"It did!" he mouthed, still feeling the heat of that sip.

"Pass it on. The lad'll need it, too," Swacky said, nodding to Asgenar's right.

All in the same state, Asgenar thought and passed it. He experienced a mild shock at his first glimpse of his neighbor's face; the boy was older than he had looked in profile, and his expression was far more grim than cold. He mouthed a thanks and sipped easily, seemingly accustomed to such rough liquor.

Not just grim, Asgenar thought, returning the bottle to Swacky. His neighbor was more intense than that: vindictive and bloodhot, despite the freezing cold. Asgenar hoped that there was experience there as well as incentive. A false move would flush their quarry, and they would have to go through the whole thing all over again. He wanted the matter settled that morning. There were other important things to attend to.

The sun was finally above the eastern peaks, its clear light painting the snow in gold dappled with shadowed blues and blacks. The plateau above and to their right glistened, sparkling as sun struck ice like beams of light bouncing off diamonds.

Suddenly the signal was given, and the men who had lain or crouched just in front of the trampled-down forecourt of the hold sprang to their feet and charged forward, wielding a ram to force the door, but the door proved to be unbarred, and the impetus of their forward motion put the men of the first troop into the main cavern before they could unsheath their swords. Larad pushed past them toward the chamber that he felt his sister would be using. But there were sleeping bodies along the corridor, and someone had wit enough to trip him, yelling at the top of his lungs while Larad sprawled untidily on the stone floor. Asgenar helped him to his feet while Swacky and his other companion plunged on down the gallery, swinging left and right at the sleepers who, awakened by the racket, rose to fight.

Even as Larad yelled at them to take the right fork, Swacky and the younger trooper turned to the left. Others surged in behind them, and Larad and Asgenar went on alone. When they reached their destination, they found the door barred and had some difficulty angling the ram for maximum effect.

When the door was finally hanging on its hinges, the room they entered was empty except for scattered pieces of clothing. Asgenar spotted the other doors, and the battering ram was brought into use again. Each successive room showed signs of frantic packing. Asgenar consulted his map of the complex and tried to relax. True, there was a series of smaller chambers off the main one, but all exits were well guarded. No one could escape.

Shouts resounded, often making the words unintelligble. A messenger found Larad and Asgenar to tell them that the main chamber was secure, all the left-hand tunnels cleared of their quarry, and prisoners taken.

"Any chance that Thella's among them?" Asgenar asked.

"No, sir, I've her face right here," the man said, holding out the sketch in his hand. "Several women but not one like her!"

"This is the best set of apartments," Larad said in a quiet, taut voice. "These have to have been hers."

Asgenar did not remark upon the obvious, that there had been unmistakably male accoutrements in two of the rooms. They moved forward to crouch in a narrow, low tunnel. Asgenar dropped to crawl on hands and knees and ended up, with Larad, in what appeared to be a dead end.

"Can't be," Larad said. "Glows! Forward some glows!"

"There was an exit to this group, I know it," Asgenar said, frustrated.

Before illumination could be brought, they heard an ominous rumble, and felt the stone beneath their fingers and knees shake. The sound seemed to continue for a long time.

"Lord Asgenar, Lord Larad? Are you there, sirs?"

"Yes, Swacky. What was that noise?"

"Here, Jayge, take the basket—you're more agile than I am. Sirs, it was an avalanche. We're going to have to dig our way out."

"Avalanche?"

Larad's anxious expression, lit by the glow basket, matched his worried tone, but the crouching young trooper seemed to make nothing of their cramped and closed-in condition. His face reflected so much hatred and frustration that Asgenar was stunned. A man that young ought not to feel such passions, he thought.

"Yes, sir," Jayge said. "They'd a deadfall arranged. Someone got out to release it. They've used that trick before. Didn't anyone think to check?"

"You forget yourself," Larad said icily.

"Jayge?" Asgenar slewed around and took the glowbasket from him. "You were in that ambush at Far Cry, weren't you?"

"Yes . . . sir."

"Bloodkin lost?"

"Yes, sir," he replied, the courtesy not as sullenly added. "This isn't the dead end it looks like! See the marks there on the ground. Something's scraped."

Larad and Asgenar heaved and pushed, thinking of a cantilevered slab.

"Lords," Swacky called. "You're needed out front. We'll keep on here."

Larad and Asgenar crawled back out to where they could stand erect again, and Swacky gave a fuller report.

"The Benden Weyrleader's got his dragons digging us out. We've accounted for all but three of the faces in those drawings, and some who weren't, plus one guy who swears blind he's got to talk to whoever's in charge. And there're troops following every alley and furrow in the place."

Larad swore under his breath, his expression unreadable.

"Which three faces, Swacky?" Asgenar asked.

"The woman they call Thella, the empty-faced man someone said was dragonless, and one other, a real brute."

"Swacky, you're too broad to crawl that tunnel," Asgenar said, letting Larad digest the news. "Find someone else to go down and help Jayge. And a crowbar or chisel would be useful if you can find such tools in here."

"We found an awful lot of stuff, Lord Asgenar. They'd settled in with nothing missing."

"Thank you, Swacky. The tools, please, and as many men as needed to find that exit." He took Larad by the arm and escorted him back to the main chambers.

The smallest room, which had only one entrance, was where the prisoners were being guarded. One of Larad's men greeted the two Holders and returned the drawings. "There're all here, and sixteen more, Lord Larad."

"Any casualties on our side?" Larad asked, noticing bloody head wounds and other signs of injury among the prisoners.

"A broken bone or two when the avalanche caught people unawares. Them," the trooper said contemptuously, "we mostly caught still in their bedrolls. There's one over in that small room that you should speak to." He nodded to his left, in the direction of the main hall of the complex, where one of Asgenar's foresters stood guard. "And there's some fresh klah in the pot," he added, gesturing to the bigger hearth where a fire had been freshened and a huge kettle was slightly steaming. "They lived pretty good all right."

Asgenar steered Larad toward the hearth, and a trooper sprang to serve them. Then they went to see the man the guard had mentioned.

When they entered the room he rose, smiling with obvious relief. "Did they escape after all?"

"I'll ask the questions," Larad said sternly.

"Certainly, Lord Larad." He turned his head to nod politely at the Lemosan. "Lord Asgenar." Then he waited.

"Who are you?" Larad asked after a long pause. The man showed not the slightest bit of tension or insolence.

"My name is Perschar, Lord Larad, a journeyman whom Master Robinton hoped could penetrate this band. I gather that someone finally sent you the sketches I've been dropping whenever and wherever I could. I'd swear Thella has eyes in the back of her head. Did she escape? Please, the suspense is very hard on my stomach."

"Perschar? Would the name Anama mean anything to you?" Asgenar asked, pulling at Larad's sleeve before the other could interrupt.

"Of course!" The man's long face was wreathed with a happy smile. "Lord Vincet's second daughter. I did her portrait, oh, far too many Turns back, I fear. She'll be grown and married, with children of her own to be painted, I've no doubt."

"He's Perschar, all right," Asgenar assured Larad. Taking a seat at the table, he noticed that Perschar had not been idle while waiting. There were more sketches.

"It was the only way I had of dropping information. Not that they suspected me, but it was as well not to raise any doubts whatsoever. The Lady Thella—"

"The woman is holdless," Larad said harshly.

"Exactly her problem," Perschar replied with some acerbity, then sighed. "She styled herself Lady Holdless, and, while not appropriate, as she *did* hold here—" His long hand made a graceful gesture indicating the room they were in. "—she was devilish quick, quite brilliant with her schemes— flawless almost, so I had to be cleverer still. Did she escape?" His eyes sought Asgenar's, almost pleading, certainly urgent.

Asgenar nodded, disgusted. "We think so. But until we've reestablished communications with those outside, we can't be certain."

"We had *every* hole out of this warren covered," Larad said, stalking about the small room.

"I heard the avalanche," Perschar said in a lugubrious tone. "That means someone got out. I'd lay odds with a Bitran, she did. Unless you caught Giron or Readis. Those three used the right-hand rooms."

"The guard said all but three of the faces in your invaluable drawings are accounted for—Thella, the dragonless man, and the heavyset man."

"That'd be Dushik. Thella sent him off on some special affair as soon as we made it back here. So at least Readis is accounted for, if they're the only ones missing. Yes, either Giron or Thella herself loosed that avalanche. She was rather taken with the notion. Had all of us working on it during the last Fall. Bloody cold work." Perschar shivered dramatically. "Is there any more klah in the pot?" he asked hopefully.

It took just as long for the dragons to dig them out as it did for Perschar to discover, after he had drunk his klah, that Readis was not among the prisoners. And it took twice as long for Jayge to discover how to open the clever door.

"And there was where we underestimated Thella," Asgenar said with as grim a smile as Larad's. "Gone up a bit, you might say," he added, unable to stifle the observation as he stared up the vertical tunnel through which escape had been effected. "Your charts were a trifle out of date, Larad."

Larad cursed and Asgenar listened sympathetically.

Jayge had scrambled up the rungs of the ladder and come out well above the entrance stormed by the troops. "The avalanche was set off from here," he hollered down. Both men clasped hands on their ears against the echoes his call set up. "A bronze dragonrider says that he's sent out sweep riders. They can't have gotten far on foot."

Larad leaned disconsolately against the wall, shaking his head, and sighed at the futility of their efforts. "She knows how to use snowstaves. She's very good at it."

"We can send messages ahead to be on the lookout for three refugees. Send copies of Perschar's sketches," Asgenar said as Larad once more got down on hands and knees to navigate the low tunnel. "We've blocked up most of the caves we think she's been using. She's going to have a long cold trip before she finds any safety at all." He saw Larad, just in front of him, shaking his head. "If we can get just a little cooperation from Sifer, Laudey, and Corman, surely someone will notice three such unusual people out and about at this time of year."

Once they emerged from the tunnel, Larad strode purposefully through the rooms where troopers were already gathering up the more expensive-looking articles of clothing and miscellaneous items. Asgenar followed, storing up hopeful suggestions, racking his brains to think of some logical and ultimately successful course of action. It was ludicrous that they should have failed. Yet they had.

When Asgenar saw Larad making for the eating area, he paused, looking around for one of the Benden dragonriders. F'lar, F'nor, and three troopers, still busy jotting down notes on improvised slates, came out of the storage area of the cavern.

"I found the Kadross Hold grain. They've got stables back there, baled fodder in quantity, and supplies enough to eat as well as Benden Weyr does," F'lar said, slapping his heavy fleece gauntlets against his leg. "What're we going to do with those, anyway?"

"Whose hold does this place fall in, Larad? Yours or mine?" Asgenar asked.

"Does it matter?"

"Well, sort of. You've got all those mines, and I have trees, but trees don't need much tending in the winter, and your mines can be worked year round."

Larad turned, a look of surprise on his face, but Asgenar felt that was an improvement on despair.

"I tell you what," Asgenar went on. "Let's leave them with enough to keep them going through the winter—what with the snowslide and all, I doubt they can get out, and I'm certainly not going to ask Benden dragons to give them the treat of their sordid lives. Let's see who's alive come spring."

F'lar and F'nor found that solution amusing, as did the troopers, who tried to disguise their grins. At the last, a slight smile tugged at Larad's mouth, and he began to regain his usual manner.

"I think I had better leave someone in charge, after all," he remarked. "Thella *has* really improved this place—it's isolated, but a stout holding."

"All right then, let's get busy." Asgenar clapped his hands together to call the troopers and foresters to attention. "What've you got on those sheets? I don't want to keep the dragonmen here any longer than necessary. We'll want to move the bulk out as fast as we can."

"Lord Asgenar, some of the supplies still have purchasers' markings."

"Good man, that'll spare us a lot of trouble. Swacky, organize your troop to haul identifiable things up front. I'll go separate what this lot—how many are there? Forty? Well, I leave rations for forty for three months. Then we'll come back to see who wants to work for a living."

"Meanwhile?" F'lar asked politely, his eyes dancing at Asgenar's masterful organization.

"Oh, please, F'lar, find that unholy trio!"

8

TELGAR HOLD TO
KEROON BEASTMASTERHOLD,
SOUTHERN CONTINENT,
BENDEN HOLD, PP 12

When the dragonriders brought Jayge, Swacky, and the other volunteers back to their camp, Jayge collected his pay and a written warranty from Swacky attesting to his character and service, then strapped his gear on Kesso's saddle and left. Swacky did his best to talk the younger man out of making such a long trip in winter; even the fairly temperate Lemosan valley would soon be clogged with snow. But seeing that his efforts were in vain, he let the boy go and promised to take the note Jayge wrote his father back to Far Cry. When Jayge took his leave of Lord Asgenar, the Holder expressed his regret at losing such a clever auxiliary.

Perschar was distressed when he discovered that his sketches of Readis were strangely missing from the roll that Asgenar had copied and distributed. Dushik, whom Perschar called the most ruthless and cruel of all Thella's followers, had not returned from the errand Thella had sent him on. So, in effect, they had failed in achieving the primary aim of the dawn sortie. Thella, Giron, Readis, and Dushik were still at large—and, as Perschar said without mincing words, exceedingly dangerous. There were plenty of holdless folk desperate enough to throw in their lot with such successful renegade leaders. Finding a new base in the hills behind Lemos and Bitra would not be difficult, and the band could start up all over again.

Perschar drew several views of Readis to be distributed along with those of Thella, Giron, and Dushik. Ever cautious, he asked Asgenar and Larad to hint to the captives that he, Perschar, had managed to escape. For, he said with a heavy sigh, he might be called on to help again and wanted to do so with impunity. Meanwhile, he rather thought he would like to go back to Nerat. He had not really felt warm since he left, and he had heard that Anama, Vincet's pretty daughter, now had children whom he would like to paint.

Lord Larad assigned Eddik, a trustworthy, diligent herdsman, as temporary holder. Most of Thella's band were genuinely relieved that they were not to be made holdless again. They were all afraid of the possibility of Dushik's reappearance and were reassured by Eddik's presence. Larad and Asgenar reinforced that sense of security by offering a substantial reward for any sight of the man in the vicinity, and double that for his capture.

Jayge was driven by mixed emotions, chief of which was revenging the deaths of Armald and his other friends and exacting retribution for the economic losses sustained by the train from Thella's attack. And in the back of his mind was always the thought that if Readis had had sufficient loyalty to risk death to stop the attack on his Bloodkin, then perhaps he could be persuaded to leave Thella's malign influence. Jayge had always admired his big uncle. Readis's departure from Kimmage Hold had seriously depressed the young Jayge, who could not comprehend why Readis had deserted them in that terrible situation. His father had explained that Readis had every right to leave in search of more suitable employment. And before long Jayge had come to recognize Childon's many little ways of humiliating the impoverished traders, giving them the most unsavory chores and condescending even about the food they ate and the quarters they were crowded into. Proud Readis could not have endured such treatment. Jayge, only ten Turns old, had had no choice. Even if he had been old enough to strike out on his own, he would never have left his sick mother, Gledia, behind.

But at twenty-three, and driven by revenge rather than humiliation, Jayge could take the winter, while the trader train was snowbound, to set out to settle his debt. He reasoned that if he could stay close to the amazing girl who heard dragons, whose ability had caused so much trouble for those he loved, he might also find Thella. He did not think that Thella would give up on her own pursuit of Aramina, either because without her secure mountain camp she would need the girl's talent more than ever, or out of revenge for the loss of that fine base. When Jayge had seen her there on the track to Far Cry, surveying the damage her plans had wreaked on his train, he had thought her malevolence unusual. Her knifing that burden beast had been an act of savage, almost deranged, vengeance. And her imbalance had been further demonstrated by her willingness to let everyone in her hold be killed by that avalanche—once she and her chosen followers were safe.

Aramina might have been taken to Benden Weyr. But was she truly safe there if Thella was still at large?

The fugitives had been forced to flee with little preparation and would certainly steal without hesitation. To make it across the winter trails to Benden Weyr, they would need supplies and information, both of which were most easily acquired at Igen low caverns. According to Perschar, Thella, Giron, Dushik, and Readis had often gone there, so Jayge made the caverns his first stop, pushing Kesso to his limits in order to arrive before his quarry.

To his chagrin, he learned that the best "eyes and ears" of the place had been found dead of a broken neck. Everyone was bemoaning the death of the footless old seaman, Brare, out of one side of their mouths, while calling him a dreadful cheat, rogue, extortionist, and pervert out of the other. Still, the Igen low caverns seemed a good place to start looking.

The cavern was buzzing about the spectacular raid on Thella's base, all sorts of people relating the tale with many fanciful embellishments that Jayge did not bother to correct. There was considerable confusion about how many raiders there had been and what had become of them. Some believed that Lord Larad—and who could have blamed him—had had them transported to his mines. Everyone knew the Holder needed help in those black pits of his, considering the shortage of metals needed to make the weapons for fighting Thread, not to mention those other queer things the Mastersmith was always banging away at. Others were of the opinion that the offenders had been shipped South, and there was a curiously fearful sort of envy over that fate. Jayge listened closely, wondering if there were any substance to the rumor. Would Thella and Giron have gone South with Readis—to disappear in what some claimed was a vast continent and others thought was merely an island, like Ista, only larger? Were they on their way to the boiling waters of the Southern Seas? Everyone knew how hot it was there, hotter than Igen ever could be. No, somehow he was positive that Thella would still attempt to secure Aramina—if only to kill the girl. And he particularly did not want Readis to be involved if it came to that.

By Jayge's reckoning, the fugitives would have made very slow progress out of the mountains, even using snowstaves, which were more help on snowy hillslopes than in wooded areas. Benden dragonriders were making frequent random sweeps over the mountains during the daylight hours; and even desperate people would not attempt to travel that terrain in the dark. Despite a grudging admiration for dragonriders like F'lar, T'gellan, and the young K'van, Jayge did not hold out much hope that they would actually catch the fugitives. That would spoil everything. He did not wish it to be that easy.

Jayge felt he had time to spare to search for a possible lair within the complex. Exploring the less frequented passages, he found several promising sites, none with any signs of recent occupation but all with small entrances partially or completely concealed from casual observation.

From one old trader friend of his father's, Jayge did establish that Thella and Giron had been in the low caverns during the time the Lilcamp-Amhold train had been taking on its shipments for Far Cry. He showed the sketch of Readis to the trader, and although the man had not seen Readis with Thella at that time, the sketch was much admired for itself.

"Why, you expect the man to draw breath. Nice-looking chap. Your kin, you say? Aye, no one could deny the Blood between you. Now whoever did this so handy? What'd they use? Charcoal would have smudged. Leads, you say? They'd be expensive—a' course, you being trader connected, you'd have the chance."

With one of his few marks, Jayge bought from a trader a tattered but fairly accurate map of the eastern stakes shores: Keroon to Benden, including Bitra and the easternmost section of Lemos. While in several spots the creases of the hide made the lines difficult to decipher, caves were marked, large and small, watered or dry, as well as all the holds and the best routes for various sorts of haulage. He also listened carefully to the nighttime conversations around the main fires, when the jugs were passed, encouraging conviviality. Apparently Dowell and his family had been such long-term residents that they were well-known. Everyone was still amazed that "their " Aramina had made it to Benden Weyr, where eggs were hardening. Everyone was rather pleased with the notion that "their" Aramina, raised in Igen low caverns, was certain to Impress the queen egg on Benden's Hatching Ground, and they were basking in her achievement. It had become known fact that Dowell, Barla, and the other two children had gone back to Ruatha, reinstated into their original home by Lord Jaxom, who had given them workmen to repair it, and who generally treated Barla as long-lost Bloodkin. The family was half the world away from Thella, and Aramina was safe in Benden Weyr.

Jayge did not agree. No one was safe from that woman while she drew breath. In his travels as a trader, Jayge had met all sorts of people, most of whom he could forget as soon as he moved on. But Thella was unique. She was the most evil person he had ever encountered. She deserved to be dropped down a smooth hole in the ground and left there.

Finally, with the valuable map and the sketches of Readis carefully wrapped and secured against his chest, Jayge turned Kesso southeast along the bright waters of Keroon Bay. He kept to the well-traveled routes, as a lone rider on back trails would be easy prey for petty thieves, looking for what they could get. Thella's gang may have been the best organized and most successful, but it was hardly the only one.

Despite the fatigues of travel Jayge did not sleep well. He kept going over and over that fateful raid: the rockfalls, the wagons toppling, and the stones that missed their targets and went on rumbling down the river ravine. He kept reliving his own part in the fight and wondering how he could have saved Temma from her frightful wound; protected Nazer; killed more of the raiders. He was haunted by the sight of that foot and hand sticking out of the rubble. They seemed to twitch in his dreams, as did Armald's pitiful hulk sprawled on the gravel road. He kept seeing Temma with her shoulder pinned by that barbed spear to the wall of her own wagon, and always Thella, poised on that boulder, directing all that horror—and throwing the knife that severed Borgald's pet beast's tendons. To keep from dreaming, he would walk, around and around, watching the sharp, clear stars out over the sea, conjuring the vision of himself lowering Thella by rope into a deep, smooth-sided pit and hearing her screams and then her pleas to be released.

At Keroon Hold, a trader friend of Crenden's suggested that Jayge help out one Beastmaster Uvor, who was taking four fractious mares to the stallions at the Beastmasterhold in Keroon. At the moment he was resting them from their sea voyage. "Resting his belly from seasickness," the trader remarked with a sniff. "Anyway, he lost his apprentice to a broken leg, so he's on his own. You're good with the beasties, young Jayge, and he's going your way. Doesn't hurt to close your hand on the odd mark, as well. He'll be in this evening, like as not. Come back then."

With Kesso comfortably stabled and muzzle-deep in a good grain feed, Jayge set out to explore Keroon Hold. He had never been that far south before, and the busy Hold was full of new sights, including a port facility that handled cargo bound for Ista and the west. Jayge walked down to the port and spent a long nooning in a harbor alehold, listening to seamen, listening to people, and listening for any word of Thella. He never asked about her directly but instead discreetly inquired about a dragonless man or showed the sketch of Readis.

He always asked about Benden Weyr, for news of the dragonriders. Courteous interest went down well with the Holds and Halls, which were intensely loyal to their Weyrfolk. He learned that there had been a Hatching and a queen egg but the lucky girl who Impressed Beljeth was Adrea and came from Greystone Hold in Nerat. The Neratians had been exceedingly proud of her, and she was said to be a very attractive but biddable girl.

When Jayge returned to the trader's, Uvor was there, a lean, likable man who cared for the mares and his own sturdy mount as if they were his children. On the circuitous route to the Beastmasterhold, Uvor named sire and dam of each of his mares for generations back, and never once put a name to his wife or any of his sons. He taught Jayge a few tricks of living off barren land, and what insects and semitropical plants could supplement a diet of the ever present snakes.

It was in the Beastmasterhold that Jayge first got wind of the unusual tradings with the Southern Continent. Four breeding pairs of fine burden beasts and four of runners were to be shipped to Toric at Southern Hold as soon as the winter storms had abated. A Master Rampesi would collect them in a ship outfitted with special belowdeck accommodations for such valuable animals. Jayge questioned the journeymen closely, for it had been his understanding that the Benden Weyrleaders had interdicted all commerce between north and south while the Oldtimer dragonriders remained in the Southern Weyr.

"There're reasons, you know, new reasons to reestablish trade south. There're reasons," an older journeyman assured Jayge, looking as if there was plenty he could add but he was being discreet. "Some say it has to do with mines dwindling down and plenty of rich ore just lying loose over the ground in the South. Some say it's because the Holders have put pressure on the Weyrleaders to give land to younger sons. A couple of Fort Holder's Bloods are going, and now that that raider group has been knocked into a deep pit, some of Corman's might foller."

Jayge snorted. "And what about the holdless folk in Igen low caverns who've no decent place of their own?"

"Them!" The journeyman's expression was disdainful. "There's plenty of jobs for them what's willing to work and please their Lord Holder."

"Now, Petter," a younger journeyman said, "you know that's not always the case. You remember that ragtag of folk that came through from Bitra when Thread started. Lord Sifer had turfed 'em out, and they was hard-working people."

Petter sniffed. "Lord Sifer may have had good reasons; it's not for you and me to question. Where there's smoke, there's fire. They'd no warranty to show like this young man."

Had Jayge not had other considerations foremost in mind,

he would have argued the journeyman on that point. Holders, major and minor, had taken advantage of Fall: he remembered all too vividly the humbling and belittling work that Childon had taken great pleasure in forcing him and his family to do. He knew of other cases where pride—and sheer exhaustion—had forced people to holdlessness rather than endure such drudgeries any longer.

"Is the Southern Continent so big it can handle more Fort and Keroon holders?" Jayge asked, directing his comments to the younger journeyman. "Seems to me the first thing you'd need are men and women who know how to work, not holders' sons."

"You thinking of resettling, trader?"

Jayge was put in mind of what Temma had said to him before he left Far Cry. "You know traders," he countered with a disarming grin. "Always looking for new routes, new items that travel well and sell better. The beasts would be sailed across then? And their handlers chosen?" It might be best if Jayge could persuade Readis to shift south for a while. He could always give his own warranty to his uncle.

"I wouldn't know about that," Petter said stiffly. "Uvor was chatting w' the Master about it. C'mon, you." He tapped his foot on his junior's boot. "We've got feet to trim and teeth to rasp."

Jayge asked the Smithcrafter's permission to use his forge to make new shoes for Kesso.

"D'you know how, an' all?" the smith asked, skeptical.

"Traders learn a lot of this and that," Jayge replied, selecting the iron bar, already fullered and swaged, and crunching off the length he needed. It was not the first time he had shod Kesso, and by no means the first time he had made shoes from scratch. Crenden had taught him what he had known, and then had him work under Maindy's farrier for a season. He was aware of the smith's scrutiny. But when he had heated, hammered, shaped, and clinched the first hind shoe, the smith turned back to his own work.

Jayge made two sets and paid for them and a small packet of nails. He had a long way to go to Benden Weyr. While he was eating his evening meal, Uvor and the Masterherdsman came up to his corner seat.

"I've told Master Briaret that you're a sensible young man and know how to care for animals properly," Uvor said with the air of someone happy to confer a favor on the worthy. "He's got a well-trained young runner to be delivered to Benden Hold. I know you're heading that way and that you'd take good care of her, fog, fire, or Fall."

Briaret was a short man, balding, with a rider's lean stature and the odd, bowed legs of someone who had ridden all his life. His keen eyes searched Jayge as intently as those of a Bitran giving odds. He smiled at Jayge, and the young man knew that he had passed the test.

"You've a warranty, I understand," the Master said in a slightly raspy voice.

Jayge passed over Swacky's useful recommendation and finished his meal while Briaret read. Finally the older man folded it neatly and gave it back. Then he held out his hand.

"Will you take charge of the mare? She's nearly as well bred as that runner of yours." He grinned. "As well he's a gelding. My drovers are going as far as Bayhead, so there's safe passage for you, and the journey's been timed to get all to safe cave during Fall. We haven't been as much troubled by raiders as the northwest, but there's comfort in numbers. I've a mark for you now, plus travel food and grain, and you're to get two marks at Benden Hold if the mare arrives in good condition."

Jayge shook the man's hand, well pleased. He would have some escort, he would make some marks, and he would still be making better time than Thella and her companions could.

Piemur was back at Southern and had finally cornered Toric into fulfilling his promise to let him explore freely in the

South. He had arrived armed with a polite request from Master Robinton, a request that, since it bore F'lar's signet, was more of an indirect order.

"I've got my journeyman's knot, I spent hours with Wansor, Terry, and that oaf of a Fortian, Benelek, so I'm qualified to keep Records that will be accurate as long as the Dawn Sisters remain in place. So you'll know, my Lord Holder—"

"Don't call me that," Toric snapped, his eyes flashing so angrily that Piemur wondered if he had overplayed his hand.

"I get the impression," the boy said in his most conciliatory tone, "that that is a formality that the Benden Weyrleaders will bring before the Conclave at the next possible occasion. You're as much a Lord Holder as Jaxom is, and you're working at it. *But*—" He held up his hand. "It would be wise to know how much you're going to Hold. You prove, one—" He ticked off each point on his fingers. "—how diligent you've been; two: how serious you are about all this; three: limit what their idiot sons—presuming some of them survive their initiation here—can possibly think to control; and four: make legal and binding your own claim by virtue of the fact that that's how much you've *been* holding."

Toric stared across the room to the map of what he already, by virtue of having accurately charted it, held. Much of the cartographic detail had been filled in by Sharra, Hamian, and Piemur, but that only whetted Toric's appetite to establish how much more there was. He had no intention of sharing it with any northern holders' sons—possibly not even his own, although he was proud of the twin sons Ramala had just delivered . . . again. Piemur was astonished, and secretly envious, of Toric's large family. The man would need every one of them to hold for him, that was certain. And Toric had plans for Sharra's offspring—whenever he did find someone he felt worthy of his beautiful sister. Piemur had about given up that daydream. He knew that Sharra liked him, enjoyed his company, and accepted him as a partner in their explorations, but whether she was careful to keep the friendship objective because she felt nothing stronger for him than platonic affection, or because she did not wish to bring Toric's wrath down on him, Piemur was not sure.

Maybe if he successfully broadened Toric's holding, he might also broaden Toric's appreciation of him. Maybe not broad enough to encompass Sharra, but then Piemur's motto always had been ''You never know till you try.''

What Piemur kept very much to himself was that he would be doing the survey as much for Master Robinton as for Toric. Just where his loyalties would be tested remained to be seen. In no fashion would Piemur risk Master Robinton's good relationships with the Benden Weyrleaders. He had a suspicion that perhaps F'lar and Lessa wanted a good bit of Southern to be dragonriders' territory. He hoped that the continent would be big enough for all. How much did Toric possibly think he could manage to Hold? Should someone—maybe Saneter could get away with it—remind Toric of what had happened to Fax, the self-styled Lord of Seven Holds? In any event, as long as Piemur got to set one foot in front of the other until he ran out of land, he would let the disposition of it rest with others—such as the Masterharper and the Benden Weyrleaders. *They* deserved more of the South than Toric ever did. But then, Lessa had a habit of giving perfectly good Holds away.

Piemur stopped his speculations. ''You'll never know till I go look, Toric,'' he said wistfully. ''Just Stupid and me, with Farli to send back my findings. I plan to live off the land.'' He knew that Toric hated to give out supplies that he could count on Piemur to break or lose.

The holder's ill humor began to fade. ''All right, all right, you may go. I want accurate maps, accurate readings, all along the coast. I want details about terrain, fruits, edibles, depth of rivers, navigable or otherwise . . .''

''You don't want much from one pair of feet, do you?'' Piemur asked sarcastically, but he was secretly elated. ''I'll do it, I'll do it. Garm's sailing to Island River tomorrow. Stupid and me'll hitch a ride. Why waste my time walking what's already well and truly mapped, huh?''

Garm sailed him to Island River, and Piemur spent the night with the holders there, an enthusiastic fisherman and his wife who turned out to be cousins of Toric's. They had dug out the ruins Piemur had noticed, painstakingly slated the roof, and rebuilt the wide porches that allowed air to circulate during the hottest weather through the rather spacious, high-ceilinged rooms. They chattered about their plans, which Toric had approved, and they wearied Piemur with all the good qualities they ascribed to the marvelous cousin who had rescued them from a holdless existence, quite by chance, and now they had such a bright future and weren't they the luckiest of folk?

Piemur felt himself the luckiest of folk the next morning, as he hauled Stupid from the fishing skiff in which the holder had ferried him across the Island River delta. In an hour he was slicing his way through bushes to reach a coastline where no man had ever set foot, happy as a fed weyrling despite the sweat running down his face, back, and legs and down to the thick cotton socks Sharra had knit for him.

Jayge got on well with the drovers, even though Kesso won every informal race from their prize runners. He would have liked to have raced the mare, too, for she was beautifully conformed for speed, but he had promised to deliver her safely to Benden Hold, and an overreach or a cut, while bad enough on Kesso, was not to be risked on Fancy, as he had taken to calling the mare. He was almost sorry when they got to the Keroon River, where he would go north and the drovers would go east to Bayhead. However, he was able to move much more quickly without having to hold Kesso to the herd's plodding progress. He made good time the first full day on his own and reached the fork where Little Benden River struck right toward Benden Hold, while the broader waters of Big Benden took a curve to the left past the cliffs. He chose the ferry over the sway bridge across the gorge at High Plateau Hold. To make the crossing, he had to put a twitch on Fancy to keep her quiet over the turbulent rough waters, and even Kesso was restless. Most people, according to the ferryman, preferred to swim animals across where Big Ben met the waters of Nerat Bay.

There were some grand trails up the banks of Little Benden River, and several times he galloped Kesso, the mare beside him stride for stride. She had the most enjoyable paces. Not that Kesso was not a very comfortable animal for long-distance riding, but Kesso had just happened; Fancy had been bred for it. Such a quality animal was certainly destined for one of Lord Raid's own women, he thought. He had the impression that the Lady Holder was an older person, so perhaps the horse was a gift for a daughter or a favored fosterling. He hoped she would be a good rider, with light hands for the mare's soft mouth.

On the second night the weather turned fierce, with high winds blowing right up the mare's tail and dirty sheeting rain, and Jayge was forced to approach a farmhold for shelter. When he produced both the travel note from Master Briaret and his own warranty, the slightly suspicious holder agreed to share quarters and meals. When Jayge admitted that the mare was to be delivered to Benden Hold, the holder's wife, a romantic type, went through the list of fosterlings at Benden Hold, trying to decide who the lucky recipient was. There seemed to be ever so many fosterlings at Benden, she said. She did hope there would be a Gather soon—it had been such a long tedious winter, and the children had had a tenacious fever, and she had had to drum for a healer to come down from the Hold, and the Lady Holder had sent her own special medication for rasping cough.

Jayge made his escape the next morning, limiting his time at her hearth to a cup of klah, even though she urged porridge on him, as garrulous as if she had not stopped talking all night. The trace by the river soon widened out to a wide roadway, well surfaced and maintained, and intersected a similarly good road heading north. His map indicated excellent roads all the way to Benden Weyr. All he had to do was deliver the mare at the Hold, and then he could complete his journey to the Weyr, and Aramina.

He paused at noon to eat, letting the two runnerbeasts graze. He brushed mud off the mare's legs and tail, and gave Kesso a few swipes, too. He would rub Fancy down again before they actually got into the Hold, so that she would look her best as they entered. He was soon close enough to Benden Hold to see its splendid proportions, the multitude of windows in the sheltering cliff face, and the south end of the broad east-facing inner yard. It was an hour or so of good riding away, but already small cotholds were visible on either side of the river, making use of cliff and cave. Behind and to the northeast were the Benden Mountains, and almost directly north—Benden Weyr.

Suddenly a group of riders burst out of a ravine just beyond him, startling the two runnerbeasts. By the time Jayge had Kesso under control, he was surrounded by a party of young people, admiring Fancy and Kesso and demanding, in a high-spirited fashion, all sorts of answers from him.

"My name is Jayge Lilcamp, and I'm to deliver this mare to the Beastmaster at Benden Hold. Without injury," he added in a louder tone as some of the boys began to crowd in around Fancy, who rolled her eyes and threw up her head in fright.

"Jassap, Pol, rein back. You're riding stallions," a girl said. Jayge threw her a grateful glance that turned into a long and incredulous stare.

She was not the prettiest of the three girls in that group. She had black hair, plaited in one long, thick braid down her back and covered with a blue scarf; her face was oval, strong-featured without being the least bit coarse. He could not tell what color her eyes were under rather level black eyebrows, but she had a nice straight, longish nose, a sweet shape to her mouth, a firm chin—and an odd sadness in her expression.

"Go on, Jassap and Pol. You, too, Ander and Forris. It's not fair, and she's such a pretty thing. She shouldn't arrive all sweated up. Lord Raid won't like it, you know." She was handling her own mount with quiet competence, and the others complied with her suggestion. It had not exactly been an order, but she had quietly taken charge.

"You're mean—a—!" one of the boys protested, but he obeyed, and they all set their mounts to a trot, chanting "meana, meana, meana!" They were laughing, but Jayge did not see what amused them so.

"She's a very elegant runnerbeast," one of the other girls said, pulling her mare abreast of Kesso on Jayge's left. "Did you come all the way yourself?" She smiled winningly at Jayge, who smiled back, knowing a flirt when he saw one.

"Master Briaret put her in my charge," he told her.

Another girl had kneed her mount beside the flirt, her expression fearful. "From the Beasthold itself? But that's a long way, and there was Fall, wasn't there?"

"Fall was allowed for, and we were safe in a beasthold," he said. He had discovered that most holdbred people found it upsetting to learn that he was not frightened by Fall. Casually, he glanced to his right and was relieved to see that the dark-haired girl had pulled into line with him, leaving a good space between her mount and Fancy, who was settling down again.

"We've been hunting," the flirt said, pointing to the boys ahead of them, on whose saddles hung some plump, young wherry bucks.

"We're going to have a Gather in a few sevendays. Will you be around?" The second girl had turned as coquettish as the first.

Jayge looked at the dark girl who was watching Fancy's

high movement, smiling to herself as the mare gave that extra little flick to her front hooves. The girl appreciated a good mover, he saw. He found himself wondering if there was any chance that he could complete his mission before that Gather. In the dancing square all were equal.

"I wouldn't miss it, fog, fire, or Fall," Jayge said with a courtly half bow to the tease and the flirt, but he ended with a questioning glance directed at the black-haired girl. She smiled, a very nice smile without a hint of the others' coy archness.

"We'd better catch up with the others," the first girl said. "See you later." She waved as she dug her heels into her mount. Fancy pulled back on her tether rope, and Jayge wound it more tightly around his hand, waiting for the others to charge off. The dark-haired girl rode ahead more slowly, looking back at him over her shoulder.

When he delivered Fancy to the Beastmaster at Benden Hold, Jayge handed over Master Briaret's packet of information about her breeding, and the mare's hair whorls checked against those on her papers. The man inspected the mare thoroughly, legs, hooves, barrel, neck, and teeth, and had Jayge trot her up and down the inner court until the young trader was a bit short of breath. Master Conwy could find no fault in her condition or appearance. Jayge waited silently, indolently feeding Kesso's reins through his fingers.

"You've earned your marks, Jayge Lilcamp," the man said finally. "She's a fine animal. Come with me. You can put your own mount up for the night here. Benden Hold keeps a good table. I'll speak to the steward about your pay and see if there're any messages you can take back with you."

"I'm not going back to the Beasthold," Jayge said. Then he caught himself. "I have to go north to Bitra."

"You'd best leave your marks here with honest men, young man. Those Bitrans are terrible folk for relieving a man of his coin."

Jayge could not help but grin at Conwy's dour and disapproving expression. "I'm a trader by craft, Master Conwy. It'd take more than a wily Bitran to relieve me of my marks."

"If you say so, so long's you know their tricks." Master Conwy clearly thought little of Jayge's understanding and less of Bitran "tricks," but he did not let that interfere with hospitality. First he put the mare into her stall, telling Jayge to put his runner next to her so that she would settle down more quickly. Then he took Jayge to the bathing rooms, offered to have a drudge launder his clothes, directed him to where he could find a cubicle for the night, and told him where to go before mealtime.

Clean and dressed in his newly pressed spare clothes, Jayge found Master Conwy's hold and was given the marks. To his surprise, the Master asked for the warranty again and added a second recommendation on the end of Swacky's.

"Doesn't hurt for someone out and about to have proof of honesty and diligence."

Master Conwy then walked him up the steps of the main Hold and into the dining hall, which was full of bustle and enticing aromas wafting up from the kitchens below. Jayge took the place offered him, on the far right with the other men and women of journeyman rank, and Master Conwy left him.

Such a main Hold was sinfully luxurious, Jayge thought, looking at the smooth, painted walls, the deep window apertures, and the burnished and etched shutters. The upper portions of the walls were embellished with brilliantly colored paintings, some of them quite old, to judge by the clothing depicted. It was the habit of the very old Holds to include portraits of notable lords, ladies, and prominent crafters. Some had been done in miniature on the borders, and some were so high up the wall as to be practically invisible. Idly Jayge wondered if any of those portraits could be Perschar's work.

He answered the polite queries put to him and responded noncommittally to a rather blatant come-on from the handsome journeywoman beside him, but he listened more than he talked. When the soup was passed around—Jayge was rather flattered to be served first—the journeywoman contrived to brush her full bosom against his shoulder. Her touch reminded him of how long he had been on the road alone.

But all thought of casual dalliance faded from his mind with his first clear look at the head table on its dais and the black-haired girl seated at the right-hand edge. A fosterling then, Jayge realized, but not of sufficient rank to sit closer to Benden's lord, lady, and their own children. She wore a low-cut deep maroon dress that offset her creamy skin. She smiled often, laughed seldom, and ate neatly—and Jayge could not stop staring.

"She's not for the likes of you, journeyman," his seatmate said in his ear. "She's for Benden Weyr. Next Hatching, and she's sure to be Impressed."

Jayge had thought that girls found on Search went immediately into the Weyr, but if she was a fosterling of Benden's, maybe that made a difference. He did know that there was no clutch on the Hatching Grounds at the moment.

"She was in the hunting party that passed me on the track," Jayge said casually. He tried to keep his eyes from her but could not. There was a sweet calmness about her; it was soothing just to watch her deal with her food platter. Jayge thought that he had never seen a girl quite like her. And she was not for him. He wrenched himself away and turned, smiling, to the journeywoman, who was eager to continue conversation.

The next morning, somewhat to Jayge's dismay, the first person he encountered was the black-haired girl. She was in Fancy's stable as he arrived from a quick breakfast to saddle Kesso.

"I think she's going to settle in all right," she said, smiling with obvious relief up at Jayge. "Master Conwy said you'd brought her all the way from Keroon Beasthold without so much as a scratch. Do you like all animals? Or just runners?"

Jayge was having trouble organizing a suitable answer, so

he just smiled. Yes, he thought, he had been right about that sadness in her face. "Oh, I get on well with most animals. Treat 'em right, they work well for you. Feeding's important. Enough for the work they've got to do."

"Are you a beastman, or a herdsman?"

"I'm a trader."

"Ah, so you'd know burden beasts better." For some reason the girl's smile was tinged by wistfulness. "We had a yoke—I called them Nudge and Shove. They did a lot of it, but they never let us down."

Jayge had completed saddling and stowing his pack without realizing that he had done so, and he was suddenly very shy in her presence. "Gotta go," he said. "Long way still. Nice meeting you. Keep your eye on Fancy."

"Fancy?"

"I always name animals. Even just for a journey." He shrugged diffidently, wondering what had gotten into him. He usually had no trouble talking to girls at all. Last night had proved that, though if he had known that he would be talking to *her* again today, he would not have settled for a quick tumble with that journeywoman. He backed Kesso out of the stall.

"Fancy's a very good name for her." The girl's voice followed him out of the beasthold. "Thank you. I'll take good care of her. Good luck."

Jayge swung up on Kesso and trotted smartly out of the beasthold, wishing he could have thought of some excuse to stay. But she was for the Weyr, and that was that!

9

BENDEN HOLD,
BENDEN WEYR, PP 13

Though the trail was good, the weather was cold and the hilly going sometimes so treacherous in the early mornings that Jayge delayed starting until the sun was well up. He preferred to find or make his own overnight shelters, though several times he shared a midday meal with holders he met up with. He lent assistance to one farmer, changing a damaged wheel, and when Kesso's shoes were noticed and admired, he made the man a new set for his barefoot runner. That time he agreed, when pressed, to stay the night, as it was too late to continue.

But despite the occasional encounter, Jayge spent far too much time on his own, thinking of the black-haired girl. He ought to have asked her name. That would not cost him anything, he thought. He would have liked to know her name. He ran through all the variations of women's names he knew but could not find one that suited her. He found himself fretting over that indefinable sadness in her eyes and in the slight droop of her mouth. She was probably the same age as the other two girls in the hunting party, but she had exhibited an air of maturity that the others lacked. His dreams at night took on an erotic flavor, but they amused more than embarrassed him. On the dancing square all were equal, he reminded himself again. He would get back to that Gather. He would dance with her and clear that sadness from her eyes.

Benden Weyr's peak grew to dominate the horizon, serene and invulnerable with its high steep sides. The bigger it got, the faster Jayge urged Kesso, and the longer he traveled each day. He was up at dawn on what he judged to be the last morning on the track, when he saw the unmistakable bloom of a fire being stoked up on a ledge across the river. He was instantly alert.

Studying his map again, Jayge saw that his campsite was not the only cave in the immediate vicinity. Could Thella have come over the mountains directly? Without bothering with her informants in Igen low caverns? And who had killed old Brare? He told himself that the fire could well have been made by a herdsman, checking on his flocks, but he felt compelled to take a look. Aramina was in Benden Weyr, and if Thella was outside it, the dragonriders should know.

He tied Kesso up again, gathered some dry grasses to keep the runner occupied, and after testing the edges of his daggers, he made his way in the dawn-dark down to the river. A bridge, somewhat rickety and probably dating from the time the Lord Holders had attempted to storm Benden Weyr, provided him with a quick, dry, and quiet crossing. He caught sight not of the fire itself but of its glow on the rock face that sheltered it from the northeast. There was light enough now in the sky for him to pick a careful route. He soon crossed a narrow, twisting path and nearly slipped on some herdbeast dung. Judging that the faint path was safer than a more direct line, he followed it, climbing to a point higher than the spot from which he had seen the fire. Then he left the trace, parting the scraggly bushes with a care to thorns and stiff branches, and crept ahead a step at a time.

He heard their voices—two men, and a voice he recognized

as Thella's. He could distinguish no words, nor could he get any closer, as the steep ridge before him was too smooth to be climbed and he could not see a way around it in the semidark.

Hunkered down, he waited—until suddenly he realized that the voices had stopped. He moved as quickly as he could in the growing light, but when he reached his objective, the only evidence that anyone had been there was the warmth of the stone where the fire had been, and a few fragments of charcoal. The interior of the small cave was clean—far too clean, Jayge realized. He could see the river below him, and not a sign of travelers. Could his quarry have gone west, up and over the hill, and down to another concealed spot?

Just as Jayge craned his neck to examine the slope above him, he caught sight of dragons emerging from the crater mouth of Benden Weyr, soaring majestically into the sky as if welcoming the sun's rising with their own. His first encounter with a dragonrider had given him a warped opinion of them, but that had been tempered gradually as he met others when working ground crew. He had heard the high opinion in which Benden riders were held, and had actually ridden Heth to Thella's hideout. The early morning flight before him was so beautiful that his whole perception of dragons and riders altered completely.

Absorbed in that beauty, Jayge gave no thought to the possibility of his being discovered there. He watched until they had either returned to the Weyr or winked out *between*, an ability that the young trader found frightening even after surviving a demonstration of it on Heth. Then it occurred to him to wonder why the dragons, known to be long-sighted, had not reacted to his presence, sprawled there as he was across the rock face. They had not seemed to be alert at all. True, he had not moved, but surely Thella and her companions were on the move! Were the dragons even watching out for her? Clearly not. Those dragonriders were so secure in their bloody Weyr, they did not bother to keep sentries, he thought in disgust. And what was to keep Thella from brazening her way right into the Weyr and making off with Aramina?

Jayge took the fastest way down, racing across the bridge and back to the cave, hoping that a dragon would appear to bar his way, his rider demanding to know who he was and the nature of his errand. But no one stopped him, and Jayge tightened Kesso's girth with unusual violence. Vaulting to the saddle, he had the gelding galloping at full stretch up the valley to the tunnel that was the only surface entrance to Benden Weyr.

There he met with resistance. And while he was somewhat reassured by the evidence that not everyone could enter the tunnel, he was irritated at the way his concise statement of danger to Aramina by Thella's covert presence in the valley was questioned by every member of the guard, none of them dragonriders and all of them taking far too long looking over his warranty. Then his sketch of Readis, which he accidentally dislodged from his chest pocket in his haste to show his warranty, was picked up by one of the guards.

"This guy was here yesterday. Kin of yours?"

Jayge was paralyzed for a moment with shock. "He's in Benden?"

"Why should he be? He only wanted to deliver a packet of letters to Aramina, and she's in Benden Hold."

"And you told him that? You smokeless weyrling, you consummate dimwit." Jayge was primed to elaborate on the antecedents of all six guards when the oldest man suddenly held his spearpoint right against Jayge's throat.

"State your business." The spearman pricked the sharp point encouragingly.

Jayge swallowed both ire and insolence and, raising his hand, moved the point away from his neck, all the while staring back at the hard-eyed guard. "I must see K'van, Heth's rider, immediately," he said more reasonably. He kept his tone urgent. "Thella was camped last night in the valley. I heard her this morning. And if she knows Aramina's at Benden Hold, the girl is in grave danger.''

The spearman gave him a faint reassuring grin. ''Someone who hears dragons has all the protection she needs. But if that raider female is in the vicinity, Lessa will wish to hear all about it. Ride through. I'll inform them you're coming.''

Kesso did not like the tunnel despite the glows that illuminated it at frequent intervals. He sidled, spooked, and twitched his ears constantly at the echoes of his own rattling hooves. When he stumbled on the ruts made in the floor by hundreds of Turns of cart wheels, Jayge kicked him smartly to make him pay attention. Finally they came to a second, inner gate, whose guards waved him on through into a vast, high-ceilinged area furnished with platforms of varying heights for the unloading of any sized wagon or cart. From there Jayge was directed to a second, longer tunnel, its far end a mere circle of brightness. He trotted Kesso, disliking the sensation of being enclosed in rock. He kept hearing noises that reminded him a shade too much of the avalanche in Telgar, and he resisted the urge to gallop Kesso out of the place.

Then he was out in the Bowl of Benden and gawking like the most ignorant back-of-the-hill hold apprentice. The immense crater was an imperfect oval—actually two coalescing craters, rather than a single one. The irregular sides loomed high and were dotted with the dark mouths of individual weyrs. Many of the protruding ledges already held dragons lolling in the sunlight. One whiff of the dragons' scent, and Kesso threw his head up until Jayge could see the whites of his frantic eyes.

A youngster came trotting up to him. ''If you'll come with me, Trader Lilcamp, you can put your runner where the dragons won't scare him.'' The boy pointed to his right. ''The blackrock bunker's not too full right now, so there's enough space. I'll get him some water and hay.''

Jayge had his hands full with the beast's terrified behavior, and by the time they got safely inside, Kesso was lathered with sweat. Fortunately the acrid dusty smell of the blackrock masked dragonspoor, and Kesso, his fright forgotten, was glad to slake his thirst in the water pail. After checking that the hay was of good quality, Jayge left him to it.

"Now, if you'll come this way, Lessa's waiting for you," the boy said.

As Benden Weyr was an amazement to Jayge, Lessa was only slightly less of a surprise. He could feel the force of her personality as strongly as he had felt Thella's, but there all resemblance ended. Despite her slight stature, Lessa carried herself with authority, gracious but firm. She was more courteous to a trader than he had expected, and she listened with such interest that he found himself telling her the whole story, from his first encounter with Thella and Giron, to that dawn's surveillance, and his fears, assumptions, and anxieties—with one exception. He made no mention of Readis.

"Please, Lady Lessa, bring Aramina back here before it's too late," Jayge said, stretching his hand across the table to Lessa's and then pulling it back as he realized his forwardness.

"As soon as I learned of your errand, Jayge Lilcamp, I sent word to Lord Raid. They'll keep her safe, I assure you." She gave him a radiant smile, then explained her method. "Ramoth, my queen, told Benden's watchdragon."

"But the girl'd be safer here," Jayge insisted, fretting. Anyone could walk into Benden Hold; anyone could find her out on a hunt.

Lessa frowned just slightly, then leaned toward Jayge, putting her small hand on his arm, strong fingers pressing in reassurance. "I do understand your concern. And I would prefer to have Aramina right here in Benden until she Impresses but . . . the girl *does* hear dragons." She grimaced in frustration. "All the time, and every dragon." She sighed extravagantly, then tilted her head slightly and smiled at him.

Suddenly Jayge knew why so many people respected, even worshipped her, and he found himself smiling back at her, half-embarrassed by his reaction. "The conversations were driving her crazy."

"Not as crazy as Thella could," Jayge heard himself saying.

"Tubridy at the outer gate said you had a picture of a man who purportedly had letters from her family," Lessa said.

Jayge pulled his warranty from his pocket, opening it as if expecting to find the sketch folded up in it. Then he fumbled in his chest pocket, feigning dismay and annoyance and checking the other pockets in his jacket. "I must have dropped it. My runnerbeast did not like the tunnel, or the dragons." He attempted an ingratiating smile and an abashed shrug.

To his surprise, she spread out a sheet, much bigger than any of the ones Perschar had used, but which included all the sketches the craftsman had done, including a new pose of Readis, by no means as accurately drawn from memory as from life. The resemblance of uncle to nephew did not seem as pronounced—at least Jayge hoped that Lessa would notice none. Without hesitation, he pointed to Dushik.

"I'd know that one anywhere," he said. He knew he was taking a chance but he was irrationally determined to save his uncle. How, he did not know—but he had to try.

Lessa was looking at him oddly, her eyes slightly narrowed. "How did you have come to have a sketch?"

"Well, as I told you, I thought they'd make for Igen low caverns. On my own like that, I might just be told something holders, and dragonmen"—his smile was respectfully apologetic—"might not get to hear. So I was given one of Perschar's sketches to show. I've a score to settle with Thella and her friends." Jayge had no need to counterfeit the hatred and determination that welled up in him. Then he was startled to hear a dragon rumble nearby.

"Private scores have a habit of getting out of hand, Jayge Lilcamp," Lessa said with a strange smile.

Suddenly Jayge was reminded again of Thella. He shook the comparison out of his head and got to his feet as the Weyrwoman rose.

"And getting in the way of more honorable qualities," Lessa continued. "You can leave this matter in Weyr hands. We'll protect Aramina." A dragon bugled, and the noise reverberated. Lessa smiled dotingly. "You have Ramoth's word on it."

"Does she hear everything?"

Lessa laughed. It was an astonishingly young laugh. She shook her head reassuringly. "Your secrets are safe with me."

Jayge turned away to avoid her shrewd eyes and perceptive mind. He had never heard anything about dragons being able to hear everyone's thoughts—just those of their riders.

"Go across to the kitchen on your way out, Jayge Lilcamp. You'll need a good meal to start your way back home."

Thanking her, he followed the boy out of the weyr but came to an abrupt halt at the sight of the golden dragon sitting on the ledge. She had not been there when he had entered. Her tail was wrapped around her front legs and her wings tucked flat to her dorsal ridge, but she was looking squarely at him as he came out.

"She likes it if you speak to her. 'Good morning, Ramoth' is appropriate," the boy suggested when he realized that Jayge had not moved.

"Good morning, Ramoth," Jayge repeated in a dry voice and edged carefully toward the first step. The dragon loomed above him, and he had never felt so insignificant in his life. Although he was of reasonable height, he came no higher than her short foreleg. He swallowed and took another step. "Give my greetings to Heth, would you? I liked meeting Heth." Jayge knew he was babbling, but somehow or other his words seemed appropriate.

"Really," the boy said, tugging his arm, "she won't do anything."

"She's bigger than I thought," Jayge said, speaking rapidly and in an undertone.

"Well, she *is* the Benden queen. And," the boy added proudly, "the biggest dragon on all Pern."

Ramoth canted her head upward suddenly, rumbling at three dragons circling to land on ledges above her. Two of them answered her. Jayge took advantage of that distraction to go down the weyr steps as fast as he could, passing the boy on his way out. When he reached the Bowl floor safely, he took a deep breath and wiped his sweating forehead with one hand.

"C'mon, you're to have a meal. Weyr food's good," the boy said encouragingly, catching up.

"I think I'd rather—"

"You can't leave the Weyr without a decent meal," the boy insisted. "Look, Ramoth's curling up for a snooze in the sun."

Lessa's reassurances lasted only until Jayge's first overnight camp. He had been heartened to see sweep riders quartering in the distance, farther down the roadway. Then the overlapping branches obscured his sight of them. He fretted until almost dawn, sleepless, remembering each word of his interview, trying to allay his doubts about dissembling to the Weyrwoman herself, and trying to puzzle out her warning about settling private scores.

He wished he could see some way of getting Readis free of his association with Thella. And who was the third man he had heard? Dushik? Or Giron? He rather doubted it was Giron, not that close to a Weyr. Dushik was reputed to be the more formidable opponent.

Jayge drove himself and Kesso hard down the trail, eschewing more comfortable lodging in the interest of pressing on. Someone at the Weyr had kindly tied a sack of grain to his saddle so that he could feed the hard-working Kesso properly. He stopped only to buy travel meal and more grain before moving on. He kept looking for any signs of other recent travelers, although it would have been too foolish of Thella and the others to move on the well-used road.

Then he knew what he would do when he reached Benden Hold. He would ask to see the black-haired girl. She had seemed sensible enough to take him seriously. He would show her the sketch of Readis and warn her about him. Dushik was ferocious enough so that people would automatically be wary of *him*. But Readis looked respectable and he had a clever tongue in his head. Too clever by half. Still, Blood loyalty had compelled Readis to draw Thella's raiders off the train, and Jayge had to do as much for his uncle.

He was tired, still wet from the previous day's rain, and hungry on an exhausted, foot-dragging mount when he arrived at Benden Hold. To his immense relief, activity around the Hold seemed to be normal. He asked for Master Conwy, who was surprised to see him but who welcomed him cordially.

"Have there been any strangers asking for . . . the girl who hears dragon?" Jayge asked immediately.

"Aramina?" Master Conwy's bushy eyebrows lifted. "So, you're the one who rode all the way to Benden Weyr to warn them. Lad, you'd only to tell me that was your worry. We'd've sent the watchdragon up and spared you a long journey."

"Then I wouldn't have seen Thella's band camped near the Weyr."

Master Conwy nodded as one did to a nervous person, deftly took Kesso's reins from Jayge's hand, and began shooing him into the beasthold, helping Jayge unsaddle and stable the tired beast. "That's true enough, but you did see them and, I hear, spoke to the Weyrwoman at length."

Jayge's hopes flared briefly. "Then the dragonriders found Thella?"

"No, but not for want of trying. And we've guards out in plenty and every holder on the lookout, as well."

Jayge paused in the act of placing his saddle on the partition between the two stalls. "The mare I brought to you was in the next stable. Where is she?"

"Out. Aramina went—with two guards—to help with a staked burden beast. She's very good with animals and they sense that—"

"You let her leave the Hold? Shards, man, you're as mad as they are up at the Weyr! You don't know what Thella and Dushik are like! You've no idea what they're like! They mean to kill the girl!"

"Now, see here, lad, leave go of me. And I don't take that kind of language from anyone." Master Conwy pulled Jayge's hands from his shirt. "You're tired, lad; you're not thinking straight. She's safe. Now you come with me, have a bath and something to eat. She'll be back shortly. Won't take more than a few hours."

Jayge was trembling with stress, and since Master Conwy sounded so certain of Aramina's safety, he allowed himself to be persuaded into the hold and the bath. It was only when Master Conwy's eldest boy brought him hot klah and fresh bread smeared with sweetsauce to eat while he soaked off the travel dirt that he realized that Aramina was the black-haired girl he had so admired. Fortunately the food distracted his thoughts from the girl, thoughts that had been taking a decidedly erotic turn. He concentrated instead on the disquieting fact that the dragonriders had not flushed out the fugitives. They were hiding, biding their time until the alertness of the Hold and guard relaxed. Thella was good at waiting—witness the way she had built those deadfalls, spaced to catch every wagon. But she could make mistakes. She had made another in building a fire that could be seen, and had been.

"Jayge Lilcamp!" Master Conwy charged into the bath, throwing a towel at Jayge, then dragging him out of the water when he did not move fast enough. "You were right, and we were shamefully slack. Gardilfon just now came up the Hold road, driving his tithe beasts. He had sent no word to the

Hold about a burden beast, certainly not to Aramina, and he's seen no one on this road since dawn.''

Hurriedly drying himself and fumbling with the clothes the Beastmaster flung at him, Jayge heard the rumble of the Hold drums, his blood pounding as much to their beat as to the heat of the bath he had just left. His boots were clammy and mud-caked, but he crammed his feet in.

"Lord Raid wants a word with you. He's mustering everyone, and yes—" Master Conwy glanced skyward as dragons appeared in the sky, "We've all the help we need. Aramina will tell the dragons where she is."

"If she knows," Jayge murmured, suddenly seeing the flaw in their thinking. "And if she can talk."

At first Lord Raid discounted Jayge's remarks, repeated to him first by an angry Master Conwy and again by Jayge, who was then told to sit down and be quiet. Of medium height and somewhat plump, with a discontented droop to his mouth, long lines from nose to mouth, and puffy bags under his eyes, Lord Raid had a habit of posing himself; as he turned from one advisor to another he was almost a caricature of himself. Meanwhile someone gave Jayge a bowl of porridge, which he ate quickly, despite the fact that his stomach was tense with worry.

When the hours passed with no word from the search parties, Benden Hold's many fire-lizards, or the dragons, Lord Raid strode over to where Jayge was half-dozing by the hearth. The young trader had tried to stay awake, but the warmth and his fatigue had overcome his anxieties.

"What exactly did you mean by your remarks, young man?"

Jayge blinked to clear his eyes and tried to remember what he had last said. "I meant that if Aramina isn't conscious, she can't hear dragons. And if she can't see where she is, how can she be rescued by them?"

"And just how do you arrive at those conclusions?"

"Thella knows she hears dragons." Jayge shrugged. "It

stands to reason a clever woman like Thella would make certain Aramina had nothing to tell the dragons."

"Exactly," a cold voice said. Lessa was pushing through the knot of men around Jayge. "I apologize, Jayge Lilcamp. I didn't heed your warning closely enough."

"Isn't it possible this young man is in league with them?" Raid said in an audible aside to Lessa.

She raised her eyebrows in a slightly contemptuous quirk, and her lips thinned. "Heth and Monarth both vouched for him to Ramoth at Benden. Lords Larad and Asgenar confirm his description."

"But—but—" Raid stuttered impotently.

Lessa sat down beside Jayge. "Now, what do you think has happened to Aramina?"

"None of the dragons have heard her?"

"No, and Heth is nearly hysterical."

Jayge exhaled, sick with worry, but he made himself say what he feared most. "I don't put it past Thella to have killed her."

"No, the dragons say not," Lessa said positively and looked at him for his next suggestion.

"What about the guards with her?"

"They are dead," Lessa said, her voice full of regret. "Stuffed out of sight, which is why it took so long to locate them."

"Then she's been knocked unconscious." Jayge shut his eyes against the image of Aramina's limp body, blood staining the blue scarf on her head, hanging across Dushik's powerful back.

"Then waiting until she recovers consciousness is unlikely to be useful?" Lessa asked somewhat sardonically.

Depressed, Jayge nodded. "Thella will have found a dark cave. Or a deep pit. If Aramina can't tell the dragons where she is, it doesn't matter if she can hear them or they her."

"Exactly my thinking. Raid—" Lessa got to her feet. "You surely must have Hold maps that indicate where the deeper cave systems are. They've had a head start of roughly six hours. We can't tell when they reached their destination, so even nearby caves must be searched. We must bear in mind how far they could have marched over this terrain; we know they weren't seen on the roads, haven't been spotted since the dragons started looking three hours ago. Let us not waste more time.''

Haunted by memories of the black pit of Kimmage Hold, Jayge volunteered to go with one of the search teams. There were fire-lizards beholding to three members of the ten-man team, so they were in constant communication with Weyr and Hold. That night as they wearily exited the seventh cave they had thoroughly searched, word reached them that Aramina was still alive, and had spoken to Heth. She could not see anything in the pitch black, and she could take only six steps before reaching the other side of her prison. It was damp and smelled foul—more like snake than wherry.

''That's a brave girl,'' the team leader said. ''Let's eat, roll in, and start looking as soon as we can count our fingers.''

Bloodkin be damned, Jayge thought to himself as he tried to sleep—he was going to kill Readis, as well as Thella and Dushik, with his bare hands.

They searched for two more days, until a rockfall tumbled down on top of them. Two men were injured badly—one with a broken leg and the other with a smashed chest—and had to be dug out. Instantly suspicious about such a convenient rockfall, Jayge told the team leader that he wanted to check it out while the others took the injured men down to a nearby hold for treatment.

He was careful about his ascent, choosing a ridge that would overlook the point of the minor rockslide and picking a route that provided the best natural cover. Then he settled down to watch.

For a long time nothing happened. When a whiff of some foul odor tickled his nose, he had been cramped too long in one position to be able to move fast enough—one strong hand caught his arm behind him and wrenched it up high on his shoulderblade, and another was clapped over his mouth. Jayge had always considered himself strong, but though he struggled, he could not pull himself from those clever and painful holds.

"Always said you had the brains in the family, Jayge," Readis whispered softly in his ear. "Don't struggle. Dushik's watching somewhere nearby. We have to get down behind him, go in from the other side, and get her out of that pit before the snakes eat her alive. That's your aim, isn't it? Nod your head." Jayge managed some movement, and the hand over his mouth eased. "Dushik'd kill you as soon as look at you, Jayge."

"Why did you kidnap that girl?" Jayge twisted around to look at his uncle, who maintained the tight armlock. The man was filthy with slime, haggard, and red-eyed, with gaunt cheeks and a very bitter line to his lips. His clothes were ragged and equally slimy, and he had a length of slime-coated rope slung over his shoulder.

"I didn't! I'm not mad or malicious." Readis's whisper ended in a hiss. "I didn't know what Thella had in mind," he continued, mouthing the words with little sound.

Jayge kept his answer as muted as his fury would permit. "You knew she wanted to kidnap Aramina. You arrived at the Weyr with that bogus packet of letters."

"That was bad enough," Readis said wincing. "Thella has a way of making things seem rational. But throwing a young girl down a snake pit is not rational. Not rational at all. I think Thella went raving mad when the dragonriders attacked the hold. You should have heard her laughing all the way up that tunnel she made the drudges cut. I don't think you'll believe me, but I tried to stop her loosing that avalanche. Then I was stuck, trying to save Giron. He's dead, by the way. She nicked his throat that first night." Readis shuddered. "I'll show you where the girl is, and I'll help you get her out. Then I'm disappearing, and you bask in the glory of your heroic efforts.''

Jayge believed his uncle; believed the desperation behind the scoffing words. ''Let's get her out then.''

Readis headed around the ridge, pushing his nephew in front of him. ''I threw her down a water bottle and some bread when I had a chance. Hope she heard it coming and ducked. Duck!''

Jayge's head was pushed down, his cheek slamming against a boulder. He could feel Readis suspend his breathing and did the same until his lungs threatened to burst. Finally a nudge told him that he could move and he inhaled gratefully, taking great, deep breaths. Then Readis signalled to move forward again.

It took a long time to negotiate the slope to the spot that Readis was aiming for. Jayge's muscles were cramped with strain by the time they reached an overhang, and the sky was beginning to darken. Jayge was not comforted by the thought that it would be darker where Aramina was. Readis crawled under the ledge and disappeared. Jayge followed, inching along on his belly and elbows and pushing forward on his knees and toes. He felt the slime that coated the ground, and he wondered how anyone had managed to push an unconscious girl down the hole.

At the touch of a slimy hand on his face, he pulled away, banging his head on the roof of the low tunnel and just barely managing to bite his tongue on his curse.

''Touchy, aren't we?'' Readis commented in a low voice. ''We can walk from here, and it's not far this way. Dushik must be guarding the more accessible entrance.''

As Jayge got to his feet, he was surprised to see a dim light coming from a thin fissure far above their heads.

''Don't speak loud when we do get to the pit,'' Readis instructed, ''but *you* do the talking. We're going to have to haul her up. The faster the better.''

The dim light from the ceiling crack faded, and then they were in a very dark tunnel. Readis laid an arm across him, signalling for silence. For a long while they listened and heard nothing but the dripping of the water down damp walls—until the silence was abruptly broken by a soft moan that reverberated hollowly, as if from a long way down.

Suddenly a light blazed and Jayge crouched in alarm, but as his eyes adjusted, he realized that Readis had lit a dim, almost spent glowbasket. And in the faint light he could see the yawning open pit before them.

"Talk to her, Jayge," Readis murmured. "I'm rigging a loop at the end. She's to put it under her arms and hang on tight."

"Aramina," Jayge said tentatively, cupping his mouth with both hands to focus the sound as he bent over the awesome edge of the pit. "Aramina, it's Jayge."

"Jayge?" His name began as a scream and ended in a gasp.

"Tell her not to let everyone know," Readis said acidly.

"Quietly, Mina," he called, the nickname he had misunderstood that day near Benden Hold coming easily to his lips. "You're found. A rope is being lowered." He turned to Readis. "Can't we send the glow down? She can bring it back up with her."

"Good thinking." Readis slipped the noose around the glowbasket and lowered it quickly hand over hand down the pit.

They could see the light descending deeper and deeper. Just when Jayge was beginning to think that the pit was bottomless, the glow stopped.

"Put the loop under your arms," he told Aramina. "We're going to pull you up fast, so hang tight."

"Help me, Jayge," Readis said. Jayge gripped the rope along with Readis, and it writhed in their hands as she secured it under her arms. Then they began to pull.

Aramina was not heavy, but the coarse rope was slimy, and Jayge was afraid of losing his grip. He dug his fingers into the hemp. When the rough upward movement slammed her into the pit wall, she grunted, and Jayge winced. But steadily the light came closer. Finally Jayge leaned down and grabbed her arm, nearly wrenching it from the socket as he heaved her up over the edge. She clung to him, shuddering and panting. He was lifting her farther away from her ghastly prison when they heard Readis's gasp of warning. A black shape launched itself on Readis, and before Jayge could put out a hand, two bodies went hurtling into the pit, the screams reverberating in horrifying echoes that made Jayge clasp the girl tightly to him, trying to blot the sound from her ears.

"Come. If Thella's near . . ." He tugged the shaking girl to her feet, grabbed the dying glow, and started back the way they had come.

Aramina stumbled but refused to fall. Jayge could feel the tremors shaking her. She was sobbing, and her fingers dug into the flesh of his hand. He hated to ask her to crawl up the cramped dark burrow.

He turned to her to tell her to take the glow and go first. It was only then that he realized that she was not just slimy—she was naked. Her shivering was more from the cold than from reaction or stress, and she would tear the skin from her bones crawling up that tunnel. He stripped off his jacket and thrust her arms into it. It covered her to the hips. Then he pulled off his shirt and tore it into strips to wrap around her knees and feet.

"That'll help," he said. "Push the glow in front of you. It's not far to the surface. Watch your head. Go!"

An eerie moan resounded down the tunnels and corridors of the ghastly cavern system. The weird sound was enough to send her to her hands and knees to crawl, sobbing with fright, into the burrow. Jayge fervently hoped that it had been Thella who had fallen down the pit with Readis.

Somehow they made it out into the twilight. Enough of the glow remained to light their way down the slope to easier ground. He managed to locate the pack he had left behind when he had set out to investigate the rockslide and unstrapped the blanket to put around her before fumbling for his numbweed jar.

"Can you call the dragons now and get them to come take us away from here?" he asked, slathering numbweed on her legs and feet.

"No."

He looked up at her face, confused. "Say again?"

"No, I will not call dragons. If I didn't hear them, this never would have happened to me. Jayge," she said, putting her cut and bruised hands on his arm, "you can't know what it's like. I can hear them now. Particularly Heth, who's crying inside. I'm crying, too, but I won't answer him. I can't! They'd make me stay at Benden Weyr, and I'll hear, and hear, and hear!" She was weeping, her fingers flexing on his arms. "It was better for a while at Benden Hold. There was only the watchdragon, and he was asleep so much of the time. If I heard the sweepriders talking, I could get very busy and pretend not to hear them."

"But—you hear dragons! You belong in the Weyr."

"No, Jayge, I don't think I do," she said, daubing numbweed on a bleeding knee. "Not the way I am. Oh, I stood on the Hatching Ground, and the little queen made a straightline dash for Adrea. A very nice girl and welcome to Wenreth. And I'm very fond of K'van and Heth. They saved me from Thella once already. You saved me this time. You went all that long way to Benden Weyr, and they didn't believe how serious it all was. Yes, I heard them talking about you. But I had two strong fine men with me when I went to Gardilfon's." She took a long shuddering breath. "I saw Dushik break Brindel's neck and Thella slit Hedelman's throat. They liked doing it. The third man had the grace to look sick. Was he helping you get me out of there? Was it Thella or Dushik that dropped?" Her voice was low and urgent, but she sounded rational.

"I don't know who took Readis down, and I'm not going

back to look. We'd better get out of this vicinity. If you won't call the dragon . . .'' Looking down at her he saw that she had set her jaw resolutely, so he shrugged. He slung the pack over his shoulder and picked her up.

At first, she seemed to weigh nothing in his arms, but gradually he tired. He had to rest several times.

"I'm trying to think light," she said once, and he patted her shoulder reassuringly.

The glow died just as they reached the cave he had been looking for. He stumbled in, nearly dropping her. It was little more than a hollow where a large boulder had once lodged, but it was free of snakes and would do for shelter for the night. When he had shared his rations with her and made her take several long pulls at his spirit bottle, he got her to wrap up in the blanket.

"You get a good sleep and it'll all seem better in the morning," he said, echoing his long-dead mother's advice.

"At least there'll be light," she said in a composed voice. Then she yawned, and very shortly he heard her breathing slow to a sleeping rhythm.

Jayge was accustomed to night vigils, but he wished that a dragonrider would land nearby whom he could shout to, or that he dared risk a fire without being sure if Thella had died down in that pit. And most earnestly he wished that Heth or Ramoth would hear him shouting at them with his mind.

Aramina's cries roused him. She was thrashing about, sobbing, and she fought at first when he tried to quiet her. He had to wake her up with a rough shake, and then she collapsed against him, panting.

"See, there's the moon," he said, slewing about so she could see Belior setting. Her face was ghastly in the pale light, but he was relieved to see her taking deep breaths to calm herself. "You're not in the pit, you're not in the pit!"

"Giron! He was there! Chasing me. Only he suddenly turned into another man, much bigger, who turned into

Thella. And then I woke up in the pit again. And the other voice I keep hearing, that had turned into a roar. It had been such a comfort to me, much more than just hearing dragons, even if I couldn't understand what it was saying to me. But it was there, just as lonely as I was and wanting so much to be *with* someone. Only it wasn't comforting in my dream. It was screaming at me."

He comforted her, murmuring soothing nothings and not arguing with her irrational words. He rocked her in his arms, and eventually she fell asleep again, twitching and moaning occasionally. Her movements served to wake him up when he dozed off, but eventually both slept quietly.

In the morning he found her sitting cross-legged, gazing out at the rain that cascaded down like a waterfall over the cave mouth. She had built a little dam of earth and stones to keep the water from running into their shelter.

"Jayge, you must help me," she said when he hunkered down beside her. "I cannot go back to either Hold or Weyr."

"Where will you go? To Ruatha? I heard Lord Jaxom gave your father back his old place."

She was shaking her head before he finished his sentence. "They would be appalled." She gave a weary smile. "Me hearing dragons embarrassed them enough. To think I would leave the Weyr would crush them."

Jayge nodded, since she seemed to expect some response of him.

"I shall go to the Southern Continent. I hear that there's lots of it no one's ever seen."

"And that the Oldtimers don't take their dragons out often," Jayge said with a sly grin.

"Exactly," she said, with a gracious nod. Then her expression altered. "Oh, please Jayge, help me. The dragons say that they've found no one." Seeing his unspoken query she explained, "I can hear them whether I want to answer them or not." She laid another pebble carefully where water threatened to spill over her little dam. She seemed so absorbed in her occupation that for a minute Jayge did not realize that she was adding slow tears of despair to the rainwater.

"What do you want me to do?"

Closing her eyes, she let out a relieved sigh and looked up at him, eyes still brimming with tears but a wan smile on her mouth. "Would that lean, wicked-looking-runner of yours carry two?"

"He could, but there're plenty of others to buy around here. I'm a trader, after all. And?"

She pulled at the edge of his jacket, a rueful expression on her face. "I'll need something to wear. Dushik slit mine off me . . ." An involuntary convulsion shook her, and he put a comforting arm about her shoulders until it passed.

"I'm a trader, remember," he said again.

"On rainy days, they often hang clothes to air in the bathing rooms." She bit her lip, realizing that she had just suggested he steal for her.

"Leave it to me." He dragged the pack over and sorted out the rest of the food; she refused to keep the spirits bottle, though he made her take a drink for its warmth.

"You have to take back your jacket," she said. "I'll have the blanket to keep me warm. No one will question your losing a blanket, but shirt and jacket . . . and as soon as you leave here, I'm going to go out in that rain and get clean."

"Then you'll need the sweetsand." He found the little bag in his pack and gave it to her. "Don't stay out long. Thella could still be hanging around."

Aramina had swathed herself in the blanket and was wriggling out of his jacket as he spoke. "I don't think so. It had to have been Dushik who charged Readis. Thella would have thrown a knife."

Jayge grimaced at the acuteness of Aramina's observation. She *was* thinking clearly. So he would do exactly as she asked and get them out of Benden Hold. Back to . . . then he remembered the shipment of breeding pairs, slated to go to the Southern Continent. Well now, he might just do a bit of real trading and see if it solved Aramina's problem. So long as he went, too. He had found her! He loved her! He would help her. The Weyrs and the Holds be damned. Hold and Weyr could not provide her with safety. He could and would!

10

SOUTHERN CONTINENT,
PP 15.05.22–15.08.03

As Piemur entered Toric's private room, he shot a quick glance at the inner wall to his left and saw that the hold map was, as usual, covered. Since Piemur had contributed many of the latest entries, he was amused by the man's paranoid secrecy. Saneter was sitting on the edge of his bench, agitatedly rubbing his swollen knuckles. Piemur could tell nothing from Toric's expression, which was a bad sign, especially when considering that he had returned from Big Lagoon to find the entire hold in a frenzy of indignation, outrage, and fright. Farli had chittered irrationally about dragons flaming her, then had disappeared. He had noticed that there were not many fire-lizards about, but there had been no time to look into the matter, as he had been ordered to report to Toric immediately.

"So, what have I done wrong this time?" Piemur asked brazenly.

"Nothing, unless your conscience is heavy," Toric said edgily and Piemur immediately altered his expression and

manner to respectful attentiveness. "Why would all the dragonriders leave?" the Holder went on.

"They've left?" Piemur wondered that Toric was not ecstatic. He glanced at Saneter for confirmation and the old
harper flapped his fingers in a confusing sign that the boy
could not interpret. When T'ron had died, T'kul had insisted
that he was Weyrleader, and the situation at Southern Weyr
had deteriorated rapidly. None of the other bronze riders had
contested T'kul, but no one was happy with his irrational attitudes and demands.

"There isn't a male dragon anywhere," Toric said, rubbing
his chin on his fist. "Only Mardra's queen is weyred, and
she's more dead than asleep." Toric was rarely without some
course of action; not always one that Saneter—and sometimes
Piemur—approved, but one generally guaranteed to protect
Southern Hold. "There isn't Threadfall," he went on, not
hiding his contempt for the Southern dragonriders who so
seldom stirred themselves to perform traditional duties. "So
I can't think why all the males would just take off."

"Nor I," Piemur agreed. His voice must have sounded a
little too cheerful, for Toric gave him a long measuring stare.
Piemur waited patiently. Toric obviously had something in
mind.

"You like it here, don't you?" the holder finally asked.

"My first loyalty is to my Craftmaster," Piemur replied,
holding Toric's gaze. So far Piemur had managed to retain,
his first allegiance warped a trifle but unsullied.

"Understood." Toric flicked his fingers in acceptance of
Piemur's response. "But *my* first loyalty is not to those—those
sisters' mothers."

"Understood." Piemur grinned at the description of the
Oldtimers, though the incestuous implications drew a gargled
protest from Saneter. "And I'm sure you already know that
you've got your Southern holders behind you all the way,"
he added, thinking that was the reassurance Toric wanted.

"Of course I do!" Toric flicked his fingers again impatiently. "What I *need* is to be distanced, officially, from whatever that lot is now up to."

"What could they be up to?" There were not that many Oldtimers to be effective at anything: both men and dragons were old, tired and more pathetic than dangerous. Except T'kul—lately no hold woman was safe from that womanizer.

"If I knew, I wouldn't worry. I do so now, officially, in the presence of two journeyman harpers, disclaim any knowledge or part in any Southern dragonrider activity."

"Heard and witnessed," Saneter said, and Piemur echoed the formal words. "But I do think that you should inform the Weyrleaders. They are, after all, the best ones to deal with other dragonriders."

"They can't, and they won't," Toric said, his voice grating angrily, "interfere with the Oldtimers. They made that clear enough to me."

"At least Benden keeps *its* word," Piemur muttered, aware of just how much latitude Toric had given himself after his discussion two Turns before with the Benden Weyrleaders. When Toric gave him a cold and calculating stare, Piemur held up both hands in apology for his impudence. "I could send Farli—if I can get my hands on her—with a warning to T'gellan that the Oldtimers have all vacated. You owe Benden that."

Toric considered, scowling and rattling his fingers on the worktable.

"I did report those peculiar exercises they were doing a few days ago, popping in and out of *between*. It still makes no sense, but maybe the Weyr can figure it out." Piemur realized that Toric would rather see the Oldtimers do something so dire and unforgivable that the Northern Weyrs would be forced to confront the problem they posed.

Neither could have guessed what the Oldtimers were attempting until three days later. Abruptly Mnementh appeared in the sky over Southern, Ramoth following a second later, swooping across the Hold clearing toward the Weyr. Piemur was astonished enough to see the two great Benden dragons, but when he realized that they were riderless, his heart began to pound with dread. Had some incredible disaster occurred in Benden? What could possibly have caused Mnementh and Ramoth to come here on their own? He raced for Toric's hold to find the holder and old Saneter outside, staring skyward in consternation.

"Why would dragons come here without their riders?" Toric asked, his eyes never leaving the beasts as they wheeled above the Weyr, heads down, eyes a brilliant orange. "Those are too big to be Oldtimer beasts."

"It's Ramoth and Mnementh," Piemur replied, his anxiety increasing as he noted the color of their eyes.

"What are they doing here?" Toric's voice sounded slightly strained.

"I'm not sure I want to know," Piemur admitted, shading his eyes and hoping to see the dragons' eyes turning a less agitated shade.

"They're searching the Weyr. What for?" Saneter asked in a fearful murmur.

Suddenly Ramoth flung her head up, uttering the most poignantly sorrowful cry Piemur had ever heard. Not the keen of mourning, but a weird and terrible anguished plaint. Despite the heat of the day he shuddered, the flesh on his arms rising in chill bumps. Even Toric paled slightly, and Saneter gave a moan. Mnementh's deeper voice echoed his queen's in a discordant tone that increased the pathos of their call.

Then, as abruptly as they had arrived, the two dragons disappeared. For a long moment, the holder and the two harpers remained motionless. Finally Toric exhaled in gusty relief. "Now what was that all about, Piemur?"

Piemur shook his head. "Whatever's happened, it's bad."

"Bloody Oldtimers! If they've compromised me . . ." Toric shook his fist at the Weyr.

"Oh!" Saneter's astonished exclamation brought their attention to the nine bronzes that were sweeping in. One circled to land, while the others began a quartering search, their feet flicking the topmost foliage, making it look as if they were walking on the forest roof.

"That's Lioth and N'ton," Piemur said. He was relieved until he saw the bronze rider's dark expression as he dismounted and strode purposefully up to them. Then anxiety came flooding back. "Ramoth and Mnementh were just here—riderless. What's happened?"

"Ramoth's queen egg has been stolen from the Hatching Ground."

"Stolen?" The word erupted from Toric's lips as he stared with utter disbelief at the bronze rider. Saneter gasped and covered his eyes. Piemur swore.

"It is regrettable that we hesitated to inform you of their recent erratic behavior—" Toric lifted both hands in mute apology. "But who would have expected them to commit such a heinous crime against the Weyrs?" He sounded unusually subdued. "How could they hope to . . . how could that help? Where could they *hide*—no, not here!" He lifted his hands, fending off the mere hint of any complicity. "Search! Search!" He gestured expansively. "Look everywhere!"

"It is apparently a matter of every*when*," N'ton said grimly. Piemur groaned, suddenly understanding the significance of the Oldtimers' latest exercises: They had been practicing going *between* times, a dangerous use of draconic abilities, even for the best of reasons—which Lessa's famous ride had been, but which stealing an egg was not.

Toric looked inquiringly at N'ton, expecting an explanation; then he gave Piemur a hard and significant look.

"Toric has nothing to hide, N'ton," Piemur said solemnly, recalling their recent interview and Toric's request. "Saneter and I give you our oath on that!"

N'ton nodded gravely and returned to Lioth, springing to take his place on the bronze's back. Toric and the two harpers watched until the dragons had swept beyond their line of sight, frantically inspecting the surrounding forest.

"What do we do now?" Toric asked in a low voice.

"Hope," Piemur replied, wishing fervently that he had sent Farli when he could. Although who could have suspected those depraved fools to be mad enough to *steal* an egg from Ramoth? How could any strange dragons have got into the Benden Hatching Ground? Ramoth rarely left it. And how could they have left the Ground without being intercepted?

The next few hours were exceedingly anxious. But just when Piemur had made himself ill with imagining the consequences—for the Oldtimers as well as for Southern Hold—Tris, N'ton's brown fire-lizard, appeared with a message on his leg for Piemur. He was also wearing an intricate neck design, an addition so recent that the paint still glistened.

Unrolling the message as he ran, Piemur raced for Toric's office. "It's all right, Toric! The egg's back!"

"What? How? Let me see!" Toric grabbed the note from Piemur's hands and, with unusual openness, muttered the tightly written words aloud.

"The egg has been returned—no one knows by what agency. Ramoth had left the clutch to eat. Three bronzes appeared, and before the watchdragon realized their intent, they'd flown into the Ground. Ramoth screamed, but the bronzes were away and between with the queen egg before she could act. As you will appreciate, Ramoth and Mnementh suspected the Oldtimers and instantly overflew the Southern Weyr without finding any trace. It was then obvious that the absconding dragons had gone between time to secure their theft. Before a disciplinary move could be made, the egg was returned. One moment it was not in the Hatching Ground, in the next breath it was there. However, it was taken somewhen for long enough to be quite hard, a condition that incenses the Weyrwoman, for it confirms the

*elapse of considerable time. Where is not known. The Oldtimers
are suspected, for what other Weyr would steal what it can
produce? Master Robinton urged caution and deliberation, even
spoke out against a punitive search, and has been peremptorily
dismissed from Benden Weyr. N'ton."*

"So!" Toric said, leaning back in his chair. He tapped the
message against his desk. "So the Oldtimers have compromised only themselves. That is a relief."

"If you see it as one," Piemur murmured, and abruptly
strode out of the hold. Toric could be as relieved as he wished,
but Piemur was far from easy. The Masterharper exiled from
Benden? That was bloody awful. The more he thought of the
consequences of such an estrangement, the more depressed
he became. It had come so frighteningly near the worst catastrophe that could afflict Pern—dragon fighting dragon. Those
accursed Oldtimers! What consummate fools! Especially T'kul,
who undoubtedly had instigated the senseless scheme. There
would be retribution for their act, and Piemur devoutly hoped
that the future of Southern Hold—and Toric's ambitions—had
not been jeopardized. But he worried most of all about Master
Robinton's anomalous situation.

The Oldtimers returned late that afternoon. It was a small
satisfaction to Piemur, when Toric sent him to check, to note the
utter dejection and the drained color of every single Oldtimer
dragon. The dragons were too exhausted by their failure even
to eat and most of the riders were intent on getting very drunk.

"That's nothing new," Toric replied when Piemur reported
to him. "Shards, but I don't think there's much to choose
between Northern and Southern dragonriders," Toric went
on, pacing the length of his workroom. He did not seem to
notice that he was kicking furniture out of his way and knock-
ing objects off tables with impatient sweeps of his hands. He
had kept his temper during the day and was still wound tight
as a screw. "But how could I have suspected they'd try something like stealing Ramoth's queen egg? Believe me, boy, T'kul

and those randy riders of his *did* steal that egg. No question of it in my mind.'' Piemur nodded agreement, hoping Toric would just leave matters lie for a while. ''I should have guessed that they'd be desperate for a queen to mate with those bronzes while there's enough energy in any of them to fly her. I'd say they waited too long! I don't know who did restore Ramoth's egg, but by Faranth, I'm grateful to him. It was close there today, boy. Damned close. Those Northern dragons could have charred everything—Hold and Weyr.'' Another wide sweep of Toric's hand knocked Records to the floor. ''I don't like the Oldtimers, but not even I would want dragon to fight dragon.''

''Don't even think about it, Toric,'' Piemur said and shivered. That possibility had been so frighteningly imminent.

''For a little while there, I saw everything I've worked twenty Turns to accomplish about to be ruined.'' Another sweep of Toric's arm knocked a glowbasket from the wall bracket and spilled its contents over the Records. Piemur grabbed them out of the way and closed the basket, stamping at the spillage. ''I'm going to set a watch on those Oldtimers, Piemur. I'll have Saneter draw up a roster. I can't let something else happen. I was hoping to have a few words with F'lar . . .'' Piemur nearly choked at that bit of arrogance. ''No, I guess this wasn't the time for it,'' the holder added with a rueful shake of his head. ''That Masterharper of yours has good ideas. I'd like you to get in touch with him about this.'' Toric turned to look sharply at Piemur.

The boy cleared his throat and scratched his head, avoiding Toric's eyes. He did not wish to mention Master Robinton's now tenuous influence on the Benden Weyrleaders.

''I took a close look at the dragons, Toric, and honestly, I think time is on your side. Stealing the egg, and I agree with you that they did even if Benden couldn't prove it, took almost every ounce of strength they had. I think you're absolutely right that we should keep a discreet watch on them. It'd be easier if the fire-lizards would go anywhere near the

Weyr, but Farli's still chattering about dragons flaming her. Have yours?''

''I haven't had time for fire-lizards today, with full-grown Northern dragons breathing firestone stench in my face,'' Toric replied acidly.

''So this time we inform Benden Weyr the moment suspicious behavior starts,'' Piemur went on blithely, hoping to talk Toric out of any plans that included Master Robinton. ''I want to tell you, Toric, I really admired the way you handled yourself with N'ton!''

''Thank you,'' Toric said sarcastically.

''You're welcome,'' Piemur snapped back in the same tone. Then he grinned smugly and remarked with calculated insolence. ''You'd have been in far worse case if Saneter and I hadn't stood your witness!''

At that reminder, Toric reacted, first with a hard stare and then with a bellow of laughter. ''Yes, you and old Saneter did come across, and for that I am genuinely grateful, Journeyman Harper.''

''Indebted, in fact,'' Piemur suggested with a wry grin.

''Now, another thing . . .'' Toric—the laugh had relaxed him a little—sat on the edge of his worktable, arms folded across his chest, his right hand fiddling with the holder knot on his shoulder. ''You've ridden dragons. Just how much do you think they saw?''

Piemur snorted. ''Shards, Toric, they were looking for a place an egg could harden, or for Oldtimer browns and bronzes. They wouldn't have noticed anything else in the state they were in. Well, T'bor might have, but you've been mighty careful where you've allowed all our new arrivals to site their holds.'' Piemur grinned slyly. ''Hamian's mine would appear to be basically the same from the air; all the other adits look like the holes in the ground they are; the wharf and hold on Island River shouldn't be visible from the sky; Big Lagoon Hold is large, that's true, and there'd have been fishing ships out in that direction . . .'' Piemur shrugged. ''Maybe later

T'bor or F'nor, someone familiar with Southern, will ask some awkward questions. I doubt it. The interdiction still holds. They came to retrieve the egg. It got back all by itself. They left." Piemur was beginning to suspect who might have returned the egg, but he had absolutely no evidence with which to prove it.

"And we still have those bloody Oldtimers to deal with." But there was less force in the kick Toric gave the table leg.

"They haven't hindered your plans all that much, now, have they?" Piemur said drolly. "What they don't know won't hurt them. I'd bide my time, Toric."

"You're with me, then?"

"If today didn't prove that, I don't know what will," Piemur said, cocking his head to one side. He liked Toric, admired him, but he did not entirely trust him. Which was fair. Toric did not completely trust Piemur, especially not too often in Sharra's company. Piemur had noticed how Toric tried to keep them apart; the holder had just given Sharra her long-sought permission to go on an adventurous trip south, beyond Hamian's mines. "So, if we're back to normal tomorrow, I'd like to see what's beyond that headland east of Island River. Maybe even get as far as the cove that Menolly found when they were storm-lost." He noticed the alertness in Toric's eyes. The holder had not liked that inadvertent excursion; he had always been suspicious of just how far Menolly and the Masterharper had gone, though he could never deny that they *had* been storm-driven, and that only Menolly's sea skills had kept the small boat afloat. "A dragon can't go *between* to a place he's never seen," Piemur reminded the Southerner. "Likewise, a man can't hold what he hasn't beheld! How about it, Toric?"

Stupid led the way out of the brushland, pushing through the tangle with his sturdy front end, his hide too tough to be pierced by branch and thorn. From above, Farli was giving directions, and Piemur thrashed at the vegetation with the thick blade Hamian had forged for him.

He came out on a beach that sloped down to the sea, a pale green expanse of water ruffled with whitecaps from the on-shore breeze. He sighed at the splendid view, then looked back the way he had come, at the thick trees waving their fronds and leaves. He took a redfruit from the pack on Stupid's back, nicked it expertly with his chopper, and sucked at the sweet, thirst-quenching flesh. Stupid complained. He chopped off a hunk and fed it to the little runnerbeast, who munched contentedly.

But when Piemur turned to look down the narrow bay, he froze. He could not believe his eyes. He fumbled for the small distance-viewer he had wheedled away from Master Rampesi, who had just received a more powerful device from Starmaster Wansor; it had not done him much good with his nighttime star-gazing, but it had been useful in surveying terrain. When he had focused it, there was no doubt that smoke was rising languidly from the chimney of a good-sized building, high up on the riverbank. It was roofed, big, and had a wide porch, probably on all four sides, with steps leading up to it on the two sides visible to him. Other buildings, large and small, were positioned nearby, making it a sizable settlement. A small sloop was drawn up on the shore, although he could see the stumps of pilings jutting out into the river that might once have been a pier, and fishnets hung on a rack to dry. Colored fishnets! Even through the distance-viewer, he could make out the yellows, greens, blues, and reds.

"There isn't anyone in all this part of the world, Stupid. There just isn't. I haven't seen anyone in months. Toric certainly doesn't know. Shipwreck?" Piemur searched his memory. There had been quite a few shipwrecks—and the number was growing. "That's what they are. Shipwrecked. And colored fishnets? Toric won't like this."

A fair of fire-lizards appeared overhead, but they did not fly low enough for him to get a close look. Farli joined them in the usual aerial dance. He had seen numerous fire-lizard nests along the coast, even some unplundered golds. But Toric had definitely stated that there would be no more trade of eggs with the north. Farli swooped to his shoulder, wrapping her tail about his neck and chittering unintelligibly about men and lots of things piled on the beach.

"Houses are not piles," Piemur stated firmly. But the incident with the northern dragons had taught him to pay attention to Farli's incomprehensible statements. For the last few days she had been trying to tell him something that she had learned only recently. Eventually it would all make sense to him, just as he had deciphered her comments about the Black Rock River, which they had had such trouble negotiating. He had not expected such an immense inland sea, with distant islands lost in the misty rain.

Piemur's cautionary instinct had sharpened on the long and solitary eastward journey. And though he was eager to talk to someone besides himself, he was also strangely loath to initiate a meeting. Nevertheless he proceeded down the long strand to the river's mouth, struggling up dunes and treading carefully through the salt grasses, prodding ahead of his feet with his snake-stick, Stupid a pace behind him, Farli swooping up and back, flitting away and returning.

There were people, she told him, but not the men. Not the other men.

It was almost time for the precipitous sunset of those parts when Piemur finally got close enough to see that some of the buildings were derelict, with plants growing out of the windows and through cracks in the roofs. Several were bigger than anything Toric had yet permitted to be built, and they tended to be more wide open to air and sun than anyone dared build in the north, though the facing material was beautifully fit stone. The roofs seemed to be sheer slabs, finger thick. He remembered the exceedingly durable mine props that Hamian had found solidly in place after who knew how many Turns.

And there were people. He dropped down on the sand, getting a mouthful, when he saw a man walking from what had to be a beasthold toward the steps of the wide verandah. Canines, large ones to judge by their deep voices, began to bark somewhere behind the house.

"Ara!" The man's call brought a woman out of the house, followed by a toddling child. There was a touching moment of embrace, then the man scooped the child up and, with one arm around the woman, entered the house.

"A family, Stupid. There's a family living here, with a big house, lots of rooms, more than three people need. Why'd they build it so big? Or are there others inside?"

Four fire-lizards, two gold, a bronze, and a brown, suddenly came out of nowhere and hovered on wing above him before disappearing. Although Farli was not alarmed, Piemur was.

"O-ho, we've been spotted. Well, fire-lizard friends can't be all bad, can they, Stupid? Let's go forth like brave men and get this over with." He got to his feet and approached the building, shouting at the top of his well-trained lungs. *"Hello the house! Let's hope there's enough dinner for four, huh, Stupid? Hello there!"*

There was glad astonishment and a warm, if shy, welcome from the shipwrecked couple, as well as an immediate invitation to share their meal, which was cooking over a most fascinating stove. The man, Jayge, tanned and well-muscled, was several Turns older and taller by several handwidths than the harper. He had an open face, a nose slightly bent out of line from some brawl, light-colored eyes, and a steady gaze. He wore a sleeveless vest and short pants of roughly spun cotton, and around his lean hips was a fine leather belt from which hung a bone-handled knife. On his feet were rather ingenious sandals that protected toes and heels but were open across the foot. They looked much more comfortable and cooler than the heavy boots Piemur wore.

Ara was younger, with an appealing face that looked both innocent and yet was oddly mature; at times she looked sad. Her black hair was braided down her back, but curls escaped the plait to frame her face. She wore a loose, sleeveless cotton dress, dyed a deep red and embroidered on scoop neck and hem, a narrow leather belt dyed a red to match her dress, and red leather sandals. She was utterly charming, and Piemur did not miss Jayge's proud and proprietary gaze.

While Piemur ate his way through the best meal he had eaten since he had left Southern, he listened to Jayge and Ara tell of their adventures, occasionally throwing in a question or a comment to encourage them to add details.

"We were hired at Keroon Beastmasterhold," Jayge told him, "about thirty months ago—we lost an accurate track of time in the storm and during our first days here. We were transporting some expensive breeding stock for Master Rampesi, to be delivered to Holder Toric at the Southern Hold. Would you know him?"

"I do. I remember how mad Rampesi was when he had to admit your ship must have gone down. You were lucky to survive."

"We very nearly didn't," Jayge said, giving Ara a sideways glance and laying his arm across her shoulders, his expression tenderly amused. "Ara here insists that we were dragged to shore by shipfish."

"Quite likely," Piemur assured him, grinning at Jayge's surprise and Ara's triumphant cry. "Every Masterfisherman worth his knots will agree: Master Rampesi has told me of men falling overboard and being lifted up by shipfish. He's seen the phenomenon himself, and he's not given to harper tales. That's why Fishcrafthallers are so glad to see them escorting a ship out to sea. Means good luck."

"But the storm was incredibly powerful," Jayge objected.

"So are they—and quite at home in stormy seas. You're the only survivors?"

When Ara looked stricken, Jayge answered quickly. "No, but one man was so badly hurt, we never even learned his name. Festa and Scallak had broken leg and arm bones; I'd snapped my wrist and a few ribs; but Ara set us all and healed us straight." He twisted his left hand to prove the mend, smiling at Ara. "We were quite a sight then, only three good arms and four legs among us, except for Ara, who nursed and fed us all." He shot his young wife a look of such tender pride that Piemur almost blushed. "We were getting along fine here, even tamed some wild beasts—Ara's got a gift with animals—when first Festa and then Scallak caught some kind of a fever, terrible headaches . . . they went blind." He broke off, frowning at the memory.

"Fire-head, probably," Piermur said, breaking the silence to relieve Ara's obvious distress at the memory. "It has a high mortality rate if you don't know the cure."

"There is one?" Ara's eyes widened. "I tried everything I knew. I felt so helpless, and ever since I've been afraid. . ."

"Don't fret yourself. Look—" Piemur hauled his pack over and pulled out a small vial, which he handed to her. "I've medicine here. Instructions on it, as you see. Just don't go near beaches stained yellow. It's at its worst in mid- or late spring. And now that we know where you are, I'll see that Sharra—she's had Healer Hall training—sends you a record of symptoms and treatment for some of the southern nasties."

"I hope we've found most of them," Jayge said with a rueful grin, rubbing the scar on his forearm. Piemur recognized the blemish as an old needlethorn infection.

"That's the hard way to learn what to avoid. I'd say you'd done pretty well here." Piemur was fascinated with the material of the house.

"We *found* all this," Jayge said, his gesture including the house and the buildings beyond.

"*Found* it?"

Jayge grinned, his teeth very white in his tanned face. He had curious yellow-green eyes, with flecks of dark in them, and a one-sided smile that Piemur liked. "Found the whole settlement. Mind you, it saved our lives. There were appalling storms for weeks after we were swept in here." He paused, hesitant. "I didn't think anyone had been allowed to settle in the south, except at Southern Hold. This isn't part of Southern, is it, and we just didn't search far enough west?"

"Ah, to be honest with you . . ." Piemur hesitated only a moment, for Toric could not possibly expect to claim the entire south. "No, this isn't Southern Hold!" Seeing that his vehemence had surprised both Jayge and Ara, he smiled to reassure them. "You're a long way from where you were supposed to land those beasts. A long way." Piemur decided it would also be a very long time before Toric discovered their existence. "Hold hard to what you've got here," he added blithely, and looked admiringly around at the gracious proportions of the room in which they ate. With its wide windows, louvered on the inside, it was unlike even freestanding hold rooms. The inside walls were not of the same stone as the outside and were colored very cool green blue. Jayge had fashioned sconces for candles Ara had made from berry wax, so the room was pleasantly lit. "How big is this house you *found*?"

"More than we need right now," Ara said, swatting at Jayge affectionately when he winked at Piemur. Though her figure was not yet distorted, the harper had suspected she might be pregnant again. There was a luminous quality to her eyes and face that Sharra had told him often enhanced the beauty of a gravid woman. "Twelve rooms, but some would be awfully small to house a whole family. We had to shovel out the sand in the front rooms. The walls were filthy; I was afraid we'd have to scrub them clean, but the dirt sort of slid off when we washed them. I haven't quite got the stains completely off, but now you can see what pretty colors they used."

"We fixed this roof with slabs taken from the other ones," Jayge said. "I've never seen material like this before. And we shouldn't have been able to nail it, but Ara found a keg of nails that would penetrate and hold."

After a moment's hesitation, Ara went on with an air of confession. "The house is unusual, but the thick walls keep us cool in the heat of the day and warm enough on cold ones. We found the strangest-looking containers, most of them empty. Jayge laughs at me, but I know we'll find something to tell us who lived here before we did."

"I'd like to know when you do," Piemur said. "Did you find those colored fishnets here?"

They both grinned, exchanging glances, and Jayge explained. "We found lots of empty nets stored in one corner of the largest building. It had neither porch nor windows but it did have vents along the roof, so we figured it may have been a storehouse. Snakes and other insects had destroyed whatever was in the crates and barrels and those nets, but the material they were made of seems indestructible."

"It'd have to be, to last any length of time here in the south," Piemur said casually, though he was more excited about the settlement than he dared express. The Harper should know about it. He wondered if he should send Farli with a message to Master Robinton but decided that it could wait until morning. "So you've fished, and you've stock . . ."

"I'll have to introduce you to the dogs tomorrow," Ara said. "We have them against snakes and big spotted cats."

"You have them here, too?" Piemur asked eagerly. Sharra had thought those cats a local sport—she would be interested to know that they inhabited other parts of the Southern Continent.

"Enough so that we don't hunt without the dogs," Jayge said. "And we carry spear or bow and arrow once we pass the clearings."

"But there's wild rice," Ara put in enthusiastically, "and all kinds of vegetables—even a grove of the oldest fellis trees

I've ever seen!'' She waved to the east of the hold. ''We've floods of wild wherry, and runner and herd beasts grazing in the river valley, a day's good run from here. Jayge is a good spearman.''

''And you've never missed with bow and arrow,'' Jayge said proudly. ''And—'' Jayge grinned at Piemur. ''We've a fair home brew.'' He went to a wall cupboard, fashioned out of one of the crates he had mentioned, and opened it to display two small barrels, their shape reminiscent of much larger ones Piemur had seen at the Benden Mastervintner's. ''We've been experimenting,'' Jayge went on, pouring three cups and serving them. ''And it's improving!''

Piemur sniffed and found its aroma odd, not as fruity as he had expected. He took a sip.

''Ooooh, that's great stuff!'' His appreciation was genuine as he felt the shock of it coursing pleasantly through him. He raised his cup to the smiling Ara and Jayge in a toast. ''To friends, near and far!''

''I think it'll improve with age,'' Jayge remarked with quiet satisfaction after he and Ara had solemnly returned the toast. ''But for a trader's brew, it's passable.''

''I could be prejudiced, or maybe I've just lost my palate, but Jayge, this's smooth to lip, mouth, and throat, and a tonic to blood and bone.''

They talked long into the crystal clear, chill early hours of the morning until sheer fatigue slowed both question and answer. If Piemur had extracted from them an account of their establishment there, he had replied with eagerly received news of the North—expurgated, of course, and embellished when the incident deserved his harper's touch. Piemur had introduced himself with rank, craft, and hold affiliation and explained that his current task was to explore the coast. Jayge had responded that he was a trader by craft and that Ara was from Igen. There was something that they were not revealing, Piemur was quick enough to realize, but then, he had not told them the entire truth either.

Piemur remained with Jayge and Ara for longer than he should have. Not only did he admire their fortitude and industry—even Toric would consider them resourceful and diligent—but also he wanted time to delve into the mystery of the buildings there on the far edge of nowhere. In the oldest of the Harper Hall Records, there had been elusive fragments, which Piemur, as Master Robinton's special apprentice, had been allowed to see. *When man came to Pern, he established a good Hold in the South*, one fragment had begun, only to conclude ambiguously, *but found it necessary to move north to shield*. Like Robinton, Piemur had always wondered why anyone would have left the beautiful and fertile Southern Continent and settle the far harsher north. But it must have happened—the discovery of the ancient mine had been evidence of that. And now these incredible buildings!

Piemur could not imagine how building materials could have lasted so long. It could only be more of those forgotten methods and lost secrets that Mastersmith Fandarel had complained about so often, and which his Crafthall was trying to revive.

That first morning, with young Readis toddling when he could and carried when he tired, Jayge and Ara showed Piemur around what had clearly once been an extensive settlement.

"We've torn down most of the creepers and shoveled out some of the blown sand," Jayge said, leading the way into a one-room building. The two big, rangy canines—the black one was Chink and the brindle, Giri—always preceded their masters into buildings and rooms, an exercise to which they had clearly been trained. A snap of fingers brought them back to heel, or sit, or stay. "We found this." Jayge pointed to a piece of enameled metal, a man's hand wide and two arms long, leaning against the inside wall.

"There's lettering on it," Piemur said, angling to one side to read it. "P A R . . . can't read the next one . . . D I S . . . nor the next." He hunkered down and fingered the metal.

" 'RIVER' is perfectly legible!" He grinned at Ara, then tried to decipher the final word. "Looks like 'stake' to me."

"We think the first word is 'Paradise,' " Ara said shyly.

Piemur glanced out the open door to the idyllic surroundings, peaceful, private, beautiful with blossom and fruit. "I'd say that was a fair description," he said.

"I'm positive this was a teaching room," Ara went on in an embarrassed rush. "We found these!" She hefted Readis into his father's arms and beckoned Piemur to a corner where she lifted the cover of a box of the ubiquitous opaque material. She held up a short, fat record, neatly squared off like one of Lord Asgenar's newly bound leaves.

As Piemur turned it in his hand, its texture, despite the stains of age, was somehow soapy. The leaves fell open to clever illustrations so humorous that he smiled; he glanced at the words beneath them—short sentences all, and the letters, while recognizable, were absurdly big and bold. Master Arnor would never have let Harper Hall apprentices waste so much space; he taught them to write in small but legible letters, so that more could be crammed onto each page of hide.

"Clearly a youngster's book," he agreed. "But no teaching song I've ever read."

"I can't imagine what these were," Ara said, holding up some flat rectangular objects, fingerlength and fingernail thin. "Even if they are numbered. And this . . ." She drew out a second, slimmer lesson book.

"I don't know how much figuring a harper has to do," Jayge said, "but it's far beyond a trader's need."

Piemur recognized the combinations as equations, far more complicated than those Wansor had managed to drum into his head for use in figuring distances. He grinned, anticipating the expression on the Starsmith's face when he opened that book.

"I know someone who might like to look at that," he said casually.

"Take it with you," Jayge replied. "It's no good to us."

Piemur shook his head regretfully. "I'd be afraid to lose it in my travels. If it's lasted this long, it can wait here awhile longer." Then he made a show of examining the box itself, which was made of more of that strange and durable material, without joins at its corners. "Master Fandarel is going to drive himself crazy trying to duplicate this material. How far have you gone inland and along the coast?" he asked Jayge.

"Three days west and two east." Jayge shrugged. "More coves and forests. Before he took sick, Scallak and I followed the river, oh, four or five days, to where there's a deep bend in its course. We could see mountains in the distance, but the river valley was much the same as it is here."

"And no one else," Ara added.

"You're lucky I came!" Piemur spread out his arms, smiling mischievously to lighten their somberness.

On his second night he brought out his reed flute and the multiple pipes he had made, copying Menolly's design, to cheer his lonely evenings. Jayge and Ara were grateful to hear music, Jayge mumbling along in a raspy light baritone while Ara lilted in a clear, sweet soprano. He showed them both the rudiments of playing and made them pipes.

Piemur made an outline of their holding, noting the positions of the restored house and each of the ruins. He knew exactly how far a man could walk the coast in a day and marked out an appropriate border on each side of the river. An inland boundary would have to wait, but he mentioned Jayge's bend. He witnessed the sketch and wrapped it apart from his other records, to keep until he had a chance to discuss it with Master Robinton. If the Harper proved still too estranged from Benden, then he would speak to T'gellan about Jayge and Ara. If necessary, he would stand witness for them with Toric and the Weyrleaders himself.

He made Farli memorize the unique landmarks so that she could find her way back to the Paradise River Hold. Observing that exercise, Ara and Jayge asked him about his fire-lizard. They had Impressed eight between them—two queens, three bronzes, and three browns—but they had not trained them to any particular duties, apart from watching out for Readis's cry. So on the fourth day, Piemur helped them with the most basic training. They were amazed at how well the creatures responded.

On the fifth morning, when Piemur went to the spacious beasthold to feed Stupid, he found Meer and Talla perched on Stupid's back. Meer had a message from Sharra strapped to his bronze leg.

"They can even carry messages?" Ara asked, surprised.

"Useful that way, though they have to know where they're going." Piemur's reply was somewhat distracted, for the message told him that Jaxom was gravely ill with fire-head at the Masterharper's Cove. How Sharra knew where that was, Piemur could not guess. He himself had been hunting for that particular cove for the past three months. "I've got to leave. A friend needs me," he added. "Look, Farli now knows who you are and where you are. As soon as I can, I'll send you a message by her. When you've got it, just tell her to find Stupid—who isn't."

He gave Jayge a friendly clout on the back, made bold to hug Ara, and tweaked Readis's chin, making the little fellow giggle. Then he started off in an easterly direction, wondering why Jayge did not come after him, demanding what he expected to find in that direction.

11

SOUTHERN CONTINENT,
PP 15.08.28–15.10.15

Saneter had never felt so ineffective, though since coming to Southern, Toric had given him a good deal of practice. The old harper fervently wished that Piemur was not somewhere tramping through the eastern wilds; that Sharra, who was always clever at diverting her older brother, was not who-knew-where nursing Lord Jaxom of Ruatha Hold. Only the previous day her bronze had arrived with a message reporting that she could not yet leave her patient. Toric had irritably demanded to know how long it took to recover from the disease.

The current catastrophe added insult to Toric's list of aggravations. T'kul on Salth and B'zon on Ranilth were both missing from the Southern Weyr. The remaining dragons, despite their frailty, were creating the most dreadful din, making everyone uneasy and certainly exacerbating the volatile Southern holder. Furthermore, every fire-lizard in the hold had streaked off, just when Toric urgently needed one.

"How," Toric demanded, kicking at the furniture in his

workroom, "can I get word to Benden Weyr when there isn't a fire-lizard to send?"

"They never fly off like that for very long," Saneter suggested hopefully.

"Well, they're gone now, and now is when I need to inform Benden of this development. It may be critical. Surely you realize that." With a savage scowl, Toric kicked a chair out of his way. He whirled on the elderly harper, pointing a thick forefinger at him. "You must bear me witness in this! I had no means to send an urgent message, and that wretched journeyman is gone when I need him most! My hold may depend on informing Benden! *How*, Saneter? *How?*" Toric bellowed.

For one horrified second, Saneter heard an echo of that shout. Only it was not precisely an echo of Toric's bellow. It was the sort of noise that lifted the hair on the back of the neck, the keening that Saneter was all too familiar with: dragons announcing the death of one of their kind.

"*Who?*" Toric demanded of the walls at the top of his voice. He wheeled to Saneter, then obviously remembered that the old harper was unable to run any errands and charged from the chamber in search of an answer.

Toric was halfway down the path between hold and Weyr when a bronze dragon, giving a consoling bugle, swooped in over his head to land before the Weyrhall. Toric did not recognize the rider when he stripped off helmet and flying gear and stood looking around him. The keening of the resident dragons, however, had dropped to a bearable moan, and the unfamiliar bronze changed his tone to something that sounded, even to Toric, like encouragement.

"Dragonrider, I'm Toric of Southern. Which dragon died?" The Southerner strode across the clearing, taking the measure of the older man. Despite his fury and frustration, Toric found some reassurance in the confident manner in which the dragonrider awaited him.

"D'ram, rider of Tiroth, formerly Weyrleader of Ista. F'lar has asked me to assume the leadership of Southern. Other young riders have volunteered to help and will arrive shortly."

"Who died?" Toric demanded again, impatience getting the better of courtesy.

"Salth. Ranilth is badly spent but may recover. He and B'zon remain at Ista." D'ram spoke with such deep sorrow that Toric felt the tacit rebuke.

"What happened?" he asked more politely. "We knew the bronzes were missing, but so," he added through clenched teeth, "was every fire-lizard we could have sent to warn Benden."

D'ram nodded acknowledgement of Toric's quandary. "T'kul and B'zon brought their bronzes to Caylith's mating flight, which had been thrown open to decide the new Istan Weyrleader. Salth burst his heart trying to fly the queen . . ." D'ram paused, terribly distraught, then sighed heavily and continued without meeting Toric's eyes. "Having nothing to lose by it, T'kul challenged F'lar."

"F'lar is dead?" Toric was appalled, seeing all he had worked so hard to obtain lost through more of T'kul's stupidity.

"No, the Benden Weyrleader was the stronger. He mourns T'kul's death as all dragonriders do." D'ram gave Toric such a challenging look that Toric nodded in a gesture that was close to apology.

"I can't say I'm sorry T'kul is dead," Toric replied, though he was careful to speak with no heat, "or Salth. They've both run mad and uncontrolled ever since T'ron—and Fidranth— died." Toric had struggled to recall T'ron's dragon's name. But he was rapidly realizing, and hoping, that F'lar's appointment of a new Weyrleader heralded the changes he had so long sought: open commerce with the North, allowing his hold to expand as he had always planned.

Just then Mardra appeared, sobbing hysterically in a maudlin show of grief that disgusted Toric, who knew very well how often she had quarrelled with T'kul. He excused himself, telling D'ram that the Weyrleader had only to ask what he could do to assist him.

"There will be other dragonriders joining me here, both Oldtimers and those of this Pass. You will see the Weyr restored," D'ram said with quiet confidence before he went to comfort Mardra.

Toric walked slowly back to his Hold, deep in thought about the implications of such a promise. Anything would be an improvement—just so long as it was not a hindrance. How was he to retrieve Sharra? How was he to contact Piemur? He needed the quick wit and solid Northern associations of that devious young man more than he had remotely appreciated. It was then that he noticed the return of the Hold's fire-lizard population. But when his little queen tried to settle on his shoulder, chittering agitatedly about something, he was in no mood to heed her.

The cove that Piemur had heard so much about from Menolly and Master Robinton was every bit as beautiful as they had said. A perfect deep half-circle, with wide sandy beaches sloping slightly upward to meet the lush forests, trees and shrubs a riot of colorful blossom and leaf. Ripe fruit was evident on a half dozen trees. And he had seen no snakes, their absence due, no doubt, to the presence of Ruth, Jaxom's dragon. A rough building was set well back in the shade, a well-trodden path leading to it from the shore. The water, ranging from a pale green to the deeper blue of greater depths, was deceptively pellucid, and the gentlest of waves rolled over the sand.

"So Sharra," he said after the three had exchanged joyful greetings. "What is it that Meer, Talla, and Farli are trying to tell me? And where's Ruth?"

"You'd better sit down, Piemur," Sharra said gently.

Piemur stood stolidly on both feet, his expression belligerent. "I can hear it just as well standing!"

Sharra and Jaxom exchanged looks that spoke too loudly to Piemur of a well-developed understanding—and of something he was not going to like to hear.

"T'kul and B'zon tried to fly the Istan queen Caylith this morning," Jaxom began. "Salth burst his heart, T'kul attacked F'lar—are you all right?" Piemur had sat down, very hard, his face ashen under the dark tan.

"F'lar's alive, unhurt," Sharra cried, going to Piemur's side and slipping an arm about his shoulders. "B'zon and Ranilth will stay at Ista awhile."

"D'ram is now Southern Weyrleader." Jaxom added.

"Really?" Piemur's color returned, and mischief glittered briefly in his eyes. "Toric's going to love that. Another Oldtimer to deal with."

"D'ram's different," Jaxom said encouragingly. "You'll see."

"Well, that's not so bad. A change in the wind always helps." Piemur glanced at Sharra to see if she had considered what the new development might mean to Toric's ambitions, but the distress on her face had not lessened. He turned back to Jaxom. "And?"

"Master Robinton has had a heart attack!"

"That arrogant, addlepated, insufferably egotistical, altruistic know-it-all!" Piemur shouted, springing to his feet. "He thinks Pern won't manage without his meddling, without him knowing everything that happens in every Hold and Hall on the entire planet, North and South! He won't eat properly, he doesn't rest enough, and he won't let us help him even though we could probably do the same job even better than he can because we have more sense in our left toenails than he does." He knew that Sharra and Jaxom were staring at him, but he could not stop. "He's wasteful of his strength, he never listens to anyone, even when we *try* to get him to see sense, and he's got this wild idea that only he, the Masterharper of Pern, has any idea of the destiny of Weyr, Hold, and Hall.

Well, this serves him right. Maybe now he'll listen. Maybe now . . .''

Tears came to Piemur's eyes, and he stared from one to the other, begging them to say that it was all some kind of hideous joke. Sharra embraced him again, and Jaxom awkwardly patted his shoulder. Above him the fire-lizards chirruped in far too happy a tone. Piemur had not wanted to understand Farli. He had not let himself understand her.

''He's all right,'' Sharra was saying over and over, and he could feel her tears on his cheek. ''He'll be fine. Master Oldive's with him and Lessa. Brekke's just gone. Ruth insisted on taking her. And you know that Master Robinton will have to recover if both the Masterhealer and Brekke are attending him.''

Piemur felt Jaxom's hand on his shoulder, shaking him. ''The dragons, Piemur—the dragons wouldn't let Master Robinton die!'' Jaxom spaced his words out so that their sense would penetrate the young harper's shock and fear. ''The dragons wouldn't let him die! He's going to live. He'll be fine. Really, Piemur, can't you hear how happy the fire-lizards are?''

Piemur only believed in Master Robinton's eventual recovery when the white dragon, Ruth, burst back into the clearing, his clarion bugle sending Stupid careening into the safety of the forest. Ruth was so eager to hearten Piemur that he ventured to nudge him gently with his white muzzle, a gesture of extreme affection, while the facets of his beautiful eyes whirled slowly with their reassuring green and blue.

''You know that Ruth can't lie, Piemur,'' Jaxom said earnestly. ''He says Master Robinton's resting easily, and he tells you that Brekke told him herself that he will recover. Mainly he needs rest.'' Jaxom attempted a one-sided grin. ''With every dragon on Pern watching him, he won't get away with any of his usual tricks.''

Piemur had to concede that point. Gradually he began to relax and answer his friends' questions about his travels. He did not mention Jayge and Ara, though with Master Robinton ill, he would have to confide in someone else. Sebell was the one most likely to assume the Mastery of the Harper Hall—he had long been trained to that onerous position. He would know all Master Robinton knew, and Piemur would have no hesitation about informing his Craftmaster friend—once everything had settled down again. For the time being, the secret of Jayge and Ara's Paradise River Hold was safe enough.

In answer to Piemur's questions, Jaxom explained how he had found the cove. The young dragonrider had first been to the cove when searching for D'ram who had stepped down from Weyrleadership of Ista after the death of his long-time weyrmate, Fanna, and disappeared. Later, delirious with the fire-head fever he had contracted on his first visit, Jaxom had directed Ruth to bring him back to the cove.

"It's a beautiful enough spot," Piemur agreed. "But you were out of your shell to come here to die!"

"I didn't know I was. In fact, neither Brekke nor Sharra here told me just how sick I'd been until I was much better." He gave his healer an intense look that held more than simple gratitude.

"And Toric just let you come?" Piemur demanded of Sharra.

"As a favor to the Benden Weyrleaders and Master Oldive, I think." She gave the journeyman harper a wink, then sat up straighter and stuck her nose in the air. "I do have an exceptional record of nursing fire-head victims through fever and blindness, you know."

Piemur knew that, but he just did not like the idea of Sharra and Jaxom together. Perhaps Toric saw it another way. An alliance with the Ruathan Bloodline, and a kinship with the Benden Weyrwoman, Lessa, might prove invaluable to him.

And there was something else niggling about in the back of Piemur's mind, especially as he noticed how many fire-lizards, mainly wild ones with no hall or hold neck markings, engulfed Ruth wherever he went. And he could not ignore the brief flashes he was getting from Farli now that she was back in the white dragon's presence. The more the young harper twisted the matter around in his head, the more certain he became about how that stolen queen egg had gotten back to Benden Weyr Hatching Ground. But it was not something that he, for all his intimacy with Jaxom, could come right out and ask.

By the time they had settled down to eat grilled fish and fruit on the beach that night, they had caught up on the main exchange of adventures and news. Piemur was unhappily sure of Jaxom's feelings toward Sharra. And, knowing her as well as he did, he was dismally convinced that the attraction was mutual. Even if neither of them knew it yet. Or maybe they did. But Piemur did not intend to make it easy for them. He would have to think of distractions.

The next morning Piemur told Jaxom that Stupid had eaten every nonpoisonous blade he could find near the shelter and that the runner flatly refused to emerge from the denser undergrowth when Ruth was around. "He's a bit puny from all the traveling we've done, Jaxom," Piemur said. "He needs feeding up."

So Jaxom offered to fly him on Ruth to the nearest meadow to collect fodder for Stupid. Piemur always enjoyed riding a-dragonback; riding Ruth, who was so much smaller than the full-sized fighting dragons, added a more immediate dimension to the experience, slightly scary, though he had every faith in the amazing white beast. If he had a dragon, he thought, he would have had a much easier time exploring . . . or would he, having trod the ground and learned much that he had not appreciated of the shrubs, trees, and brilliant flowering plants? Flying straight on a dragon gave one other perceptions of vast and beautiful terrain.

Ruth landed them neatly in the center of an expanse of waving grasses dotted with wildflowers and, rolling carefully over, stretched out wing and limb to bask in the sun. But when Jaxom asked him to help harvest the grasses, he willingly set to with gusto.

Jaxom burst out laughing. "No, we are not feeding him up for you to eat." Affectionately he lobbed a dirt ball at the lounging dragon. Later, as they watched Stupid munching happily away, they gazed at the giant mountain visible in the distance and discussed the possibility of trekking to the peak while Jaxom waited out his convalescence. The trip would take four or five days on foot—Ruth could not carry all three, and Jaxom could not risk flying *between* so soon after his bout with fire-head—but that did not daunt Piemur, nor did he mind the fact that it would keep him close by Sharra and Jaxom for a time longer.

Sharra was amazed that Piemur had traveled so far with a runt of a runnerbeast and one fire-lizard as his only companions. Over a midday meal, Piemur told them at some length how he utilized Farli's wings and Stupid's sturdiness to make them a team. That led into a discussion of how to interpret a fire-lizard's sometimes incoherent imagery, and to theories about the wild fire-lizards' adoration of Ruth. Until Jaxom had fully recuperated from fire-head, the three of them might be forced to remain in the cove, but they were by no means out of touch. Ruth kept them current with news of the Masterharper's recovery. And Sharra had another, more impatient, note from her brother, which she showed to Piemur but did not mention to Jaxom.

"If he really needed you, Sharra, it'd be one thing," Piemur told her. "Fire-head season's over. Tell him you're helping me with the mapping. Besides, if it *is* urgent, his new Weyrleader's one of the few who knows exactly where the cove is." In an absurd way, he was enjoying being a third wheel. "Of course, maybe Toric doesn't want to ask that sort of a favor of D'ram. And it's not long now, is it?"

Mindful of his own duty to Toric, he enlisted Jaxom's aid in translating his travel notes into maps. Sharra bleached wherhide skins into usable form and concocted a good ink from local plants. They fished, they swam, they got to know the cove and the little streams feeding into it, and they explored the eastern horn of the cove until they came to a less passable rockstrewn region. At mealtimes, Piemur regaled them in his best harper fashion with tales of hazards and unusual things he had seen.

"Those big spotted felines, by the way," he told Sharra, "are not local to Southern. I saw them all along my way." He tapped his elongated map. "Farli always warned me soon enough to avoid a direct encounter, and I've also seen some huge canines no cook would ever want to use as a spit turner."

As a further diversion, the three of them hiked westward to collect a queen fire-lizard's clutch that Piemur had noticed on his way to the cove. The eggs of a queen fire-lizard were much prized in the north, and both Jaxom and Sharra had been trying to find a clutch. So they carefully packed the eggs they found in baskets filled with hot sand and struck off, Piemur whacking a way through the underbrush. But heat and unaccustomed exercise took their toll on Jaxom's returning health. He was exhausted by the time they reached the cove, and Piemur was soberly repentant. He really had not meant to jeopardize the Ruathan's recovery. Magnanimously he went so far as to admit that the trip had tired him, too, and he was going to go to bed as soon as it was dark. The maps could wait—and, clearly, so could the planned trip to the mountain.

They were all awakened the next morning by Ruth's bugling announcement of the imminent arrival of Canth and F'nor from Benden Weyr, along with some dragons and riders. Immediately Ruth's adoring circle of wild fire-lizards disappeared; only Meer, Talla, and Farli remained to greet their immense cousins.

When F'nor told them why he and the other riders had come, Piemur had mixed reactions. He was delighted by the plans to build the Masterharper a convalescent home right there in the cove that he had found so beautiful and restful. But he did not like the idea of the incredible place becoming too well known—at least not until he had had the chance to discuss Paradise River with someone. He could just imagine

Toric's reaction to the wonderful surprise for the Masterharper. Sharra seemed unperturbed, but then, she was far more involved with Jaxom than with her brother's aspirations.

Up until the day of the Masterharper's arrival in the newly named Cove Hold, there was little peace there. Sharra, disabusing F'nor of the suitability of the plans he had brought, promptly drew new ones, designed for living in Southern, where it was more important to encourage breezes and mitigate the summer heat than to keep out cold or Thread.

Then Mastercraftsmen in every Hall got wind of the project, and dragons arrived with men and material in such quantity that Piemur was overwhelmed. As he sought privacy in the dense forest, he knew that it might seem that he was deserting his friends. But there were more than enough hands to complete Master Robinton's new hold, and besides, so many dragons frightened Stupid into a quivering wreck. No one, it turned out, expected either Sebell or T'gellan at Cove Hold, and Piemur had counted on one of them to appear.

He debated sending a message by Farli to Sebell. But if Sebell had been named Masterharper, he would have more than enough problems to sort out. Also, Piemur would have to know exactly where Sebell was, or wear out poor Farli with *betweening*. In any case, he was reluctant to mention Jayge and Ara in writing. Sebell, in his quiet and understated way, was as astute and clear-eyed as his Master and had been in Southern often enough to have Toric's measure. And if F'lar had replaced D'ram as Southern Weyrleader, maybe everything in the South had altered. Maybe that was why Toric had been ordering Sharra to return. It looked as if for the time being the secret of Jayge and Ara would have to keep.

Having listened to F'nor talking rather proprietarily of that part of the South, it occurred to Piemur that the dragonriders might have thoughts of taking hold there in the next Interval, where they would not be dependent on the generosity of Holds. Piemur knew how that dependence had vexed Lessa and F'lar before the current Pass had begun.

Well, he was only the explorer, not the dispenser of the land. He and Jaxom had made several copies of his journey map, one for himself, one for Toric, and a third to occupy the Masterharper on his long sea voyage to Cove Hold. He could no longer delay dispatching Toric's copy by Farli, and he would have to add some details. Admittedly, Toric had sent him no message to report back, nor a spare dragonrider to convey him, but he had come as far as he had at Toric's request, and until he had been officially recalled to the Harper Hall by Sebell, he was still an official member of Toric's hold.

Piemur decided not to mention to Toric Sharra's fondness—who was he kidding? Sharra's love—for Jaxom, so obviously reciprocated. He would certainly omit any details of the beautiful Paradise River, but he thought he ought to mention the existence of ancient ruins to someone, and get that extraordinary Record to the Mastersmith.

He wandered as far as the meadow where he and Jaxom had cut grass and gazed long and hard at the distant mountain peak, so serenely symmetrical. And he slept surprisingly well those nights, with no repeats of the erupting volcano dream that had plagued him earlier. Farli no longer chittered excitedly at him about men and big objects in the sky. He had understood finally that she had not meant dragons. She also conveyed some vivid images of erupting volcanoes, and Piemur wondered who was dreaming whose dreams. Finally, on the fifth day, she interrupted his ruminations with an ecstatic message that the ship was very near the cove.

He returned to find the new Hall at Cove Hold completed, all the craftsmen and women already conveyed back to the north. Sharra and Jaxom were delighted to see him again and showed him all that had been accomplished in his absence.

"Shards, but this is magnificent," he said, wishing that he had not taken off like a scared wherry as he stared around at the spacious main hall where Master Robinton could entertain half a Hold, if he chose. He loved the Harper, and he knew that almost everyone on Pern did for one reason or another, but to have so many skilled people express their respect and admiration in such a way brought a lump to Piemur's throat. "This is just magnificent," he repeated and noticed the amused grins. He wandered about the hall, touching the carved chairs and the fine chests and tables.

He said the same thing when Sharra brought him into the corner study, with its incredible view of the sea and the eastern headland, the clever storage racks for Records and musical instruments, and the impressive supply of Master Bendarek's leaves to write on. He admired the guest rooms, large enough to be comfortable but small enough not to encourage too long a visit, and complimented Sharra on the kitchen she had spent so much time organizing, with the special cupboards to store the Benden wines that the Mastervintner had sent in extraordinary quantities. Yes, Piemur thought, brushing irritably at his brimming eyes, the Master would find everything to his taste and convenience at Cove Hold. And live long and happily, safe there from all strife.

The day that Master Robinton was expected, Piemur volunteered to oversee the roasting of the fresh wherry in the firepit constructed in a convenient rock pile on the right-hand side of the cove's semicircle. Piemur had become obsessed by the idea that the Harper might have dwindled the way T'ron had, becoming aged and bowed overnight by his illness. He would hate to see his proud, vital Master in such a state. But he had to see him with his own eyes.

He had the best view of the westward reach of the cove while he tended the roast, and he was the first to see the three masts of Master Idarolan's finest ship, the *Dawn Sister*, with all sails set, keel showing as she raced along the clear green waters. He watched as she altered her course, sailors climbing her yardarms to furl sails, and as she smoothly slid in to dock at the fine pier that had been constructed to receive her and her special passenger. He watched as Lessa, Brekke, Master Fandarel, and Jaxom assisted the Harper down the bobbing gangplank, and he was relieved to see Master Robinton stride down the plank with his customary vitality. Watching Menolly follow him off the ship, Piemur felt oddly removed from all those old friends of his. He told himself that too many people could be stressful. He could wait. So he continued to baste the succulent wherry.

"Piemur!" The familiar baritone sounded as firmly supported as ever, and that voice, ringing and clear, did much to restore him.

"Master?" he called out in reply, startled by the familiar summons.

"Report, Piemur!"

D'ram, Sebell, and N'ton, the young Fort Weyrleader, came to the Southern hold, asking to speak to Toric.

Recently there had been much coming and going of dragonriders bringing supplies and people and generally working on D'ram's promised restoration of the Southern Weyr. The newly augmented wings had begun to fly regular practice flights. The Weyrhall had been scrubbed and painted by the younger riders, and encroaching forest growth had been trimmed from individual weyrs. D'ram had been exceedingly circumspect, but took entirely too much notice, Toric thought, of what went on in the Hold. Far too much.

To show united Bloodkin, he had sent his fire-lizards to Hamian at the mines, Kevelon in Central Hold, and Murda and her husband at Big Lagoon, telling them to return immediately. He had also sent a note to Sharra, insisting on her return. Surely she could talk some dragonrider into conveying her back. Uncharacteristically, she had sent no reply, though the message had been removed from his little queen's leg.

"We'd like to help you, Holder Toric," D'ram said when

Ramala and Murda had offered them all klah or the cool fruit drink that was particularly refreshing in Southern.

"Oh?" Toric cast his eyes quickly over each of the three men. Sebell, who had always been discreet and had helped him out on several occasions, was now Masterharper of Pern and might very well hold views different from Robinton's. The Harper's expression at the moment was pleasantly attentive. N'ton had the same sort of energetic, inquiring look about him that Piemur had, and to Toric, that could mean that the young dragonrider would be troublesome. What was a Fort Weyrleader doing there anyway?

D'ram cleared his throat, obviously finding it difficult to continue.

"Help me in what way?" Toric asked testily.

"Now that Masterharper Sebell has brought me up to date on the many abuses and incivilities you have suffered from the Southern Oldtimers, and their rather conspicuous demands over and above the lawful tithe, I think there should be some changes."

Toric merely nodded, aware that the Fort Weyrleader and Sebell were watching him closely.

"I—we—in this bountiful place," D'ram went on, "feel that the Weyr should substantially reduce its requirements of you, especially in the matter of feeding our dragons. They actually prefer to hunt, and once we know where your livestock is pastured, we will avoid the area. We expect to have five wings, as well as—" D'ram paused "—those no longer able for active service."

Toric accepted with a nod what D'ram was implying, though he did not quite like the suggestion that dragonriders would soon be overflying the land. Just how much did dragonriders notice when they flew? They might not have seen much when they had searched for Ramoth's egg—but while hunting wild game? He found himself mulling over that problem as D'ram continued.

"We have brought with us sufficient weyrfolk to handle all

domestic duties, so those holders whom you have been good enough to attach to the Weyr can return to their normal duties."

Toric cleared his throat. He could appreciate D'ram not wanting those slatternly drudges about a freshened Weyr. He did not want them about Southern, either. But there was an easy solution for that.

Then Sebell held out a long cylinder, encased in a finely tooled leather sheath. "Mastersmith Fandarel wishes you to have this," he said with a slight smile.

When Toric unwrapped it, he could not suppress his delight at being given a distance-viewer of his own. Master Rampesi had managed to acquire a small one but nothing so fine as this. He turned it over in his hands, putting it to his eye and reacting with a startled cry at the magnification of what he knew were minute fissures in the wall.

"You should be able to see the length and breadth of Southern Hold with that," Sebell said.

That got Toric's complete attention. "Master Fandarel doesn't waste his efforts," he said obliquely. Length and breadth of Southern Hold, indeed!

"Yes, I also bear a message from Master Fandarel," Sebell went on smoothly. "Metal is, as you know, in short supply in the North. You have been supplying the Smithcrafthall with much needed zinc, copper, and other ores, for which that is a token of gratitude."

"We've shipped what we could," Toric said carefully. It was one thing for the dragonriders to hunt for meat in the hold. How much else were they expecting to find for themselves?

"I think arrangements can now be made for more regular commerce," D'ram said, "as compensation for what you've endured."

Toric eyed him warily.

"A regular trade would be extremely beneficial for both North and South," Sebell continued, betraying no hint of his knowledge of Toric's already steady activities in that area. "And Mastersmith Fandarel is certainly eager to have as much ore as you can ship to him. You, and quite likely your Smithmaster brother, will have to advise him as to how much you can manage to supply. To this point, I think N'ton has something to say."

"Please understand, Holder Toric," N'ton began in a slightly rueful tone, "that I was not at the time concerned with anything other than finding Ramoth's egg, but I noticed some mounds along that great inland lake that cannot be natural. I heard, from someone," he said, jiggling his hand to indicate a faulty memory that Toric did not believe for an instant, "that the new zinc and copper deposits you've been working might have been worked a long time ago."

No, it was not compensation he was getting, Toric reflected. No matter how smoothly their ideas were presented, his full cooperation was expected. Those bloody Oldtimers and that wretched queen egg had done him more damage than he had supposed! But he could make certain not to lose so much as a fingerlength of land he already held, or the riches above and below the soil. He also knew the place N'ton must have seen. Sharra had reported it to him the previous Turn. He had marked the huge lake and the three rivers that flowed from it on his private map. He must be very careful. He must seem to cooperate while sending reliable men and women to hold what ought to be his.

"There's always been that rumor," he said skeptically.

"More than a rumor," Sebell said in that quiet unemphasized voice of his. "There are some ambiguous Fragments among the Harper Hall Records that indicate that the Northern Continent is the more recent settlement."

"Recent?" Toric let out an incredulous guffaw.

"I believe you established a prosperous hold in ancient ruins on the western bank of Island River," Sebell said.

"I wouldn't call such old stonework 'recent.' "

"May I make it plain, Toric?" Sebell said, leaning forward, his manner earnest and subtly ingratiating. "No one contests your holding. But we would very much like to extend our knowledge about our ancestors. It becomes a matter of intense

Craft pride, you know. We're supposed to keep the Records of Pern.'' He gestured again to the distance-viewer Toric was fondling possessively. ''We can learn a lot from the past that will assist us in our future.''

''I wholeheartedly agree, Master Harper,'' Toric replied as earnestly as he could when he saw how little option he had.

''Naturally, I'd be glad to convey you to that place I have in mind, Holder Toric,'' N'ton said with a boyish eagerness that Toric found puzzling.

But he accepted the offer graciously. With so much to plan and to manage, he had been forced to let his kin do the explorations. Hurried trips to Big Lagoon or Central Hold, and one sail down the Island River, had given him only a shallow glimpse of what he held. If he got on good terms with N'ton, who knew what else he might see? Dragonriders had an unfair advantage over any holder: quick, sure movement from place to place.

What was it that rascally journeyman had quoted to him before he left? ''A dragon can't go *between* to a place he's never seen. Likewise a man can't hold what he hasn't beheld.'' He caressed the distance-viewer again.

He rose then, pretending a geniality he did not feel. ''I've a fair map of the area we've managed, over the Turns, to investigate afoot. It really is a relief to me to have a proper Weyr and good relations with my Northern neighbors.''

The morning after his arrival, Master Robinton was up early, to the disgust of his young friends who had enjoyed the evening's festivities. Despite the restrictions imposed on him by Brekke, Menolly, and Sharra, he was determined to extend their knowledge of the south in all directions. For that purpose, he convened a meeting of Jaxom, Piemur, Sharra, and Menolly.

The Harper's particular interest was in finding further evidence of the original inhabitants of the Southern Continent. He mentioned not only the ancient iron mine that Toric had found, but some unnatural formation that he himself had spotted with N'ton. Piemur grinned, betting with himself that Toric did not know about that. Had it happened when Master Robinton had voyaged with Menolly to Southern for personal talks with Toric? The Southern holder had gone to Benden Weyr shortly after, and returned very pleased with himself. Thinking of the houses at Paradise River, Piemur vowed that he would speak to the Master Harper on that point as soon as he could get him alone.

Master Robinton's plans called for a dual attack, both ground and aerial. He was adamant and enthusiastic as he ordered them to begin, once Jaxom had been pronounced fit by Master Oldive, who was due to arrive that afternoon. Piemur, because of his experience, would be in nominal charge, an arrangement to which Jaxom had no objections. Jaxom would fly Ruth ahead each day to settle a new camp and do an aerial survey, while the girls and Piemur followed on foot for more detailed examinations.

The young people were quite content to fall in with his scheme, happy to do anything that would keep Master Robinton pleasantly occupied while his strength returned. Master Oldive, after examining the Harper, lectured them on how to help Robinton in his recuperation. Despite his enthusiasm, the Masterharper was still weak and vulnerable to another attack, so they promised to do all they could to protect him from himself. Jaxom, however, was declared fully recovered.

Despite the good intentions of his nurses, Master Robinton was full of projects, all of which he fully expected to see carried out. He was especially excited when Mastersmith Fandarel and Master Wansor arrived from the Telgar Smithcrafthall with Wansor's new distance-viewer, the most recent product of the Starsmith's experimentation. It was a tube as long as Fandarel's arm and thick enough so that he needed two hands to surround it; carefully encased in leather, it had a curious eye-piece set not on its end, where Piemur thought it ought to be, but on its side.

Wansor, in an explanation that explained very little to his rapt audience, told them that the distance-viewer was designed somewhat along the same principles as the ancient instrument, found in one of the unused rooms of Benden Weyr, that made small things appear larger.

That very night a viewing took place, the instrument mounted on a frame erected on a high point of the stony eastern tip of the cove. And what they learned in their first clear view of the Dawn Sisters made, in Piemur's eyes, the discovery of Paradise River insignificant. For those stars were no stars at all! They were man-made objects—and very likely they were artifacts of those mysterious Southern ancestors. Perhaps they were even the actual vehicles that had brought those ancestors to Pern in the beginning. And when Piemur got his turn to gaze through the device, he felt his heart leap at the splendor he glimpsed.

12

SOUTHERN CONTINENT,
PP 15.10.19

Young Lord Jaxom, with Piemur, Sharra, and Menolly, has found a vast settlement, buried under volcanic ash and dirt," D'ram announced excitedly. He had brought the news to Toric immediately, a sign of the growing mutual respect between Weyrleader and Southern Holder.

Toric hid his dismay as he read through the lengthy message that D'ram had brought from Master Robinton. He had swallowed his chagrin the previous month when he learned that the cove had been claimed for the Masterharper. One small cove Toric could allow without regret, however beautiful the place was rumored to be. With the help of Piemur's maps and more eager dragonrider assistance than he really wanted, he had made other advantageous discoveries. For the first time, he had been able to fly over a good deal of his own holding—and he could begin to appreciate how large the continent was. But it had also been made tacitly clear to him that he could not have it all. The latest discovery made clear that "one small cove" was the thin edge of a big wedge.

He would have liked to digest the news without the pres-

ence of the new Masterharper, Sebell, but they had been trying to reach an understanding about which and how many
new settlers Toric would permit in his hold. He was going to
have to remind the Benden Weyrleaders of the promise made
to him two and a half Turns before—and hold them to it.
Aware that Sebell was watching his reactions, he expressed
amazement at the new discovery.

"I shall, of course, convey you there myself," D'ram replied, looking more like an eager weyrling than a seasoned
leader. "I saw that mountain peak when I was in Cove Hold.
I saw it, and never realized how significant it was."

" 'When man came to Pern, he established a good Hold in
the South,' " Sebell murmured, his eyes shining almost reverently, " 'but found it necessary to move north to shield.' "

Toric snorted at such ambiguous nonsense, although he had
to admit that the first part of the Fragment did seem to be
true. Had they held the entire South? "I'll get my flying gear,
D'ram."

"Oh, no, not now, Toric," D'ram said, grinning. "It's late
in the night there now. I assure you, we shall leave here in
an appropriate time to arrive when the interested persons have
gathered tomorrow morning. But I've matters to organize.
And so must you. I'm as eager to go as you, Holder, believe
me." D'ram's smile faded as he saw the concern on the Masterharper's face. "Sebell?"

"I just don't like so much excitement for my Master. He's
not fully recovered."

"He has Menolly in constant attendance, as well as Sharra,"
D'ram assured him. "They won't let him tire himself."

Sebell gave an uncharacteristic snort. "You don't know
Master Robinton as I do, D'ram. He'll wear himself out, puzzling through the whys and wherefores of this."

"It'll do him good, Sebell," D'ram replied. "Keep his mind
occupied. Not that he would interfere with your Mastering,
but an—" He changed word midthought. "An older man
needs interests that involve him in life. Don't worry, Sebell."

"At least about your Master's health," Toric said sardonically. "He's got both Menolly and Sharra, hasn't he?"

D'ram realized that his mention of Toric's sister had not been as circumspect as it might have been, just as he also remembered that Menolly was Sebell's wife. "I'll leave you to the reading and collect you in six hours' time."

"Isn't there a lad from Ruatha Hold in this new batch of dimwits?" Toric asked Sebell when D'ram had left. He wanted to settle the latest arrivals immediately.

"Yes." Sebell skimmed over the careful lists he had helped Toric make of abilities and ambitions. "Dorse: comes with a good recommendation from Brand, steward of the Ruatha Hold."

"I don't remember him offhand."

"I knew him from Ruatha," Sebell began in a tone that Toric was coming to identify as discreet. "You can trust Brand's warranty. Says he does well if overseen."

"Anyone does well overseen," Toric said in a derisive tone. "What I need is someone who can initiate and carry through."

"There's a very competent man, Denol—came here from Boll on Lady Marella's recommendation. Brought many of his family with him. Crop pickers by occupation, but they've settled in here well and obey him implicitly . . ."

"Ah, Denol. Yes, I know the man you mean. Well, then, give him a gaggle of these Northern louts, have him take his kin with him to that new holding at Great Bay, and we'll see what he makes of it."

"Send Dorse with him?"

"Not yet. I've something else in mind for that lad."

As the bronze Tiroth emerged from *between* just east of Two-Faced Mountain, the volcano dominating the plain on which the settlement had been discovered, Toric tugged at D'ram's sleeve and inscribed circles with his gloved finger. He wanted a good look around. Clearly he was not alone: two dragons were still airborne, and four more sat on the ground below, Ruth's white hide standing out among them. Groups of people were wandering aimlessly around, and Toric wondered just how many had been informed of the amazing discovery. A positive rainbelt of fire-lizards, soaring and diving, was exulting in a cascade of sound that Toric could hear even through his padded helmet as a swarm swooped in greeting to Tiroth.

He bitterly resented the fact that the news had been spread with such a lavish hand. Southern had been his! It was enough that he had had to spend much of the past month delegating holdings to Northerners who would probably kill themselves with either enthusiasm in the heat or their igno-rance of Southern dangers. He had been forced to recognize that the Southern Continent was *not* his to dispose of. But was it really Benden's, either?

He shook his head. One man could only Hold so much. Fax's depredations in the north had proven that. He had not made Fax's greatest mistake, controlling by fear. Greed, he knew, served as well for holdless men and women. But such speculations were useless at the moment, so he concentrated on the truly awe-inspiring panorama that spread below him as Tiroth circled slowly over an incredible sweep of meadow, broader and deeper than any expanse Toric had seen before.

The mountain dominated the scene. Its eastern lip had blown out, and the three smaller volcanoes crouching on its southeastern flank had also erupted at some time. Lava had flowed down, south toward the rolling plains. Was that what his fire-lizards had been screaming about recently? Toric was rarely aware of his dreams, but lately he had recalled vivid ones, totally incomprehensible. A man should not be plagued by fire-lizards in his sleep—yet there he was circling over the very site that matched their mental images.

He had no doubt that the plain at the foot of the volcanoes had once been inhabited. The morning sun threw outlines in bold relief. Such outlines could not have been the result of natural forces. The mounds, with straight lines setting them apart from one another, were formed in squares and rectan-gles. There was row upon row, square upon square of mounds, some large, some small; those nearest the lava flow had collapsed, proving that not even the ancients had been impervious to the planet's restless internal forces. Rather stupid, Toric thought, to have built out in the open, totally vulnerable to Thread and volcanic eruptions.

D'ram looked back at him with an unspoken query, and reluctantly Toric nodded. He was honed with eagerness to see what Benden proposed to do about the discovery. And to see who else had gathered to view this wonder. Toric was not often impressed, but today he was awed.

Tiroth deposited them on the plain, not far from the distinctive figure of Mastersmith Fandarel, towering above the diminutive Benden Weyrwoman. Toric strode toward them, nodding to Masterminer Nicat, Mastersmith Fandarel, F'nor, and N'ton.

As he greeted F'lar and Lessa, he glanced sharply over at the small knot of younger folk standing beyond, noticing that Menolly and Piemur acknowledged his presence. He decided the tall young man standing by Sharra must be Jaxom, Ruathan Lord Holder, still a boy, much too young and insignificant for his sister. He would put a stop to that immediately—as soon as he was through dealing with Benden's encroachment on his continent. He returned his attention to F'lar.

"Actually, Toric," F'lar was saying, "it was young Jaxom who made this discovery, along with Menolly, Piemur, and your sister, Sharra."

"And quite a discovery, it is, too!" Toric replied, seething inside. Smoothly he steered the discussion to the question of the ruins themselves. Soon he found himself caught up in the excitement as, shovel and picks in hand, he joined the others in attacking the mounds.

With its thick grass cover and dry, grayish soil the ground was not easy to break, but Toric, working alongside Mastersmith Fandarel, soon made good headway. The Southern holder was in excellent condition, but quickly found that he had to extend himself to keep up with the indefatigable and powerful Craftmaster. Toric had heard about the man's energy: now he believed it. He used the infrequent rests he permitted himself to observe the impudent young scut who had kept Sharra away so long. Weyrless lordling boy, he thought. A few scowls would send him scurrying.

The next time he took a breather, he saw that Jaxom's runt of a white dragon and some of the fire-lizards had joined in the digging. Dirt was being shifted at an amazing rate. He called his own fire-lizards to him just as Ramoth, Benden's proud queen, began to assist at the small mound that Lessa had chosen to excavate. Toric redoubled his efforts beside Fandarel.

Lessa and F'lar, each working at separate mounds, were the first to reap any results of their hard work, and everyone rushed to see. Toric followed the crowd, but he was confident that all the digging would prove to be wasted effort. All previous evidence suggested that the ancients would have stripped everything before they left their settlement behind. He took only one look into each dragon-dug trench. What he saw was the same rocklike substance that had been used in the mine building he had found, except that in F'lar's an amber panel was set in the curve of the mound. Uninterested, he stood to one side while the others argued about what to do next. Finally the Mastersmith took charge: they would unite their efforts and concentrate on Lessa's mound.

Toric was disgusted that people he had admired should be so caught up by vain hopes. But he found that he, too, could not turn his back on the project, even supposing he was able to talk D'ram into leaving. There was always the chance, despite all his previous disappointments, that there *was* something left behind, and he could not miss that. It would show him what to look for in the other mounds Sharra and Hamian had discovered, the ones whose existence had *not* been reported to the world at large.

Late in the day a door was discovered, and amid much excitement, the mound was entered. And, as luck—good or bad, Toric wondered—would have it, Toric was the one who found the strange spoon, made of a smooth, clear, and incredibly strong nonmetal substance. Lessa was thrilled, and as they all enthusiastically trooped out to excavate another mound, Toric wished he had not encouraged them. Night had fallen before they quit for the day and he could make his escape. When Lessa invited him to join them overnight at Cove Hold, he summoned up as much politeness as he could manage and declined, calling for D'ram to give him a ride home.

That night Piemur composed a message for Jayge and Ara. With all the new wonders of the excavation to fully occupy the Halls and Weyrs, he was more sanguine about the couple's safety. If they had found the *only* remaining settlement of the ancients, he would have felt compelled to mention it, out of Hall loyalty, to Master Robinton. But there was plenty of time for that—he could wait until the excitement about Two-Faced Mountain died down. In his message, Piemur told Jayge briefly that a huge settlement of great antiquity had been found and that he would try to visit them again soon. He sent Farli with the note.

In the morning she swooped to his shoulder, a brief message on the reverse side of his. "We are well. Thank you." He just had time to thrust it into his pocket when Menolly appeared, wanting to know if he had seen either Jaxom or Sharra. Before he could frame an answer, Jaxom and Ruth, accompanied by a multitude of fire-lizards, burst into the air above the cove. The noise roused Master Robinton, who roared for silence.

"I have found the ancients' flying machines," Jaxom insisted, his eyes wide with wonder and excitement. "The fire-lizards have been driving me and Ruth crazy with memories of the scene. As if they could have a memory that old! I had to see, to believe," he explained earnestly. "So Ruth and I dug down to the door into one of them. There are three, did

I mention that? Well, there are. They look like this—'' He grabbed a stick and, in the sand, sketched an irregular cylindrical design that had stubby wings and a straight-up section over the tail. He drew smaller rings at one end and outlined a long oval door. "That's what Ruth and I found!''

At every sentence, there were choruses of approval from the fire-lizards outside and inside Cove Hold until Master Robinton once again begged for silence. By that time, both Menolly and Piemur had been bombarded with confirming images from their own fire-lizards, vivid scenes of men and women coming down a ramp, interwoven with views of the cylinders gliding in to land and taking off again. Everyone was thrilled at the idea of seeing the actual ships that had very likely brought their ancestors from the Dawn Sisters to Pern. Jaxom's only disappointment was that Sharra was not there to share in his glory; she had, he learned, been called back to Southern Hold to deal with some illness there.

F'nor arrived on Canth just after they had eaten, none too pleased to be rousted by F'lar and sent out at such an early hour. But he changed his tune when he learned why Master Robinton had sent word to Benden Weyr. He was instantly ready to head right out to see the ancient ships.

When the Harper insisted on going along, they all protested, but he refused to be left on his own again at Cove Hold—it would be inhumane, he said, to deprive him of witnessing such a historic moment. He promised not to dig, but he simply had to be there! So despite their misgivings, they set off, F'nor taking Robinton and Piemur on Canth, and Jaxom taking Menolly, accompanied by an increasing storm of fire-lizards that could only be silenced by Ruth.

The excavation that followed yielded marvel after marvel, only beginning with the green button that, when pushed, caused the vehicle's door to open on its own. But for Piemur and Master Robinton, the most wonderful find was the maps, covering the walls of one of the rooms, showing both continents in their entirety. Thinking of his own arduous mapping expeditions, Piemur was awed by the extent and the detail. Briefly he struggled with the dilemma of conflicting interests. He admired Toric and respected what he had achieved, but such a vast land was more than any one man had a right to Hold. From now on, Piemur would take a harper's view.

Toric did not expect Sharra to appreciate what he was doing for her sake. He did not expect wife, sister, and both brothers to oppose him.

"And what's wrong with Sharra making such a good match?" Ramala demanded, displaying an anger and force of will that astonished him.

"With Ruatha? A table-sized Hold in the north?" Toric dismissed it with a flick of his fingers. "Why, you could fit the place in one corner of my hold and it'd rattle."

"Ruatha is a powerful Hold," Hamian said, his face expressionless except for an angry tightening around the eyes. "Don't dismiss Jaxom because he's young and rides a sport dragon. He's extremely intelligent . . ."

"Sharra can do better for herself!" Toric seethed. He was tired. After two days of digging and trying to keep up with that blasted smith, he wanted a bath, a good meal, and a chance to go over the maps Piemur had sent him. He was determined to learn exactly where the incredible Plateau was located—flying *between* with D'ram had given him no useful direction other than east.

"Sharra has done very well for herself," Murda said, raising her voice as if volume would impress their opinion on him. She did not bother to conceal her approval and scowled fiercely at Toric.

"How would you know?" Toric demanded. "You've never met him."

"I have," Hamian said. "But that's not as important as the

fact that Sharra has chosen him. She's been too long complying with your demands and suppressing her own needs. I think she's done bloody well."

"He's younger than she is!"

Ramala shrugged. "A Turn or two. I'm warning you, Toric. Her feelings for Jaxom are genuine. She's old enough to know her own heart and marry to suit herself."

"Any one of you, *any* one of you," Toric exclaimed, shaking his fist at each in turn, "meddle in this, and you can leave! Leave!" With that he dismissed them all, slumping into his chair and fuming over their reception of his decision.

A man should be able to trust his own family. That was the basis of the Blood relationship: trust. Give her a few days back home, away from that gawky lordling and the glamorous atmosphere of Cove Hold, and she would see reason. Meanwhile, he would see she stayed at home. He sent a drudge in search of the Ruathan he had previously noticed.

"Dorse, do you know that Ruathan lordling well?" he asked when the young man arrived.

Dorse was surprised and then guarded. "I gave you the warranty note from Brand, steward at Ruatha."

"He said nothing to your discredit." Toric put an edge on his tone. "I repeat, did you know this young Jaxom?"

"We were milkbrothers."

"Then you'd know if he'd ever come to Southern on any errand?"

"Him? No." Dorse was positive. "He was never let go anywhere without everyone knowing. Afraid he'd lose himself or crease the hide of that precious white dragon of his."

"I see." And Toric did: milkbrothers were rarely fond of each other, despite the popular myth. "You know that my sister, Sharra, has returned." Very few in the hold would have failed to note that. "I want her to stay here, see no one, and neither receive nor send messages. Do I make myself understood?"

"Perfectly, Lord Holder."

That had a nice ring to it, Toric thought. Another important matter to be resolved. "Use Breide as relief guard. He's in the same dormitory. He's got a good memory for faces and names. If the pair of you keep her safely here, I shall find a special hold for you later."

"That's easily done, Lord Toric." Dorse grinned. "I had a lot of practice keeping my eyes on people, if you know what I mean."

Toric dismissed him and, calling up his two queens, gave them particular instructions about Meer and Talla, Sharra's fire-lizards. Satisfied with his preparations, he then bathed, ate, and figured out which reliable aspiring young holder he could spare to keep an eye on his interests at the Plateau. If something useful was found in any of those abandoned buildings, he wanted full details. He had secured a magnificent hold, far richer and more extensive than even Telgar. Dorse had automatically accorded him the title that he should long before have been accorded, and it had sounded very pleasant indeed. While the Benden Weyrleaders and the others were dazzled by the empty promises of that Plateau, he must force the issue on the matter of rank and be confirmed by the Conclave as Lord Holder of Southern.

Maybe then Sharra would appreciate how much he had achieved for them all and consent to his arrangements. She did need a husband and children. Why had Ramala turned against him? Fatigue eroded his concentration. He rolled up on the floor in a spare fur he kept in his work chamber. When he returned to the Plateau he would warn off that boy, and that would be the end of it.

The next day, when Tiroth and the other dragons deposited him and his holders on the mound, Toric looked first for Lessa and found her standing with others at Nicat's mound door. Then he saw Jaxom with the Harper and changed direction. Let the Harper know, he thought, and all Pern would.

"Harper!" Toric came to a halt with a courteous nod to the old man, who looked surprisingly hale for one whom half Pern had had in his grave.

"Holder Toric," the boy said casually, over his shoulder.

"Lord Jaxom," Toric replied in a drawl that made an insult of a title.

Jaxom turned slowly. "Sharra tells me that you do not favor an alliance with Ruatha."

Toric smiled broadly. This was going to be entertaining. "No, lordling, I do not! She can do better than a table-sized Hold in the North!" He caught the Harper's surprised look.

Suddenly Lessa, a hint of steel in her eyes, appeared beside Jaxom. "What did I hear, Toric?"

"Holder Toric has other plans for Sharra," the boy said, more amused than aggrieved. "She can do better, it seems, than a table-sized Hold like Ruatha!"

Toric would have given much to know who exactly had repeated his words to Sharra. "I mean no offense to Ruatha," he said, catching the flicker of anger in Lessa's face though her smile remained in place.

"That would be most unwise, considering my pride in my Bloodline and in the present Holder of that title," the Weyrwoman said.

Toric did not like the casual tone of her voice.

"Surely you might reconsider the matter, Toric," Robinton said, as affable as ever despite the warning in his eyes. "Such an alliance, so much desired by the two young people, would have considerable advantages, I think, aligning yourself with one of the most prestigious Holds on Pern."

"And be in favor with Benden," Lessa added, smiling too sweetly.

Toric absently rubbed the back of his neck, trying to keep his smile in place. He felt unaccountably light-headed. The next thing he knew, Lessa had put her arm through his and was escorting him to the privacy of her mound.

"I thought we were here to dig up Pern's glorious past," he said, managing a good-natured laugh. His head still swam.

"There's surely no time like the present," Lessa continued, "to discuss the future. Your future."

Well, that was more like, Toric thought. F'lar was there, beside Lessa, and the Harper had followed them. The Southern holder shook his head to clear it.

"Yes, with so many ambitious holdless men pouring into Southern," F'lar was saying, "we've been remiss in making certain you'll have the lands you want, Toric. I don't fancy blood feuds in the South. Unnecessary, too, when there's space enough for this generation and several more."

Toric laughed. The man didn't realize just how much space there was in the South. He seized his opportunity. "And since there's so much space, why should I not be ambitious for my sister?"

"You've more than one, and we're not talking of Jaxom and Sharra just now," Lessa said with a hint of irritability. "F'lar and I had intended to arrange a more formal occasion to set your Holding, but there's Master Nicat wanting to formalize Minecraft affairs with you, and Lord Groghe is anxious that his two sons do not hold adjacent lands, and other questions have come up recently which require answers."

"Answers?" Toric leaned against one wall of the cot and crossed his arms on his chest.

"One answer required is how much land any *one* man should Hold in the south?" F'lar said, idly digging dirt from under his thumbnail. The light emphasis was not lost on Toric.

"And? Our original agreement was that I could Hold all the lands I had acquired by the time the Oldtimers had passed on."

"Which, in truth, they haven't," Robinton said.

"I shan't insist on waiting," Toric replied, nodding, "since the original circumstances have altered. And since my hold is thoroughly disorganized by the indigent and hopeful lordlings and holdless men and women, as well as, I am reliably informed, by others who have eschewed our help and landed wherever their ships can be beached."

"All the more reason to be sure you are not deprived of one length of your just Hold," F'lar said—far too agreeably, Toric thought. "I know that you have sent out exploring teams. How far have they actually penetrated?"

"With the help of D'ram's dragonriders"—and Toric saw that F'lar did know of that agency—"we have extended our knowledge of terrain to the foot of the Western Range." That was safe enough to admit. He had not said when he had extended that knowledge.

"That far?"

"And, of course, Piemur reached the Great Desert Bay to the west," the Southerner went on determinedly.

"My dear Toric, how can you possibly Hold all that?"

Toric knew the rights of Holding as well as the Weyrleader did. "I've small cotholders with burgeoning families along most of the habitable shoreline and at strategic points in the interior. The men you sent me these past few Turns proved most industrious." The Weyrleaders would have to accept the accomplished fact.

"I suspect they have pledged loyalty to you in return for your original generosity?" F'lar asked.

"Naturally."

Lessa laughed. She was really a very sensual woman when she wanted to be, Toric realized. "I thought when we met at Benden that you were a shrewd and independent man."

"There's land, my dear Weyrwoman, for any man who can hold it."

"I'd say then," Lessa went on, "that you'll have more than enough to occupy you fully and to Hold, from sea to Western Range to the Great Bay . . ."

Suddenly Toric heard his fire-lizards' warning. Sharra was running away. He had to leave the Plateau, to get back to the hold.

"To the Great Bay in the West, yes, that is my hope. I do have maps. In my hold, but if I've your leave . . ." He had managed one stride to the door when the Benden queen bugled a warning. Another male voice chimed in, all but drowning his fire-lizards out. F'lar moved swiftly to block his way.

"It's already too late, Toric."

And so it was. For when they all filed out of that all too provident meeting, Toric saw the white dragon landing, Sharra and the young lordling on his back. Unsmiling and impotent, Toric watched them approach.

"Toric," Jaxom said, "you cannot contain Sharra anywhere on Pern where Ruth and I cannot find her. Place and time are no barriers to Ruth. Sharra and I can go anywhere, anywhen on Pern."

One of Toric's fire-lizard queens attempted to land on his shoulder. He ignored her piteous chirps and brushed her away. He hated disloyalty.

"Furthermore," Jaxom went on, "fire-lizards obey Ruth! Don't they, my friend?" The white sport had followed his rider. "Tell every fire-lizard here on the Plateau to go away."

In an instant the meadow was empty of the little creatures. Toric did not like the young upstart's demonstration. When the fire-lizards returned, he allowed his little queen to land on his shoulder, but he never took his eyes from Jaxom's.

"How did you know so much about Southern? I was told that you've never been there!" So that milkbrother had lied. Toric half-turned, looking across the meadow, wondering if Piemur had had a hand in this. That unweyred lordling could not have snatched Sharra back from Southern all by himself: he wouldn't have had the courage or the knowledge.

"Your informant erred," Jaxom continued. "Today is not the first time I've retrieved something from the Southern Weyr which belongs to the North.'' He laid his arm possessively about Sharra's shoulders.

Toric felt his composure leave him. *''You!''* He thrust his arm out at Jaxom, wanting to do many things at once, especially swat down that—that—impudent excresence. He was livid with the indignation of being under obligation to that—that lordling! That leggy, undeveloped *boy*! He wanted to rend Jaxom limb from body, but little though the white dragon might be, he was bigger than Toric, stronger than any man, and both dam and sire were not far away. There was *nothing* Toric could do but swallow his humiliation. He could feel the blood suffusing his face, pumping through his extremities. Impossible as it was for him to believe, he was faced with the fact that the boy had dared to retrieve Sharra—dared and done—and now faced him coolly. He had been in error to call the lad a coward! He had allowed himself to be swayed in his judgment by the jaundice of a milkbrother. Young Jaxom had acted like a proper lord, reclaiming the woman of his choice in spite of precautions. *''You* took the egg back! You and that—but the fire-lizards' images were black!''

''I'd be stupid not to darken a white hide if I make a night pass, wouldn't I?'' Jaxom asked scornfully.

''I knew it wasn't one of T'ron's riders.'' Toric was reduced to clenching and unclenching his fists as he struggled to regain his composure. ''But for you to . . . Well, now . . .'' He forced himself to smile, a trifle sourly, as he looked from the Benden Weyrleaders to the Harper. Then he started to laugh, losing anger and frustration as he roared away the stress. ''If you knew, lordling,'' and this time it was a respectful title as he pointed his finger at Jaxom, ''the plans you ruined, the— How many people knew it was you?'' He turned accusingly on the dragonriders.

''Not many,'' the Harper answered, also glancing at the Weyrleaders.

''I knew,'' Sharra said, ''and so did Brekke. Jaxom worried about that egg the whole time he was fevered.'' She gazed up at the boy proudly.

They made a handsome pair, Toric thought inconsequentially.

"Not that it matters now," Jaxom said. "What does matter is, do I now have your permission to marry Sharra and make her lady of Ruatha Hold?"

"I don't see how I can stop you," Toric had to admit, sweeping his arm up in irritation.

"Indeed you couldn't, for Jaxom's boast about Ruth's abilities is valid," F'lar said. "One must never underestimate a dragonrider, Toric." Then he grinned, softening the implicit warning. "Especially a Northern dragonrider."

"I shall bear that firmly in mind," Toric replied, letting chagrin color his voice. Indeed, he *had* become far too complacent about the distinction. "Especially in our present discussion. Before these impetuous youngsters interrupted us, we were discussing the extent of my Hold, were we not?"

He turned his back on his sister and her lordling and gestured to the others to return to their temporary hall.

13

SOUTHERN CONTINENT, NERAT HOLD, PP 15.10.23

Two days after Jaxom had triumphantly returned to Cove Hold with Sharra, and Toric had concluded his Holding agreement with the Benden Weyrleaders, contingent on confirmation by the Lord Holder Conclave, Piemur managed to find an opportunity to tell Master Robinton about Jayge and Ara.

"Another ancient settlement? Restored and lived in?" Astonished, Master Robinton leaned back in his great chair. Zair, asleep on his desk in the sun, woke up, blinking. "Bring me the relevant map." He tossed Piemur the key that unlocked the drawer in which his secret documents were kept. Masterscrivener Arnor had had his most discreet and accurate journeyman make three copies of all the maps found on the walls of the "flying ship," after which access to the ship had been restricted to Master Fandarel's most trusted Mastersmiths. "How kind of you, Piemur, to save something to amuse me just when it was beginning to be humdrum again," Robinton went on.

After Piemur had shown him the location of Paradise River, the Harper pored over the map a long time, murmuring to himself and occasionally grimacing. Well accustomed to his Master's ways, Piemur filled Robinton's goblet with wine and put it by his right hand. Piemur had been officially reassigned by the new Masterharper Sebell as journeyman to Cove Hold. He did not bother asking the new Masterharper if Toric had refused to have him back, or if Master Robinton had specifically requested him. What mattered to Piemur was that he was back with Master Robinton where, despite the old man's wistful complaints, things were never dull—especially since, having been given a clean bill of health by Master Oldive, the Harper had great plans for further exploration.

"A vast and marvelous land, Piemur," Robinton said, taking a sip of his wine. "And when one thinks of the plight of the holdless in Igen low caverns, those terrible rock cells in Tillek and High Reaches . . ." He sighed. "I think—" He broke off with a dismissive wave of his hand. "I let them talk me into retiring too soon is what I think."

Piemur laughed. "You're no more retired than I am, Master Robinton. Merely looking for a different kind of mischief to get into. Let Sebell cope with the Lord Holders, Craftmasters, and Weyrleaders. I rather thought you liked delving into the mounds?"

The Harper's gesture was testy. "If they'd find anything! Fandarel and Wansor have the best part of what has been discovered so far and are happy as gorged weyrlings with those totally undecipherable star maps. The few empty bottles—albeit made of a very curious substance—and broken mechanical parts simply do not stimulate my imagination. I want to know so much more than what the ancients threw away or left behind as too bulky to dismantle. I want to know their style of living, what they used, ate, wore, why they moved North, where they came from originally, how they got here, apart from using the Dawn Sisters as vehicles. That really must have been a staggering voyage. I want to reconstruct Landing and . . . Just how much was left there at—what did you call it?''

''Paradise River? You'd best judge yourself,'' Piemur said, at last getting his suggestion in edgewise. The journeyman was certain that once the Harper had met the resourceful and thoroughly likable Jayge and Ara, he would sponsor them—certainly against any claims Toric might make against them. ''They've a stoutly built and pleasant house; they've tamed wild stock and made do with what they could find and put to use. As you can see, they're far away from Southern's boundary.'' Journeyman and Master shared a smile, and then Piemur ventured a question. ''What, may your humble journeyman ask, is going to determine who holds what and where from now on?''

Master Robinton eyed his journeyman closely. ''A very good question, humble Journeyman Piemur.'' He winked. ''But not my problem.''

''I'll believe that when watchwhers fly.''

''Seriously, I've been provided with this magnificent residence''—the Harper's eyes sparkled—''sufficiently far away from stress and strain to preserve me. I cannot offend the many who built it for my use by leaving it even if I could talk a dragonrider into taking me North now and then.'' He frowned. ''Lessa took too narrow an interpretation of Oldive's advice.'' He sighed and, glancing out his window at the turquoise sea, smiled with resignation. ''And I am nominally in charge of excavations above.'' Then he said more briskly, ''Of course, if Weyrleaders or Lord Holders care to ask my opinion—'' He ignored Piemur's derisive snort. ''—I would remind them of the long-standing tradition of autonomy: Hall, Hold, and Weyr their own masters except when the safety of our world is at stake.''

''There's been a lot of traditions lying about in shards these days,'' Piemur remarked dryly.

"To be sure, but some were long past their usefulness."

"Who decides that?"

"Necessity."

"Does 'necessity' decide who gets to hold what where?" Piemur asked acerbically. Privately he felt that Toric had been granted far too much by the Benden Weyrleaders, even if, at that time, Lessa had also been bargaining for Jaxom's happiness with Sharra. He had the feeling that Master Robinton agreed with him on that score.

"Ah, we're back to your young friends again, are we?"

"That's where we started, and no more diversions, Master Robinton. *I'm* asking you for your 'opinion' on this matter. And, with you in charge of *excavations* and other ancient puzzles, I feel you should meet Jayge and Ara and see what they've found!"

"Quite right." The Harper drained his wine, rolled up the map and stood. "As well Lessa assigned old P'ratan to Cove Hold. He's discreet and willing enough if I don't ask him to do too much," he said as he reached for his riding gear. "Why do you call it 'Paradise River?' "

"You'll see," Piemur replied.

Jayge was hauling in his net when he saw the dragon in the sky.

It came gliding in from the east. He watched it in awe for all of a minute as astonishment and then anxiety made him relax his grip on the full heavy net. As it slid from his grasp, he recovered enough sense to snap a buoy on the last strand so he could retrieve the valuable net later. In another moment, he had hoisted the skiff's sail, seen the fresh offshore breeze fill it, and wondered if he could possibly beat the dragon to the shore.

Maybe, just maybe, Aramina was still asleep. He knew she

only heard dragons when she was awake, and he had left both his wife and the boy fast asleep when he had crept out to catch the dawn run of fish. If he could just warn her. While she heard fire-lizards—they both did—and had laughed about their recent astonishing images, she generally found their meaningless chitter more amusing than disturbing.

The green dragon, an old beast to judge by her whitened muzzle and the puckering wing scars, carried three people. She appeared to be taking her time about landing, circling slowly down. It even seemed as if she had timed her landing with Jayge's arrival at the strand. Just as Jayge hauled up the rudderboard, one of the passengers dismounted and came running down to the beach, unlatching his helmet. Piemur!

"Jayge, I've brought the Masterharper. P'ratan kindly conveyed us on Poranth." Piemur spoke quickly, smiling to reassure Jayge about the unexpected visitors. "It's all right. It's going to be all right for you and Ara," he added, lending a hand to help Jayge pull the little skiff above the high-tide mark on the sand.

Movement on the verandah of the house attracted Jayge's attention, and he caught just a glimpse of Ara collapsing in a faint.

"*Ara!*" he cried, and without even a nod in the direction of the two older men, he pelted up to the house and Ara's unconscious body. Hearing a dragon after all those years must have given her a terrible fright.

He had laid her on her bed and Piemur was offering her a cup of Jayge's brew by the time the Harper and the dragon-rider had joined them in the house. Readis, bawling with fright at the sight of the strange faces, turned rigid in Piemur's arms when the journeyman attempted to comfort him. Then he abruptly stopped his squawling. Piemur caught the direction of his look and saw Master Robinton making such absurd grimaces that the baby was too fascinated to howl, his tear-filled eyes fixed on the Harper.

When Ara regained consciousness, she stared white-faced at the visitors. Jayge felt her relax only a fraction, and somehow the pressure of her fingers on his arm suggested to him that she knew neither of them.

"Ara," he told her in urgent reassurance, "P'ratan's Poranth has brought Piemur and Master Robinton. They mean us to have what we've got here. It'll be our hold. Our own hold!"

Ara kept staring at the men, who were attempting by their manner and smiles to reassure her.

"I can appreciate the shock, dear lady, to be confronted with visitors so unexpectedly," Master Robinton said. "But today was really the first opportunity I've had to come."

"Ara, it's all right," Jayge reassured her, stroking her hair and patting her fingers where they clutched frantically at his vest.

"Jayge," she said in a low, constricted voice. "I didn't hear her!"

"You didn't?" Jayge thought to keep his voice low. "You didn't?" he repeated with more confidence. "Then why did you faint?"

"Because I didn't!" In that pained reply, Aramina managed to convey her conflicting emotions to Jayge.

He pulled her into his arms, rocking her gently and murmuring over and over that it was all right. It did not matter if she did not hear dragons anymore. She had no need to. And she must not be afraid. No one would censure her. She must relax and compose herself. Such a shock was not good for the baby.

"Here! This'll help," Piemur said, again offering the cup of fermented drink. "Believe me, Aramina, I know how it can be when you don't see anyone else for Turns and suddenly you've got callers."

At the use of his wife's full name, Jayge looked up in wary surprise.

"I recognized you from a sketch that was circulated after

your disappearance," the Masterharper explained kindly. He was jouncing Readis on his knee, and the toddler was gurgling with delight.

"My dear child," he went on when Aramina had recovered sufficiently. "It will be the best of all possible news that you are alive and so well, here in this fine Southern Hold. We all thought you dead at the marauders' hands!" There was a hint of rebuke in the glance he gave Jayge but none in his voice for Aramina. "I've had more surprises these past few weeks than ever in my lifetime. It's going to take me Turns to absorb it all."

"Master Robinton is very interested in ancient ruins, Jayge, Ara," Piemur said. "And I think yours have more to offer than the empty ones up on the Plateau."

Still amusing the baby, Master Robinton went on eagerly. "Piemur mentioned that you have found and are using articles of obvious antiquity, besides this most unusual dwelling. I saw the nets, boxes, and kegs, and I am amazed. The Plateau settlement will take us Turns to dig out, and so far we've found no more than a spoon, while you . . ." He gestured with his free hand to the various items he could see in the main room and included the dwelling itself.

"We haven't been able to do much," Ara said modestly, her courage restored. "Once we had the house finished—" she broke off apologetically and looked anxiously at Jayge. He was sitting beside her, one arm lightly around her shoulders, the other hand clasping hers.

"You've done marvels, my dear," Robinton corrected her firmly. "A skiff, fishing; we saw the animal pens and your garden—the undergrowth you've cleared!"

"Haven't you been troubled by Threadfall?" P'ratan asked anxiously, speaking for the first time.

"We stay out of it," Jayge replied with a wry grin, then smiled apologetically at the startled dragonrider. "I'm of trader Blood and survived the first Telgar Fall. So I'm used to being holdless."

"We never know just how our lives take shape, do we?" Master Robinton remarked, smiling with great good humor.

Jayge offered their guests klah and slices of fresh fruit, and bread Aramina had baked the previous day. She apologized for the texture, saying that she had not quite worked out the right grinding stones. Then she insisted on joining the Harper and the green rider on a tour of the other buildings on the river banks. Readis was persuaded to leave Master Robinton and go with his father and Piemur to salvage the nets and any fish they still contained.

"Impressive, truly impressive," Robinton kept saying as they moved from one place to the next, touching a wall, checking a door's closure, scuffing his boots on the floor. P'ratan said little, but his eyes were round, and he kept shaking his head in wonder, regarding Aramina with some awe. "Quite an extensive place. There must have been at least a hundred people living here, working the fields, fishing and—" He waved his hand distractedly. "—doing whatever else they did to create such durable materials."

When they reached the shed that was being used as a beasthold, he leaned against the rail, another remnant of the ancients' manufacture. "And you say you tamed all these animals yourself?" He smiled at her as a little queen swooped gracefully to land on her shoulder. "Do you hear what they say?"

He spoke kindly, but Aramina flushed and ducked her head in momentary embarrassment. "They talk a lot of nonsense," she said so disparagingly that the Harper sensed that recent fire-lizard conversations might have distressed her. "They *are* very good, minding Readis when we both have to be out of the hold. And Piemur showed us that they can be far more useful than we thought." She slid open a high, wide door in the biggest of the buildings. "This is where we found most of the useful stuff," she told them just as Jayge and Piemur rejoined them. With a brief apology, P'ratan wandered back to his green, who was basking on the sand.

"What we need," the Harper said, planting his fists on his belt, "is an accurate rendering of the settlement." He looked around the dim storehouse, at the pile of nets and the tumble of crates and barrels. "Where each building is, the state of it—a list, if you wouldn't mind, of the items you've made use of, what's left! I think I must send for Perschar. He finds it tedious to draw straight rows of empty buildings."

"Perschar?" Jayge exclaimed.

"You've met him?" Robinton was surprised.

"I was one of those who assaulted Thella's mountain base," Jayge replied with a bark of laughter. "I know him! I didn't know that you did."

"Of course I did. I prevailed on him to use his talents for the Harper Hall, and so I'd been informed of many of the thefts and the ingenious ways in which they were carried out long before Asgenar and Larad realized what was happening. Would you mind Perschar coming here for a few days on my behalf?"

Jayge hesitated, caught Ara's nod, and agreed. "A very clever man, and brave."

"Likes a bit of a challenge now and then, but he's as discreet as they come." The Harper smiled reassuringly at Ara. "I think some company would do you both the world of good. You can be on your own too long." Piemur noticed the sly glance directed at him and snorted. "My Zair," Master Robinton said, indicating the bronze fire-lizard that had landed on his shoulder only moments before, "could also take a message to your parents at Ruatha Hold if you'd like, Aramina. In fact, he's quite capable of carrying several, you know," he added, looking inquiringly at Jayge.

"Master Robinton—" Jayge began in a rush and then hesitated, looking helplessly at Aramina. She put her arm about his waist.

"Yes?"

"What are we?" And when the Harper regarded him in surprise, he elaborated. "Trespassers? Or what?" He gestured to the other buildings and the rich fields beyond. "Piemur says this isn't anybody's hold?" His voice lifted questioningly, and his eyes held an eloquent appeal.

Just as Piemur had hoped, the Masterharper had taken a liking to the couple. He beamed at them. "In my opinion," he said, shooting his journeyman a stern look, "you have undeniably established a secure and productive hold here. In my opinion, Holder Jayge, Lady Aramina, you may now do as you see fit. You have two Harper witnesses here to properly attest to your claim. We'll even wake P'ratan up," he offered, gesturing to the beach where the old green and his rider were dozing in the sun, "and ride a sweep of what should be included in this Paradise River Hold."

"Paradise River Hold?" Jayge asked.

"That's what I've been calling it," Piemur explained a bit sheepishly.

"It's a perfect name, Jayge," Ara put in. "Or should it be called 'Lilcamp Hold?' " she added noncommittally.

"I think," Jayge said, taking her hands in his and looking deeply into her eyes, "that naming it 'Lilcamp Hold' just because we got shipwrecked here would be presumptuous. I think out of gratitude we ought to use the name the ancients had for it."

"Oh, Jayge, I do, too!" She threw her arms about his neck and kissed him.

"Is becoming a holder as simple as this, Master Robinton?" Jayge asked, his face a bit red under his tan.

"In the south it will be," the Harper announced firmly. "I shall, of course, submit this matter to the Benden Weyrleaders, who should be consulted, but you have demonstrated your ability to Hold on your own, and according to traditional methods"—he gave Piemur a stern glance as the journeyman guffawed—"that has *always* been the rule!"

"Then if you don't mind, sir, if a message could be sent, could it be more than just that we're alive?" Jayge's face was eager, all trace of patient resignation erased. "There's so much more that could be done with more hands. If that's allowed?"

"It's your hold," the Harper said, and Piemur thought his tone defiant. The journeyman wondered just what the new Lord Toric's reaction would be.

Jayge was looking across the river with a proprietary smile, reexamining buildings and the lush forestry crowding against them. Aramina whispered to him, and he looked down at her, giving her shoulders a squeeze.

"I'd like to send for some of my Bloodkin," Jayge said.

"Always a good idea to have them share your good fortune," the Harper said approvingly.

Although the Harper would have been happy to sift through the contents of the storehouse, Piemur, with some assistance from Jayge and Ara, urged him to come back to the cool house and compose the messages. Zair was dispatched to Ruatha Hold with reassurances to Barla and Dowell, while Farli went to the harper at Igen Hold, who would locate the Lilcamp-Amhold train and deliver Jayge's missive.

"I've asked my aunt Temma and Nazer if they'd be willing to join us," Jayge said tentatively as he finished writing. "Only how will they get here? I'm still not sure where we are!"

"Paradise River Hold," Piemur replied irrepressibly.

"The Southern Continent is much more extensive than we originally believed," Robinton said after a reproving glance at his journeyman. "Master Idarolan is still sailing eastward and updating me by means of his second mate's fire-lizard. I believe that Master Rampesi is continuing westward past the Great Bay. In the meantime, I think we might prevail on P'ratan to convey your kin here, if they're willing to come and wouldn't overload Poranth. Would Temma and Nazer object to flying *between* on a dragon?" His eyes twinkled.

"Nothing fazes Temma or Nazer," Jayge replied with conviction.

After a refreshing lunch, Piemur suggested firmly that perhaps the time had come for Aramina to give the Harper a full
account of the past two years, while he and Jayge figured out
boundaries for Paradise River Hold.

"A fine thing when a harper has to teach a trader to bargain," Piemur said, mildly scoffing, though he found Jayge's
reluctance a refreshing change from Toric's rampant greed.
Jayge had to be reminded of Readis's and any future children's needs, as well as the requirements of Temma and Nazer, if they joined him. "You told me how far you and Scallak
had walked west, east, and south. Well, we'll just make those
your boundaries. I'm good at figuring out how far one can
travel in a day over what kind of terrain. This'll be a good
spread and still won't take that much of a bite out of the
continent."

When the heat of the day had passed, P'ratan was quite
willing to take harper and holder on an aerial sweep. Bright
red stakes of the ancients' durable manufacture were taken
from the storehouse and pounded into the ground; trees were
distinctively cut and distances confirmed. Piemur marked two
maps, properly witnessed them with the Master Robinton and
P'ratan, and left one with Jayge.

The Masterharper assured the young couple that he would
personally speak to the Weyrleaders and the Conclave on their
behalf at an imminent meeting.

"Please come back whenever you can, Master Robinton,
Rider P'ratan," Aramina told them as they escorted them to
green Poranth. "Next time it won't be such a shock not to
hear the dragon coming!"

Master Robinton took her hands in his, smiling kindly down
at her. "Do you regret that you no longer hear dragons?"

"No." Aramina shook her head violently. Her smile was
more wistful than sad. "It's better this way. Listening to the
fire-lizards is quite enough, thank you. Have you any idea
why I should stop hearing them?" she asked shyly.

"No," the Harper replied honestly. "It's an unusual enough ability. Only Brekke and Lessa can hear other riders' dragons—and then only with conscious effort. It could have something to do with moving from girlhood to womanhood. I'll ask Lessa—she will not chide you, my dear," he added when Aramina's hands clenched nervously in his. "I'll see to that."

When the dragon took off and suddenly disappeared, the baby in Jayge's arms was startled into crying, looking wide-eyed at his mother for reassurance.

"They'll be back, lovey. Now it's time for you to be in bed."

"Are you truly glad you don't hear dragons anymore, Ara?" Jayge asked much later, after they had lain in bed for long hours discussing their plans for Paradise River Hold. He raised himself on his elbow to see her face in the moonlight flooding in through the window.

"When I was a little girl, I loved to hear them talking. They didn't know I was listening." Her mouth curved in a little smile. "I could pretend to have conversations with them. It was exciting to know where they were going, or where they'd been, and desperately saddening when I knew who had been injured. But I used to pretend, and this used to be terribly important to me, that they knew who Aramina was." The smile disappeared. "Mother was always very strict with us. Even when my father was working at Keroon Beasthold, she wouldn't let me play with many of the cothold children, and we weren't allowed in the main Hold. When we were forced to live in Igen low caverns, Mother got even stricter. We weren't allowed to play with anyone. So the dragons became even more important to me. They were freedom, they were safety, they were so marvelous! And when the hunters started taking me with them, my hearing dragons was my way of getting a larger share of what was available in Igen low caverns."

She was suddenly silent, and Jayge knew she was remembering the trouble that her ability to hear dragons had caused.

Gently, to remind her he was there, he began to stroke her hair.

"It was a wonderful gift for a child to have," she murmured. "But I grew up. And the gift became dangerous. Then you found me." She began to fondle him, as she often did when she wished them to make love. He held her closely for a long moment, trembling with the gift that Aramina gave to him.

Perschar was more than willing to go to Paradise River. "Anything to get me away from Master Arnor's precise journeyman. I detest having to measure everything before I draw it. My eye is quite keen, you know. It will be nice to have something other than squares and rectangles to draw. Did the ancients have no imagination at all?"

"Rather a lot," Robinton replied. "They got here, you know." He pointed downward, meaning Pern.

"Oh, yes, rather." Perschar was hauling watercolored scenes of things other than straight lines out of his carrysack.

"Where's this?" Piemur asked, nicking one out of the pile and holding it up.

"That hill?" Perschar craned his neck. "Oh, that's down by the grid that Fandarel's young men are trying to pry out of the ground."

Master Robinton turned the drawing so that he could see it. "I don't think that's a real hill," he mused.

"Of course it is. Trees, bushes—quite irregular. Nothing like the others. Too tall for their one-level buildings, and sort of—" He paused, his eye arrested suddenly by what the harpers had seen. "You know, it just could be." He made gestures indicating several levels with his hands. "Well, don't dig it all up until I get back, will you?"

After Perschar was handed over to P'ratan to be conveyed to Paradise River, Master Robinton propped the sketch up on his desk and stared at it. Piemur picked up a charcoal and, thriftily using a corner of a scrap leaf, did some alterations.

"Hmm, more than one level, huh?" Robinton murmured.

"It's sort of halfway down the grid strip the flying ships used," Piemur said.

"We could go have a look," the Masterharper suggested. "I'd like to find something myself! Wouldn't you?"

"Not if I have to dig it out by myself," Piemur replied.

"Would I ask you to do something I wouldn't do?" Master Robinton demanded, wide-eyed with an innocence that appeared remarkably genuine.

"Frequently! Fortunately there're enough willing hands up at the Plateau, so I'll see that I have help."

P'ratan returned from Paradise River later that afternoon, apologizing for taking so long on a simple errand. "Rather a lot going on down at your Paradise now," he told the harpers as they left Cove Hold for the beach to rouse Poranth. The old green tended to doze off whenever she was not moving. "He's got Temma, Nazer, and their youngster, and the young holder traded some of those things he's got stored for Master Garm to sail some holdless Craftsmen down. There's talk now of setting up a seahold. Told 'em to get in touch with Crafthalls. They've usually got a few journeymen'd like to change around for the experience. Place is bustlin' now. Nice to see."

Fortunately Poranth was of the opinion that it did not matter where she did her dozing and conveyed them to the Plateau. As she circled lazily for a landing, Piemur noted that the work was progressing systematically: Minercraftmaster Esselin was in charge of the excavations, using the larger building F'lar had discovered as storage for the artifacts so far uncovered, and Lessa's building as an onsite office. Several more in her section had been dug out and were being used as living quarters for the diggers and rodmen. At least one building in each immediately adjacent section had been cleared enough to permit inspection.

Master Robinton and Piemur found Master Esselin in his

office and begged the loan of several workers. Breide, Toric's ubiquitous representative, hurried in to hear what was going on.

"The hill, you say?" Master Esselin said, consulting his map. "Which hill? What hill? There's no hill down on my list for excavating. I really can't divert men from my schedule to dig out a hill."

"Which hill?" Breide asked. He and Master Esselin had an uneasy truce. Breide, blessed with an unusually sharp and copious memory, could remember such details as how many teams to excavate which shaped mound, how much water and how many meals they needed, and exactly where what had been found in which building. He knew which Crafthall and hold had sent men and supplies, and how many hours they had worked. He was useful, and he was a nuisance.

Silently Master Robinton unrolled Perschar's sketch and presented it to them.

"That hill?" Master Esselin was clearly not impressed by its potential. "It's not even on the list." But he looked inquiringly at Breide.

"A few sample rod holes, including the walk to and from the site!" Breide said in the flat voice of the slightly deaf. "It would take about an hour." He shrugged, waiting for Esselin's decision.

"It's a hunch," Master Robinton said. He spoke with so much winning confidence that Breide gave him a sharp glance.

"Two rodmen, for an hour," Master Esselin conceded and, according Master Robinton a respectful bow, left his office to give the necessary orders.

"I should think, Master Robinton, that those flying ships would have a priority," Breide said as he followed the two harpers, the rodmen resignedly plodding after them.

"Well, *they* are clearly Master Fandarel's responsibility," Master Robinton said, dismissing Breide's implicit and repeated argument. "He is so ingenious. These rods he designed especially for excavation work, for example, make it possible to tell, with a few strokes of the hammer, the depths of earth above a mound. I understand that he's trying to develop a more efficient way of digging, a revolving scooping apparatus.''

Piemur admired the way the Harper handled Breide. The man's persistence annoyed the journeyman. A person could not go anywhere on the Plateau without him popping up and asking questions.

''I really don't see why you would want to bother with this,'' Breide said as they came down the slope to the site in question. He was a man who sweated hard and wore a band on his forehead to keep the moisture from spilling over his brows into his eyes. He was perspiring freely and uncomfortably. Piemur wondered why he did not get himself one of the grass hats that some enterprising craftsman had been weaving as head protection. ''An hour, Master Esselin said,'' Breide reminded them as if he had a timekeeper in his head.

''I'm sure we're keeping you from other duties, Breide. Look, there, Piemur!'' The Harper pointed to the south, where Smithcrafthall journeymen were trying to dig up a section of the massive grid that the ancients had laid. Something glinted brightly in the sunlight.

''They do seem to have raised something,'' Piemur remarked, quick to catch the Harper's intention. Breide, his attention caught by the sight of men wrestling with crowbars and shouting, trotted off to investigate.

Free of Breide's unwelcome presence at last, the harpers neared their destination and scrutinized it carefully.

''I think Perschar's right about levels,'' Robinton said, taking off his hat and mopping his brow. They walked all around it, then stood off a ways and inspected it, the rodmen waiting patiently.

''I'd say three levels,'' Piemur remarked judiciously. ''A central tower on a wider base. The lip of the south wall has fallen in, which makes that side look like a natural slope.''

''How convenient,'' Master Robinton said, grinning mischievously at his journeyman. ''Then let us try the other end, which hasn't collapsed and is out of Breide's sight.'' He gestured to the rodmen. ''The ancients were rather big on windows. We'd best try here, where a corner might be.''

Piemur held the point of the rod at shoulder height while the hammer man tapped. The rod went in two handspans before they all heard the *thunk!* as it met resistance.

''Could be a rock,'' the hammerman said with the shrug of experience. ''Try it a little higher.''

Soon they had made a series of vertical thrusts, each meeting resistance within a finger joint of the others.

''If you ask me, you've got a wall in there,'' the hammerer said. ''Want to try for a window? Or d'you want us to get some diggers down here? We're rodmen, you know.''

''I certainly appreciate that,'' Master Robinton assured him. ''Now, in your experience, where would a window be situated? That is, if indeed we've struck a wall.''

''Oh, you have, Master. And I'd say, if this is your ordinary sort of place, there'd be a window . . . here.'' The man measured off ten handspans and, resting his fist on the place, turned for the Harper's approval. ''That is, a' course, if this *is* your ordinary sort of place.''

''Clearly you don't think it's ordinary,'' Master Robinton ventured.

''Not being so far away from all the rest of 'em, I'd say it isn't.''

''Hour's near up,'' the rodman who had not spoken before said. Continual work on the Plateau had burned his skin a deep brown.

''Humor an old man and drive the rod in,'' Robinton said, gesturing with uncharacteristic impatience.

The rod was set, and the fourth blow sunk it to its head.

"Got a hollow in there," the hammerman said as the rod-man struggled to pry the probe out. "Not a window. You crash in windows. Can hear it. Sorry about that."

"Time's up," the other said and, settling the rod to his shoulder, began to hike back up to the main settlement.

"Want I should ask Master Esselin to send you some diggers?" the hammerer asked helpfully, wiping the inside of his grass hat with a colorful kerchief.

"We've hit a hollow, haven't we?" The Masterharper said dispiritedly. "Well, it was just a hunch." He sighed heavily, leaning back against a tree and fanning himself with his hat.

"Lots of people got hunches in this place," the man replied. "Breeds 'em, you might say. Good day to you, Masterharper, Journeyman!" He resettled his own hat and followed in the other's footsteps.

"I want to widen that hole, Piemur," Master Robinton said when he was sure the men were out of earshot. "See what you can find."

"They took the hammer with them."

"There's plenty of branches and rocks," the Harper said, beginning to search.

Piemur found a sturdy stick and began to pound around the rod hole. The Harper kept ducking around the side of the hill, to be sure that the men were still trudging back to Master Esselin's and that Breide was occupied with the Smith's men. Then, becoming impatient, Piemur held the branch firmly and made a run at the wall. The branch knocked a substantial hole in the dirt and took Piemur off his feet. He brushed himself off and peered inside.

"It's hollow all right, Master. And dark!"

"Good. Zair, come over here and be useful. Piemur, call Farli to help. They're better diggers than anyone Esselin has."

"Yes, but that'll leave a hole for Breide to see."

"Let's worry about that when the time comes. My hunch is stronger than ever!"

"This place breeds 'em, you know!" Piemur muttered, but Zair and Farli busily began to dig. "Easy, easy!" he cried as clods of grass and dirt flew out in all directions.

"Can you see anything yet, Piemur?" Master Robinton asked from his post.

"Give us time!" Piemur could feel the sweat running down his back under the loose shirt he wore. I should get a sweat-band like Breide's, he thought, if the Harper plans more of this sort of activity. When the opening was large enough for entry, Piemur peered through. "Not enough light to see much, but this is definitely manmade. Shall I send Farli for a candle?"

"Do, please!" The Harper's voice was full of pained entreaty. "How big is the hole?"

"Not big enough." Piemur paused long enough to retrieve his thick branch before he renewed his efforts alongside Zair, battering the soil into the hollow in preference to removing it.

By the time Farli had returned with a candle in each claw, Piemur had an opening large enough to crawl through. The two fire-lizards, upside down on clawholds at the top of the hole, peered in. Their inquiring chirps echoed. Then Zair pushed off and Farli followed him, their chittering reassuring Piemur as he struggled to strike a sulfur stick ablaze and light a candle.

"Anything? Anything?" The Masterharper fairly jiggled with impatience, anxious to succeed without Breide's interference.

"Give me a chance!" As the journeyman extended the candle inside, the flame bent and nearly went out before it straightened and illuminated the interior. "I'm going in."

"I'm coming, too."

"You'll never make it! Well . . . don't bring in half the hill with you!"

Piemur grabbed Master Robinton's arm to steady him. They both heard the crunch of something under their feet. Adjusting their candles' light, they saw the shimmer of glass shards littering the floor. The Harper toed a clear space and hunkered down to touch the floor.

"This is some kind of cement, I think. Not as smooth a job as in others." As he rose, both candles flickered. "Air's fresher in here than it usually is in long-enclosed places," he remarked.

"That collapsed side may account for that. We should have looked on the side of the hill for fissures," Piemur remarked.

"And let Breide come bouncing up for something to tell Toric?" The Harper snorted and began to look around, now that his eyes were accustomed to the dim light. Holding his candle high, Piemur took a few steps to his left, then uttered a suppressed "yipe!" of discovery.

"Your hunch pays off, Master," he said, striding to the wall. Candlelight illuminated a group of dusty rectangles pinned there. "Maps?" With a reverent touch, Piemur brushed aside the accumulation of grit and ash to reveal a transparent coating that had protected its treasure for unknown Turns. "Maps!"

"What did they use?" Master Robinton whispered, softly brushing dust from another. "By the First Egg!" He turned with incredulous disbelief to his journeyman. "Not just outlines this time, but names! Landing! They called the Plateau 'Landing.' "

"How original!"

"Monaco Bay, Cardiff! The biggest volcano is Garben. It's all here, Piemur."

"Even Paradise River!" Piemur had been following the coastline with his index finger, making a zigzagging trail in the dust as he moved it eastward. "Sadrid, Malay River, Boca . . . and would you look at this, they hadn't got as far as Southern!"

Zair and Farli flitting back from their own explorations recalled them from their wonder.

"Quickly, Piemur. See if you can pry the nails up. We mustn't let Breide find *these*!" Robinton had his beltknife out and was working on one of the larger maps. The nails popped easily out. "Roll them up. We'll give them to Zair and Farli to convey for us. Quickly. Take a strip off your shirttail to tie them. It would be premature indeed for Toric to discover what a relatively small portion of Southern he has actually acquired. Then we've got to see if there's anything else important on this site."

"Breide was way off up at the other end, wasn't he?"

"Yes, but he'll have seen the rodmen leaving without us. He's a suspicious sort."

"I'm amazed that he's allowed here," Piemur said, tying up his three maps.

"Better the rogue you know," the Harper said. "Zair! Take this to Cove Hold. Quickly now!"

Zair clutched the tube, as long as the span of one wing, settled it to a balance between his claws, and promptly disappeared. Piemur gave Farli her burden and instructions, and she followed the bronze.

Distantly the harpers heard someone calling them.

"Let's see what's to be seen," Master Robinton said in an unnecessary whisper and moved to the door still half ajar.

"What if there's more that should be hidden?" Piemur asked, but he followed.

"If there is, I'll think of something."

They were in a corridor, with doors opening onto it. Quick glances inside each discovered nothing more promising than the usual discarded bits and pieces. At the end of the corridor there was a hall, filled with the debris of what must have been stairs before the collapse of the southern wall and seeping water had destroyed that end of the building. They both heard the unmistakable soft noises of tunnel snakes retreating.

"Do you think snakes breed in here like hunches, Piemur?" The Harper held his candle high, craning his neck to see up the stairwell. "How unusual! So much of what they built seems indestructible."

"Maybe this was a temporary building, something to do with the flying ships."

"I wonder what's up there," the Harper said, gesturing for Piemur to add his light. They saw glimpses of white root tendrils and the glisten of wet walls but nothing informative.

"*Master Robinton!*" The strident shout made the Harper wince.

"Let's put a brave face on our disappointment, Piemur!"

As they retraced their steps, Piemur noticed a square placard on the door of the room by which they had entered the corridor. It came off easily. He held up his candle to see the usual bold letters, as bright as the day they had been first inscribed.

Breide came stumbling into the room. "Are you all right? Did you find anything?"

"Snakes for the main part," Piemur replied glumly. "And this!" He held up the sign, which read "OUT TO LUNCH."

The Benden and Fort Weyrleaders, Lord Holders Jaxom and Lytol, and Masters Fandarel, Wansor, and Sebell met at Cove Hold to view the new maps. A damp cloth had cleaned away the dust and grit, and Master Fandarel was in awe of the clear film that had protected the surfaces. Some of the numerals that had been printed on the covering had apparently faded, though Piemur's careful washing had not blurred others.

There were two maps of the Southern Continent, each with different legends on them: the largest one was inscribed with the ancient names and showed clearly defined areas. A second showed the terrain in great detail, including hill and plain contours, and river and ocean depths. The third and smallest

continental map, the labels done in minute lettering, had su-
perscriptions of numerals below each name. The fourth map
was of "Landing" itself, with each of the squares named and
other sections marked INF, HOSP, WRHSE, VET, AGRI, MECH,
and SLED REP. A fifth plate, which Piemur and N'ton suggested could represent the area to the south of the grid, indicated underground caves. The last one showed several sites,
one clearly labeled MONACO BAY, another the pointed penin-
sula just east of Cove Hold, and the third Paradise River. The
wide strand along the sea on both sides was covered with
figures in orange, yellow, red, blue, and green.

"Ah, yes, Paradise River," Master Robinton said in a
fond voice and then cleared his throat. Piemur closed his eyes
and held his breath. He was at the meeting only because he
had been with the Harper when the maps had been found.
"Lovely place. Piemur, we really must trace that river to its
source."

"Oh?" Lessa said, looking up from the maps to give her
old friend a long look. "You are supposed to be taking it easy,
Robinton." A worried frown creased her forehead.

"Well, it's really not that far away, as you can see for yourself," Robinton replied, sounding slightly annoyed as he used
finger and thumb to measure the distance between Cove Hold
and Paradise River. "And I am also supposed to be supervis-
ing excavations and artifacts."

"The excavations at the Plateau," Lessa stated, eyeing the
Harper suspiciously.

"It was Piemur who found these fascinating ruins on his
way here," Robinton replied, looking abused. "Inhabited."

"Inhabited?" everyone echoed.

"Inhabited?" Lessa asked pointedly, her eyes wide.

"Only a pair of shipwrecked northerners and their baby
son," Piemur began and saw from the gleam in the Harper's
eye that he had made a good beginning. He glowered back
before he returned Lessa's inquiring stare. He was not certain

why he was to become the culprit in the matter. He looked across the table at Jaxom, who shrugged helplessly. Lytol merely watched, his face unreadable. "A resourceful couple. They've survived two Turns or more."

"These illegal sailings . . ." Lessa began, scowling and sitting back in her chair. She crossed her arms, emphasizing her dislike of such adventuring.

"Not at all," Piemur replied. "They were on an authorized voyage from Keroon Beasthold, bringing Toric—I mean, Lord Toric—some breeding pairs. Five people survived the storm, but injuries killed one before they found out his name, and two died of fire-head the following spring."

"And?" Lessa's foot tapped, but Piemur noticed a gleam of interest in F'lar's eyes and a sympathetic grin on N'ton's face. Fandarel listened, one eye on the ambiguous chart before him, while Wansor could be heard tutting happily to himself, his nose a scant fingertip from the map he was assiduously studying.

"They repaired some dilapidated buildings they found on the riverbanks and have done pretty well for themselves, I think," Piemur continued. "Knocked together a little skiff, tamed some runnerbeasts, planted a garden . . ."

Jaxom leaned forward on the table, keenly interested.

"Paradise River?" Lessa closed her eyes and uncrossed her arms to throw them up in an exasperated gesture of surrender. "And you like them, Robinton, and want them to hold?"

"Well, someone will have to, Lessa," Robinton said, looking abashed. "If you ask my opinion . . ." He glanced at Lytol and Jaxom for support.

"I haven't." Lessa glared at Jaxom and Lytol in a clear order not to encourage the Masterharper.

"I think too much is being made of 'permission' to come here," Robinton went on, ignoring her sarcasm. "Master Idarolan has, it is true, issued warnings that all shipmasters must report Southern landings to him. But just look at the breadth of land here. This big map—'' He rapped his knuckles on the largest continental map. ''—shows us just how *much* inhabitable land there is.''

''And no Weyrs,'' F'lar put in sardonically.

Robinton waved that aside. ''The land here protects itself.''

''D'ram's worrying himself to the bone over the Plateau and Cove Hold as it is,'' Lytol said, speaking for the first time.

''The young Lilcamps have been careful to shelter both themselves and their beasts,'' Robinton went on, ''in buildings they've restored from ancient remains.''

''What kind of remains?''

''These.'' From a cabinet behind him Robinton produced a sheaf of sketches; Piemur recognized Perschar's work. The Harper skidded each sheet down over the map, casually describing the scene. ''The beach as seen from the verandah of the house. The house—it has twelve rooms—as seen from the eastern strand, with Jayge's boat. Another view of the harbor with the fishnetting—Jayge cobbled up nets from material he found in one of the storehouses. This is the storehouse. You can just make out the beasthold. Ah, this is looking south from the verandah. And another of the western bank and some of the ruins. This charming little fellow playing in the sand is young Readis.'' By the clever order in which Robinton was presenting the pictures, Piemur guessed his intention. ''This is Jayge—son of the traders Lilcamp-Amhold. Quite a reliable train. He plans to bring over some of his Bloodkin. And this is his wife!''

''Aramina!'' Lessa snatched up that sketch before it could settle to the table.

F'lar gave an exclamation of surprise and looked over her shoulder, a startled expression on his face. ''Robinton, you have some explaining to do!''

Seeing that Lessa had gone quite pale under her weather-tanned skin, Piemur quickly poured out a cup of wine for her. She took it absently, her narrowed eyes on the Harper.

''Do calm yourself, my dear,'' Robinton said. ''I've been

trying to think of a way of breaking this good news, but there have been so many demands on your time and energy, and so much has been happening over the last few months . . ."

"You've known Aramina was alive for months?"

"No, no. No, only a few days, in fact. Piemur met them months ago, before he got to Cove Hold. The very day that—"

"That Baranth flew Caylith," Jaxom put in when the Harper faltered. Glancing sharply at Piemur, the young Ruathan Lord Holder added, "A lot happened that day, too."

"Piemur wouldn't have known about Aramina, my dear Lessa. He wasn't even north during that period. But she confided in me, if you'll listen."

Lessa was quite willing to hear everything that Aramina had told the Harper, though she was furious that Benden had been allowed to believe the girl dead. The heat in her eyes suggested that her first meeting with Jayge and Aramina might include some recriminations.

"She no longer hears dragons," the Harper said gently when the retelling was done.

Lessa sat very still, except for her fingers, which tapped out an uneven rhythm on the armrests of her chair. She looked up at F'lar, then across to N'ton; her gaze flicked from Jaxom to Lytol's expressionless face and rested on Fandarel, who looked back at her without concern.

"And she is happy with this Jayge?" the Weyrwoman asked.

"One fine son already and another baby due." When Lessa discounted that as a measure of contentment, the Harper continued. "He's a resourceful and provident man."

"Jayge adores her," Piemur said with a broad grin. "And I've seen the way she looks at him. They could do with some company, though." As neatly as the Harper could have done it himself, Piemur suggested the possibility of what had already been accomplished. "It's been pretty lonely. Even for Paradise!"

"How big is Paradise?" Lessa asked. There was noticeable relief as she appeared to relent.

Piemur and N'ton both reached to pull the appropriate chart in front of Lessa.

"Not as much as this is marked, certainly," Piemur said, tapping the squared-off section. The site actually extended much farther east and west; the map went as far as the bend in the river that Jayge had mentioned.

"A rough estimate," Lessa suggested, a half-smile turning up the left-hand side of her mouth. She knew very well that Piemur could provide a reasonably accurate one.

The Masterharper handed over his copy of the witnessed hold map. "Here!"

"Does this establish a precedent, old friend?" Lytol asked quietly.

"A better one, I feel, than the method Toric employed." He held up his hand to ward off Lessa's rebuke. "Different circumstances now obtain. But very soon now, you Weyrleaders, Craftmasters, and Lord Holders must decide which precedent to follow. Toric's or Jayge's? In my opinion, a man ought to be able to Hold what he has proved."

Master Wansor's rather squeaky voice broke the silence that followed Master Robinton's quiet challenge. "Did they have dragons then?"

"Why?" Realizing that she had spoken more curtly than she had meant to, Lessa softened her bluntness with a smile.

Wansor blinked at her. "Because I don't see how the ancients got about such vast holdings. There are no tracks or trails listed. The coastline or river situations would be easy enough to reach, but this Cardiff isn't near a river and not very close at all to Landing. I suppose the mining facilities marked here at Drak-ee's Lake used to be one of the rivers, but that isn't specified, or a seaport marked. I really don't understand how they kept in touch unless they had dragons."

"Or other flying ships?" Jaxom asked.

"More efficient sailing vessels?" N'ton suggested.

"We have found many broken parts that were beautifully crafted," Master Fandarel said, "but not a single complete motor or engine or other mechanical device that requires such pieces. Not in the oldest of the Records in my Hall. We have found three immense disabled vehicles that the fire-lizards inform us once were airborne. I do not think their design would be efficient over short distances—too awkward and heavy. The tubes in the rear suggest that their motion was upward." He tilted his hand and massive forearm in demonstration. "They must have had other vehicles."

"This is so exasperating," Lessa exclaimed, scowling. "We cannot do everything at once! You may be reasonably safe from Threadfall in the South, but every wing is vital in keeping the north and all its people protected. We just can't move everyone South!"

"Once everyone moved north," Robinton said, beaming at her. "To 'shield.' "

"Until the grubs spread themselves to protect the land," F'lar added, laying one reassuring hand on her shoulder.

"While the Weyrs protected Hold and Hall," N'ton put in.

"We have such a lot to learn about this world," Robinton said quite happily.

"There are answers somewhere." Master Fandarel sighed heavily. "I would be content with just a few."

"I would be content with one!" F'lar said, looking out the window to the moonlit scene. Jaxom nodded in sympathy.

"So, the Paradise River Hold is confirmed to Jayge and Aramina Lilcamp?" the Harper asked with sudden briskness.

"It is much the better precedent to follow," Lytol agreed. "I shall, if you wish, suggest this at the next Conclave."

"That's going to be a full meeting," F'lar said wryly, but he nodded.

"Why is it that what is forbidden," the Harper said drolly, "is all the more exciting?"

"You can take it from one who knows," Piemur made bold

to add, "that the Southern Continent has a way of making or breaking you."

"Just what is it doing to you, Master Robinton?" Lessa asked in her sweetest and most dangerous voice. But she smiled, and the smile was genuine.

The news of a second hold gradually filtered to the North, to be commented on by Lord Holders and Crafthall Masters. There were those who delighted in Jayge's elevation, and some who found his new eminence distasteful for a variety of reasons. Toric was one such, but he slowly overcame chagrin and resentment. In the North, a gaunt, scar-faced woman swore savagely when she heard, kicking her saddle across the narrow interior of her cave dwelling, throwing about her other belongings, and damaging the breakable without relief to her fury and bitter disappointment.

When her temper had abated sufficiently for her to think clearly, she sat down by the ashes of her fire and the spilled kettle that had contained her evening meal and began to plot.

Jayge and Aramina! How had he found the girl? Surely Dushik would have been on guard. She had had cause to doubt Readis's loyalty ever since she had killed Giron, who had become a useless handicap in their desperate flight from her hold. Readis had openly opposed her plan to abduct Aramina and then, suddenly, he had acquiesced, a reversal she had not trusted. But once down that pit, the girl had been as good as dead. *How* had that wretched little trader man rescued her?

Her mind seethed over that now indisputable fact. Aramina had been rescued and was alive and well in the south, enjoying prestige and comfort while she, Thella, had nearly died from a noxious and debilitating infection that had left her scarred. Had either Dushik or Readis reached the appointed meeting place, she would have fared much better. As it was, it had been weeks before she had recovered from the fever.

Weak and unable to focus her mind on new plans, Thella had drifted, carefully avoiding holds until she found herself a secluded valley in Nerat, where quantities of food easily gathered had somewhat restored her to health. She had been appalled at the scarring on her face and the wisps that were all that was left of her once luxuriant hair. All Thella's misfortunes could be traced back to that whelp spawned by an insignificant trader, who had prevented her from finding a miserable girl who could have made life so much more predictable.

Periodically she had comforted herself with the torments Aramina would have suffered before succumbing to terror and starvation in that dark and slimy pit. She still had to settle accounts with the trader, and she thought long and pleasantly about how she would wreak her revenge on Jayge and the entire Lilcamp train.

To do so, she would have to recover full strength, and though the time it took to do so became another cause to resent Jayge, Thella achieved it. A deep tan reduced the shock of her facial scars, and her hair was reasonably thick again by the time she saddled her runner to take up her task.

She replenished her empty pouch with marks after a fortunate evening encounter with a farmer journeyman. She appropriated his clothing once he no longer needed it. Before his demise, he had genially brought her up to date on nearly a full Turn's news. His enthusiasm for the opening of the Southern Continent almost made her abandon her initial plans to go south and stake out in the tropical wilderness the holding which had so long been denied her.

As she knew the Lilcamp-Amhold train initiated its sweeps from Igen, she took herself back to the low caverns. To her satisfaction she learned that, while Borgald Amhold had given up trading, the Lilcamp folk were still traveling. She began to make plans, first revisiting all her old caves to see which were still undiscovered and usable. And she began recruiting.

At first she was not too successful. The stories about her had made many people wary of flouting the authority of Hold and Weyr; so although the population of the low cavern had changed sufficiently that most of those who might recognize her were gone, and those that remained were confused by her altered appearance, she found few willing accomplices. But once she had heard of Paradise River Hold, her energies were redirected and galvanized. Jayge and Aramina would live only as long as it took her to recruit sufficient men, acquire a ship, and sail south.

14

SOUTHERN CONTINENT, PP 15–17

Over the next two Turns, Piemur had reason to recall Lessa's comment—or had it been a challenge?—to Master Robinton. There were changes of all kinds, but that was only natural, though some were rather spectacular, such as Menolly, Sharra, and Brekke all having sons on the same day. According to Silvina, Menolly gave birth to Robse between one note and the next; Sharra had slightly more difficulty producing Jarrol; and Nemekke arrived, two weeks before he was due, just before midnight, Benden Weyr time. Robinton and Lytol, deciding that they were the spiritual grandfathers of Menolly's and Sharra's sons, drank to their health, and that of Brekke's second boy, with sufficient wine to have drowned all three.

And there were other changes: Piemur's prediction that Southern hazards would sort out aspiring holders proved correct. As tales from discouraged immigrants circulated north, the wave of northerners venturing south lost its impetus. Piemur knew that Master Robinton had had a hand in that through Master Sebell's offices. The Southern Continent was having an effect on the Harper, fascinating him, as it had Piemur, with its lush beauty and incredible bounty and the allure of the mystery still locked in the ruins of another time.

During the first Turn, Master Rampesi and Master Idarolan finally sighted each other, halfway around the world from Cave Hold. To mark the historic occasion, the two captains hammered a stout red stake into a hillside above the bay, and the festivities lasted well into the early dawn hours. There was a good deal of friendly banter over which ship had sailed the farthest, but as *Dawn Sister* was clearly the bigger, faster vessel, Master Rampesi finally gave way to his Craftmaster. Then they continued their explorations of the Southern shores, one heading eastward and the other westward, back to their ports of origin. Both shipmasters' reports, delivered to the Conclave of Weyrleaders, Lord Holders, and Craftmasters, indicated a varied terrain, including precipitous cliffs and arid desert with sparse and unattractive vegetation but also a reassuringly large portion of inhabitable lands. That information considerably reduced the friction that was developing over titular possession of choice areas. The Weyrleaders were implacable on the point that northern Lord Holders, already well established, should not look to the South for their own benefit.

Piemur was proud of and impressed by Master Robinton's continued insistence on small holdings. Paradise River Hold, rather than Southern, was constantly cited as the acceptable precedent. The Weyrleaders, besieged by petitioners, finally conceded that point, adding the provision that no one already in possession of a hold could expect to be granted one in the South. With greatly increased supplies of all raw materials available from the South, Craftmasters increased their numbers of apprentices and more walked the tables as journeymen to support broader holder requirements.

With no need any longer to limit mating flights to keep the

dragon population down to that which the existing Weyrs could accommodate, there were soon sufficient weyrlings to populate a new Weyr in the thick forest between Landing and Monaco. T'gellan, rider of bronze Monarth, was appointed as Weyrleader to the Eighth Weyr, designated as Eastern until a suitable name could be agreed upon. T'gellan found his new position no sinecure, since he had to deal both with older dragons and riders, unable to fly full Falls, and weyrlings sent to Eighth for a season to perfect their fighting skills before being added to Northern wings.

Southern dragonriders turned out to be useful after all, despite the land's defenses—in the form of those amazing grubs—against Thread. After a storm of nasty tangles ripped through some of the dense forests, Weyrleader T'gellan increased sweepriders, and even Lord Toric, once he had seen the damage done by a series of tangles, lost his complacence and organized ground crews.

A nearby Weyr, with an old friend as Weyrleader, provided Piemur and his master with any number of willing beasts to help them explore, far more extensively than perhaps Benden might realize. To their delight, they found more ruins along the river that flowed on Mount Garben's western flank. And Master Robinton knew of suitable folk to move into those old holdings—ostensibly for onsite excavations.

D'ram passed his leadership on to K'van, whose Heth surprised complacent older bronze riders by flying Adrea's Beljeth in her mating flight. D'ram retired to Cove Hold, where he was well received by Master Robinton and Lytol, the retired Lord Warder of Ruatha Hold.

The fears that another Toric, or worse yet, a second Fax, might emerge began to recede as more and more small holds were established along the coast and rivers. The sheer size of the Southern Continent, and the difficulty of communications—solving that problem was a major priority of the Smithcrafthall—served as inhibiting factors.

There were regular passages back and forth between the continents, both by sail and by dragon. The harbor facilities at Monaco Bay were still functional, though the dwelling at the point had been battered into ruins by storms. The harbor was superb, and several Masterfishermen vied with each other for Master Idarolan's permission to take hold there. Paradise River Hold was thriving; it had its own seahold, Mastered by Alemi, formerly of Half Circle Seahold, who had command of two small coastal skiffs and one deep-water vessel.

During those Turns, excavations continued at the Plateau, though the work became somewhat slow and desultory during the long stretches during which little or nothing was found. Whenever minor finds were uncovered, interest would be temporarily revived, and Master Robinton would seize that renewal of energy to get other sites dug up, clinging to his belief that somewhere in the ruins would be the answers to his questions about the Dawn Sisters and the origin of their ancestors. The maps had only whetted his appetite.

Meanwhile Master Fandarel had assembled an astounding array of mechanical pieces, including the shell of what he insisted had to be one of the ancients' small flying ships. The starboard side had been badly dented, the durable material fractured, stained, and mottled with tiny cracks. The stripped hull raised more questions than it answered, but encouraged the hopes of those who thought that a complete vessel might be found abandoned at one of the ancient sites.

To assist in the tagging and cataloging at Cove Hold, Menolly and Brekke sent a variety of young people, serving informal apprenticeships. Piemur suspected his friends of matchmaking, but there was no doubt that the girls were useful—and, Piemur conceded, decorative. They seemed to enjoy D'ram's occasional teasing and were understanding of Lytol's quiet introspection. Still, none of them caught Piemur's fancy, especially since they had a tendency to moon over Master Robinton.

For the additional residents at Cove Hold, small private cots had been constructed, though most evenings everyone met for their meal in the main Hall. A large area adjacent to D'ram's cot was cleared for Piroth's weyr. A second guest house was constructed when the facilities in Cove Hall were constantly strained; then an archive hall—Lytol's domain—was added as repository for the mass of records, sketches, charts, maps, ruin diagrams, and artifact samples. Soon an annex was required to allow space for the craftswomen determined to piece together some of the splinters and shards. Wansor's large distance-viewer was housed on the eastern point, where he continued his observations of the Dawn Sisters, the baleful Red Star, and those other celestial bodies which, with the help of the ancients' star maps, he managed to identify.

And still the excavation of Landing continued. Fandarel's mound, the last of the original choices to be excavated, had added to the frustration. He had been correct that the heat of the volcano had kept the building from being cleared by the ancient refugees, but whatever had been in it had been so badly damaged—or, in some cases, completely destroyed—that it was impossible to identify. A flurry of further digging in that sector proved unenlightening: the buildings thus found seemed to have been used as beastholds.

That raised the questions of how so many beasts could have been accommodated in the Dawn Sisters, how many people had made the voyage, how far they had come, and how long had Landing been inhabited. The fire-lizards' peculiarly tenacious memory evidently contained only unusual occasions: the initial landing, the volcanic eruption, and the far more recent incident of the retrieval of Ramoth's stolen egg, when dragons had actually flamed at fire-lizards. It was still not common knowledge that Jaxom and Ruth had stolen back the egg for the North—all most people knew was that the miraculous return of the egg had made it unnecessary for the Northern dragon wings to exact retribution from Southern

Oldtimers and prevented the worst catastrophe anyone could imagine: dragon fighting dragon.

There was a certain contentment on both sides of the sea now that the Southern Continent had been opened up, leaving those interested in the ancients free to pursue the puzzles posed by the excavations. One rainy week, the frustration level of those kept holdbound at the cove was particularly high, and even Piemur, racking his brain, could not come up with a diversion.

"It may well be, Robinton," Lytol suggested, "that we shall never know the answers."

"Now *that* I won't accept!" The Harper propelled himself out of his chair, pausing the tiniest bit as his joints prevented a smooth rising. "Bloody rain always seizes me up." He straightened his back, stood on one leg to jiggle the other, then repeated the process with his right leg. "What was I going to do?"

"Pace with frustration," Piemur said, looking up from the object he was studying under an enlarging glass. "I'll join you. There is no way this—thing—was useful." He flicked the rectangular board away from him. "Beads and wires and tiny joins!"

"Decorative?" D'ram asked.

"Unlikely. It's more of the same sort of thing we found in the forward portion of the flying ship."

"What was I going to do?" Robinton demanded of no one in particular, one hand on his forehead, the other propped at his belt. "And I've got enough wine."

"I was talking about generations," Lytol patiently cued him. "You wouldn't accept the delay . . ."

"Ah, yes, thank you." Robinton went over to the map stand that stood across one window. He leafed through the charts until he found the one he wanted and then pulled it up to hook it to the top of the frame. "Has anyone done anything about these?" He indicated the symbols in red, blue, and green, positioned like miniature flags between the landing strip and the far southern edge of the settlement.

Piemur swiveled in his chair to look. "No, sir. There doesn't seem to be anything there now."

"But caves were discovered in that general area, weren't they?"

"Yes, caves that had obviously been adapted for use as living quarters," Piemur admitted. "Probably for greens, since the dragon couches were very small."

"What if—what if the caves here," Robinton said excitedly, tapping the flags, "had concealed entrances?"

"Master, haven't we found *enough* junk?" Piemur's sweeping gesture took in the entire Cove Hold complex.

"But no answers!" Robinton shook his head. "There have to be some answers, so that we can understand more than what we've gleaned from fire-lizards!" Roused from his sleep on the back of Robinton's chair, Zair chirped in reassurance. "And that's enough from you, impudence with wings. As I've said before, people who could execute the wonders we have seen would have kept records!"

"They did, and they're the dust in the back corridors of Fort Hold and Benden Weyr," Piemur broke in. "And we're none the wiser."

"They can't have kept so *few* copies!" the Harper insisted. "And we have the maps as examples of the durability of their materials—so where are the rest?"

"There were lapses in record-keeping," Lytol agreed solemnly. "We now know there must have been a terrible fire in one portion of Fort Hold's lowest level; we are also agreed that plague decimated Hall, Hold, and Weyr on three separate occasions. We may never learn our history." He seemed as resigned to that possibility as the Harper was resistant to it.

"So, when the rain decides to stop," Piemur asked on a long-suffering note, "do you want me to take some rodmen and find these caves for you?"

When the next day brought a clearing of the heavy rains, Piemur sent Farli to Eastern Weyr for a dragon to convey himself and the Harper to the Plateau. V'line, a young bronze rider, arrived and duly transported them. Once at the Plateau, the Harper requested V'line and Clarinath to circle over the site. So often an aerial search produced visual clues not apparent on the surface. Carefully scrutinizing the terrain below, neither Piemur nor Robinton noticed the absence of fire-lizards.

But as the wide circling brought them to face north, they could not fail to notice the map building, which had been completely unearthed, visibly tremble and slowly, almost majestically, collapse. Then people were erupting from the Plateau buildings in panic.

"Clarinath says the ground isn't steady," V'line exclaimed.

"Earthshake?" Piemur suggested.

"Can we land?" V'line asked.

"I don't see why not," the Harper said. "There's nothing out here to fall on us. Pity about the 'hill.' Perhaps we shouldn't have uncovered it."

"Perhaps you should have let Master Esselin shore up the weak section," Piemur replied.

"Shall we land?" V'line was dubious, and Clarinath was swinging his head anxiously, peering down at the unreliable surface. "Is it still rocking?"

"How can we tell up here?" Piemur demanded. "Tell Clarinath the Harper says it's all right to land."

"I'm glad you're so certain about it," the Harper said, his expression reflecting his qualms. "But I feel we ought to proceed first to Plateau and see if all is well."

The rest of that day was spent in establishing that there had been little damage, with the exception of the old "hill," at the Plateau. The earthshake had been more noticeable at Monaco Bay and Eastern Weyr, but had been the merest shiver at Cove Hold, noticed only because of the disappearance of the fire-lizards.

Masters Nicat and Fandarel were sent for—Piemur thought it a waste of their valuable time, since it was his experience that shakes were common in the South—to look into the phenomenon and figure out what precautions could be taken for the future. Earthshakes were exceedingly rare in the North, and no one knew what to expect.

"It's really rather simple," Piemur muttered to the girl who was passing around soup and klah. "The next time all the fire-lizards flick off in a storm, you can expect another shake."

"Are you certain of your facts?" she asked skeptically.

"Yes, on the basis of personal observation," Piemur replied, not certain if he liked being challenged so quickly. Then he noticed the twinkle in her eye. She was not unattractive, with a mop of very curly black hair, gray eyes, and a fine long nose—he always noticed noses, since he regretted his own snub of a nose. "I've been in the South nearly ten Turns and that shock was nothing."

"I've been here ten days, and I found that shock unsettling, journeyman. I don't recognize your colors," she added, nodding at his shoulder knots.

He winked at her and assumed an arrogant pose. "Cove Hold!" He was extremely proud to be one of a half dozen entitled to wear those colors.

His reply brought the gratifying reaction he had expected. "Then you're journeyman to Master Robinton? Piemur? My grandfa mentions you frequently! I'm Jancis, Telgar Smithcrafthall journeywoman."

He made a disparaging sound. "You don't look like any Smithcrafter I've ever seen."

A dimple flashed in her right cheek when she smiled. "That's exactly what my grandfa says," she said, snapping her fingers.

"And who might your grandfa be?" Piemur asked obediently.

Her smile had a touch of mischief as she turned with her tray to serve others. "Fandarel!"

"Hey, Jancis, come back!" Piemur shot to his feet, spilling soup over his hands.

"Ah, Piemur," the Harper said, appearing before him to catch his arm and thwart his pursuit. "When you've finished eating— What's the matter with you?"

"Fandarel has a granddaughter?"

The Masterharper blinked and then focused a kindly gaze on his journeyman. "He has several that I know of. And four sons."

"He has a granddaughter here!"

"Ah, I see. Well, when you've finished eating . . . now what was it I wanted you to do?" The Harper placed his fingers on his forehead, frowning in concentration.

"Sorry, Master Robinton." Piemur was sincerely contrite. He knew that the Harper hated his lapses of memory; Master Oldive had explained that they were a natural part of the aging process, but Piemur found such reminders of his Master's mortality distinctly unsettling.

"Ah!" the Harper exclaimed, remembering. "I wanted to get back to Cove Hold. Zair has gone off with a multitude of other bronzes, chasing some queen, and I've really had quite enough excitement today. Would you, in the light of your new acquaintanceship, care to accompany me?"

Piemur did not, but he went. Two could play a disappearing game, he thought wryly.

The next morning, a fire-lizard brought an urgent message for the Harper from Master Esselin.

"Well, it seems that between the rains and the earthshake, an interesting subsidence has occurred, and it looks as if an entrance to those caves has been revealed," Robinton said cheerfully. "I think we'd better ask V'line to come as soon as possible." He rubbed his hands together in anticipation.

A large depression in the ground, along with a substantial fracture of the surface, had been noticed early that morning by the ever observant Breide. Master Esselin had assembled a crew at the site, but no one had been permitted to descend into the cavern until Master Robinton arrived. In preparation, Esselin had tested the safety of the fissure's edge and found it solid enough. Glows had been collected and a sturdy ladder lowered and settled firmly on the cave floor. When Robinton arrived, he found Breide in a sweat, arguing vehemently with Master Esselin, who was guarding the ladder with his own body.

"I'm in charge of the Plateau," the Harper said, sweeping both Breide and Esselin out of the way when he realized that the contention was about who should take the "dangerous" step of entering first.

"But I'm more agile than you, Master," Piemur said. "I go first." He slipped onto the ladder and was down the rungs so fast that the Harper had no time to argue the point. Someone began lowering glowbaskets on ropes to illuminate his way. Not wasting a moment, Master Robinton eagerly followed him down, then Esselin, and then Breide after him.

"This is amazing!" the Harper exclaimed as Piemur helped him over the broken earth where the ceiling had collapsed. They seemed to be in a narrow aisle. Piemur held a glowbasket above his head and turned slowly around.

Within the circles of light cast by the glowbaskets was an astonishing clutter of crates, boxes, and transparently wrapped items, some heaped haphazardly and some more neatly stacked along the irregular walls of the cavern. The cavern had a vaulted ceiling and seemed to be one of several interconnecting chambers. All four explorers peered around in a daze of wonder.

"All these Turns, they've been here, waiting for their rightful owners to reclaim them," the Harper murmured, almost reverently touching one finger to a crate. He stepped carefully over a box to peer into the shadows beyond the light. "An immense storehouse of artifacts."

"I'd say they'd been in a hurry," Breide remarked, "if you compare the relative order of things along the walls to the disorder here. Ah, and this seems to be a doorway." He gave the door panels a couple of stout blows, but he could not find any latches or handles with which to open it.

"Boots," Piemur said, picking up a pair and brushing the dirt off the transparent envelope that had protected them. He tried to pinch the film, but it resisted. "Feels like the same stuff that coated the maps." His low voice was awed. "All sizes of boots! Sturdy ones. They don't look like leather."

Master Robinton was on his knees, trying to figure out how to open a crate that seemed to be sealed tight. "What does this say?" he asked, pointing to lines of differing widths and shadings on one corner of the lid.

"I don't know," Piemur replied. "But I do know how to open it!" There had been identical crates at Paradise River Hold. He took hold of two metal flaps centered on the short sides, pulled them sharply to fold down, and the lid came free.

"Sheets!" Master Esselin shrieked, the noise echoing through the tunnels beyond them. "Sheets of the ancients' material! Master Robinton, just look! Sheets of it!"

Master Robinton lifted out a flattish transparent envelope, a handspan wide and two long and two fingers thick. "Shirts?"

"Sure looks like one to me," Piemur said, briefly shining his glow over it, and moved on to search for something less prosaic.

Later, when they had recovered from the initial excitement, Master Robinton suggested that records be made of the contents of the storehouse, listing at least those objects that were easily identifiable. Nothing must be removed from its protective covering, he said. The Benden Weyrleaders and the Mastersmith would have to be informed . . . and perhaps the Masterweaver, since clothing was his Craft.

"And Masterharper Sebell," Piemur added teasingly.

"Yes, yes, of course. And . . ."

"Lord Holder Toric!" Breide put in, indignant at having to remind them.

"Oh, this is truly amazing," Master Robinton said. "A major discovery. Untouched for who knows how long . . ." And then his face fell.

"Well, maybe they stored away duplicate records here, too," Piemur said encouragingly. He took the Harper's arm and gently pushed him down to a large green crate. "It's going to take a long time to sift through this lot."

"I don't think we should touch anything more," Breide said nervously, "until everyone has gathered here."

"No, no, you're quite right. They should all see it as we just have," the Harper agreed, his expression slightly dazed.

Piemur scurried up the ladder, popping his head out of the hole and surprising those trying to peer down. "Jancis?" he called, looking impatiently around. The throng parted as she came up to him. "Get some wine or klah for the Harper, please."

She nodded and dashed off, returning moments later with someone's belt flask. Piemur gave her a thankful grin and slid down the ladder to revive the Harper.

What do you mean? Denol and his kin have taken possession of the island?"

"What I said, Lord Toric," Master Garm replied unhappily. "He and all his kin have crossed the channel to the island and plan to hold it themselves. Denol says that you've got more than enough for one man, and the island can easily be an independent, autonomous hold."

"Independent? Autonomous?"

Master Garm had had occasion to remark to Master Idarolan that Lord Toric had mellowed over the past few Turns since he had achieved his ambition. Clearly that tempering did not extend deeply enough to accept mutiny calmly.

"That's the message, Lord Toric. And those left at Great Bay Hold are the most shiftless, indolent lot I've ever seen." Garm did not hide his disgust.

"That is not allowed!" Toric exclaimed heatedly.

"I agree, sir, so I sailed directly back here. No sense leaving good supplies for those lazy lugs. I knew you'd want to take appropriate action."

"Indeed I do, Master Garm, and you will reprovision your ship immediately for an afternoon sailing." Toric stalked to the magnificently embellished map of his Holding, which now took up one whole wall of his workroom.

"As you say, sir." Garm knuckled his brows and exited hastily.

"*Dorse! Ramala! Kevelon!*" Toric's roar echoed down the corridor after Master Garm.

Dorse and Kevelon arrived at a run, to find the Lord Holder writing a note, his fury evident in the bold, hurried letters scrawled across the narrow sheet.

"That ingrate, Denol, has mutinied on the Great Bay and is claiming my island as an independent, autonomous holding," he told them. "This is what comes of assigning lands to any rag, tag, or scum. I am informing the Benden Weyrleaders of the course I intend to take, and I expect their cooperation."

"Toric," Kevelon said, "you can't expect dragonriders to take punitive action against people—"

"No, no, of course not. But this Denol will soon see that he cannot maintain his position on *my* island!"

Ramala entered the room. "A message just in from Breide at the Plateau, Toric."

"I don't have time for him right now, Ramala."

"I think you'd better, Toric. They've discovered storage caves full of ancients'—"

"Ramala," Toric snapped, frowning irritably at his wife. "I have *present* concerns. That wretched crop picker from South Boll has occupied *my* island and intends to make it *his*. The Weyrleaders . . ."

"The Weyrleaders will be at the Plateau, Toric. You could combine—"

"In that case, I shall send this message to them there. Ramala—" Toric thumped the table with his fist. "This is far more important than any scraps and shards left behind by the ancients. This is an arrant challenge of my authority as Lord Holder and cannot be permitted to continue." He turned to Dorse. "I want all the single men aboard the *Bay Lady* by midday, with suitable supplies of weapons, including those barbed spears we've been using against the big felines." Then, waving Dorse out, he rolled up the two messages, which he handed to Ramala. "Give these to Breide's fire-lizard and send it back to him. Kevelon, you remain here in Southern to manage things. I can trust you." Toric gave his brother a warm embrace and then returned to study the map, focusing on the threatened island.

Never had Toric expected to be challenged in his own Hold, and by a jumped-up drudge of a crop picker. He would pick him over, so he would!

Denol, you say?" the Master Harper exclaimed. "A crop picker from South Boll?"

There was such amusement in his voice that Perschar, who was busily sketching the scene around the collapsed cave roof, looked up in surprise.

Breide gave him a quelling stare. "My remarks were addressed to Master Robinton," he said haughtily, gesturing with his free hand for the artist to go back to his business. He handed Toric's message to the Harper.

"Well, that's a facer for Lord Toric, to be sure," Perschar went on, ignoring Breide.

The Harper grinned. "I don't think Lord Toric will be over-faced, however. A man of his infinite resourcefulness will soon put matters right. And the diversion at this particular moment in time is fortuitous."

"Yes," Perschar replied, a speculative gleam in his eye. "You may be right at that." He resumed his deft quick lines, a broad smile on his face.

"But Master Robinton," Breide went on, mopping the sweat running down his temples. "Lord Toric has to be here."

"Not when matters of Hold importance come up abruptly." Robinton turned to Piemur, who had listened with great interest, especially since Breide was so patently distressed. "Ah, here comes Benden," the Harper added, pointed skyward. "I'll see that the Weyrleader gets his message from Toric." He nipped the other roll from Breide's hand before the man could protest, then walked across the well-trampled field to greet F'lar and Lessa.

More ladders had been lowered and a quantity of glowbaskets placed below to enable the Weyrleaders and Craftmasters to explore easily. A number of people were already doing just that, and the Masterharper and the Weyrleaders joined them.

It was then that Piemur noticed Jancis coming down. "Hi, there," he said. "We're not supposed to go off on our own, so how about I go with you?" He helped her down the last step.

"I'm here officially," she said with a grin. She opened her shoulderbag to show him a board and writing materials. "To measure and diagram the corridors before you get completely lost." She handed him a folding measuring stick. "You just got seconded to help."

Piemur did not mind in the least. "The door's back this way," he said. "I think that would be a good starting point." He cupped his hand under her elbow and guided her in the right direction.

While she was diligent about measurements, both took time to peek into crates and examine a variety of the stores.

"Mainly things that they either had plenty of or didn't immediately need," Jancis remarked, looking through a large case of encrusted soup ladles and jumping back as one disintegrated in her hand.

"You always need boots!" Piemur replied. "And they're in an excellent state of preservation. I make this chamber twenty paces by fifteen." They had moved some distance from the original chamber, through interconnecting caves, some of which showed evidence of having been reshaped and squared off.

"*How* could they manage to shear through solid rock like a carver through roast wherry?" Jancis asked, running one hand over an archway.

"You're the smith. You tell me."

She laughed. "Even Grandfa can't figure that one out."

"You haven't actually worked metal, have you?" Piemur finally blurted out, unable to contain himself any longer. She was not a fragile-looking girl, but neither did she have the bulging muscles of most male smiths he knew.

"Yes, the Crafthall required me to, but not the heavy stuff," she answered absently, more intent on measuring the archway than on his questions. She gave him the measurements. "There's a lot more to smithing than working hot metal or glass. I know the principles of my Craft, or I'd not have walked the tables." She cocked her head at him, the dimple appearing with her grin. "Can you craft every instrument a harper plays?"

"I know the principles," Piemur said with a laugh and then held up the glowbasket to see into the next chamber. "What have we here?"

"Furniture?" Jancis added her glows to his, and the dark shadows took on form, light shining off smooth metal legs. "Chairs, certainly, tables, all of metal or that other stuff they used so much of." She was running knowledgeable hands down legs and across surfaces.

"Hey, drawers!" Piemur exclaimed, wrestling with a tier down one side of a desk. "Look!" He held up a handful of thin cylinders with pointed ends. "Writing sticks? And these?" He held up clips and then a transparent stick, a nail thick, a finger wide, and more than a handspan long, both edges covered with fine lines and numerals. "What standards were they measuring by?"

He gave her the stick, and she turned it over and over. "Handy enough, since you can see through it," she remarked and then put it in her shoulderbag, making a notation on her diagram. "Grandfa will want to see it. What else have you found?"

"More of those useless thin placques of theirs. If all the drawers are full of th—" He stopped complaining as he opened the deepest drawer and saw the neat arrangement of hanging files. He removed one. "Lists and lists, on that film of theirs. And color-coded—orange, green, blue, red, brown. Numbers and letters that don't mean a thing to me." He passed the file to her and picked up another one. "All red and all crossed out. Records my Master wants, and records I can now give him! For all the good it does."

"Aren't there these sorts of bandings, numerals, and letters on those crates?" Jancis asked.

Piemur groaned, thinking of the piles of crates and boxes and cartons they had seen. "I have no wish to cross-check. Couldn't they have left anything in plain language for us?"

"What upsets Grandfa," Jancis went on, exploring more of the accessible drawers, "is that we've lost so much of their knowledge over the hundreds of Turns. He calls that criminal."

"Not just inefficient?" Piemur grinned, hoping no unexpected summons would interrupt them and that somehow he could get her mind off their main reason for being here.

Jancis had just opened the wide shallow drawer in the center of the desk and removed some very thin loose sheets of the same durable material on which the maps had been printed. She peered at the letters across the top. "E-V-A-C-U-A—

funny shape to these letters . . . Ah, evacuation plan. More numbers." She folded the top sheet back and gasped. "A plan of the Plateau, with names, and—HOS-PI-TAL, WA-RE-HOUSE, VET, LAB, ADMIN, AIVAS. They have everything named as to function," She turned to him, her eyes glowing as she passed the sheets to him. "I think this is an important document, Piemur."

"I think you're right. But let's see what else we can find."

The furniture was packed so carefully that in the end they were able to reach only a few more drawers without unstacking things—and there was no space for that. Not all the drawers were as full as the one Piemur had first opened, but each contained interesting detritus in the form of brief notes, more obscure lists, and the thin rectangular placques that appeared to have no obvious function. Jancis made the final discovery: an oblong of black material with raised buttons, twelve bearing numbers and four arithmetic signs, all flanked and topped by buttons, but they both agreed that her grandfather should see. Most of the furniture was in remarkably good condition as the cave complex was dry and the material impervious to penetration by tunnel snakes, though excretal evidence of those creatures marked the surfaces.

"Poor hungry critters," Jancis said in mock sympathy. "All this for centuries and not one thing edible!"

"Or long since consumed." Piemur noticed that their glow-baskets were getting dim. "How long have we been down here?"

"Long enough for me to get hungry," she replied, her dimple showing.

They had already started on their way back to the entrance when they heard their names echoing down the corridors. When they got back to the entrance, they found Master Esselin halfway down one ladder in an urgent discussion with F'lar, who was a few rungs up another, peering more at the sky than at the man he was talking to.

"Ah, Piemur, there's a squall bearing down on us," Master

Robinton said. His eyes twinkled as he acknowledged Jancis's presence. "Esselin is certain we'll all drown along with our treasures."

"Well, we won't," Lessa said, chuckling. "Dragons have many unlikely uses."

A little baffled, Jancis looked sideways at Piemur.

"Ramoth and Mnementh both?" the journeyman asked the Weyrwoman, craning his neck to look up the fissure. He could not see any stormclouds from that limited range.

"Their combined wings will overlap quite nicely," Lessa said. "It's Esselin who thinks it's beneath Benden's dignity. Just as well he wasn't there to see Ramoth and Mnementh digging out the mounds that day. Esselin, do send us down something to eat while we wait out the squall," she added, raising her voice as the Masterminer disappeared up the ladder.

The light dimmed abruptly as two great dragon pinions spread over the hole. F'lar, Lessa, and Robinton looked smugly satisfied.

"I've never appreciated dragon wings quite so much before," Jancis remarked softly to Piemur. "No, I mean it. Look at the delicate veining. So fine a membrane and yet so incredibly strong. A rather magnificent design, you know."

Lessa took the few steps across the aisle that separated them and smiled at Jancis. "According to Master Robinton, some of the very old Records suggest that the dragons were indeed designed," she remarked, settling herself on the crate beside the younger woman.

"Not cousins to the fire-lizards?" Jancis asked.

"Oh, they admit that," Lessa said with a shrug. "Though how they know," she added, her expression fondly doting, "is beyond me."

"About something to eat, Lessa," Piemur said. "I think we'd better not wait on Master Esselin's assistance. If Ramoth and Mnementh can shelter us, then Farli and Zair can feed us.'' He gave Lessa a sideways grin that bordered on a challenge. He held up his hand, and Farli abruptly appeared, squeaking with surprise at finding herself so close to the Weyrwoman and nearly dropping the basket she carried in her talons. ''If you'll pardon the impudence, Weyrwoman.'' He rose, relieved Farli of her burden, and with a gesture sent her off again. ''Well, it's something to start with at any rate,'' he said after he had examined the contents. ''She's coming back with more.''

''You are irrepressible!'' Lessa exclaimed, but her laugh was gay, and she was quite willing to share the sandwiches that the fire-lizard had brought.

With Zair supplying the Harper and F'lar, the group stranded in the cavern was able to make quite a satisfactory meal while rain pelted in a torrential downpour on shielding dragon wings.

''Well, and what did you discover on your search, Jancis, Piemur?'' Robinton asked.

''Famine or feast, Master Robinton,'' Piemur replied. He held out the file, flipping the pages until he came to the one with the map. ''This seems to indicate which buildings were used for what.''

Master Robinton took the file, bending closer to the nearest glowbasket to read it. ''This is marvelous, Piemur. Marvelous! Just look, Lessa. Each square is named! And HOS-PI-TAL—that was an old name for a Healer's Hall. ADMIN?—administration, no doubt. Ah, and that one hasn't been excavated yet. Marvelous. What else, Piemur?'' The Master's expression was eager.

''Not until you tell me what *you* found!'' Piemur replied.

''Gloves!'' F'lar said, holding up three wrapped pairs. ''Different weights for different jobs, evidently. I think they'd be cold to fly in, but we'll let the experts decide.''

''We could clothe the weyrfolk in what I found,'' Lessa added.

"She even found boots her size," F'lar said, grinning at his diminutive weyrmate.

"I can't imagine why they left such necessities as clothing behind," Lessa commented.

"And I," Master Robinton said, still clutching the file, "found pots and pans of immense size; and more spoons, forks, and knives than you'd need at a Gather. I also found immense wheels, small wheels, medium wheels, and crates and crates of tools. Master Fandarel has already absconded with a selection of their implements. Some were well smeared with a protective oil or grease. He's fearful that sudden exposure to the air might cause them to become friable and dissolve, or something." He winked at Jancis.

The rain was still pounding down.

"If we could locate the original entry," F'lar remarked, glancing up at the shielding dragon wings, "it would be wise to cover that hole over completely. Fine thing it would be to have all this mystifying and unusual stuff survive earthshake, eruption, and the centuries only to ignominiously drown."

"That certainly can't be allowed to happen," Master Robinton agreed.

"It wouldn't be efficient," Jancis murmured in Piemur's ear.

"And you're incorrigible," Lessa said, her keen hearing having picked up the soft remark. "Your grandfather has probably already solved that minor problem. He's eager to use some of the building materials Master Esselin discovered. You weren't here when they hauled some of the slabs up to the surface. I think every Mastersmith on Pern will be congregating here. And, by any chance, do you have some spare sheets I might use, Jancis?" she went on, briskly rubbing crumbs from her fingers and jerkin. The girl nodded. "Excellent, because I feel that a strict list should be made of things removed from here—though what we found were certainly not one of a kind. The quantities of *things* all of a kind are amazing.''

''Amazing what they left behind here,'' F'lar said wonderingly. ''They must have intended to return . . .'' A thoughtful silence followed his remark.

''They have,'' the Master Robinton said gently. ''They have returned in us, their descendants.''

15

SOUTHERN CONTINENT, PP 17

Due to Jancis's excellent measurements, the original entrance to the cavern was found the next day, dug out, and shored up, and the fissure closed using—at Master Fandarel's insistence—one of the sheets of the ancients' translucent material.

"It's efficient," Jancis told Piemur, her eyes dancing with merriment, "because it provides a certain amount of light. It's strange, really," she added, tilting her head in a manner that Piemur found exceedingly endearing, "to think that here"—she gestured toward the unearthed mounds—"they seemed to encourage light in their dwellings, and then they go carve out cliffs to live in and hide away from it."

"Baffling, indeed. It seems such a drastic change to make," Piemur said. "Is it possible that they didn't know about Thread when they first landed?" He had not even mentioned that idea yet to Master Robinton.

"And Thread sent them scurrying north to caves?"

"Well, there are more caves in the North. Mind you," he said, qualifying that statement, "there's a good-sized complex at Southern Hold, and this rambling one here, and I've only been along the coast, so there could be hundreds inland . . ."

"Yes, but you've been to most of the ancients' sites, haven't you? And you mentioned that they built above the ground, in freestanding buildings." She gave him a measuring look and then shyly added, "I really would like to see one of those sites."

"That can be easily arranged," Piemur said, trying not to read into the wistful request more than a professional curiosity.

They had been together almost constantly for the last ten days, either as assistants to Master Robinton and Master Fandarel, or on their own, itemizing the contents of some of the smaller, well-packed chambers. Master Fandarel had ordered several crates of machine parts to be transferred to a warehouse where he and other mechanically oriented Masters and journeymen were attempting to make sense out of such quixotic wealth. Piemur and Jancis, meanwhile, were attempting to match banding, color, and numerals on the crates and cartons to those on the lists Piemur had found in the desk that first day. They had been eating lunch when Jancis made her innocent comment. Piemur called Farli to him and wrote a message to V'line, Clarinath's rider at Eastern Weyr.

"I do envy you Farli," Jancis said when the little queen had disappeared on her errand.

"How come you don't have a fire-lizard?"

"Me?" She was astonished by the question. She also had a smudge on her cheek and another on her forehead, and Piemur wondered if he should tell her. She was neat in her habits and motions, but he kind of liked to see her disheveled—it made her seem more approachable. "Not likely. With every Craftmaster and senior journeyman ahead of me in the list, I'll be waiting a long time. Unless you know of a nest around here?"

He gave her a long look, suppressing the laughter that threatened to fracture his solemn regard. He knew very well that she had spoken artlessly, but that did not keep Piemur from daring. "Nest hunting is the preoccupation of every rod-man and digger. But you—you'd make a good fire-lizard friend."

Jancis's eyes went wide, and then her expression changed. "I think you're teasing me."

"No, really, I'm not. After all, I've got a queen."

"You mean Farli's clutched?"

"Frequently." And then Piemur was forced to admit the embarrassing aspect of that: "Trouble is, I don't know where!"

"Why not?" Jancis asked, surprised.

"Well, you see, queens instinctively return to their original clutching place and choose a free site nearby. Only I don't know where that was."

"But you Impressed her when she hatched? Surely—"

Laughing, Piemur waved his hand to halt her comments. "That's another long story, but basically I don't *know* where she was clutched and she can't seem to give me directions beyond sand dunes and heat."

Just then Farli returned, flying into the chamber and chittering agitatedly about things in her way. But the message she bore was affirmative.

"We're taking the afternoon off, Janny. We deserve it," Piemur said firmly. "We'll ruin our eyes, trying to match up all this banding. So we'll go visit a restored ancients' ruin at Paradise River Hold. You'll like Jayge and Ara! I told you about them being shipwrecked and all."

Her answering expression was inscrutable, but she smiled before she gathered up their work materials.

"This is official, isn't it?" V'line asked Piemur, glancing at Jancis when the two presented themselves to the bronze-rider.

"Sure is," Piemur assured him airily, helping Jancis to mount Clarinath. "Got to cross-check carton markings on the ones left at Paradise River. It's one of those boring things that's got to be done, and Jancis and me got chosen!" He climbed on behind the girl, well pleased with himself. It would be perfectly legitimate for him to put his arms about her during flight.

Jancis gave him a speaking look and a grin for his outrageous invention, and then gasped, grabbing his arms as Clarinath launched himself skyward.

"This isn't your first time a-dragonback, is it?" Piemur asked, his lips close to her ear. Tendrils of her curly hair escaped from her helmet and tickled his nose. She shook her head, but her grip on his arms did not relax, so he knew that she could not have ridden often.

Then they went *between*, and her fingers tightened spasmodically. The next moment they were above the clean sandy stretch, Clarinath gliding in to land on the riverbank a few lengths from the hold. The heat was considerably greater there than on the relatively higher, cooler Plateau. Fleetingly Piemur wondered why Alemi had a ship anchored that far to the west of Paradise River. Then Farli came streaking in over Clarinath's shoulder and, bugling in her silvery voice, joined the stream of welcoming resident fire-lizards, who all swooped into the hold.

"Look, I don't know how long this will take, V'line," Piemur began, hurriedly unbuckling helmet and jacket as the heat enveloped them, and helping Jancis remove hers.

"I've got to hunt Clarinath," V'line said. "That's how come I could get off sweepriding to bring you. Would you ask Jayge where's the best place to go for wild runners?"

Piemur dismounted and helped Jancis down just as Jayge came onto the verandah to see who had arrived. Piemur hurried over to the dark shady expanse of the porch, introduced Jancis to Jayge, and asked where Clarinath could hunt.

"Tell him to go on down the river, about twenty minutes straight. He'll catch 'em browsing close to the water this time of day," Jayge suggested, adding that V'line should return to the hold to bathe the bronze and to join them in the evening meal while Clarinath digested his.

"You're crazy, Piemur, coming down here before the heat's passed," Jayge said, yawning hugely. He turned to Jancis. "Want something cool to drink?"

"Thank you, Holder Jayge," Jancis said, giving Piemur a sly glance, "but we ate just before we left the Plateau and we really must check the coding on the cartons in your store-room, if we may."

Piemur was stripping down to the loose vest he wore under his shirt. Jancis seemed unaffected by the heat, which irritated him, but then, smiths were used to warmth. "Now, Jancis, I only said that—"

"That's true enough, Piemur," Jancis went on equably, "but it was a clever notion, and I think we should check it out."

"You two do as you wish," Jayge said, grinning as he looked from one to the other, "but I'm going back to my hammock and wait till the afternoon shower cools us off. Anyone with any sense stays out of the hot!" he muttered as he went.

"Now, Jancis," Piemur began, using his shirt to mop his forehead.

"It can't take that long to *look*!" she said, peering around the verandah at the empty rocking chairs and baby swing. She started down the neat shell-lined path toward the other buildings, and Piemur, cursing under his breath, followed her. "Are all these occupied now?" she asked when they were halfway to the storehouse.

"As far as I know," he answered grumpily. He knew she was teasing him and that he should not react. And then he began to wonder why she was doing it; he had believed that she liked him and even enjoyed working with him. Why was she being perverse? Was it a character flaw? "Jayge and Ara invited some Bloodkin to join them from the north," he went on, attempting a more cheerful, if resigned, attitude. "And then Menolly suggested her brother, Alemi, who's Master Fisherman here, and there's a Glassmaster now because there are some really fine white sands, and, well, Paradise River was gradually repaired and occupied. Here we are!"

The high-ceilinged building was cool, with what breeze there was entering at the ventilating slats at the top. Empty crates and cartons were still piled neatly in one corner, but there were more that had been put to use and were stacked close to the entrance. Jancis made a small disapproving sound.

"Why *not* use 'em?" Piemur asked. "They weren't full; they were all Jayge and Ara had when they were shipwrecked. Besides, I think the ancients would like to see them in use again."

"A lot of people are second-guessing what the ancients would and would not like," Jancis said.

"Including your grandfa," Piemur reminded him. "You didn't object to him using the sheet to cover the fissure."

She gave him a quelling look. "Master Fandarel had his reasons."

"So did Jayge and Ara. Why ignore useful things?" Piemur asked. "It's one thing if they contain artifacts—but otherwise they are being useful, efficient." He threw in that word more out of pique than as a humorous reference. "They're not being desecrated or misused. They're not inviolable. They're certainly durable."

"Then you believe we should *use* the shirts and boots and other materials in that cavern?" Jancis turned on him, her eyes flashing and her jaw set in a determined line.

"If they fit, why not?"

"Because it's—it's profane, that's what!"

"Profane? To wear a shirt because it's a shirt and was made to cover nakedness; boots because they're boots and made for walking? I don't understand you."

"It's a misuse of historical relics."

"Besides the building slab, Master Fandarel's using some of those drills—sharpest steel he's ever seen."

"Grandfa is *not* wasting them!"

"These aren't being wasted either," Piemur declared. He raised his hands up high in frustration, then brought them down smartly to his sides. "Go read the bloody carton labels! That's what you came down here to do. I'm going back to the hold. Jayge's right about the heat of the day. It affects some people's thinking."

Farli accompanied him, chittering questions at him which he could not have answered even if he had understood them. When he got back to the wide verandah, he went to the clay pitcher that hung at the shady corner and poured himself several long, cool drinks. Then he strung up one of the hammocks and tried to figure out why he and Jancis were quarreling.

The canines' excited barking roused him from a light doze. Then Farli swooped, tugging at his sleeveless vest to emphasize her urgent little squeaks.

"Huh? Whassamatter? Easy, Farli. You scratch!" But the instancy of her alarm was inescapable. He blinked sleep from his eyes and made an awkward attempt to jump out of the hammock; it swung out from under him, and he landed with an ignominious thump on the porch floor.

The resident fire-lizards were swarming into the house through window and door, chittering with great agitation. Piemur could hear Jayge's drowsy protest. Outside, the pitch of the canines' alarm went up several notches to a frenzy, a commotion that further agitated the fire-lizards.

Just as Piemur was getting to his feet, he saw furtive movements on the beachfront, and the last of his torpor abated. Small wonder the canines were hysterical. Piemur had relied on Farli and Stupid too long to argue with animal instincts or wonder why anyone was creeping up on Paradise River Hold. At the sound of a strangled cry from the line of fishers' cots farther up the beach, he unsheathed his hefty jungle blade, crept to the porch railing, and peered cautiously out.

There! More movement! It looked as if a number of people were spreading out to surround the hold—and more invaders seemed to be crawling down to the other holds. He heard Jayge muttering irritably at the interruption to his nap. Silently Piemur crept to the hammock, reaching up to release first one end from its wall hook and then the other. Maybe he could use it as a second weapon. Dragging the hammock with him, he scooted around the corner of the porch and climbed in through the side window, anxiously scanning the walls for possible weapons.

"Jayge!" he called softly, seeing the holder sleepily stumbling down the corridor.

"Huh?" Still groggy, Jayge just stared at him.

"Grab something. You got invaders!"

"Don't be silly!" Jayge said in a normal voice. Then his fire-lizards came swooping into the room, squeaking in their panic. "Huh?"

Outside, the canines' racket took on a new note, almost jubilant. Someone had had the wit to loose them from their pen. Galvanized, Jayge yanked two kitchen knives from their rack just as they heard a sudden shout from the beach.

"Ara! Get the children and run!" he roared, bounding forward with Piemur to meet the enemy outside.

It proved an embarrassingly short defense. Six sunburnt tattered men, brandishing swords, pikes, and long daggers, rushed Piemur and Jayge at the base of the short porch steps. Piemur slashed with his knife and thrashed about with the hammock, which was soon cut to shreds despite the clumsiness of the attackers. Curses and shrieks told him that Jayge was making full use of his knives. Someone was yelling orders in a strident voice, screaming with impatience at the attackers' ineptitude and demanding results. A concerted rush by the attackers pushed both Piemur and Jayge awkwardly against the steps. Piemur heard someone behind him, but before he could react, he felt the crashing blow on his head and slid into oblivion.

Jayge came to, facedown in sand, head pounding fiercely, ribs and right shoulder aching, aware of the burn of sand-filled cuts all over him. He quickly discovered that he could not shift and ease his discomfort—he was trussed up like a wherry on a spit. He was about to spit out a mouthful of sand when he heard a groan, then a thud, and finally a smug chuckle.

"Back to sleep, harper," a harsh-voiced woman said. "And that's how to deal with jumped-up holders, lads. It also prevents them from getting any assistance from those fire-lizards. or anyone else. Now—" Her voice went from cajolery to sheer venom. "I want the woman and her brats. Without them, this whole effort is worthless."

Inadvertently Jayge stiffened, straining against his bonds. Thella! He had never believed his own words when he had reassured Aramina over and over that the woman must have perished, or been apprehended. Of late, when their formal acquisition of the Paradise River Hold had meant that their names would be circulated, he had had twinges of anxiety. If Thella lived, would she hear? Would she care? Would she act? Common sense made that seem unlikely. But common sense was not a likely virtue in someone as vindictive as Thella.

Fortunately Ara had managed to escape with the children. Also, he was relieved to recall that V'line was due back to collect Piemur and Jancis! A dragon in the sky could be quite a deterrent to the type of holdless men that would fall in with a renegade like Thella. How long had he been unconscious? The heat was still oppressive, so he might have been out . . . just long enough, he thought sourly, to be trussed up so thoroughly.

"I thought it was him you wanted to kill?" someone complained indignantly.

"Killing's easy. I want him to suffer! As he's made me suffer for the past two Turns. But that can be best accomplished by forcing him to watch what I've planned for her! And you imbecilic dolts let her get away from you!" Jayge heard the sound of startled grunts.

"Why kick us? We did our best," someone complained. "You never said nothing about canines! Vicious, they was. Couldn't get past 'em. Fangs a hand long. Great brutes as big as herdbeasts!"

"There were six of you, with swords and spears! More than enough to take a drudge slut. Are these all tied up now? And the women in the fisherholds? All right, then, now we go after her. She can't go far with small kids. She may be holed up in those big ruins. If she took to the forest, that underbrush is so thick she'll have to have left some sort of a trail even tunnel turds like you could find. I want her and those children. She'll wish she'd never been born before I'm through with them. And her."

"Now, look, Thella," the spokesman protested. "You didn't say nothin' about savaging anybody! I don't hold with—" There was a loud and sickening gasp, and then a silence more telling than any words.

"I trust that answers any question?" Thella challenged, her voice edged despite a mockingly light tone. "Bloors, your leg may be sliced, but you've two good arms. Take this club, and when anyone so much as twitches, you clout 'em good. Just behind the ear! Got it? If I find that one of them has moved so much as a muscle when I get back, I'll hamstring you. You, pick up that rope. You, the nets, to wrap our guests up in. You others, grab some of those spears. Those should do for the canines. Now, follow me."

Jayge tried to figure out how many men Thella had with her. He knew that he had sunk the longer knife in someone's belly and blooded some of the others who had pressed in on him. Piemur had made good use of that jungle blade of his before he had been overcome. He heard the grate and grind of sand underfoot and cracked his eyes a bare fraction to count four sets of feet going past him, flicking sand in his face. Thella's voice went off to his right, down past Temma's and Swacky's holds and toward the warehouse. Jancis? Had it been she who had loosed the canines?

More sand spattered across his face. He was aware of a fetid odor—blood, stale sweat, and fish oils—and something looming over him. He almost winced as a club prodded him experimentally. This Bloors took his duty seriously. In the distance Jayge could hear Thella directing the search of the ruins. Let her! Aramina would have made for the woods and most likely headed for the great fellis trees that stood in a grove beyond the first thickets. If Ara could hide in one of the great densely leaved trees—and keep the children quiet—Thella could be searching a long time. Long enough, he hoped, for him to somehow free himself and overcome the one guard.

Bloors had stopped moving, but Jayge could hear sounds that suggested that the man was evidently settling himself on the verandah steps. He strained against painfully tight bonds and pumped up his chest, despite sore ribs, to try to loosen the ropes binding his arms to his sides. His wrists were secured behind his back, and his ankles were so constricted that he could barely feel his feet. Grimly he twisted his wrists, seeking any slack in the ropes, while he listened to Thella banging about in the warehouse, looking for any sign of the fugitives.

As he carefully worked his wrists, he became conscious of other silences. There were no canine sounds, not a single whine, bark, or growl. The beasts could all have been killed, but reviewing the comments he had overheard, Jayge thought that some had survived to protect Aramina. Most conspicuous was the absence of fire-lizards. His were not as well trained as Piemur's, but they, too, had been present during the fight, diving at the invaders, scratching and biting. With Bloors on guard, he could not risk calling to them. Besides, Piemur was the only person they knew to go to with messages. Where was Piemur's Farli? The harper claimed that his queen showed more initiative than most. Was she off trying to rouse help? If only Bloors could be gotten out of the way, perhaps Jayge could get his fire-lizards to bite through the cords around him.

Where was Farli likely to go for help? To V'line and Clarinath? Brief hope encouraged Jayge. The sight of V'line and his bronze might be enough to send Bloors scarpering off, if only to warn Thella. Once Jayge was free, he would settle Thella for once and for all. He was consumed with the desire to feel his sword slide into her belly, to hear that arrogant voice beg for mercy.

A comforting thought, but it brought no slack to his bindings—the constriction was slowly taking all feeling from his fingers. His dry throat began to tickle, but he dared not cough. He pushed the sand from his mouth, holding on to a small shell, which he sucked to encourage salivation. Someone beside him groaned and stirred in the sand, and Bloors applied the club. How many such blows could a skull absorb without permanent damage? Jayge wondered desperately.

He heard some distant shouting and crashing—and still no canine growls. Thella had a huge area to search. If Ara could manage to keep the children quiet . . .

There was another thunk of club against flesh. Something heavy and damp fell across Jayge's back, forcing a gasp from him.

"Easy!" a quiet voice cautioned.

"V'line?"

"K'van." The bronze rider was already sawing at Jayge's bonds. "Aramina yelled—a good knack to rediscover at a moment of crisis. Heth responded. I can see why. Did Thella leave only the one guard?"

"Yes. She took the rest off to hunt Aramina and the children. I don't know how many she has. K'van, I don't need to remind you how dangerous Thella is."

"No, you don't." K'van cut the final strand and turned Jayge over. As blood rushed into starved tissues, Jayge gasped and writhed with pain. K'van massaged his limbs to help encourage circulation. "Easy now. It'll be awhile before Thella realizes her quarry is well away." He helped Jayge to his feet. "Stamp your feet." Then he projected his voice cautiously toward the hold. "It's all right, Mina. Get some of that rotgut Jayge makes. He needs it and so will the others."

"You rescued Ara?" Jayge reeled more from relief than physical weakness.

K'van steadied him, eyes twinkling. "Plucked her *out* of the trees this time—her, Jancis, and the two children. Had to leave the canines behind." He began tying up the gagged and unconscious Bloors.

Jayge shook his head at the dragonrider's levity. "Look, K'van, ask Heth to contact Ramoth and Mnementh. They'll want to know . . ." Jayge's stiff, thick hands refused to close on the dagger in Bloors' belt.

"I expect they will, but as Benden Weyr's fighting Threadfall, Heth can't bespeak them yet."

"Then call up your own Weyr!"

K'van gave him a long, measuring look. "You know I can't do that, Jayge."

"I don't understand you, K'van. I thought you were our friend, and now when we really need your help . . ."

"I've already done more than I should," K'van said, a trace of impatience in his tone as he bent to cut Temma loose.

Jayge had no chance to argue with him, for at that moment Aramina came running down the steps and into his arms. The skinful of spirits banged against his sore ribs. His embrace was perfunctory as he was still seething at K'van's unwillingness to help more. Then he saw Jancis, carrying Janara on one arm while Readis clutched her skirt, and he had to reassure the children, as well.

"Jancis, that was quick thinking, to free the canines then," he said fervently.

"Seemed the logical thing to do," she said, shrugging off his praise. Placing Janara on the ground, she knelt by Piemur, who was pallid under his deep tan. "Awful woman! Isn't she the one Telgar and Lemos were hunting so earnestly? Well, drink up and then hand the wineskin to me, will you, Jayge? I don't like Piemur's color."

Jayge obeyed and found that a long swig of the strong spirits proved to be a powerful restorative.

"Temma could use some as well," K'van said, helping the groggy woman to a sitting position. Aramina gently began to rub the older woman's red and swollen wrists and ankles. The two children, still subdued by their experiences, stood close together, wide-eyed, watching the adults.

"Free Swacky, Jayge," K'van suggested, ignoring the furious look Jayge shot him as he cut Nazer's bonds.

"If you'd only send for a wing, K'van, or even a few more riders . . ."

"Much as I would like to, I can't compromise the Weyr, Jayge, not without Benden's permission," K'van said impassively. "It could be constituted as direct interference in hold management. You have to rescue yourself from Thella."

"He's right, Jayge," Jancis said, briskly massaging Piemur's bruised arms and wrists.

"But you . . ."

"Heth heard Aramina, and he rousted me out of the Weyrhold in only my pants." K'van shuddered involuntarily. "We came out of *between* right over her head. There wasn't much else I could do except pick her out of that tree." He gave an exasperated snort. "I'll take knocks enough for that later, but Heth didn't *ask*. Maybe F'lar will permit the lapse on those grounds: a rider rarely wins an argument with his dragon."

"But you *had* to save Aramina and my children!"

"And so I did!" K'van's patience was wearing a little thin, and he frowned at the irate holder. "I would again, even if I knew the circumstances beforehand. The rest, my friend, is now up to you. There's another couple of hours before I can contact the Benden Weyrleaders, and I don't think Thella's going to be barging around in your orchard that long. Pass me that wineskin. Swacky looks like he needs a long pull.''

"There are five of us," Jayge began, forcing his anger with the bronze rider out of his mind and trying to organize a strategy.

"Seven." Jancis said firmly.

"I don't know how many Thella has with her."

"Well, she's lost a few," Jancis said helpfully, pointing to five bodies laid out to one side of the porch.

"Six came at us," Temma said hoarsely, shaking her hands to increase the blood flow. "I managed a couple of good blows, and I know Nazer knifed one in the chest."

"Three attacked me, and I got one, but I don't think I killed him," Swacky said.

"Are all the canines dead, Ara?" Jayge asked. They would attack anything on command.

"Only one. The rest are up the tree," Aramina said with a brief grin. "Jancis heaved and I pulled. They're perched out of sight—I hope—and on a stay command. I was going to organize the fire-lizards, but then Heth appeared and they all departed."

From the woods the shouts of the frustrated searchers could be plainly heard, with a louder female voice exhorting them to climb up into the trees if they could not check from the ground.

"Was Farli among the fire-lizards?" Piemur asked weakly, a healthier color gradually reducing his pallor.

"I didn't see her," Jancis replied.

"She probably went for help once I was knocked out."

"To the Master Harper?" K'van asked.

"I suppose!"

"Alemi and the fishermen would be nearer to hand," Aramina said, shielding her eyes to peer out at the sea-reach. "Would she have the wit to go to them?"

"Finding them and getting them back here in time are two

separate matters," said Swacky, who did not think that much of fire-lizard abilities. "And where are Alemi's womenfolk?"

"Tied up in their holds," Jayge said, gesturing toward the cots farther up the river bank. "Ara, you and Jancis take the children and go free them. If, by any miracle, Thella left the skiffs intact, I want everyone to pile into them and sail out into the bay until Alemi returns."

Aramina bristled. "I'm not running away again, Jayge Lilcamp!"

"I think you'd make it a lot easier for Jayge if you were out of Thella's range," K'van said firmly. "You and the children. Let him deal with her. It's going to come to that one way or another, you know." And with that the bronze dragonrider looked Jayge squarely in the eyes.

"And long overdue!" Jayge said savagely. "Go on, Aramina. She won't find me such an easy mark this time."

"Or any of us!" Swacky said fiercely, his eyes bright with anger. He had been searching among the weapons piled on the porch: he found his own sword and passed Piemur his broad jungle blade. "You, me, Temma, Nazer, and Piemur, if he's got his wits back . . ." He grinned when Piemur cursed him roundly. "We can cause a lot of damage against such an undisciplined bag of scum with no need to compromise the dragonrider. Dragonriders," he corrected himself, pointing one of the hunting spears downriver, where a second dragon was lazily gliding in to land.

The newcomer settled on the beach not far from Heth. Then his eyes whirled from placid green to agitated orange, and he emitted a startled bleat.

"Heth just brought Clarinath up to date," K'van said with a wry grin.

V'line was scrambling down his dragon's side and came racing toward them, his expression anxious. "Is it true? You've been attacked, Jayge? By whom? It's outrageous. This sort of thing can't be permitted."

"Permission is never the issue," K'van said grimly. "And our hands are tied in such matters."

"Oh, yes, that's true, you're right," V'line said, belatedly recalling Weyr strictures.

A frantic fire-lizard erupted into the air above Piemur's head and then wrapped herself around his neck, threatening to strangle him with relief.

"Hold it, Farli, hold it! I can't understand you," Piemur exclaimed, protecting his face from her lickings and unwinding her tail from his neck. "Once again, more slowly. Ah, really? Weren't you a clever one!" Piemur managed a grin as he explained. "She found Alemi, and he's just beyond the point. He sent her to see what's happened. Jancis, you got anything to write on? And what do I tell him, Jayge?"

"Alemi had six crew—that gives us twelve." Swacky looked pleased.

"We can't wait," Jayge said. "We'll have to rely on surprise—and luck."

"They won't expect canines to come out of a tree," Aramina suggested.

Jayge pawed through the weapons, searching for a dagger. Solemnly K'van handed him his own blade.

"They're heading into the grove now," Swacky said, cocking his head at the sounds of men crashing through the undergrowth. "We can sneak after 'em, pick 'em off one by one." He flexed his sword arm, grinning in anticipation.

Jayge caught Aramina's hands as she hefted a fishing spear. "Oh, no, my love. You will take yourself and our children as far away from here as possible. Do you understand me? There's no time to argue the point. You're going."

"And Heth and I will make sure she does," K'van said unexpectedly, taking Aramina by the arm. "That much I can do."

She hesitated one brief moment, then acquiesced, her shoulders drooping. "Just don't let her slip away again, Jayge. I don't ever want to be faced with this again!"

Piemur dispatched Farli with the message to Alemi. Swacky fortified himself with one more pull from the wineskin, settled the fishing spears to his shoulders, and looked attentively to Jayge. They were all armed now, bristling with assorted weapons, their manner determined. Under the worried gaze of V'line, the Paradise River Holders jogged east, slipping past the thickets that bordered the holds.

The tree in which Aramina and Jancis had taken refuge with the two children was in the approximate center of the grove that Thella was currently searching. The ancient fellis trees, their massive trunks larger than three men could span with fingers touching, spread densely leaved branches to form a large, dimly lit park. Air vines looped in intricate patterns, further obscuring any sun that tried to penetrate the luxuriant foliage. A thick, deep mulch covered the ground and aided the soundless advance of Jayge and the others as they slipped from the shadows of one wide-boled trunk to another.

"Hey, over here! I saw the branches move," someone called. "Over here!"

Jayge swore under his breath, praying that the canines would not break until he and the others got close enough to make use of that diversion. Thella's men—he counted eleven, no, fifteen—closed in on the tree.

Then Thella swaggered forward. Even in the dim light, Jayge realized that the woman who had caused him and Aramina so much pain and anguish had altered considerably since their first encounter on the trail. Though better clothed than her ragtag minions, she was as gaunt, and her close-cropped hair framed a face made ugly by scar pocks and privations.

"Aramina!" She peered up into the branches, and her call was brightly wheedling. "We know you're up there. Your man and all your other friends are tied up tight and out of their senses. This time—" Thella's throaty laugh was malicious "you haven't any handy dragons to help you."

Jayge edged closer, hefting the spear in his hand, marking a burly man as target, but he was not close enough for a killing throw yet. He checked the others. Piemur and Jancis were on his left. Swacky, on his right, crouched low and darted forward, Temma and Nazer moving like shadows beyond him. They would all have to get closer. If each disabled one man, there were still nine to contend with. Though maybe now that the renegades were confident of their quarry, they would relax their guard and lower their blades. He gestured to catch Swacky's eye and pantomimed his instructions. The man nodded.

"You—Obirt, Birsan, Glay," Thella said. "Gather up some of those loose branches. I don't know how well fellis burns, but we'll soon find out, won't we?" She laughed nastily. "It's one way to get someone out of a tree, isn't it, men? I can just see the flames crackling, climbing quickly up this hairy bark, thick smoke roiling up, choking the brats, making them lose hold and fall to their deaths. Is that what you want, Aramina?" Thella's jocularity ended. "Come down out of there. Now! Save your babes from suffocating."

The three men she named had set aside their weapons and begun to gather kindling. The others continued to peer up into the tree, circling it, oblivious to the holders' stealthy advance. A fourth man began to kick the dry ground cover into a pile against the trunk and knelt to start a blaze. Suddenly he collapsed across the pile of brush, the flickering flame extinguished by his body.

"What the—" some else declared. "Hey, there's a knife in Birsan's back!"

"Attack!" Jayge yelled, and sprang from behind his tree.

He launched his spear at the back of the burly man and swerved to one side to throw one of his daggers at the nearest wood gatherer. A dagger whistled past his ear to thunk into the fellis trunk behind him.

"Attack!" he repeated, hoping the canines would respond. The upper branches began to shake, and then the canines sprang from above. Jayge heard their snarling challenges as he raced toward Thella. The din of screams, curses, growls, and the clang of metal against metal filled the air.

She was waiting for him, blatantly ignoring the pleas for help from the man on the ground a scant stride away, struggling to keep the canine from tearing out his throat. Jayge saw the arrogant smile on her face—and then her raised arm. As her hand snapped forward, he flung himself sideways and heard the thrown blade whir through the air where he had been standing to hammer into the tree that guarded his back. She flipped a third dagger into her left hand and, grinning balefully at him, drew her sword.

Jayge watched the curved sword and the straight dagger as he edged closer, wishing for another spear and the greater range it would have given him. His own sword scraped from its scabbard, and he twisted it to make the sound as loud and threatening as he could. Thella was not impressed.

"So," she said, "it seems I was foolish to leave just one guard. How did you escape? I tied you up myself, little trader man." She was circling slowly, and the point of her sword dabbed out like a feline's paw, chiming against Jayge's blade, testing his wrist. "Is all the strength back in your arm?" The blades chimed again, and Jayge's sword wavered off line as the impact thumped his jangling sinews. Thella grinned more widely still. "It seems not. Even so, I should have followed my own advice and chopped off your hands, but those oafs let your woman escape."

"That's been your problem all along, Thella—things get out of your hands. Maybe weapons, too." Jayge wondered why she was circling that way. Looking for an escape route? Maybe her touted ability with a sword was all bluff, too. "This is your final mistake, Thella. Because this is where it ends. You won't slip away from me, not this time. Not here. Not *now!*"

The slow circling broke as he thrust forward suddenly, violently—but the blades met with a clash and a grinding sound like huge, murderous scissors as Thella's defensive sweep became a parry and riposte that licked her sword's steel tongue straight at his face. Jayge broke ground with a barely balanced backward leap and heard her laughing at him. There was blood on his cheek, from a slice he had not even felt—not until the wet heat dribbled from his chin and the sting of the cut ran from his eye to the corner of his mouth.

"I wouldn't be too sure of that, little holdling," Thella said with a sneer. "First blood's mine!

"Only heart's blood counts." He slammed his sword's edge against her knuckleguard, hoping for a flinch, for the weapon to twist in her grip, maybe even for it to fly from her hand. Jayge had no such luck; she let the stroke glissade and expend its force along the sweep of her own blade—and then the dagger in her left fist jabbed at his face, his throat, his belly, three flickers of bright metal that reminded him where her true skill lay.

Jayge smashed the daggerpoint sideways with the guard of his sword, feeling it pluck at his clothing as it came close, far too close. But he refused to make the break Thella had hoped for, and instead forced her back, back, back, until she slammed hard against the immovable trunk of a fellis. Her widened eyes told him that she had not expected to be trapped that way, and Jayge anticipated her attempt to beat her way free with a series of savage cuts. He met them and blocked them, every one, and forced her hard back against the tree again.

"And it's your heart's blood that will spill today." His point flicked through her guard and left a long rip down her left arm. The dagger went flying. "That's for Armald!" He came at her again, feinting at her weakened arm and then closing, K'van's knife in play now for all that its lack of a guard might cost Jayge fingers. Their swords ran together at the hilts, a tangle of sharpened metal held crisscrossed by main force as Jayge's dagger pulled to gash her right arm. "That's for Borgald's best team!" Another swift feint led her blade far off its defensive line, swept further by the knife in his left hand as the sword in his right raked across her exposed midriff. "And that was for Readis!"

"Readis?" Her voice was trembling, from surprise as much as from pain. "What was Readis to you?"

"My uncle, Thella. My uncle!" Jayge backed off, seeing the pallor in her pocked face as shock changed to despair. The rage in him abated briefly, and he charged it again to do what was necessary and end it all.

Is it necessary, Jayge? Is it really? The voice in his head, and in his memory, belonged to Readis—but the voice in his ears belonged to Aramina. "Enough, Jayge! Or you'll be no better than she is."

For all his surprise at hearing his wife when she should have been safely away, Jayge did not let his gaze waver from Thella's face. But hers, startled, went over his left shoulder, and her face contorted with loathing. Eyes blazing, she lunged in a savage futile attack at the girl who had eluded her. Jayge was in the way.

Thrusting as hard as he could, he felt the appalling jolt along blade and hand and arm as his curved sword went into Thella's flesh, its edge grating against one rib as the point punched through to her hating heart. Stolidly, he wrenched the sword free.

Thella's sword spun from her hand, thudded deep into the dirt at Aramina's feet, and stuck there, swaying. With a little sigh, she dropped to her knees, one hand against her breast as if to stem the flow of shocking red that seeped through her fingers. And then she crumpled to the ground unmoving.

The deep hush that settled once again over the fellis tree grove was punctuated by Jayge's hoarse breathing and the whimpers of wounded men and animals. Gulping air into pumping lungs, Jayge gradually became aware of Alemi and the other fishermen moving about the glade. Aramina, carefully avoiding the dagger, bent down to study Thella's face. Without speaking, she rose and turned to Jayge, noting the bleeding cuts that his exertions had opened.

"Those will need to be cleaned, Jayge," she said in a curiously detached tone. "And we'll have to tend the canines."

"Go on, Jayge," Alemi said. "We'll take care of all this." His gesture consigned Thella and her dead supporters to oblivion.

Lessa and F'lar arrived two hours later, straight from Threadfall. As K'van had anticipated, he was soundly berated by Lessa for involving himself in a holder dispute.

"I'd have done the same thing even if I'd known what the problem was when Heth shouted at me, Lessa," K'van said stoutly, although Piemur thought the young Weyrleader was pale enough under his tan. "A rider doesn't ignore his dragon's summons."

"A rider makes certain a dragon doesn't endanger himself," the Benden Weyrwoman replied, "much less his entire Weyr! Did you forget your position, Southern Leader?"

"No," K'van replied. "But neither did Heth."

"At least, you had the good sense to limit Weyr involvement to the one rescue." F'lar's expression was as grim as Lessa's. "Jayge honorably concluded the affair."

The Weyrleaders had seen the dead woman where she and the other renegades lay in sacks, prepared for immediate sea burial.

"That's the end of that," Lessa said, frowning. Then she began to take off the rest of her heavy flying gear. "Did the renegades destroy everything in the hold, or do we have to fly back to Benden to refresh ourselves?" she demanded petulantly. She was tired, hot, and at the end of an exhausting Fall, the last thing she needed was another crisis.

"No, indeed not," Jancis said, taking Lessa's jacket. "There's redfruit, juice, klah, some of Jayge's rotgut spirits, and if you can spare the time, broiled fish fresh from the sea."

The hospitality brought a smile to Lessa's face, reluctant at first, but more relaxed as Jancis led them up the porch steps. The first of the evening breezes had freshened the sultry air, and the house was pleasantly cool.

"What sort of casualties did Jayge suffer?" F'lar asked.

"None of the hold was badly hurt—bumps, lumps, superficial cuts, and bruises mostly," Jancis said, "though Ara had to take a few stitches here and there. She's very neat."

"And the renegades?" Lessa asked, sipping the drink Jancis had given her.

"Six survive, all badly wounded." There was a note of satisfaction in Jancis' voice. "One of them captained the ship that brought them here."

"Master Idarolan should be informed." Lessa grimaced. "He doesn't like his masters disloyal."

"The man wasn't a master, Lessa," Piemur said, joining them. The bandage on his head, his bruised face, and the various small lacerations smeared with numbweed gave him a raffish appearance.

"You should be resting," Jancis told him sternly.

He caught her hand and grinned down at her. "Harpers have notoriously hard heads."

"And thick skins," Lessa added in mock derision.

"Leave it to Thella to have found a dissatisfied journeyman, denied his mastery and willing to dishonor his Hall," Piemur went on. "Stole the ship from the repair dock at Thella's instigation. Master Idarolan will enjoy making an example of him."

"And the others?" F'lar asked.

"Holdless men," Piemur shrugged. "Promised rewards and easy living in the south." He eased himself onto the broad couch beside Jancis.

"They can go back with the ship," F'lar said, "and then wherever Master Idarolan requires drudges."

"That's not the end of the problem of renegades, though, F'lar," Lessa said, frowning.

"True enough, but if Thella's death is sufficiently publicized"—F'lar looked meaningfully at Piemur—"it will deter the undecided and give us another breathing spell."

"I'll make a full report to the Masterharper—both of them," Piemur said, a twinkle in his eye.

Lessa gave an impatient exclamation. "Robinton's nearly as much of a renegade as—" She paused to think of a suitable comparison and then, with a sly smile, fixed her eyes on Piemur. "As you are, journeyman!"

"Truly spoken," Piemur said, grinning broadly.

Lessa opened her mouth to say more but broke off as Jayge, bruised, bandaged, and bedaubed even more than Piemur was, entered the room with an apprehensive Aramina.

Lessa greeted her warmly, expressing delight that Aramina had rediscovered her ability to contact dragons. She was magnanimously restrained over the brief Weyr participation, dwelling on the relief all would feel at Thella's defeat. Upon questioning, it appeared that Aramina had not heard Ramoth and Mnementh as they arrived—which, Lessa said kindly, she ought to have done since both dragons had been considerably agitated.

"I do hear the fire-lizards," Aramina offered, and Piemur was pleased to notice that for once Lessa did not respond to mention of the creatures with her customary acerbity. "And I also hear someone—something else—occasionally. Whatever it is, is very sad, and so I don't *try* to hear it."

Despite gentle probing, she could give no more information, but Lessa extracted a promise from her to be open to dragons again. "Not to intrude on your life, my dear, but merely to keep in touch. It proved valuable enough today, you'll agree.

"We're not even halfway through this Pass," Lessa reminded her as the Weyrleaders prepared to leave, "and we'll need good women for our queens. I—and Ramoth—hoped to have you in our number, but perhaps that daughter of yours . . . The ability is in the Bloodline, you know, and you're Ruathan, too, Mina!"

16

SOUTHERN CONTINENT, PP 17

Despite the exertions of the previous day, Piemur was awake at dawn, groaning when he realized how early it was. Muscles along his back cramped, and his efforts to ease them merely brought home the awareness of how very stiff he was. Slowly he elevated himself on one elbow and stretched cautiously, wincing.

"Whooo!" The exclamation escaped him as he experimentally felt the two lumps on his head. The bandage had come off during the night.

"Piemur?" Jancis's soft voice made him whirl, which proved to be another injudicious movement. She was already dressed, a cup of klah in one hand and a reed basket containing bandage rolls and two salve pots in the other. "Stiff, are you?" Her smile was fondly proud.

"You bet."

"Here." She held out the klah. "Wake up a bit more. Healer Jancis urges Harper Piemur to consider a gentle dip in the sea, and then she'll tend to his honorable wounds. Head ache?"

Piemur grimaced. "A slight improvement on yesterday." He sipped the klah gratefully. "How come you're so bright at this wretched hour?"

Jancis gave him an impish grin. "Oh, I slept, but excitement woke me up."

"Excitement? Yesterday's?" On top of the fight with Thella's men, Piemur and Jancis had had the privilege—and thrill—of riding Ramoth and Mnememth back to Cove Hold, where F'lar and Lessa had stopped to confer with Master Robinton.

"No, today's!" And she seemed altogether too pleased with herself. "But first, I want you able to concentrate your harper wits. Finish the klah, swim, I'll patch you up, and *then* I'll tell you." She hauled him up from his bed and started dragging him from the small sleeping room.

"You found something in the warehouse?"

"Not until you've swum!"

Jancis was adamant, and, annoyed as he was, Piemur had to admit later that the swimming eased the aches, though the salt water stung his cuts. He felt much better after she had slathered numbweed where it was needed. He was both pleased that she had taken no harm from her part in the previous day's skirmish and chagrined that he had sustained so much. He had kept right by her side during the ambush of Thella's band, had cheered when her spear throw had wounded her target, and had been exceedingly relieved to see Alemi leading reinforcements into the grove.

When she insisted that he eat, Piemur discovered that he was hungrier than he had realized, and they both ate a hearty breakfast. Then Jancis cleared their dishes, and only after that, with an air of triumph, did she carefully unroll a transparent sheet of the ancients' peculiar material. She held the corners down with spoons and forks and waited while he examined it.

"Ad . . . min an . . . nex," he read slowly, enunciating each syllable of the caption. "For aivas. Aivas?" He looked inquiringly up at Jancis.

"I don't know what an aivas is either, but it must be important. See? They went to a lot of trouble to reinforce it. 'Cer . . . a . . . mic tiles'—well, we know 'tiles.' Heat resistant, that's obvious, too. I don't understand what the figures mean, but 'tolerance' would indicate they were determined to protect this aivas thing." Jancis was excited.

"Admin annex? We haven't excavated that one yet, have we? It's up near the edge of the lava flow. And what're so . . . lar pan . . . els?" he asked, tapping the long strips that were apparently attached to the roof of the aivas annex.

"Solar's an old word for sun. Panels, we know."

"Sun panels? What would they do?"

"I don't know, but I'd like to find out." Jancis's eyes sparkled vivaciously.

"You were very brave yesterday, fighting right alongside us," he said irrelevantly because she looked so pretty just then. Her flush deepened. "And if you hadn't released the canines so that Thella didn't get her hands on Ara and the children at the start . . ."

"Well, she didn't, and that was yesterday. This is today, and I think we've got the clue to something very important. No other building on this plateau was especially reinforced against lava. What they couldn't move, they left to slag."

"We'll have to wait until Master Robinton's awake. After yesterday, I doubt I can coax V'line to convey us anywhere without the Harper's authority."

"And just why is that needed?" the Harper asked, yawning as he entered the kitchen.

When applied to later that morning by Master Robinton himself, T'gellan dispatched one of the green weyrlings, who had strict orders, respectfully begging the Master Harper's pardon, to go only to the Plateau and return immediately to the Eastern Weyr.

"Lessa wasted little time distancing Weyrs from our problems," the Harper said, more amused than offended. "However, you two go on. Not only is a green beneath my consequence, but I must construct a report on this matter for Sebell. Yesterday may have broken one thorn in the sides of the Lord Holders but—"He sighed deeply. "—only one, and it behooves me to sweeten the inevitable furor. I am thankful that Jayge is confirmed as a holder. I doubt Larad, or even Asgenar, will feel that the lad exceeded his authority, but he's new to his honors. Some may feel he ought not to have killed Thella. The Telgar Bloodline is an ancient, and generally an honorable one."

Piemur and Jancis were relieved to be allowed to go, Piemur now infected by Jancis's curiosity. They had assembled their tools by the mound when Piemur saw the white dragon arrive. So much had happened that he had forgotten his offer to Jaxom until that very moment. He waved vigorously to attract the Ruathan lord's attention, sending Farli to reinforce his message by way of Ruth. Jaxom and Ruth landed in the aisle in front of the annex, which put Jaxom on a level with the two on the mound top.

"What happened to you?" Jaxom asked with some concern, noting Piemur's bruised face. "Fall down one of those caves?"

"Something like that," Piemur said diffidently. "Lord Jaxom of Ruatha, this is Smith Journeywoman Jancis, Master Fandarel's granddaughter."

"Don't I remember you from Telgar Smithcrafthall?" Jaxom smiled winningly as Jancis regarded him frankly.

"Yes," she replied mischievously. "I used to serve you bread and klah when you came to the Smithcrafthall for lessons with Wansor."

'You're not that old," Piemur protested, and Jancis cocked her head at him.

"What are you doing on this building?" Jaxom asked. "I was looking forward to a prowl through endless caverns and fascinating treasures."

"We may be onto something a lot more exciting, Jaxom," Piemur said, placing the rod at the edge of the long narrow band nearest him and tapping the point gently. "We're following Jancis's hunch."

"I've had one or two of those myself," Jaxom said with a rueful grin. "About this building?"

"I—we—" Jancis stammered, breaking off uncertainly and turning helplessly to Piemur.

"Jancis found an old drawing," the harper said, smoothly taking up the tale and rescuing her from a possible indiscretion. Jaxom would learn about Thella's raid soon enough. "Gave us a hint that this might be an important site. So we thought we'd take a closer look. It's her hunch. According to the master map the Harper and I found, that"—he pointed to the mound perpendicular to them—"is marked as 'ADMIN.' This section we're standing on is marked 'AIVAS.' The ancients went to considerable trouble to protect this aivas thing from the lava flow with heat-tolerant shielding, so we're investigating."

"That's enough to make me curious, too," Jaxom said, suddenly stepping from the white dragon's back to the top of the mound. "I'll help."

"Great!" Piemur tapped his rod again and suddenly the point clicked against something. "That's odd. The click, I mean."

"Usually it's a thunk," Jaxom agreed knowledgeably.

Jancis consulted her sheet, which she had carefully taped to a writing board. "These unusual long protruberances are listed as solar panels," she said, showing Jaxom the diagram. "None of the other buildings have such features." She moved her arm in a wide sweep of the nearby mounds. Suddenly she grinned at Jaxom so infectiously that he responded with a broad smile. "D'you think it's a good hunch?"

"Sounds like it. Got another trowel?" She did, and they

carefully began to clear the accumulated dirt from one of the six long solar panels.

"Farli!" Piemur gestured for the little queen to help. They were all a bit startled when Ruth extended one forepaw, offering to assist.

"Not right now, Ruth," Jaxom said, turning to hold a finger up to his inquisitive friend. "But we're likely to need you later."

"Careful, Farli," Piemur cautioned as the fire-lizard fell to her digging with the boundless, and often misplaced, energy of her kind.

Farli chirped inquiringly. "Yes, right here," Jancis said absently. "Be careful, will you?" Jaxom winked at Piemur, who felt absurdly proud of the easy way Jancis interacted with his little queen.

Farli obediently moderated her efforts, using a slow claw-over-claw technique, until she stopped, chittering with success, when her talons exposed a dull black surface.

"Careful . . ." Jancis used her hands to comb the remaining ash aside, revealing a hand-wide square. Farli patted it, her claw tips clicking. "I don't know what this is. It's not their usual material. It's more like dense opaque glass." She rapped on it experimentally. "Doesn't sound like glass."

"Let's get the whole piece uncovered," Jaxom suggested.

But revealing a complete panel made them no wiser. So they excavated the other five panels on the south-facing roof and then, with Ruth's assistance, the entire roof, which proved to be clad in hand-square sections. Once a piece broke loose, slithering to the ground, but fortunately it was not damaged by the fall.

"Look, these tiles cover the original roofing material. Mortared on." With a sharp cutting tool, Jancis scratched at the surface of a tile. "It could be ceramic, but it's the hardest I've ever seen. However did they get such strength to ceramics?" she wondered aloud.

"Could these possibly be ceramic, too?" Jaxom asked, tapping one of the long panels.

Piemur was lying prone, poking his finger around one panel. "It's always a possibility. You know, these are attached somehow to, and maybe even penetrate, the original roof. All the tiles were carefully shaped to fit snugly around the panels and on the roof. Very curious. Why wouldn't the panels be covered against the heat, too? I don't understand this. D'you think your grandfather should have a look at this?"

"Master Esselin *should* see it first," she said, none too happily. "He's in charge here."

"Of excavating," Jaxom said, motioning Ruth to him. "But Fandarel checks new materials." He grinned as he slipped onto Ruth's back. "He'll be at these caves I came to see?"

"Have a look in passing," Piemur yelled as Ruth launched himself upward.

"You and Lord Jaxom seem to be old friends," Jancis remarked casually as she reached for her notepad and the transparent measuring stick. She saw his look and flushed. "Well, we did find several boxes of them, you know."

"Tools are meant to be used," he replied magnaminously. "There are things to be kept for what they are, and things that should be used because they're more efficient than anything we have." He grinned at her discomfort, and she got busy with her measurements.

In a very few minutes, Ruth returned with Jaxom and the Mastersmith, Fandarel's massive bulk dwarfing even the tall Ruathan and certainly looking conspicuous on the small white dragon. For a man of his size, however, Fandarel was agile and active, lying flat by one of the solar panels to examine it thoroughly, running his fingers over the puzzling new surface.

"This tiling is familiar," he said, grimacing at another loose piece and rubbing his thumb over it. "It was not meant to lie flat, either. See, there is a slight rounding to it. It might have been bedded in this mortar . . ." He pinched some of the dusty stuff visible where the section had lain. "But this was not its original purpose."

Jaxom let out a sudden whoop. "It's like the coating on the flying ships in the meadow!"

"Why would they coat a building with—" Piemur began.

"Heat tolerance. There'd be heat, or friction—" Jancis said at the same time.

They both broke off, startled by the sight of the smith precariously tilted groundward to examine the exposed corner of the roof and wall. He grunted, waving one hand urgently at the three young people. Jancis held out the trowel; he grabbed it and began chipping away the dirt around the corner, murmuring to himself. He sounded both puzzled and pleased.

"Jaxom, would Ruth be kind enough to dig out this corner section for me?"

That was soon enough accomplished, though Ruth did knock off a few more of the tiles, apologizing through Jaxom for it.

"Tell him not to worry," the Mastersmith replied. "The mortar that held them in place has accomplished its purpose. Your theory is supported, Jancis. These tiles were added to protect what's in this curious building against the heat of lava. Now what does it contain?"

"An aivas," Jancis said, clearing her throat conspicuously and passing the drawing to her grandfather. Piemur noticed how subdued she had become, turning into a very proper and self-effacing young lady.

"And what, Master Fandarel, is an 'aivas'?" Jaxom asked patiently.

"I don't know, Jaxom," the smith replied. "Let us all find out."

"Jancis had the hunch," Piemur said, wanting her to assert herself.

"Good girl. Always uses her eyes and her wits," the smith

said, surprised at Piemur's fervent agreement. Then Fandarel dropped off the roof and went to round up a full team of excavators, unceremoniously excusing them from their other projects. He rudely ignored Master Esselin and Breide when they demanded explanations, telling them absently to go do something they were qualified to do. By evening the annex was completely unearthed to reveal that, unlike all other ancient buildings, it had neither windows nor door, and that the original walls were of a double thickness. Ventilation slats were finally discovered under the eaves, but they allowed no glimpse of the interior. At sunset, the smith called a halt, giving orders that the project was now the highest priority and that Master Esselin should see that there was a full complement of workers to secure access to the ADMIN building and the mysterious aivas as soon after daylight as possible.

"Look, I've got to get back to Ruatha," Jaxom said as the smith concluded his instructions. "Sharra's going to be disgusted with not being able to travel right now. She's pregnant again, you see." His grin was both embarrassed and proud.

For the first time, Piemur discovered that he felt no pain at Jaxom and Sharra's happiness. "Nuisance, that," he said, grinning back. "Listen, would Ruth mind dropping Jancis and me off at Cove Hold? Master Robinton will want a full report on this."

Ruth did not mind at all.

Another marvel?" Master Robinton asked. His workspace was littered with examples of the cavern artifacts. "It's going to take us till the end of the Pass to document what we've already got." Almost irritably, he shoved at the mess around him. "Things! The ancients had so many *things*!"

Piemur chuckled as he automatically refilled the Master's empty wineglass.

"A building is not a thing, Master Robinton. D'ram, have you or Lord Lytol come across any reference to the 'aivas?' " he asked.

"It was not listed on the evacuation plan," Lytol said, reaching over to find the relevant notes.

"Maybe an aivas couldn't be evacuated," Jaxom suggested. "They did leave some heavy equipment behind. Not that you could guess its purpose from the slag it is now. But those remains were left in a special room with no doors or windows, only ventilation grills. And thicker walls than usual. We'll have to go through the ADMIN building."

"If we can," Piemur said gloomily.

"That's a double thickness of the heaviest gauge of their material," Jancis said thoughtfully. "So far Grandfa cannot find a way of penetrating it, even using the ancients' drill bits."

"Aivas, aivas, aivas," Master Robinton mused. "It doesn't sound like a real word. An aiva, the aiva, many aivas!" He flicked one hand in a gesture of defeat. "You will stay the night, won't you, Jancis? Our current cook has a way with fish that's magical." His charming smile brought an answering one from Jancis. "Then we can all get up to the Plateau in plenty of time for yet another revelation."

After dinner, when Piemur went to check on Stupid, he invited Jancis to come along.

"That's a terrible name to call any creature," Jancis chided him as he led the way, glowbasket overhead, toward the fenced clearing where the little runnerbeast was accommodated.

"It's an old joke," Piemur said lamely, but even Jancis was impressed when Stupid nickered in response to his name and trotted over, thrusting out his nose to nuzzle his master. "You don't mind, do you, Stupid? If I called you anything else, you wouldn't answer, would you?"

Stupid waggled his ears and nickered again as Farli joined

them, settling, as usual, on the little runner's rump. He switched his tail, and she scolded him.

"They really like each other," Jancis exclaimed. "I didn't think runners liked fire-lizards or dragons."

Piemur chuckled, leaning against the top rail of the enclosure, idly rubbing Stupid's soft nose. By the light of Belior moon, Jancis looked slightly mysterious, the planes of her face touched by the white light.

"Well, it's a fact Stupid shies away from any dragon, even Ruth. You haven't been dragon food yet, have you, friend?" he teased. "But he and I and Farli make a pretty good team."

"They say," Jancis said, scratching just the right spot on Stupid's neck and causing him to lean into her fingers, tilting his head, eyes half-closed, "that you and Stupid and Farli walked the entire coast of Southern."

"Only from Southern Hold to Cove Hold. I got excused the rest of it."

"Even that much took a lot of courage."

"Courage?" Piemur snorted at the notion. "Courage had little to do with it. I was born naturally inquisitive. And," he added in a sudden spurt of honesty, "it was one way to keep Toric from exiling me from Southern."

"Why would Lord Toric do that?"

"He didn't fancy me as marriage kin." Piemur had shifted position so that he was closer to her, though still ostensibly leaning indolently on the rail.

"You? And Sharra?"

Piemur grinned. "For that matter, he didn't fancy Jaxom as marriage kin, but he got talked into it." Finally Piemur could appreciate the full irony of that confrontation. "He didn't fancy his sister married to the lord of a table-sized hold."

"What?" Jancis, appropriately indignant, ceased scratching Stupid's neck and turned toward Piemur. "Why, Ruatha has one of the oldest Bloodlines on Pern. Everyone with marriageable daughters was hoping to attract Lord Jaxom."

"Toric had bigger plans for Sharra." Piemur worked his way a little closer to her as Stupid swung his head back to nip at a nightfly.

"How could he? Jaxom's the only young Lord Holder. And they say they're devoted to each other. She nursed him through fire-head right here at Cove Hold."

"I know," Piemur murmured. Smiling, he put both hands on the rail, one on either side of Jancis. When she became aware of the maneuver, he grinned down at her, waiting for her reaction. "And what do they say about Journeyman Piemur?"

She dared him, the dimple flashing in her cheek, a dark spot on her moonlit face. "What they say about any harper journeyman, of course. That they're not to be trusted for a moment."

Slowly, so she could escape if she really wanted to, and he hoped very much that she did not, he lowered his head and brought his arms up to hold her. "Especially not on moonlit nights like this, huh?" He touched her lips very gently with his, aware that they were parted in a smile and that she had no intention of ducking away at the last moment. Abruptly she was pushed forcefully into his arms. He tightened them to keep her from falling just as her arms went around him to steady herself. "Thank you, Stupid, that'll do quite nicely." And Piemur made excellent use of his runner's headlong assistance.

If Piemur and Jancis were preoccupied with each other the next morning at the dawn breakfast that Master Robinton had ordered, the others were far too intent on arriving on time at the Plateau to notice. D'ram would convey the Harper, Piemur, and Jancis to the ADMIN building. Lytol had declined to go along.

"I think he's noticeably fading," Robinton murmured to

D'ram as they strode to Tiroth's clearing. "Jaxom remarked on it to me."

"He's fine, Robinton, really he is. It's just that like all of us, he can't do as much as he used to," D'ram replied, his expression sad. "Jaxom's news about a second child cheered him."

"It cheered me, too. Ah, Tiroth, you're very good to haul us to and fro," the Harper said, giving the elderly bronze an affectionate clout as he climbed up to sit between the neck ridges. "Hand Jancis up to me, Piemur. I'll see she's safe. You can hold on to me as tightly as you wish, my dear."

"You keep your hands to yourself, Master," Piemur said in a mock growl, ascending first and then assisting Jancis to the position behind him. He ignored the protests from his stiff muscles and tender bruises.

"Where's your respect for my age, my position?" the Harper demanded, laughing as he mounted just in front of the journeyman.

"Where it always has been, Master," Piemur assured him heartily. "Where I can keep my eye on you!"

D'ram was chuckling as he mounted, and Tiroth's powerful upward leap brought Jancis's arms clutching at Piemur's. He covered her hands on his chest with his, very pleased to feel her pressing so tightly against him. They all had a good view of the Dawn Sisters shining in the morning sky before Tiroth took them *between*.

The Sisters were still in sight when they arrived at the Plateau and skimmed up from the landing strip to the dark shadows of the mounds and the spot where the light of many glowbaskets told them the excavation crew was all ready to go. Indeed, they learned shortly, Master Fandarel had already outlined the area to be dug and the first shovelsful had been removed.

"Master Robinton, D'ram, good morning. Jancis, Piemur. We calculate a full span's encrustation. I also deemed it wise to remove the tiles, so obviously a temporary cover. Last night

I compared them with some still in place on the flying ships, and I believe that it is the same material, though none of the ships seem to be missing any significant number. That confirms my theory that originally there were more than three ships.''

''I think that's likely,'' Master Robinton agreed, shivering a bit in the cool dawn air. ''The fire-lizards' images always suggest more than three. Twice that many, and even with six the labor of transporting all those things from the Dawn Sisters to the surface here would have been astounding.''

Someone brought stools and hot klah so that Master Robinton and D'ram could be made comfortable while the digging progressed. Jancis and Piemur stood to one side, sipping at the klah. Piemur tried to suppress the irritation he felt that their private little dig had turned so official. Jancis was rather more subdued than he liked. This was her find, her hunch. She should be directing the work. True, she could not really expect to take precedence over her grandfather, but they all seemed to have forgotten that the whole effort was due to her discovery of the ancient drawing film. It had been one thing to ask Jaxom to help, but not the whole bloody Plateau. The lumps on his head began to throb.

As the sun came up, he realized that someone had worked hard during the night to strip the tiles from the roof. The panels stood completely clear, a long finger-length above the original roof. Some of the cladding remained on the walls, but a trench had been cut through the soil, right down to the tar-based material with which the ancients had paved the walks and roadways between their buildings.

Suddenly a cheer went up. Grabbing Jancis by the hand, Piemur pushed past the crowd clustering in a loose circle about the dig area. Master Fandarel and Master Robinton had been ushered to the newly uncovered door. It was not one of the common sliding doors of the ancients but had instead two equal-sized panels.

''I beg your pardon, Master Fandarel and Master Robinton,

but this building was Jancis's hunch, and she should by rights go first!'' Piemur heard Jancis gasp in astonishment and felt her pull against his grip. He ignored the bemused expressions of the two Mastercraftsmen as he hauled Jancis right up to the doors. He heard Master Esselin's indignant exclamation and Breide's acid comment about harper arrogance, and the ripple of surprise passing back through the small crowd. Jancis tried to pull him back, tried to free her hand.

''You know, you are right, Piemur,'' Robinton said, stepping to one side. ''We have usurped Jancis's prerogative.''

''After you, Jancis,'' Fandarel said. He spoke with the utmost courtesy but looked thoughtfully at Piemur.

Seeing that Jancis was too dismayed to act, Piemur stepped beside her, looking for the method of opening the door. He could see none, but there was no way that he would have turned back to the Smith for assistance. He scrutinized the door more carefully. There was an unusual hinge arrangement, but no knob or latch. He put one hand on an obvious doorplate and pressed. There was the resistance of long unmoved parts, then dust and ash showered down from the gap between the doors. He pushed with both hands, and the door began to move inward. Jancis rallied from her embarrassment sufficiently to lend her weight, and suddenly the door swung completely inward, marking its path in the fine dust that had filtered inside over the Turns.

Piemur pulled the other side back, opening the doors wide to the fresh morning breeze blowing softly up the Plateau and swirling the dust in the corridor. Then he turned around, gesturing for one of the glowbaskets. Soon the sun would bring light into the hallway, but he did not want to delay a single moment. A judicious two paces behind Jancis and Piemur, Masters Fandarel and Robinton entered.

''A corridor to the right,'' Piemur said, holding the glowbasket up in his left hand while he kept his right one firmly around Jancis's wrist. She was not resisting him anymore, he thought, grinning to himself. She just needed to assert herself a little more and no one was going to do her out of her rights, not while he was around.

Now that he was making the first footprints the ashy floors had felt in who knew how many Turns, he was beginning to be appalled at his own brashness, but he had gotten away with it—again. He grinned. He turned to his right again, and with the added illumination from the glowbaskets carried by Robinton and Fandarel, he could see more tiling, whitely gleaming at the end of the short hallway. "They sure weren't taking any chances with aivas."

"There is an obvious door," Master Fandarel remarked. He started to move in front of them, then paused and gestured for the two younger people to continue.

Jancis shot Piemur a look of wretched consternation, but he just grinned at her, squeezing her hand. "You found it—you get to see it first!"

The hall was wide enough for all of them to stand abreast at the reinforced wall. The door had a knob, and when Jancis declined to touch it, Piemur had no hesitation. It took all his strength to turn it, for time and dust had clogged the mechanism, but with both hands and a mighty effort, he disengaged the latch. The door did not open inward, as he had half expected, but outward.

"There is little dust on this floor," the smith remarked, peering over their heads at the scene in front of them.

"There's a red light on a cupboard," Piemur observed, feeling his skin crawl with amazement.

"And more light!" Jancis said in a timorous voice.

"In fact, the whole place is lighting up," Piemur added, feeling his feet rooted in the doorway as strange and unfamiliar sensations coursed through him. This place had not been emptied. He had never seen such cabinets and closets before, but there was no doubt in his mind that they were right for this room. For once, the brash young harper was touched with awe and reverence. This was just the sort of place they had all been hoping to find.

"The red light illuminates letters," Master Robinton said in a hushed voice as he looked over Jancis's shoulder.

"Remarkable, truly remarkable!" The Smith's voice was no less reverent.

The growing light made visible some of the details within the room: the worktables on either side of the door, and the two high stools neatly placed under them. On the wall opposite the door was a large framed surface, tinted slightly green, with little red letters blinking on and off in the lower left-hand side. A chair, on a pedestal with five spokes in its base, stood in front of it and the slanting workspace. It seemed unadorned until Piemur noticed the regular squares—lighter in color than the surrounding surface—set in ranks and odd-looking protruberances in a series of rows to the right. Above them, to the right of the screen, were slots and more dial faces, one of which showed a steady green light and a needle swinging slowly from the left to a central position.

The red lights, which read *panels charging*, stopped blinking and settled to a firm color that gradually changed to green as the lighting—from whatever mysterious source it emanated—continued to brighten. Suddenly a quiet *blip* startled all of them, and a new message blazed from the left-hand corner: AIVAS FUNCTION RESUMED.

"That corner says 'AIVAS,' " Piemur said excitedly, pointing to the obvious.

Robinton had turned to view the corridor walls and recognized familiar artifacts. "Charts," he said.

"Please state ID and access code! Your voiceprints are not on record."

The voice startled all of them, and Jancis clutched at Piemur.

"Who said that?" Fandarel demanded, his voice booming in the confines of the room.

"State ID and access code, please!" The voice repeated, sounding slightly louder.

"That's not a human voice," Master Robinton said. "It has no real resonance, no inflection, no timbre."

"State the reason for this intrusion."

"Do you understand what he's saying, Master Robinton?" Piemur asked. The words sounded familiar, but the accent was too strange for him to comprehend the meaning.

"I have the feeling that I ought to," the Harper admitted ruefully.

"Unless ID and access codes are given, this facility will close down. Its use is restricted to Admiral Paul Benden . . ."

"Benden, it said Benden!" Piemur cried excitedly.

". . . Governor Emily Boll . . ."

"Boll, that's another recognizable word," Robinton said. "We recognize the words 'Benden' and 'Boll.' We do not understand what you are trying to tell us."

". . . Captain Ezra Keroon . . ."

"Keroon. It knows Keroon. Do you know Telgar?" The Smith could not contain himself any longer. "Surely it must know Telgar."

"Telgar, Sallah, married to Tarvi Andivar, later known as Telgar in memory of his wife's sacrifice . . ."

"All I understand is 'Telgar,' " Fandarel said. He raised his voice unthinkingly, in a frustrated attempt to encourage comprehension. "Telgar, we understand. Keroon we understand—that's another big hold. Boll is a Hold; Benden is a Hold. Do you understand us?"

There was a long pause and they all watched with complete fascination as a range of symbols and, occasionally, letters rippled across the panel in front of them, accompanied by a variety of sounds, mainly blips and beeps and odd whirrings.

"Did I say something wrong, Robinton?" Fandarel asked, his voice an awed whisper again.

"Are you all right down there?" Master Esselin's plaintive query reached them where they stood bunched together in the doorway.

"Of course we are," Fandarel bellowed back to the Master-miner. "Clear those windows. Let some light in. Glammie has my diagrams. Work from that and leave us alone!"

"New letters," Piemur said, digging the Mastersmith in the ribs to attract his attention. "Running . . . Running? E . . . M . . . E . . . R . . . G . . . E . . . N . . ."

"Emergency," the harper guessed before the C and Y appeared. He grinned with pleasure.

"P-R-O-G-R-A-M—program? The words we understand, but what do they mean?" Piemur asked.

"The lights are quite bright now," Fandarel said cheerfully. "Very curious." He stepped inside the room, his initial surprise having worn off, and the others followed hastily. "There are buttons on the wall." He flicked one, and a soft whirring noise began. The fine film of dust on the floor began to shift: the closeness of the air freshened. Fandarel flicked the button again, and both the noise and the stirring of air ceased. He flicked it on again, murmuring happily to himself. "Well, this aivas of yours is an ingenious creature," he commented, smiling down at Jancis. "And efficient."

"We still don't know what an aivas is!" Piemur remarked.

"*AIVAS is an acronym for Artificial Intelligence Voice Address System,*" the voice intoned. "*To be precise, a Mark 47A, programmed to interface the main computer storage banks of the* Yokohama *and the settlement on Pern.*"

"Pern—I understood Pern," Robinton said. Then, enunciating very clearly and projecting his rich baritone voice, he added, "From where are you speaking, aivas?"

"*This system is programmed for voice address. State your name. Please.*"

"It sounds testy, but I think I'm getting the hang of its accent. My name is Robinton. I am Masterharper of Pern. This is Fandarel, who is Mastersmith in Telgar Hold. With us are Journeywoman Jancis and Journeyman Piemur. Do you understand me?"

"Lingual shifts have occurred, Robinton. Modification of the language program is now required. Please continue to speak."

"Continue to speak?"

"Your speech patterns will be the basis for the modification. Please continue to speak."

"Well, Masterharper, you heard it," Piemur said, rapidly recovering his composure. "Here, sit down." He pulled the chair from under the desk, brushed the seat off, and made a flamboyant gesture.

Master Robinton looked aggrieved as he sat. "I always thought the Harper Hall had succeeded very well in keeping the language pure and unadulterated."

"Oh, aivas just doesn't understand us!" Piemur murmured reassuringly. "Everyone understands you. That thing," he said, airily dismissing the aivas, "doesn't even use words we know."

"This is all very interesting," Fandarel said, peering at every surface, poking a finger into the slots, and cautiously touching the various knobs, buttons, and toggles. "Very interesting. Much less dust has filtered into this room. No doubt due to the tile layer."

"Please do not attempt to use the touch-screen controls. That function is now deactivated."

Fandarel pulled his hands back like a small boy caught reaching for bubbly pies. The slanting board, which had been glowing amber, went dark again. Jancis had gingerly settled on one of the stools, rolling her eyes around the room and trying not to look at the screen.

"What's happening down there?" Breide called.

"A modification of the language program has been necessary," Piemur called back. "Master Fandarel has it all well in hand, Breide."

"Four persons are observed to occupy this room, but only three voices have been registered. Will the fourth person speak?"

Jancis looked around apprehensively. "Me?"

"You are requested to speak a full sentence."

"Go on, Jancis," Piemur urged. "I don't think it will bite you, and a feminine voice will give it a new perspective on life here."

"But I haven't the faintest idea what one says to . . . a disembodied voice."

"Any speech will suffice. The difference in resonance and timbre has been noted. To assist the program, question: You are a female person."

"Yes, she is a female person," Piemur repeated.

"The female person is asked to answer for a voiceprint reading."

Jancis burst out laughing at the surprise on Piemur's face, for the reproof, despite the uninflected tone, was unmistakable.

"You should see your face, Piemur."

"Well, at least you can laugh about it," Piemur said. "Thank you . . . sir, whatever. How should you be addressed?"

"This is an artificial intelligence voice address system. It does not require personification."

"Does artificial mean man-made?" Robinton asked.

"That is correct."

"The men who built the Dawn Sisters?"

"Reference to Dawn Sisters is unknown. Please explain."

"The three metallic objects in the sky overhead are known as the Dawn Sisters."

"You refer to the spaceships Yokohama, Buenos Aires, *and* Bahrain.*"*

"Spaceships?" Fandarel asked, turning to stare at the panel with its green blinking legend.

"Spaceships, life-supported vehicles that travel in the vacuum in-accurately referred to as 'space.' "

"Do the spaceships still support life?" Fandarel's eyes were wide, his usually expressionless face betraying a passionate avidity that surprised even Robinton.

"Not at the present reading. All systems are on hold. Bridge pressure is .001 standard atmosphere, or 0.1 KP. Interior temperature reads minus twenty-five degrees Celsius."

"I don't know what it's talking about," Fandarel said, collapsing onto the other stool, his face a study of terrible disappointment.

"Hey!" Jaxom came running down the hall. "No, that's all right, Breide, I'll just go right in. I'm expected." He entered the room, slightly breathless. "I thought you'd wait for me, Piemur. Excuse me, Master Fandarel, Master Robinton. What is this?" He began to assimilate the oddities of the room, the lights, the ventilation, and the expressions of his friends.

"This is an artificial intelligence voice address system . . ."

"Here we go again," Piemur said irreverently. "You do realize, Master, that here is the key you've been hoping to find. A talking key. I think if you can just ask it the right questions, you'll find out all the answers. Even some you didn't know you needed to know."

"Aivas," Master Robinton said, straightening his shoulders and directing his next remark to the green light. "Can you answer my questions?"

"That is the function of this apparatus."

"Let us begin at the beginning then, shall we?" Master Robinton asked.

"That is a correct procedure," Aivas replied, and what had been a dark panel suddenly became illuminated with a diagram that those in the room identified as similar to one found in the flying ship Jaxom had discovered. Only this diagram had such depth and perspective that it appeared three-dimensional, giving the awed observers the feeling that they were hovering in space, an unthinkable distance away from their sun. *"When Mankind first discovered the third planet of the sun Rukbat in the Sagittarian Sector of space . . ."*

About the Author

ANNE MCCAFFREY shuttles between her home in Ireland and the United States, where she picks up awards and honors and greets her myriad fans. She is one of the field's most popular authors. Her Dragonriders of Pern® novels constitute a *New York Times* bestselling series.